Books by J. FitzGerald McCurdy

THE SERPENT'S EGG TRILOGY
The Serpent's Egg (Book One)
The Burning Crown (Book Two)
The Twisted Blade (Book Three)

THE MOLE WARS SERIES
The Fire Demons (Book One)
The Black Pyramid (Book Two)

THE
BURNING
CROWN

J. FITZGERALD McCURDY

THE
BURNING
CROWN

Harper*Trophy*Canada™
An imprint of HarperCollins*Publishers*Ltd

Published by Harper*Trophy*Canada™, an imprint of HarperCollins
Publishers Ltd

First published by Saratime Publishing Inc: 2001
This Harper*Trophy*Canada™ edition: 2005

Harper*Trophy*Canada™ is a trademark of HarperCollins Publishers

HarperCollins books may be purchased for educational, business, or sales
promotional use through our Special Markets Department.

HarperCollins Publishers Ltd
2 Bloor Street East, 20th Floor
Toronto, Ontario, Canada
M4W 1A8

www.harpercollins.ca

Library and Archives Canada Cataloguing in Publication

McCurdy, J. FitzGerald (Joan FitzGerald), 1943–
The burning crown / J. FitzGerald McCurdy.

ISBN-13: 978-0-00-639334-4
ISBN-10: 0-00-639334-9

I. Title. II. Series: McCurdy, J. FitzGerald (Joan FitzGerald), 1943– .
Serpent's egg trilogy; bk. 2

PS8575.C87B87 2006   JC813'.6   C2005-905579-0

HC 9 8 7 6 5 4

Printed and bound in the United States

This book is dedicated to the inspiring
educators and librarians I have had the privilege
of meeting on my tours across Canada.
And to the kids, of course.

Thanks to Laine Cooper for her constant friendship and support, and to Gregor (a worthy King of Dwarves) for his hard work.

When the people of the world all know
beauty as beauty,
There arises the recognition of ugliness.
When they all know the good as good,
There arises the recognition of evil.

—THE WAY OF LAO-TZU, 2

CONTENTS

THE
BURNING
CROWN

THE NAMING

Inside the obsidian shell, the serpent writhed in agitation, its pinpoint red eyes blinking like twin beacons in the inky enclosure. Fully formed, and as black as a raven's feathers, it waited to hear its name, waited for the summons to rend the amnion and the chorion, the membranous walls of the egg, and break through the hard shell to freedom.

In the first months of its development, the embryonic serpent floated contentedly in the albumen, a nutritious extension of itself. As it grew, its salivary glands, spongy sacs behind its eyes, modified to produce deadly venom. The amniotic egg was its entire universe. If the creature were capable of thought, its thoughts during that time were bent on one thing—survival. Without the egg, it would die.

But all too quickly, things changed. The sustaining goo was gone, used up. The serpent's limbless body shriveled, tightening as it dehydrated and its life fluids evaporated. Without sustenance, the womblike enclosure became a prison—a death cell. Seconds became eternities. If hunger failed to drive the creature mad, it would die from boredom.

Finally, in desperation, and guided by millions of years of instinct, the thing sank its fangs into its dry, itchy skin, ripping and ripping until it hung about the creature like the wispy outer skin of an onion. Then, wearing an oily black coat, the snake slithered out of its old wrapping, and in a snap, tore into it ravenously, consuming every scaly morsel. Sated for the time being, the sleek black serpent roiled frenziedly about itself . . . and waited . . . and waited . . .

"DAUTHUSSSS!"

The snake went as still as the air just before dawn.

"COME TO ME, MY DAUTHUSSSS!"

The sound of his name pleased the serpent, sending a rush of warmth along his slick, silky length, as he hastened to do his Mistress's bidding. The creature raked his long, pointed, hollow fangs over the inner and outer membranous walls, careful not to eject even a drop of the deadly venom,

4

and shredded them into long, slimy threads. Then, he recoiled and focused on the wall of the black shell. From the serpent's eyes, thin beams of red fire shot out, blasting the shell into a million shards that rained upon Dauthus like bits of his own discarded skin.

Dauthus blinked, the rest of his body going still again as the voice of Hate filled his tiny brain with her memory and her purpose. In unspoken words and vivid images, the Demon stripped away the creature's ophidian nature, crushing his will and remaking him into herself.

Pain, sharper than a knife, exploded in Dauthus's brain as Hate worked her evil. As the serpent's life drained away, his round eyes rolled senselessly. His long body recoiled violently, flexing and knotting. His head lashed out again and again, fangs biting at air in a frenzied, futile attack. The pain went on forever. And when it finally ended, Dauthus's body was rigid with shock, drained of everything except the urgent need to free the Demon and make those responsible for her terrible torment pay with their lives.

Totally spent, the serpent rested. His forked tongue flickered spasmodically from his open mouth as his red eyes refocused and travelled about the cavernous interior of his cold, silent host. Dauthus blinked. The creature knew where he was—on Ellesmere Island, land of the loathsome Elves, deep under the city of Bethany, inside the abdominal cavity of the recently dead Elven King. He knew what he had to do. He knew everything now.

Knowing that his Mistress was trapped in a prison a billion times darker and emptier than the black egg from which he had emerged hurt Dauthus as if he were the one incarcerated in that vile nothingness. The Elves had driven her there, but others had helped. The snake opened his mouth and spat a spray of venom at the image of a slim, blond-haired girl with clear green eyes that flashed through his brain like a bolt of lightning. That was she—the human girl who had interfered in the Demon's business and whose life would soon be ended.

Yess, thought the serpent, My Lady hass planss for you, nassty, nassty meddler. Dauthus's body convulsed with pleasure. Oh yes, his Mistress had plans for the girl all right. And this time she would not have the magic Bloodstones to help her. The creature hissed softly. Without the precious stones, the human was less than nothing. Dauthus intended to get them away from her and, once he had them, he'd bite her and kill her. That's what the Great One had commanded and he, her servant, had no will except the will to obey.

The snake's eyes sought and found the soft, unmoving body of a larger serpent. He stared at it for a long time. This was his parent, the one that had sunk its poisonous fangs into the neck of the King they called Ruthar, killing the weakling in seconds. Dauthus hissed contentedly as his mind replayed the image of his Mistress snatching the parent snake from the living mass of serpents she wore like a belt about her waist, and flinging it at the King of the Elves—the Evil One.

But not so evil anymore. If the snake could laugh, he would have laughed now. Instead, he hissed again. Ruthar! What a soft, weak-sounding name, but so appropriate for the leader of the lumpen, lower order of Elves.

Dauthus didn't know his parent's name—not that he cared. The thing was dead. But even the sickening smell of its rotting carcass didn't stop him from devouring what was left of it. Finished, he looked about until he found the other four round black eggs his parent had deposited in the abdominal cavity of the dead King, seconds before it, too, had died of wounds inflicted by a small pink dog—a stupid human plaything.

The serpent inched his bloated body forward until he made physical contact with his unborn siblings. He caught and held each tiny egg in his mouth, torn between Hate's orders and his urge to crush the eggs in his sharp teeth and suck down the contents. Finally, he released them and coiled about them, drawing them to him in a strangely protective stance. Then he slept and dreamed that he was with the Demon, one of her chosen, writhing blissfully about her middle like the living bark encircling a tree.

In her prison, the Demon stirred. Two flaming red eyes blinked in the darkness. Slowly, she rose to her full height, stretched her four arms wide, opened her enormous mouth, and yawned lazily. Then she grasped the long, black iron stake with the human skull skewered on the sharp end, and raised it over her head. Crackling red fire ignited in the skull's eyes and spread down the cold iron and along the creature's arms, bathing her black, whipping tongue in fire.

When the flames died, she sank her hooked fangs deep into the flesh on her forearm and hissed with pleasure. Her plans were in motion. The one she named Dauthus knew what he must do to break the spells that sealed her dark, empty prison. Once the spells were broken, the invisible walls would melt away like snow in July. Then, Hate and the others trapped in the Place with No Name would surge forth like a violent storm, dispatching the Demon's enemies until the ground ran red with their blood.

She had thought of everything. Her plan was foolproof. It could not fail. Soon, soon, victory would belong to her. And this time when she emerged from the dark hole, she would be free forever—free to trample her enemies and expand her kingdom until she ruled the former lands of the

Dwarves and Elves. Then, when she had wiped the despised races from her world, she would turn her vast army toward that other world—the one the human girl called home.

CHAPTER ONE

THE COMING
OF EVIL

It was the dead of night when Elester, only son of the late lamented King of the Elves, awakened suddenly, his heart drumming loudly in the eerie silence, blood pulsing in his ears. A sound nearby—a stealthy footstep on the softwood floor—echoed in his subconscious. In one smooth movement, he raised his strong arms protectively and rolled off the bed, away from the menace he sensed waiting in the darkness near the other side of the bed, between him and the door. Landing on his feet in a crouch, the Prince froze, reaching out with his keen hearing, seeking the slightest sound. At the same time, his sharp eyes pierced the robes of night for the source of the evil, a thicker solid blackness among the murky shadows. He heard nothing, saw nothing. No sound. No movement. Nothing.

Silently he backed away from the single bed—his nerve ends tingling, alert for the slightest movement, the slightest sound. Still, he saw nothing, heard nothing. Then, for a fraction of a second, his throat constricted and he almost gagged on the putrid stench that spilled from the blackness and spread like poison gas through the chamber.

Now Elester was afraid.

He knew that smell as surely as he knew his own name. It was the gangrenous odour of death—the reek of evil that meant only one thing. Hate, the Demon, was here, now, somewhere in this room.

Even as his mind processed these thoughts and identified the source of the danger, the rational part of his brain screamed in denial. It is not the Demon! It cannot be! Elester knew there was no way the Demon could be here on Ellesmere Island. Not now, not ever. None knew that better than he. He had been there when Hate and the rest of her half-dead minions were driven into the Place with No Name at the Battle of Dundurum. In fact, it was he who had wielded the magic that sealed the boundaries of the creature's dark prison.

Prince Elester grinned bitterly, his mouth twisted in a hard line. Yes, he had shut the Demon away, but not in time to save his father. Now, almost three months had passed since the Elven King's death, far away from Ellesmere Island, in the land of the Dwarves; but every heart-wrenching detail of the Battle of Dundurum was burned into Elester's mind for all time. Night after night, the images replayed in his sleep like an endless horror film.

In his dreams, Elester saw the child, Miranda, cringing in terror as the huge black form of Hate, the Demon, advanced down the rubble-strewn street in the Dwarf town of DunNaith. The girl was a mere speck next to the towering creature, and the Prince's heart still ached for her, for the horrible things she had seen—things that no one, adult or child, should ever see. The dreams always ended on the same painful image—Naim, the Druid, cradling the King of the Elves in his arms as the aged monarch lay dying.

For a split second, Elester wondered if he would ever be tempted to release the Demon if such action would bring his father back. Angrily, he brushed the thought away. Much as he ached to hear his father's voice, to reach out and touch him one final time, he knew the answer: never!

Abruptly, the Prince of Ellesmere turned his thoughts to the immediate danger. He was not alone in the dark chamber and if it were not the Demon waiting motionless near the other side of the bed, then who? He sniffed, but the vile odour was gone as suddenly as it had come. Gone also was the evil he had sensed when he sent his body spinning off the bed. Was it possible that he had imagined the whole thing?

"Prince . . ."

Elester started at the sudden sound, at the same time recognizing the speaker. Breathing deeply, he rose to his full height and let his limbs relax. He moved easily across the room despite the dark, and pressed his hand against a round medallion on the wall to the right of the bed. From one of four wrought-iron sconces adorning the walls, soft golden light instantly illuminated the room, driving away the shadows and revealing the tall man waiting at the foot of the bed.

Surprised, Elester stared at the eldest member of the Erudicia, the King's Advisers, and his late father's closest friend. "Mathus?" The question hung in the air as Elester moved quickly to stand in front of the other man. His eyes scanning the corners of the room belied his relaxed manner. "What are you doing here? I could have hurt you."

For an instant, a look of suspicion or confusion crossed the old man's face. "Young fellow, I would not be here if you had not called out to me," he said, his green Elven eyes fixed unwaveringly on the Prince. "I sensed a great danger here."

As their eyes met, Elester staggered back and would have fallen if the older man had not grasped his arm. Blinking, he steadied himself and grabbed Mathus's shoulders, holding him at arm's length while peering into his eyes. Nothing. The Prince shivered. For a split second, as their eyes had met, he could have sworn that the features of the most trusted senior Adviser had blurred and shifted into a black hole with flaming red eyes and a gaping mouth showing bared fangs like spikes.

Mathus was old, but strong. He gripped Elester's wrists, breaking the steel hold on his shoulders. Then he gently released the Prince's hands, took a step back, and frowned at the younger man. "What is the matter with you, Elester? You act as though I am a stranger."

"I thought . . ." Then Elester shrugged, shook his head as if to clear away the mist, and forced himself to laugh. To his ears, it sounded forced. "Just my dreams, Mathus. You surprised me. And, I did not call you." He glanced toward the door and noticed that it was firmly locked. "How did you get in?"

Mathus cocked his head toward the double doors that opened onto the grassy terrace. Sure enough, Elester saw that one of the doors stood partly open.

"What were you doing wandering about at this hour, anyway?" asked the Prince, sitting on the edge of his bed and running his strong hands through his golden hair.

"They say the older you get, the less sleep you need," answered the old man, drawing a chair closer to the bed and sitting back. "I could not sleep. I thought a stroll in the gardens might help me relax. The past few months have been . . ."

"Yes, I know," interrupted the Prince. "It has not been an easy time."

Both men sat in silence for several minutes. Then Mathus rose, slid the chair back against the wall, and moved to the terrace door. "I miss my friend, you know. Sometimes, like tonight, I swear I hear him call my name." He sighed heavily. "Yes, yes, I know it is impossible, but that is why I came here, thinking you were in danger."

Elester rose and put his arm about Mathus's shoulder. "And I miss my father," he said, softly.

"Do you think the dead have a voice?" asked Mathus. "Oh, I know I sound like a child asking its first questions about life and death, but his voice . . . Elester, it seems so terribly real."

Elester smiled sadly. "I think it is we who do not want to sever our links with those who are gone."

He guided the older man toward the terrace doors, his heart heavy. Outside in the warm summer night, he gave the man's shoulder a gentle pat. "Try to get some rest, Mathus. It is not my father who calls you. His voice is silent."

Elester stared after the old man until he disappeared into the shadows. Wide awake now, he walked to the end of the terrace and lifted his head toward the winking stars. A meteor shot across the sky—a living fireball blotting out the stars in its fiery wake. But the young Prince saw neither the stars nor the meteor. His hand resting on one of the columns that supported the overhanging roof appeared steady, but he felt it tremble as he saw, again, the Elder's solemn face metamorphose into a fanged horror whose red eyes burned like ice.

"It is just jitters," he said aloud, but the words did nothing to quell the feeling of dread that visited him like an unwanted guest. His Crowning was less than two months away. Laury, Captain of the King's Riders, and two hundred troops had left for the Druid's Close. Their orders were to accompany the Elven Crown on its journey from its heavily-warded nether vault to Bethany, capital of Ellesmere Island. Elester had never seen the actual Crown, and he would not be permitted to set eyes on it until seconds before he took it in his hands and placed it on his head. But he had seen pictures and paintings and had heard about it all of his life.

The Golden Crown had come to this world from Empyrean with the first Elves over a hundred million years ago. Some claimed that it was a great magic, and as old as time. Elester accepted those claims with a grain of salt. But it was old, and it was magnificent—a series of interwoven golden circles, decorated with broad gold oak leaves studded with emeralds the size of large coins. In all of the pictures and paintings the magnificent Cap, as it was known, glowed with an eerie light, almost as if it were a thing fashioned out of fire.

Stifling a yawn, Elester turned toward the open terrace door. Perhaps sleep would come after all. He was glad that the Druid, Naim, would return with Laury and the Riders. It would be good to see his old friend again. But in the meantime, he'd have someone check the underground chamber where his father slept the long sleep. Not that he believed the dead King was calling Mathus, but because something was keeping the Elder awake at night and he meant to know what it was.

CHAPTER TWO

THE CAP

Naim, one of the Five Druids, rode in silence beside the Captain of the Riders. He absentmindedly stroked Avatar's mane and the big red roan stallion showed his appreciation by whickering softly. The Druid was in good spirits. They were five days out of the Druid's Close. If they continued making good time, they'd reach the Elven Kingdom before another week had passed.

It was a gorgeous summer morning. The cloudless sky was a deep iris blue, and even at this early hour, the sun shone brightly on the travellers, warming their bodies and their hearts. Naim grinned. For once, he had embarked on a pleasant mission. He was on his way to Ellesmere Island to attend the Crowning of his good friend, Elester.

In an iron box, on a wagon pulled by two grey Elven horses and flanked by the Riders, sat the Golden Crown of Ellesmere. During the time of the First Druid, the Demon and her vast army of half-dead creatures came out of the Dark Lands and poured across the earth like a pestilence. Believing themselves immune from evil, the Elves went about their business with hardly a thought for events that were happening off their island kingdom. They ignored the Demon—until she crossed the borders of Dundurum, land of the Dwarves, and turned her dark thoughts toward Ellesmere.

Only then did the Elves act. They allied with the Dwarves and prepared for war against Hate's army of evil. The Cap, as the Elves called their Crown, was moved to the Druid's Close and placed in a specially crafted vault. The vault was sealed and transported to a netherworld, beyond the reach of other beings dead or alive. As an extra precaution, the Druids used their combined powers to set wards about the vault. Then, late at night, they did one final thing.

This was only the second time in Naim's long life that the Cap had made this journey. The last event was the Crowning of Elester's father, Ruthar. But death had claimed the old King and now his son would wear the Cap.

The Druid turned to the Captain of the Riders. "I, for one, will be relieved when this Crowning business is over and done."

"My sentiments, exactly," grinned Captain Laury. "But the time is passing quickly and before we know it, the Day will arrive. The Prince will make a fine King."

"I agree," said the Druid. "But I do not approve of this practice of waiting six months after the death of the King to crown the new one. Laury, the world is changing. Half a year is too long for a country to be without a leader."

"There are many who feel as you do," said Laury. "But you know Elves. We do not take change lightly."

"Sometimes change is for the better," said Naim.

The Captain looked at the old Druid and chuckled. "I heard that you had—er—words with the Elders about that matter."

"Humph!" grunted Naim. "I might as well have spoken to Avatar," he said, running his hand along the horse's silky neck. "At least he listens. And I suspect he is also more intelligent." Avatar snorted loudly, causing both men to laugh.

"I take it the Elders said no?"

"Correct," snapped Naim, still irked at the Erudicia for telling him, politely but firmly, to mind his own business.

"Do not let it worry you," said Laury. "The Prince may not wear the Crown, but he is undoubtedly our leader."

Naim nodded. "I suppose you are right, my friend, but I have not rested easy since we found the Demon's serpent on Ellesmere Island. That was the first time evil found its way onto the Island."

Now it was Laury's turn to nod, thoughtfully. He wondered how he could have forgotten about the snake incident. It had happened in Bethany, shortly after the Battle of Dundurum. He saw it clearly now, as if the image were etched on his brain. They were in the park, outside the Council Hall, exchanging farewells with the girl, Miranda, and the boy, Nicholas, and the others. Suddenly, a small dog, belonging to one of the children, caught a serpent and chased the screaming girls, before finally dropping the limp reptile on the grass.

"The snake was never found, Laury."

"That is true," admitted the Captain.

Ahead, one of the Riders, a young man named Aaron, suddenly glanced over his shoulder and pulled his mount to a standstill. He pointed back, toward the northeastern sky. "Captain, we should make for the trees. I see bad weather coming."

Naim wheeled Avatar in the direction the young Rider was pointing. He stared, stone-faced, at the black cloud spreading like a bruise in the sky, and his body turned cold with shock. He knew instinctively what was coming at them. "That is not a storm," he said, almost to himself.

They came out of the Dark Lands like death on the wind—huge winged creatures dragging their hideous shapes across the sky, their pitiless blood-red eyes locked on the human convoy in the distance. The flapping of a thousand pairs of webbed wings created a roar like thunder. The ground beneath the horses' hoofs shook, the trees shuddered, and the proud Elven greys stomped nervously.

They were Werecurs. The Demon's hunters.

They had come to her over the years—humans whose inhuman acts had contaminated them. They came to her willingly, like thirsty men to water, seeking the greatness they craved as their due. And the Demon took them and ruined them, tearing out their minds and stripping away the last shreds of their humanity. She drained their bodies and transfused them with her own black blood. And then, she remade them.

First, she stretched their hands and feet, and fused long, curved talons onto the tips of their fingers and toes. Then, she twisted their faces into blunt muzzles for biting, broke their jaws, ripping out their useless human teeth and filling their mouths with inch-long sharp pointed fangs. Using their own skin, she fashioned bat-like wings and grafted them to the Werecurs' arms and sides. Finally, she plucked out their eyes and filled the empty sockets with fire. When the screaming finally stopped, the Demon stepped back and gazed upon her creations, hissing with pleasure at her blood hunters.

And they were hunting now.

Like the professional soldiers they were, the Riders did not show fear, but Naim knew they were afraid of the giant black cloud. They are right to be afraid, he thought.

"RIDE!" he shouted, urging Avatar into a gallop and heading toward the trees.

The Riders didn't hesitate. Shouting encouragement to their mounts, they chased Avatar as if their lives depended on it.

"What is it?" yelled Laury.

"Not it," answered the Druid. "Werecurs."

"That does not tell me what I have to fight," countered Laury, dryly.

The Druid's mouth thinned as he grinned bitterly. "The Demon's hunters are flesh and bone," he said. "And, yes, they can be killed. But there are not enough of us to fight them, my friend." He peered over his shoulder at the advancing darkness. "No, this is a time for running and hiding. They cannot fly or move easily in the forest."

"Where did they come from? What do they want?" asked Laury, his gray Elven horse keeping pace with the Druid's red roan.

"Out of the Dark," answered the Druid, curtly. "They want the Crown, and they are hungry."

"How can this happen?" said Laury, glancing sharply at the Druid. "The Demon is gone. How can these flying creatures act on their own initiative?"

"Hate may be shut away, but she has ways of communicating with her minions." The Druid shook his head. "Because I did not see them at Dundurum,

I never thought of the Werecurs, much less considered them a threat. That was a big mistake."

The first Riders barely made it into the trees before the creatures plunged from the sky. Looking about, Laury was relieved to see that most of his company had already entered the forest. Then he looked back and his heart raced faster when he saw that the wagon and the twelve Riders guarding it were still out there. Abruptly, he tugged on the reins and the horse wheeled about, reared once, and galloped to intercept the wagon carrying the Empyrean Crown.

One look and the Druid, too, knew that the driver of the wagon and the Riders were in trouble. He reached for the long wooden staff tied loosely to the saddle along Avatar's right flank. Raising it over his head, he spun the great horse about and charged toward the wagon and the doomed band of Elven Riders.

The Werecurs hit the ground hard. Ear-piercing screams and discordant squawks shattered the summer air like an explosion. They resembled a great swelling sea as they covered the ground, staggering and stumbling about to steady themselves. And then, as one unit, they surged toward the wagon and the prize they coveted.

As Avatar bolted past the wagon and the grim-faced guards, Naim shouted. "Keep moving! Do not stop!" Then he slowed, leaped from Avatar's back, and faced the winged army. "GO!" he roared in a horrible voice, pointing the staff back the way the creatures had come. "GO BACK TO THE DARKNESS!"

The sea of Werecurs faltered and then came to a dead stop. Instantly, an eerie silence settled over the plain. The creatures stared, uncertainly, at the lone man separating them from prey and prize. They sensed that he was different from the others. There was something about him that made them flinch in fear. He was dangerous. Some of them were about to die. But it took the creatures only a few seconds to do the math. There were a thousand of them and only one of him. He might kill some, but he couldn't get all of them before they reached him. Screeching in hatred, the Werecurs charged. At the same time, several dozen flapped their grotesque winged limbs, took to the air, and made a beeline for the wagon.

The Riders watching from the edge of the forest held their breaths and shook their heads. The Druid's magic was powerful, but he looked like a feather trying to stop an avalanche. Soon he would drown in the black tide sweeping toward him.

Naim gripped the wooden staff in both hands and plunged it deep into the ground. For a second, nothing happened. And then, a white spark ignited in the earth and burst into a line of flame the length of the staff. Like an electric current, it spread rapidly out from the staff and along the ground in both directions, forming a nine-foot-high wall of white fire. The creatures fell back, shrieking with rage and snapping their gross wings in frustration. But many of them, thinking they could penetrate the wall without incurring serious injuries, flew at it, and burst into flames that reduced them to pale ashes in a heartbeat.

That will hold them back for a minute, thought the Druid, wrenching the staff out of the ground and heaving himself into the saddle. Then he looked for the wagon. He saw that the driver would never reach the safety of the trees before the airborne Werecurs caught up to him.

The first creature landed heavily in front of the wagon, clawed hands raised to slash the horses to ribbons. But the pair of grays galloped straight at the menacing shape without shying. Too late, the Werecur spread its webbed arms, and then the horses were on it, knocking it back and under their pounding hoofs. The thing was already dead when the wagon wheels bumped over its broken body.

Four winged hunters dropped onto the back of the wagon and grasped the handles of the heavy iron box. Laury urged his horse alongside and slashed at the creatures with his sword, striking one in the gut. The mortally wounded Werecur stared in surprise at the thick black blood pouring from the deep gash before stumbling sideways and tumbling off the wagon. Aaron, the Rider who had mistaken the creatures for a storm, leaped off his mount onto the wagon, but another Werecur swooped from above, and before the young man even knew it was there, it drove its sharp claws through his back, piercing his heart. Death came instantly. Screaming triumphantly, the foul creature clutched its victim in its claws and lifted into the sky.

"NO!" yelled Laury, recalling the Druid's words about the hunters' purpose. "Do not let it get away!" Leaving the other Riders to combat the Werecurs in the wagon, he pursued the creature that had killed one of his men. Those Riders who were expert archers sheathed their swords and pulled bows from their saddles, unleashing a hail of arrows into the sky. One after another, arrows thwacked into the creature until it resembled a flying pincushion, but still it remained aloft.

The Druid also saw the Werecur take to the sky clutching the dead Rider in its terrible claws. He pointed the staff at the winged carrion. Less than a second later, a white ball of flaming liquid shot at the evil thing, burning a hole through its body. Hate's hunter dropped the lifeless Rider and uttered a long wailing cry as it plummeted to earth, smoke trailing from its ruined body.

Suddenly the ground shook. The Druid spun Avatar about in time to see the great flock of Werecurs lift awkwardly into the sky and streak toward the east, back the way they had come. He watched until he was satisfied that they were gone. His blue-black eyes remained locked on the box containing the Elven Crown until it became one with the black blur in the sky. Then, he went and gathered the fallen Rider in his arms and, with Avatar following, carried his sad burden toward the solemn company waiting silently near the edge of the forest. He felt a scalding anger rise up inside him as the Elves lowered their comrade onto the dry soil and examined him for signs of life. He watched in silence as they prepared a bed of dry twigs and wood, laid the body on the pyre, and set it ablaze, but his thoughts spoke volumes.

Even though she was imprisoned in the Place with No Name, the Demon still managed to reach out and bring ruin and chaos upon this world, plucking the life from those she hated. The Druid ran his hand over his eyes. He was weary of the never-ending fight, of sleepless nights, and a lifetime filled with horror and sadness. Yes, he was weary—sick to death of bloodshed and the wide, unblinking stares of all the dead, who visited his sleep, and seemed to find him wanting. He gave himself a mental shake to clear his head. He was a Druid, committed to the battle until he took his last breath. His duty was to face evil, to know it, but never, never to let his dark knowledge lead him into darkness or subvert him.

"They took the Cap," said Laury, coming up beside him, his face a mask of mingled anger and grief. "We must get it back."

The Druid's weariness passed. He grasped the Captain's shoulder. "No, my friend. You cannot follow where they are going. Only one man ever made it into the Dark Lands and back." He turned his eyes to the black cloud of Werecurs growing smaller and smaller until it was a thin black line on the horizon. Then he turned back to Laury. "We must bring this news to Bethany, and I must find a way into that evil place and take back the Cap."

CHAPTER THREE

DREAM WALKING

The man appeared out of the night, as if he had materialized out of thin air. Even though Miranda D'arte had been watching for him, waiting, hidden among the thick stand of oleander trees flanking the pathway, his sudden appearance startled her. She inhaled deeply and held it, forcing herself to be still, to be one with the trees. As he drew abreast of her, the man froze. Miranda couldn't take her eyes off the dark, motionless form silhouetted against the pale moonlight, but fear numbed her brain and turned her limbs to jelly. He was so close she could reach out and touch him.

The man remained dead still for a long count of ten, staring straight ahead at the pathway, his head tilted slightly to one side, listening intently. Miranda aped him, but the only sound she heard was the loud thumping of her heart. Surely he could hear it, too. As if he read her thoughts, the man's head whipped to the right, directly toward the place where Miranda stood with her back pressing hard against a cluster of slender tree trunks. He leaned forward, his neck stretching as he peered into the trees.

Please don't let him see me, Miranda begged silently, fighting the panic growing inside her. She desperately needed to breathe, but she had held her breath for so long that she knew the air whooshing out of her throat would be loud enough to wake the dead.

When the man reached out to part the branches, Miranda knew she had only a few seconds left before death came swiftly and terribly. Realizing it was futile, she brought her hand up to her neck, careful not to cause the branches to tremble. Her hand found and closed over the small metallic pouch dangling from a thin silver chain. Trembling uncontrollably, she opened the pouch and poured its contents into her cupped hand. Six smooth oval stones nestled in her palm, thin veins of red visible in their dull greenish glow. Quickly, she made a fist over the stones, closed her eyes, and let her thoughts flow into the cool gems.

The Bloodstones had belonged to her father, who had died before she was born, but they were hers now. King Ruthar gave them to her when she first visited the Elven capital. Miranda knew they were potent magic, but she was still a novice in their use. She figured it would take her many lifetimes to understand their awesome powers. So far, all she knew was that each of the first five stones corresponded to one of the senses. Nobody seemed to know what the sixth stone was for, but Miranda believed it had something to do with knowing. Not just knowing about things, but a very particular thing . . . evil. And, while she couldn't yet tell which stone was which, the knowing stone terrified her half to death.

Now, she felt the familiar tugging sensation as her thoughts were drawn into their buttery smoothness. The first time she experienced the feeling, it had made her sick. Even now, she didn't like the idea of giving up control over her thoughts and actions, sharing her innermost fears with six green pebbles that she hadn't begun to understand.

Abruptly, she found herself on the pathway, peering through the parted branches at the spot where she had been hiding only a second ago. At first, she was totally disoriented, unable to take in what had happened. Then, with a shock that washed over her like a plunge into an icy lake, she realized that she was seeing things through the man's eyes. Somehow she was inside his head, peering at the exact spot where she was still hiding. She also knew that, any moment now, she'd be seeing her own deathly pale face, and staring into a pair of green eyes opened wide in terror.

But, as the man looked deeper into the trees, she saw nothing through his eyes but the shadows of the branches playing in the brighter patches of moonlight on the forest floor. What am I doing here? she wondered. Who is this man? Why am I following him? He was not one of the Demon's evil creatures. She was certain of that, but she sensed that he was deeply troubled. No, he was more than troubled. He was deathly afraid. She heard someone calling his name over and over in his mind. Mathus! She knew that name. She had met all twelve members of the Erudicia the only time she had visited Bethany. Mathus was the Senior Adviser. Why was he afraid of the voice in his mind? She thought of trying to read the fellow's thoughts, but she figured she needed a bit more practice before she attempted to wring that sort of power from the Bloodstones.

Suddenly the branches slapped back into place. The man uttered a long sigh. It was a sad, defeated sound, as if he had suddenly decided to surrender to the enemy. Then he moved away. Miranda found herself among the trees again ready to sob with relief. Why was she frightened? She shouldn't fear Mathus, but she did. Why? Why? She took a minute to slow her pounding heart and ease the ache in her chest. Then she set out after him. Remembering that Elves have keen hearing, she moved parallel to the path, keeping well back and slipping through the trees as quietly as a star slipping across the night sky.

Hunter and hunted moved swiftly. Miranda had no idea of the time, but the stiffness in her legs told her that hours had passed. When Mathus finally stopped before a sturdy door built into a recess at the base of a cliff, Miranda's breathing was ragged.

The man called Mathus looked about furtively before reaching inside his cloak and producing a large key. Miranda inched steadily toward him as he inserted the key into a massive lock and turned it. The solid door clicked open. For some reason, the sight of the key surprised Miranda. She had expected the entry to be warded by spells or another form of Elven magic. What if he locked the door behind him? How was she going to get inside then?

She needn't have worried, because the man removed the key, put it in an inner pocket, and pushed on the door. It glided open slowly, without a sound, and the man disappeared into the darkness. The door swung shut with a faint metallic click.

Miranda sprinted across the grass until she stood in front of the heavy door. Pressing her ear to the damp surface, she listened. But no sound penetrated the thick barrier. She pushed on the door, and a mixture of fear and relief washed over her as it slowly swung open. Quickly, she crossed the threshold, one hand holding the door ajar to admit the feeble moonlight while her eyes adjusted to the blackness.

The room wasn't as dark as it had appeared. Off to her left, a pale, yellowish glow filtered through the cracks between a smaller door and the stone wall. Then, the faint sound of the main door closing at her back sent her spinning around, a startled gasp escaping from her throat. Realizing that she had taken her hand off the door, she forced herself to breathe softly. Then she froze and counted slowly to ten, listening for the slightest reaction to her utterance. Satisfied that the noise hadn't betrayed her presence, she gazed about at her surroundings.

She was in a small, windowless room that had been carved out of the cliff. A strong smell of mildew permeated the dankness, and Miranda's lips curled in disgust. Except for a spindly three-legged stand against the wall next to the door, the room was empty. Miranda crossed the floor in six strides and paused to examine the smaller door. She squinted through the wide cracks. The light coming from somewhere on the other side of the door was too dim for her to see anything clearly, if there was anything to see. But she heard sounds, which seemed to be echoes resounding from a great distance. Then she straightened and pulled the door open.

Beyond, there was no landing, just a flight of descending steps. Miranda started down, hurrying now to catch up with the man. She moved soundlessly, her running shoes gripping the stone. The wide steps spiralled like a screwworm through the rock, deeper and deeper below ground. She didn't know what might be waiting in the frozen silence down there, but the bristling hairs on her neck warned her to be wary.

The descent went on and on. Miranda followed the steady, soft slap of the man's footsteps on the stone. Because the stairs wound downward in a spiral, she couldn't see beyond six or seven steps. Afraid of coming behind Mathus too quickly, she slowed her pace. A sudden shiver told her that the air had been getting colder with each downward step. She crossed her arms and stuck her hands under her armpits to thaw the chill.

Despite the hour, she was wide awake. The cold made her tense and as alert as if she had drunk a vat of coffee. She tilted her head to one side, held her breath and listened, her ears straining. She no longer heard the sound of the man's feet slapping on the steps below. Spurred on by a feeling of dread, she braced herself against the cold and ran lightly down the stairs. Her breath, erupting from her throat in fierce white gusts, clung to her cheeks like ice powder.

The stairs ended abruptly. Ahead, a long passage stretched to an arched opening. There was no sign of Mathus. Keeping close to the wall, Miranda raced to the end of the passage, not stopping until she stood under the arch, before another door. He had to have come this way, she thought, looking about. There was no other way. Cautiously, she opened the door a crack and peered through the opening. It was a large room. Moving cautiously, Miranda edged through the door and slipped behind an immense square pillar.

It was colder than death in the huge, underground chamber. Miranda shivered, folding her arms across her chest, her eyes searching the shadows for Mathus. It was so dark she almost missed him, but he moved suddenly and her eyes caught the movement. He stood before a long table against the wall at the far end of the room, his back to Miranda.

She squinted, trying to see past him at whatever held his attention on the table. She had to get closer. There were three pillars between her and Mathus, all identical to the one she was hiding behind now. She crept slowly toward the table, pausing when she safely reached each pillar. Only when she made it to the last one undetected did she dare peer ahead. The light was better here. She saw that the table was really a thick marble slab resting on a solid stone base, like an altar. But it was the motionless mound on the slab that froze her blood. It was the body of King Ruthar, preserved here in this frigid subterranean room.

A dozen thoughts formed in Miranda's mind. Was this how the Elves buried their dead? Did they keep them here, under the city, preserved on cold stone, for all time? She shuddered at the thought. And where was the cold coming from? Wasn't the temperature supposed to rise as you went deeper into the earth? Was there such a thing as an underground glacier?

Mathus lowered his head and reached for the King's hand, holding it between his as if to warm the cold flesh. Miranda watched, wide-eyed, as he raised the stiff limb to his lips and kissed the emerald stone in the ring on the corpse's middle finger. Still holding the King's hand, he turned away and Miranda saw tears glistening like diamonds on his cheek.

She wondered again why she was here. Why was she following this man, who had obviously cared deeply for King Ruthar, and who now shed tears at the loss of his friend? Then a thought struck her. Maybe she wasn't following him. Maybe she was here to protect him. She was so lost in questioning the reason for her actions that she didn't notice the sudden rise of the dead king's chest or the twitch in the eyelids. It was the heat that jolted her back to reality—heat like a furnace door opening. And it was coming from the body on the marble slab.

The shock of it was like a kick in the ribs. Miranda couldn't move, couldn't breathe. She could only stare in horror, her face bleached as white as old bones, as the body of King Ruthar struggled to rise. The dead man stared at Mathus and opened his mouth as if to speak. But, instead of words, Miranda saw a forked tongue dart from the black hole. Mathus's shoulders tensed, momentarily, and then sagged in defeat. He already knew that he was going to die. Too late, he tried to release the King's hand. It was the King who finally jerked his limb from the other's grasp, but not before pressing a round black object into Mathus's hand.

For a heartbeat, the old man's eyes moved from the King's leering face to the bauble gleaming in his open palm. Then, the black object burst and the screaming started. But Miranda didn't know whether the screams were coming from her or from Mathus.

CHAPTER FOUR

MIDNIGHT CHAT ROOM

Something cold touched her shoulder.

Instantly, Miranda's body went ramrod stiff. Her hands, which were pressed tightly over her ears to shut out the blood-curdling screams, formed fists that flew at her attacker as if they were acting on their own. Her eyes were so huge with terror they threatened to pop out of her head.

"Ahhh . . .!"

"Miranda!" The sharp voice drove away the man's dying screams.

Miranda knew that voice, although now it rang with an unfamiliar urgency. She blinked rapidly as her world came into focus, and almost giggled with relief to find herself sitting bolt upright in her own bed, in her own room, in the cozy little house near the Rideau River in Ottawa, where she lived with her mother.

The older woman was leaning over her, concern furrowing her brow and clouding her usually bright green eyes. She perched on the edge of the bed and brushed her hand along the girl's pale, frozen cheek. "Are you OK now?"

Miranda nodded, still half-asleep, still a bit fearful that the dream was the reality and this comforting homey scene had been thrown in to weaken her defences.

"I thought you were being murdered," said Dr. D'arte, keeping her voice low and her tone light. After a second, she added, almost as an afterthought. "I didn't know you were still having those dreams."

"I'm not," said Miranda, squeezing her eyes shut.

"Then . . .?"

"Shhh!" interrupted Miranda, impatiently. "Be quiet!"

Dr. D'arte stood and moved to the window. Sighing softly, she parted the drapes and raised her eyes toward the sky, but the light from the room blotted out the stars. Her hands dropped to her side and she sighed again, feeling as if she were being drawn into a recurring, living nightmare—one from which there was no waking.

She remembered when the dreams had started. Was it only three months ago? Night after night, a Demon with claws like steel icicles and blood the colour of oil dripping from her long tongue invaded Miranda's sleep. Dr. D'arte had never felt so helpless, watching dark circles form under her daughter's eyes and remain there like permanent bruises. Her heart ached to think that the nightmares had returned.

In March, Miranda's dreams foreshadowed a vicious attack on the D'arte home by creatures straight out of the worst nightmare imaginable. Hate, a Demon from another, older world, escaped from the prison where she had been shut away for a thousand years. She and her cold-blooded assassins, the monstrous Thugs, along with other half-dead creatures, sped to Ottawa to find Miranda and kill her.

Dr. D'arte shivered, reliving that chilling experience. She heard again the harsh, urgent voice of the Druid known as Naim who came like a blast of winter air and sent her fleeing from her home and daughter in the middle of the night. "Leave the girl!" he had ordered. "Go now, or she will surely die!"

If it had been anyone else, she wouldn't have listened—would never have left Miranda behind. But she had known the Druid once and knew, too, that he did not lie. As long as the Demon could get her hands on Miranda's mother, Miranda was as good as dead. So, without a word, Dr. D'arte had run

42

away. And it was the most painful thing she had ever done. Even now, even knowing that she had done the only thing she could, she felt as guilty as if she had murdered her own flesh and blood.

"Aarg!" growled Miranda, pulling her short hair in frustration. "I'm losing it."

Her daughter's voice cut into Dr. D'arte's thoughts, sending them scattering like smoke in the wind. She spoke, but the words came out wrong, sounding false and clinical, as if she were calming a distressed patient. "You're not losing it. I told you before, there's nothing wrong with you, Miranda. Everybody has dreams, and some of them end in nightmares."

Miranda snorted rudely. "I'm not losing my mind," she snapped, frowning at her mother. "My dream. It's going, and it's very important."

"Don't think . . . just talk . . . take your time . . . tell everything you remember," said her mother, leaving the window and curling up on her side on the other twin bed. She closed her eyes and appeared to be asleep, but, being a first-rate psychiatrist, she was trained to listen and now, her full attention was on her daughter.

Miranda stared at her mother without seeing her, wisps of the dream drifting through her mind like dust motes crossing a beam of sunlight. "I think I was in Bethany, but I'm not sure. I was following someone . . . a man . . . I don't know why . . . I recognized him . . ." She paused for a second, frowning as she tried to picture the man's features. "But I can't remember now who it was. We went down some steps . . . a lot of steps . . . into a huge room . . . miles under the city. It was cold . . . freezing . . ."

At the mention of the frigid temperature in the underground chamber, Dr. D'arte sat up, her body suddenly as tense as a bow, her flesh crawling. Don't go there! She warned herself. I know what you're thinking. No! No! It's not possible. She was here . . . in bed . . . it was just a bad dream. But she shuddered as she remembered touching her daughter's cheek as the girl awakened. Her flesh had felt as cold as a chunk of ice. Where on earth had the cold come from . . . in Ottawa . . . in June?

"Mom, you're not listening."

Wandering lost in her own incredible thoughts, Dr. D'arte jumped at the sound of the girl's accusing tone.

"I said that's where I saw King Ruthar." Miranda's green eyes sparkled. "And Mom, he's alive."

She waited for the older woman to react.

Her mother leaned back on the bed and rested her head against the headboard. All her energy was gone, and she felt empty and dead. "What are you telling me, Miranda?"

"I'm telling you I saw King Ruthar . . . in my dream." She raised her hand. "No, don't say it. I know. I know. It was just a dream, but I think it means he's still alive."

"Dreaming doesn't make it real," said her mother, as a strong hand gripped and squeezed her heart.

"I know," said Miranda. "But it could. Why not? You're the one who's always saying anything's possible."

Her mother crossed her arms and glared at Miranda. "You know very well that when I say anything's possible I'm not talking about the dead suddenly getting up and waltzing about."

"Remember, when I was having those dreams about the Demon chasing me, you said it wasn't my dream but a replaying of something that really happened to someone else?"

Dr. D'arte swung her legs off the bed and faced her daughter. "I did not say it wasn't your dream. I said that it might be a scrap of memory you inherited from one of our ancestors, the same way you inherit your looks and other things." She thought for a second. "But if this is a memory of an event that happened to someone else, then it has to be an old memory, from a time when Ruthar was still alive. Don't you see, King Ruthar died three months ago, but any memories you might have inherited are about things that happened a long time before that."

"You could be wrong, you know," said Miranda.

"I'm too tired to argue, Miranda, but what you're saying doesn't fly. You know Ruthar's dead. You were there. You saw things through your own eyes.

And neither dreaming nor anything else can undo what happened."

Miranda shook her head stubbornly. "I still believe he's alive."

Dr. D'arte wrapped her arms about the girl. "Oh, Mir, I know how you felt about Ruthar. I know how hard it is to deal with the fact that someone you loved is gone."

"I hate it when you use your doctor's voice. I'm not one of your patients," said Miranda crossly, pulling free from her mother's embrace. "Anyway, you don't understand. It's not about me. Sure, I liked King Ruthar. He was nice. And, he was different . . . sort of like if you were in a room with a thousand people, you couldn't help noticing him. He was really good—a burning sort of goodness that seemed to light up the dark." She glanced at her mother. "Does that sound stupid?" But before Dr. D'arte could reply, she continued. "I was sad when he died, but not for me. For Elester. King Ruthar was his father. And, I was sad for all the Elves on Ellesmere Island because they lost their king. They really loved him, Mom."

"I know," said her mother softly. "I knew him too, you know."

This time, it was Miranda who reached out to touch her mother's shoulder, but Dr. D'arte didn't notice the gesture as she rose and walked back to the window. Poor Mom, thought Miranda, tears welling up in her eyes. I keep forgetting that Bethany was her home.

Miranda still found it hard to deal with the fact that her mother had a secret past that she had successfully hidden for ten years. Until three months ago, Miranda had never heard of Bethany, capital of the Kingdom of Ellesmere, and neither had anybody else in her world, except her mother. The land of the Elves wasn't on any map and it definitely wasn't something Miranda had studied in geography class.

Bethany existed in another world—a world that the Elves concealed from North and South Americans, Europeans, Asians, Africans and other peoples in Miranda's world. Wrong, she thought. It's our world that's concealed. We're the ones who didn't want to have anything to do with magic and other things we don't understand.

Until three months ago, Miranda, like any reasonable person, would have laughed herself silly if one of her friends had told her she'd been to a world where Elves, Dwarves, Dragons, and other creatures actually existed. Back then she would have described herself as a typical ten-year-old Canadian. She went to sleep at night, got up in the morning, snatched breakfast on the run, attended school, hung out with her friends, listened to music, and talked for hours on the telephone. Three months ago, she believed that her entire history and that of her family was centred in Ottawa.

But Miranda's world was turned upside down that chilly night in March when evil in the form of the nine-foot Thugs and Hate, the Demon, came to Ottawa to find her and destroy her. In desperation, she had put her trust in a harsh-speaking stranger who claimed to be a Druid from a parallel world. Together, Druid and girl had raced through the streets of Ottawa to Parliament Hill, narrowly escaping the terrifying Thugs, and before Miranda knew it, she was dropping like a stone into a vast sapphire blue lake surrounding the land of the Elves.

"I know what you're thinking," she said to her mother's back. "You think I'm different since I came back from Bethany, don't you?"

Her mother didn't turn around. "Yes, you've changed." Then she added hurriedly, "But that's not a bad thing, is it?"

"I guess," said Miranda, waiting a few seconds before asking. "What's different about me?"

When she spoke again, her mother sounded sad. "The biggest change I've noticed is that you're quieter—more serious. You don't seem to have as much fun as you used to."

Miranda smiled to herself. "Well, I am maturing, Mom. Have you thought about that?"

"I hope you're right," said her mother. "But I feel it's more than that. There's something missing—some part of you that's gone for good."

Miranda turned out the light, got out of bed and went to stand beside her mother at the window. Together, they gazed in silence at the night. Miranda had never noticed so many stars in the Ottawa sky. But tonight the city lights appeared softer, the sky blacker, the stars bright as ice, and amongst the millions upon millions of stars, she could see the hazy swath of the Milky Way, a slip of gauze stretching like a pathway across the silent sky.

They stood side by side for a long time, lost in their own thoughts. Dr. D'arte put her arm about Miranda's shoulder, shivering as cold seeped from the girl's body through her sweater, chilling her to the bone. She was here, she kept repeating, as if her sanity depended on making herself believe the words. She was here . . . asleep.

Miranda worried about her mother, wondering what other secrets she was keeping from her. When she finally yawned, Dr. D'arte gently steered her toward her bed and moved to the door. "Mom!"

"Hmmm?" The older woman paused in the doorway and looked back, the light from the hall hiding her features.

"You're right, you know. It seemed real, but now that I'm awake, I know King Ruthar's dead."

CHAPTER FIVE

PLANS AND SCHEMES

King Ruthar's alive," said Miranda, catching her best friend by surprise and grinning at the effect her words had on the other girl.

The school cafeteria was jam-packed with the usual lunchtime crowd. Arabella Winn almost choked on the remains of a peanut butter and grape jelly sandwich she had just stuffed into her mouth. She gaped at Miranda, her expression flipping from happiness to disbelief and back again. "Wha . . .?"

"You are disgusting, you know that," said Miranda, making a face at the girl across the table.

They were complete opposites in almost every way. Miranda's frame was tall and slim, like a lanky boy. Her blond hair hung just below her chin and the ends were wispy. Her pale skin made her green eyes shine like emeralds. Arabella was petite and bouncy like an India rubber ball or a Jack Russell terrier. She was dark-skinned, her short hair pitch black except for a natural white patch that hung just above her right eye. They had been best friends since nursery school.

Now, Arabella rolled her dark eyes toward the ceiling, took a gulp of chocolate milk to wash down the dry peanut butter, and listened without interrupting as Miranda told her about the nightmare.

"That's scary! But Mir, it was just a dream."

On the other hand, Arabella knew Miranda, and despite the fact that what she said was impossible, she didn't really doubt her friend. They had known each other too long and shared too many adventures for doubt to suddenly cloud their friendship.

"I guess it does sound crazy," admitted Miranda. "And I can't explain it. But Bell, I know something's wrong. I just know . . . here . . ." She pressed her hand against her heart. "And I'm afraid it's really, really bad."

"How bad is really, really bad?" asked Arabella, dreading the answer and suddenly feeling sick. She looked at her plate and decided she never wanted to see another peanut butter sandwich as long as she lived.

"I don't know." Miranda brought her fist down on the table. "Why can't I remember it?" Then, she reached out and gently slapped Arabella's hand. "I wish you could have been in my dream and seen what I saw. It was so scary. King Ruthar was lying on this sort of altar thing. I mean, he was dead, Bell. When I saw him trying to sit up, I could actually feel my heart stop beating."

"No kidding!" agreed her friend. "Please, just promise me one thing. Keep me out of your dreams. OK?" She thought for a second, her face frozen in a frown. Then her eyes opened wide and the frown turned into a look of sheer terror. "Mir! What if it's the Demon again?"

"I've thought and thought about that until my brain hurts," said Miranda. "It can't be Hate, because we were there when she disappeared into the Place with No Name."

"Then who?" asked Arabella.

"Or what?" said Miranda. She shivered as a small voice inside urged her not to dismiss the Demon so lightly. "You know, Bell, maybe you're right. It can't be the Demon, in person, but I have a feeling she's involved, somehow."

"What are we going to do?" Just thinking about the Demon made Arabella break out in a cold sweat. For a second, she didn't want to hear any more about Miranda's dream. She didn't want to do anything at all except run home as fast as her legs would carry her and hide under her bed or down in the basement behind the pile of old trunks and boxes. Why had she said, what are we going to do?

Miranda's response was immediate. "I don't know about you, but I've got to go back."

"That's definitely not a good idea," said Arabella firmly, her mind working furiously to dissuade her friend from running off to the land of the Elves at the drop of a hat. Or was she looking for an excuse to get out of having to accompany her? "For one thing, you can't rely on the dream, because you can't even remember most of it. And for another, if something really bad happened, don't you think we'd have heard from the Druid by now?"

Miranda thought about what Arabella said. "You're right," she agreed. "If something happened, I think Naim would have come for us, or got word to me somehow. But what if it hasn't happened yet? What if he doesn't know?"

Arabella sighed. It didn't do any good to argue with Miranda when her mind was made up. "I guess this means I'm going with you."

"Where are we going?" asked Nicholas Hall, slipping into a chair, pushing his unruly dark-brown hair out of his eyes, and unscrewing the plastic cap from a bottle of water. The boy lived on the street behind Miranda's in New Edinburgh. They had been friends since Miranda said her first words, and over the years, had worn a footpath through the backyards between their homes. He was tall for a twelve-year-old and excelled in basketball and soccer. It was Nicholas, along with Arabella and Penelope St. John, who had accompanied Miranda to Bethany to learn why the Demon wanted her dead.

"Miranda thinks there's something wrong in Bethany," said Arabella.

Nicholas looked at Miranda, a dozen questions showing on his face, waiting to be asked. After she repeated as much of her dream as she could remember, the three companions sat, without speaking, motionless, like figures carved in stone. It was Nicholas who finally broke the silence, cutting to the chase.

"How're we getting there?"

Miranda felt their eyes on her, waiting for her answer. She reached to clasp a small metallic pouch attached to a chain she wore about her neck, feeling panic welling up inside when she discovered it wasn't there. Except to shower, she rarely took it off. Then she remembered laying the chain and pouch containing the Bloodstones on the floor of her locker after gym. She made a mental note to be sure and fetch it on her way back to class.

"The Druid said we can't go back, remember?" said Arabella. "The Portal's closed from here."

"I never heard him say that," said Nicholas, turning to Miranda. "Is that true?"

Miranda nodded. "But later, he told me that if someone from there comes here, they can take us back with them."

"What about the Dwarves? Do you think one of them can take us back?"

"Good thinking, Nick." Miranda felt guilty every time she thought about the Dwarves. In March, Gregor, fifteenth King of the Dwarves, had sent a dozen of his short, stocky subjects to Ottawa to repair the damage Hate had wreaked on Parliament Hill. That was the last time Miranda had seen them, and she felt bad. They were strangers in her country and she had practically ignored them. Somehow, she felt she had let them down. Uncomfortable in the open, the Dwarves preferred to make their temporary home in the tunnels under the Parliament Buildings, sleeping by day and working by night.

No one but Miranda, her mother, and the three friends who had accompanied her to that other world, knew about the Dwarves' presence in Canada's capital. But strange stories about sightings of short, square ghosts who wandered the Parliament Buildings in the middle of the night were circulating around the city, taking on the mantle of urban myths.

"Did you hear the latest?" asked Nicholas, whose engineer father had the contract for the repairs to the main government building on Parliament Hill. "When Dad got to work yesterday morning, he found the stonemasons lying about on the floor, drunk as skunks. He couldn't get any sense out of them. He said they babbled on about someone crushing all the stone they were using, and they couldn't work. But, when Dad inspected the site, the work had been done. He said it was the finest stonework he's ever seen."

They all chuckled. "If you notice him acting strange, we might have to tell him what's going on," said Miranda.

"Yeah," said Nicholas. "Last night, I caught him staring off into space like his brain had been sucked out. I think he's trying to figure out how drunk stonemasons, who say they didn't do the work, did it better than if they'd been sober. He told me this morning, starting tonight he's posting guards at the site."

"We'd better warn the Dwarves," said Miranda, feeling sorry for Nick's father. She decided to run the problem by her mother when she got home. Maybe she'd know what to do. After all, they couldn't let Mr. Hall go crazy, could they?

When the buzzer sounded, summoning the kids to class, the three companions agreed to meet after school and go see the Dwarves on Parliament Hill. Even if the Dwarves couldn't get them to Bethany, it was going to be worth the trek to find out if they had any news from the old world.

"And don't tell Penelope, or the whole school

will show up," cautioned Nicholas. "And whatever you do, don't provoke Stubby. Stay cool. You don't need him hitting you with detention today."

"What makes you think we'd provoke him?" giggled Miranda, spinning about and marching toward the cafeteria doors. "Would we do something like that?"

Nicholas watched the girls walk away, doubled up with laughter. He figured they were up to something. But the big question was what?

CHAPTER SIX

MIRANDA CONDITIONING

Two more days, sighed Mr. Little, desperate for school to end and summer vacation to begin. The corners of his mouth turned down in disgust as the grade four students filed into the classroom—some of them coming alarmingly close to him. He held a long wooden pointer in one hand and poked William Potts in the ribs as that unfortunate boy dropped a pen and brushed against him as he bent over to retrieve it. "Get away from me," he barked, his face twisted in anger. The chubby boy yelped and scuttled quickly out of his way, the pen forgotten. Stubby hated the smell of the little rodents.

"Rule 3!" he barked, using the pointer to score a nasty blow on Samantha Enders's shoulder. Realizing that she had broken Rule 3, which said that students taller than Stubby must stoop in his presence, the girl's face turned red as a beet and she instantly bent her knees and shrank until her eyes were at the level of the teacher's chin.

Mr. Little pulled a crumpled, soiled remnant of cloth from a bulging jacket pocket and quickly held it over his mouth and nose. They pretended otherwise, but he knew they did it on purpose. Probably only bathed on weekends. The reason he knew they smelled just to aggravate him was because he hadn't noticed their individual and collective reeks until just after Spring Break. And, while he couldn't prove it, he knew who was behind it . . . the D'arte brat.

His flesh crawled as if all the fleas living on the unwashed bodies of the kids suddenly abandoned them for him. He whacked his chest and legs with the pointer, ignoring the curious looks turned his way. It's not fleas, he scolded himself. No, he didn't have fleas; it was a reaction to the D'arte girl. Whenever he so much as thought about her, he had to fight off an uncontrollable urge to scratch and scratch until his skin was raw.

"SIT!" he shouted, and his mood underwent a rapid transformation. He loved shouting at them and seeing the fear in their eyes as they obeyed his commands like trained dogs. Too bad he couldn't figure out a way to stop the noise, to make them stop scraping their feet, or tapping their pens, or crinkling paper, or coughing. Or breathing, he added, wistfully. Short of beating them to death, he hadn't been able to come up with a solution. Maybe a chemical spray in their inhalers, or something that'd glue them in place for the day, he thought.

Miranda looked over her shoulder and flashed Arabella a wicked grin.

At that moment, almost as if he had been waiting for a signal, William Potts stood and waddled to the front of the class. Every eye was on the boy as he turned his back on Stubby, placed one hand on the teacher's desk to brace himself and reached down to retrieve the pen he had dropped when Mr. Little prodded him with the pointer.

Caught off guard by the audacity of the Potts boy leaving his seat without permission, and after he had been specifically told to sit, Mr. Little was slow to react. He watched in horror as the boy bent over, the seams of his trousers stretching tight as his fat behind floated up, like two balloons, toward the teacher.

"Aaak!" shrieked Stubby, jumping back, like a giant flea, and coming to a stop in the corner by the window.

For the first time in his memory, instant and absolute silence fell on the classroom. Stubby couldn't believe the blessed quiet. He dropped the pointer and stuck his index fingers into his ears. Satisfied that no gobs of wax or matted hairs were blocking his hearing, he stayed absolutely still, afraid that the slightest movement would bring back the din.

He didn't move when Willy Potts straightened up and walked as quietly as a mouse back to his seat. Instead, he peered about and almost hugged himself as the most delicious feeling washed over him. It was the rodents. They weren't wearing their usual rude, smirking faces. Even Miranda D'arte and her pimply little friend were looking at him politely—with respect.

Mr. Little's heart sang. This was the greatest moment in his life—the moment he had been dreaming of for forty-five years—when the filthy brats finally recognized and bowed to his superior intellect. As he peered suspiciously from face to face, searching for any signs of trickery, and finding none, he suddenly realized that he wasn't looking at a room filled with monsters in adolescents' bodies. They were just children. How could he have imagined that such innocent faces hid diseased brains? At that moment, Stubby felt so fond of them he wanted to hug them.

He took a small step out of the corner.

Miranda didn't dare take her eyes off Stubby. She knew if she looked at one of her classmates, she'd laugh until her sides split. She saw the pleased expression settle on the teacher's face as he moved. This was the moment she'd been waiting for. She broke eye contact with the teacher and coughed. Immediately, the entire class joined her in a cacophony of sounds produced by throat clearing, fidgeting, and the shuffling of twenty-three pairs of feet.

What's happening? Stubby almost staggered and keeled over as the horrible noise reverberated off the walls. "SILENCE!" he screamed, retracing his step back into the corner. Again, the class went as quiet as the middle of the night.

So, after several unsuccessful attempts to leave the corner where he had sent students crawling for as long as he had been a teacher at Hopewell Elementary School, Mr. Little stayed there. A small voice whispered a warning in his ear, but the silence was so blissful, he quickly gagged the voice, and conducted the afternoon lessons with no other sounds competing with the pleasing quality of his own voice.

And then, a loud guffaw erupted from the back of the room, triggering prompt bursts of bottled-up laughter from other students. In less than a heartbeat, the entire class was doubled over, laughing as if they'd never stop.

"BE QUIET!" Mr. Little snatched the pointer and smacked it against the top of his desk. "SILENCE!" Still the kids laughed until tears streamed down their cheeks. He caught Miranda D'arte exchanging a smug grin with the Winn girl. "YOU!" he shouted, aiming the pointer at Miranda. "COME HERE . . . AT ONCE!"

"Who, me?" asked Miranda, all innocence again.

"YES, YOU!"

Miranda shrugged and, remembering to stoop, walked toward the teacher, eyes on the tapered end of the pointer, prepared to duck or jump aside if he raised it to strike her. She noticed that the knuckles on the hand gripping the pointer were white. As she drew near, Stubby moved quickly behind his desk and pointed to the corner. Miranda gave him a wide berth as she settled on the floor in the corner, turning her face to hide the smile that seemed stuck on her lips.

For a full minute, Stubby glared at her, desperately trying not to choke on the hatred welling up inside him. "I've had just about enough of you," he said without moving his lips and just loud enough for Miranda's ears.

Miranda kept her eyes averted, pretending she hadn't heard the threatening words. She noticed Penelope St. John eying her curiously. She stayed on the hard floor until the buzzer rang at three p.m. Jumping to her feet, she had taken only a couple of steps toward the open classroom door when Mr. Little's voice stopped her in mid-stride. "Where do you think you're going?" he asked.

"School's out," answered Miranda, turning to meet the teacher's eyes, which were boring holes through her skin.

The look Stubby returned was so horrible, Miranda drew in a sharp breath and recoiled in fear. Caught in the sunlight streaming through the window, the teacher's eyes shone like the burning ends of a pair of cigarettes. "GET . . . BACK . . . IN . . . YOUR . . . CORNER!" He spat out the words as if they burned his mouth, saliva collecting in the corners of his lips.

A surge of anger rose in Miranda's chest and made her bold. "Why?" she asked, crossing her arms, fingers automatically reaching for the Bloodstones, but they were still in her locker.

"What did I do?" she demanded, thinking as she said it about the trick she'd played on Stubby—how all the kids had laughed at him. He might think I did something, but he couldn't prove it in a million years.

Stubby snatched the pointer and sprang at her only to find his way blocked as Penelope St. John stepped between them. "Please, Mr. Little," said the redhead, a smile as wide as the St. Lawrence River lighting up her face. "It's about what you said in geography . . . about the greenhouse effect on Prince Edward Island . . . I don't understand . . ."

Mr. Little's attention dropped from Miranda and settled on Penelope like a wasp on a soft-drink can. He stood taller and puffed out his chest self-importantly. Miranda seized her chance, gave Penelope a soft nudge in the back to show her thanks and quickly slipped out the door. Then she ran along the corridor, ignoring shouts of "NO RUNNING!" from the teachers, and didn't stop until she was outside, safe, with Nick and Bell.

Back in the grade four classroom, Mr. Little beamed at Penelope. She was his favourite student. Correction, she was the only student he could stand. "My dear Miss St. John" (carefully pronouncing it "Sen Gen"). Penelope almost gagged at the false sweetness of his voice. "The greenhouse effect . . . It is a difficult concept, but yes, I'd be happy to help you get a handle on it before tomorrow's test." He lowered his voice and whispered, meaningfully. "Yes, it's one of the test questions." His voice returned to normal. "The greenhouse effect occurs in greenhouses, in which radiant heat from the sun passes through the glass, warming everything inside. The radiant heat from inside can't get out because of the glass. If we apply this effect to the earth's atmosphere . . . blah . . . blah . . . blah . . ."

"You owe me big time, Miranda," whispered Penelope under her breath as Stubby's voice droned on and on without any sign of letting up. She kept glancing out the window until she saw Miranda, Arabella, and Nicholas racing across the schoolyard. Satisfied that Miranda was safe from Stubby, she suddenly looked at her watch, fluttered her perfectly manicured fingers in the teacher's face, and broke up the boring dissertation on the greenhouse effect.

"Sorry, Sir, I just remembered I've got a nail appointment. Ta, ta!" And she turned on her heel and marched out the door, anxious to find out what Miranda and the others were up to.

Irritated at the girl's sudden departure, after she had asked for his help, Mr. Little sat on the edge of his desk and spoke to the perfect classroom— empty and silent—telling it all that he knew about the greenhouse effect. When he had finished, he sat in silence for a long time, reliving the humiliating events of the afternoon—acknowledging the awful truth that the students who habitually cringed in terror if he so much as glanced their way had ridiculed him—had actually laughed at him, laughed until their faces got red and ugly. It wasn't right. Suddenly he brightened. He knew what he must find, and he knew exactly where to find it.

Stubby hummed to himself as he opened the door and strolled along the corridor toward the monsters' lockers. In keeping with Hopewell's honour system, the kids' lockers were easily accessible. In the school's long history, no one had ever abused the code by going into someone else's locker. Well, Mr. Little had an honour system too, and he didn't give a hoot about a bunch of little warts who couldn't even spell honour. He opened Miranda's locker and there, right on top of the pile, he spotted what he was looking for. Humming at a faster tempo, he took the textbook and quickly shoved it under his jacket. Just as he was about to close the locker door, his eye fastened on a shiny metal object on the floor of the locker. Quick as a flash, he snatched the curious little pouch and popped it in his pocket. Now wasn't a good time to examine his find. Carefully closing the locker, he patted his pocket and carried the book back to his desk.

He sat and stared at the title for a long time. He wasn't a psychologist, but he knew this famous book. Boris: Introduction to Psychology. The book opened at page 171 where someone had stuck a bookmark. The chapter was entitled "Operant Conditioning in Human Subjects." His eyes narrowed and his lips tightened as he read the highlighted paragraph:

Studies conducted on human subjects have shown that behaviour can be modified by repeated application of methods similar to those employed in studies on Dogs. Every first year psychology class has successfully confined the professor in a corner by becoming noisy and disruptive whenever he attempted to move away.

Mr. Little reread the passage and gently closed the book. He sat motionless for several minutes. Then his face contorted into a mask of rage. He snatched up the book, fingers digging into the cover as if he were throttling it, and hurled it the length of the classroom. The sturdily bound text smashed against the back wall, breaking its spine before falling open on the floor. The crazed teacher strode after the book, knocking aside the desks as if they were bits of fluff in his way. He grabbed the book and tore at it, shredding the pages with his long, yellow fingernails, ripping them out and scattering them about the room. When he had destroyed the book, he sank onto the floor and hummed insanely, pouring the six curious smooth pebbles he found in the small metallic pouch from hand to hand, as he planned his revenge on Miranda D'arte.

CHAPTER SEVEN

THE TUNNELS OF PARLIAMENT HILL

"I'd give anything to have been there," laughed Nicholas, after the girls, between fits of giggling, told him how the entire grade four class had got together to control Stubby.

"It was perfect," said Arabella, her dark eyes sparkling with mischief. "We could have kept him in the corner for the rest of the week if Penelope hadn't blown it."

"It doesn't matter," said Miranda. "If she hadn't laughed, I would have."

"Watch out, Mir," said Nicholas, suddenly turning

serious. "If Stubby ever finds out it was you . . ."

"How can he find out?" Arabella cut in. "You think anybody in our class is going to tell? We were all in on it."

"He already thinks it was all my doing," said Miranda, shrugging her shoulders to show her friends she wasn't worried. "But he can't prove it or do anything about it. Only two more days till school's out, and we'll never have to see him again."

"What if he fails you?"

"Could he do that?" asked Arabella, turning as green as the copper roofs on Parliament Hill.

"He won't," said Miranda confidently. "He wants to get rid of us even more than we want him out of our lives."

With Nicholas in the lead, the companions made their way along a pathway on the cliff behind the Library of Parliament. Below, the Ottawa River flowed swiftly past, on its way to join the mighty St. Lawrence near Montreal. Miranda was glad it wasn't a sheer drop down to the river. She wasn't afraid of heights the way Bell was, but the thought of losing her footing and dropping like a stone into the roiling black water filled her with dread.

Abruptly, Nicholas stopped and pointed at something on the cliff above. Miranda squinted and looked. About twenty feet up, she saw three long, arched openings cut out of the limestone. She also saw the strong iron bars blocking them. The climb looked easy, but by the time they gained the narrow ledge in front of one of the openings, the companions' faces were red and shiny, and sweat made dark patches on their t-shirts.

Miranda doubled over, taking deep breaths as she examined the iron bars set vertically into the stone, effectively blocking any attempts to trespass. Straightening, she caught hold of the bars and shook them back and forth, but they were set in concrete and wouldn't budge. Rust shifted under her hands and shed from the bars like flecks of dry red skin.

"What are these? Air vents?" she asked, frowning as she wiped her rust-stained hands on her pants.

"Probably," answered Nicholas. Then he noticed her frown. "Forget about those bars. I tested them last time I was here. They're solid. We're going to the last opening. One of the bars there is loose and we can pry it out."

"What are we going to say if somebody stops us?" asked Arabella, following the others along the narrow ledge.

Nicholas laughed. "Don't worry, if anybody catches us, it'll probably be my Dad."

They moved carefully, in single file, the late afternoon sun warm on their backs. At the third opening, Nicholas tested the bars until he found the one that was loose. Gripping it with both hands, he lifted and pushed inward in one motion. The bottom of the bar slipped up far enough to be jarred loose. Sucking in his breath, the boy turned sideways and squeezed through the narrow opening. Then, he held the bar until Miranda and Arabella were standing beside him. Nicholas pushed the bar back in place, knelt on the hard floor and rooted through his backpack, pulling out an old map and a flashlight. Miranda and Arabella crouched over his shoulder. Nicholas spread the map on the stone floor and ran the light across its length.

"Wow!" breathed Miranda. "Look at all the tunnels."

"Yeah, it's like a maze," said Nicholas. "They run all the way from here, underground, paralleling Wellington Street to the Supreme Court Building." He poked his index finger near the bottom of the map. "We're here. But, without a map, you'd never find your way back, so let's stick together." He shone the light in Miranda's face. "Where are the Dwarves?"

"I don't know. I haven't seen them since they came back from Bethany with us." Miranda shook her head. "But if it were me, I'd pick a spot close to where I'd be working."

"Good thinking," said Arabella, peering fearfully into the darkness. "Since we're under the Library, it can't be that far to the Centre Block."

"Let's go," said Nicholas, refolding the map, but keeping it in his hand.

It was spooky in the underground tunnel. The companions walked quickly, eyes locked on the bouncing circle of light from the flashlight in Nicholas's hand, their thoughts on another journey they had made under the Parliament Buildings, when they had followed Naim, the Druid, to Bethany.

As they moved farther away from the arched vents, the darkness thickened. Miranda felt the silence settle like lead, shutting out the outside world and the familiar drone of the city. The only sounds were eerie grindings of stone against stone as the massive buildings and the rock mass shifted and settled, and the muffled echoes of their running shoes thumping on the hard tunnel floor.

Miranda kept glancing at the ceiling as she walked. She knew they were under the Library of Parliament. The thought of the huge building resting just over her head worried her. What if the tunnel collapsed from all that weight? Who'd ever find them among the millions and millions of tons of stone? She swallowed, chasing the thought from her head. But she also made a promise to herself. Next time, if there were a next time, she'd tell her mother where she was going.

"Do you think the Dwarves will remember us?" Bell whispered, her eyes scouting the shadows beyond the dancing light. "It's been three months."

"Why wouldn't they?" said Nicholas. "You can bet that every time they work in the Centre Block, they're thinking of the Demon and the mess she made here. Right, Mir?"

Miranda didn't react to her friends' chatter. She felt suddenly anxious, but couldn't pinpoint the source of her anxiety. She didn't like the heavy silence. She was constantly aware of it, pressing down on her, setting her teeth on edge. It was neither the familiar, comfortable silence she sometimes shared with her friends nor an angry, purposeful silence. This silence, trapped in the vast underground network of caves and tunnels, was different from anything she had ever experienced. It was as old as the limestone cliffs—older, even, than memory. She could hear Nick and Bell prattling amicably and she found it strange that, instead of shattering the silence, their words were absorbed into the stillness, like liquid drawn into a sponge.

Then she heard another unfamiliar sound. What was it?

She concentrated on that sound, her uneasiness growing. It seemed to be swelling, the deeper into the tunnel they went. It was different from the sighing and groaning of the rock mass as it expanded or contracted—more a rasping that reminded her of the sound she made slurping up the last drops of a milkshake through a straw. Tired of straining her ears, she finally dismissed it, not wanting to think about the kinds of insects and other crawling, scuttling things that lived in the cold, damp darkness.

They walked in silence, passing along the ghostly passage like shadows. Miranda wondered how long they'd been walking, moving deeper and deeper into the tunnel. She sensed that the afternoon had turned into evening. Surely they'd passed the Centre Block by now. Where were the Dwarves?

"Something's wrong," she said, stopping abruptly and startling her two companions. "Nick, I need the map."

"Why are we stopping?" asked Arabella, fighting to keep the panic she felt out of her voice. "Guys, what? Are we lost?"

"It's not that," said Miranda, squeezing Bell's shoulder gently, before dropping to her knees and laying the map on the tunnel floor. "Nick, give me some light. Look, we started from here, right?" She didn't wait for an answer. "We've turned at least four times, so we should be here." She jabbed her finger at a spot on the map that was at least half a mile from the Centre Block. "We've come too far."

"How do you know? They could be anywhere in here. Do you know how many side tunnels branch off from the main ones?" Nicholas knelt and traced their route with his finger.

The rasping/slurping sound came again, louder and nearer than before. "Listen!" said Miranda, suddenly tensing and dropping her voice to a harsh whisper. "What's that?"

The companions strained their ears, listening. Nicholas finally broke the silence. "What?"

"There's nothing," said Arabella, glancing about nervously.

"Don't you hear it?" insisted Miranda. "Like something breathing . . ."

Nicholas and Arabella exchanged looks and shrugged in unison. "I don't hear anything," said the boy, followed by Arabella's, "Me neither."

"There's something," said Miranda. "I noticed it when we took the first turn. There's something in here with us."

"Of course there are things in here. What did you think?" scoffed Nicholas. "Dad's worked in these tunnels for years. They're filled with giant milli-pedes and rats."

"Thanks for sharing that with us," said Arabella, furiously brushing her fingers through her hair. "Come on, let's keep going. I'm freezing."

"Shhh! Listen!" whispered Miranda, pressing her ear against the cold stone floor.

The sound was very loud. Surely the others heard it now. Miranda tried to pinpoint where it was coming from, but the design of the tunnels cre-ated echoes that resounded from every direction at once. It seemed to be coming from the ceiling, the walls, and the floor at the same time. She turned the flashlight back the way they'd come, knowing with absolute certainty that the place was alive with giant, slimy, bulb-eyed insects, their long wriggling feelers waving at her, and their bodies dragging on the stone making sounds like dying breaths. She gave a short burst of laughter when the flashlight revealed nothing but the bare stone floor.

Slumping forward on her hands, aware that the others were staring at her, Miranda slowed her breathing. Then she sat back on her heels and looked at her two closest friends. "I'm sorry. I heard this creepy noise and for a second I thought . . . never mind. It's probably nothing . . . just an echo coming from somewhere above."

"Jeez, Mir, you're weirding us out." Nicholas grabbed Miranda's arm and pulled her to her feet. "What are we going to do now?" he asked, voicing the thought that was uppermost in their minds.

Miranda shook her head. "I think we should go back. We haven't seen any signs of the Dwarves. It's like they've never been here. We can come back tomorrow and search a different section of the tunnels."

"Mir's right, Nick," said Arabella. "We should have seen something, or smelled cooking odours at least . . . you guys know how the Dwarves love to fry everything." She fell silent wondering what had happened to the stolid folk from a world as different from her own as night from day.

"Something's happened," said Miranda. "They're gone."

"Gone," echoed Nicholas, exhaling loudly. "Gone where?"

"Back home?" ventured Arabella, her voice unconvinced.

"No," answered Miranda without hesitation. "They'd never leave without finishing the repairs . . . they'd rather die than bring dishonour on their country."

"Maybe they did," answered Nicholas. "Die, I mean."

CHAPTER EIGHT

TUNNEL TURDS

"Shut up, Nick!" said Arabella, crossly. "What do you mean saying they're dead? Why did you say that?"

"Chill, Bell. It was nothing. I was just . . ."

"Being stupid, as usual," snapped Arabella, glaring at Nicholas. "Just stop sayings things like that. It's not helpful."

"OK, OK," said Nicholas, throwing his hands in the air in a gesture of surrender. "I didn't mean anything."

"Come on you two, cut it out," said Miranda. "We've got to get out of here. Mom's going to have a fit if I'm not home by dinnertime."

"Hold on a sec." Nicholas played the light beam on the walls. "We didn't come this way."

"Oh, great!" groaned Arabella. "Now we're lost."

"We're not lost," said Nicholas, bristling with indignation. "We just have to go back to the main tunnel. We must have kept going straight when we should have turned left. It's hard to see the size of the tunnels when you're looking at the light on the ground."

Miranda's eyes followed the flashlight beam as Nick played it over the walls and ceiling. The side tunnel was a fraction of the size of the cavernous main passage. The air smelled stale and damp. Both the reek and the damp seemed to seek her out and settle on her like snow on the ground. Shivering, she noticed patches of water seeping from the walls and pooling in tiny basins eroded into the rock.

"This looks like the passage we went down with Naim," she said. "If we follow it, we might end up at the Portal."

"Yeah, right!" said Nicholas. "I don't know what Naim did to open the Portal, do you?" He took a couple of steps and bent to examine something on the rock floor. "Hey, look at this."

Miranda and Arabella dropped onto their heels beside Nicholas.

"What is it?" asked Miranda.

"It's a piece of leather. It looks like part of a boot," said Nicholas, prodding it with the flashlight.

"Nick, that's a Dwarf boot!" cried Miranda, excitedly. She reached to pick up the boot, but a large, head-sized lump of something that looked like moss was partly growing on it, pinning it to the ground. "Ugh!" she frowned, making a face as her fingers touched the spongy lump. "What's that?"

"It looks like a mouldy brain," said Arabella, rising and digging at the growth with the toe of her running shoe.

"If you ask me, I'd say it looks more like a giant, green turd," said Nicholas, breaking into a grin when Miranda reacted instantly by springing quickly back from the thing, at the same time furiously wiping her fingers on the legs of her pants.

"Move," the boy ordered, getting up and elbowing Arabella aside. "I'll get it off."

For once, Arabella didn't protest. When she touched the blob of mould with her running shoe, she had felt it pulse, as if it were a living thing. It gave her the creeps. She thought about telling the others, but what was she going to say? Don't touch it, it's alive. Yeah, right, she thought. They'd think I was out of my mind after a couple of hours in this place. She gladly moved aside as Nicholas aimed a nasty kick at the lump.

"NICK, WAIT . . ." cried Miranda, suddenly sensing that what the boy was about to do was wrong. But she was too late.

SCHLOP! Nick's well-aimed kick didn't lift the lump neatly off the tatty piece of leather. His face registered surprise as his sneaker went clean through the mound, and it went off like a land mine, firing bits of tissue and streams of sticky green-black liquid at the three companions. It impacted like a ripe watermelon hitting the sidewalk.

Shrieking hysterically, Miranda grabbed Arabella's arm and pulled the girl back along the tunnel. She forgot all about the Dwarves and the nightmare that brought her here to solicit their help in getting to Bethany. The only thing that mattered now was running away as fast as she could and washing the foul-smelling gunk out of her hair and off her body. She felt like kicking Nicholas, whose laughter echoed over and over through the narrow passage.

The boy came up behind and rested a hand on Miranda's shoulder. The girl looked at him and burst out laughing. He was a mess. Green slime hung in long strands from his dark hair. His clothes were plastered to his body, giving him the appearance of a big green grasshopper. And he stank! Miranda wrinkled her nose and breathed through her mouth. "I think it was a turd," she said, suddenly aware that the stink was coming from her, too.

Nicholas didn't seem to mind the smell. He was still excited about the blob and the way it had burst apart. "Did you see that?" he breathed, using the bottom of his t-shirt to wipe the guck from his face. "It was like blowing up a jellyfish."

"Yuck!" cried Miranda. "It was disgusting." She felt the sticky tissue begin to harden on her clothes and skin, and her hair crackled and broke like strings of caramelized sugar. As Nicholas pushed past her and took the lead, she brushed away the insane thought that the smelly insides of the blob were rapidly solidifying, turning her to stone.

Arabella stopped so abruptly, Miranda's arm almost wrenched out of its socket. She turned to her friend, but without a light, Arabella was just a dark shape—a huge dark shape.

"Help me, Mir . . ." The voice was so weak, it didn't even sound like Bell.

Miranda's heart stopped. Something was happening to her legs. She tried to reach Bell, but she couldn't make her limbs obey. They moved sluggishly, as if she were wading through molasses. Keeping her eyes on the growing mass that had once been Arabella, she reached down to touch her legs. The fine hairs on her arms stiffened and a shudder racked her body as her fingers found the springy, pulsing lumps. They covered her legs like cabbage-sized warts.

And they were growing! Now Miranda knew what had been making the slurping noise.

"NICK!" She screamed, punching at the things with her fists, knowing, even as they exploded and sprayed her with slime, that it was the wrong thing to do. But it was the only way to get them off her legs. She hadn't heard a sound from Bell for the past few minutes. She was desperate to reach the girl before the blobs suffocated her.

"NIIII-IIIICK!"

A beam of light struck her in the face, blinding her.

"I'm here," said Nicholas. His voice was weak like Bell's, and muffled as if the words were spoken through a thick woolen sock. "Mir, there are thousands of them." He didn't sound the least bit scared.

For a second, Miranda wished she were more like Nick. Especially now. While she teetered on the verge of panic, she knew Nicholas was more fascinated by the lumps than afraid. Or maybe he was just better at hiding his fear than she and Arabella.

The boy suddenly seemed to notice that Miranda's arms were flailing like windmills at the blobs. "Stop!" he whispered. "Don't break them."

"I can't stop. It's the only way to get them off."

"No!" said Nicholas, straining to get the word out. "Mir, stop! Look what's happening."

Miranda looked. "Yikes!" She couldn't believe her eyes. For a split second, she had the sensation of watching a plant through time-lapse photography. All about her, velvety mounds of mould were forming and growing at an accelerated rate. Even though the sight made her sick, she couldn't pull her eyes off the swelling, throbbing blobs. Her hands dropped like dead branches to her side.

"They replicate." Nicholas bubbled as if his mouth were filled with water. "Ahead . . . the ones I burst . . . blocking the exit . . . trapped . . ." The last thing Miranda heard before Nicholas went as silent as a statue was a long, drawn-out, gurgling sound.

"NOOO! NOOO!" Miranda went crazy, screaming and screaming until her head hurt and the veins in her neck stood out like ropes. She screamed until her throat was raw and her voice was a harsh whisper.

"BREATHE!" she cried, willing her friends to live, but knowing that it was way too late. They weren't breathing and soon the things would attach themselves to her face, and she'd die, too. "Bell, please . . . breathe."

Tears filled her eyes and coursed down her cheeks. She knew it was foolish, but somehow the thought of the Library of Parliament collapsing on her head didn't seem as scary as what was happening to her now. She wondered what it would feel like when the ugly blobs reached her face and covered her mouth and nose. Were they doing this on purpose? Was this their revenge for Nicholas kicking one of them?

"HELP!" She felt the things pressing on her arms and back and stomach, heard their sickening breathing sounds. The reek of the slime filled her mouth and nose until she could actually taste it. Horrified, she watched as one settled on the flashlight in Nick's hand. As if the sun had been switched off, the tunnel went as black as a witch's robe.

"HELP!" She shouted until she was hoarse, and still she shouted. She shouted until she felt the soft, warm underside of one of the mounds cover her face and then the only sounds filling the passage were the combined sounds of the creatures slurping.

CHAPTER NINE

THE KU-KU-FUN-GI

Suddenly, Miranda's eye was forced open. A bright light shone in her face, blotting out everything else and sending a stabbing pain through her head. At first she thought it was the sun and she tried blinking to shield her eyes from its blinding rays, but whatever was pinching her eyelid was rough and strong. Then gruff voices spoke close to her ear.

"Looks deader than a boot nail!"

"She'll live."

"The others?"

"Yup."

"Got 'em out just in time."

"Yup."

"Stupid kids."

"Yup."

Miranda opened her other eye. Instantly her eyelid was released. She realized that she was lying on something hard and cold, like a sheet of ice. She felt weak and nauseous, and lightheaded, as if she were recovering from a long illness. Everything hurt. Slowly she sat up, rubbing her encrusted eyelids.

"Where am I?" she asked. And then said, "Oh!" as she remembered the horrible green mounds that, when she had last looked, were growing on her and her friends, multiplying and clinging to their bodies like clusters of giant grapes to a vine. She moved her hands to feel for the lumps, but somehow, miraculously, the things were gone. "Who are you? How did you rescue us? Where are my friends?"

"Humans." One of the voices chuckled, as if that word adequately explained the quirks and peculiarities of the entire human race. It made Miranda cross.

"Who are you?" she repeated, louder this time. "And please get that light out of my eyes."

Abruptly the light was lowered.

"What were you doing here?" demanded the voice.

"I'll tell you, but first, where are my friends?"

"Here. Alive," said the voice. "Should be dead."

Miranda blinked several times to rid her eyes of

light blindness. She gave a cry of relief when she found herself looking into a blunt, square face that featured a bulbous nose and a wide mouth. She didn't have a name, but she recognized the face. "Thank goodness!" she breathed. "How did you find us?"

The Dwarf peered at her intently. Then he stepped back, placed his hammy fists on his hips and demanded, "Who are you?"

Miranda couldn't believe how much it hurt not to be recognized. The old guilt returned. When the Dwarves had come back to Canada with the young companions, it was the last they saw of each other, until now. She should have made an effort to visit them, to make them feel welcome, and see that they had everything they needed.

"It's me, Miranda," she said. "Don't you remember?"

The same Dwarf returned and peered at her again. Then, to Miranda's horror, he pulled a crumpled wad of cloth from his pocket, spat on it, and rubbed some of the hardened green guck off her face.

"It's Miranda," he confirmed, breaking into a toothy grin, his face going red. He turned his back on the girl and discussed his findings with four similarly built fellows who were struggling to wipe the faces of a pair of wriggling shapes pinned to the ground by strong Dwarf arms.

"GET AWAY," yelled Arabella. "Don't touch me with that dirty rag!"

Miranda grinned. It was good to hear Bell acting like her old self. "Is Nick OK?"

"I'm OK, I think," said Nicholas from somewhere among the Dwarves. "Mir, tell them to let us up."

Before Miranda could open her mouth, there was a commotion near the entrance to the passage.

"Where are they?" roared a seriously angry Dwarf, pushing his way through the others and striding to where Miranda sat, leaning against the tunnel wall. The Dwarf who had been tending Miranda stepped between her and his irate countryman.

"Emmet, it's . . ."

"Out of my way, Anvil."

"It's the human girl, Miranda."

"What? Miranda? She did this?"

"What did I do? What's wrong?" asked Miranda, her stomach in knots. She couldn't imagine what she had done to make the Dwarf called Emmet so angry.

Emmet elbowed Anvil aside and stomped closer to Miranda. Leaning forward, he thrust his large face an inch from her nose. "What are you up to, girl?"

"N-n-nothing," stammered Miranda, eyes crossing as she peered at the solid rock of a man. "W-w-we came looking for you."

"Ha!" spat the furious Emmet. "Didn't look very hard, girl."

Miranda pressed her head into her hands. Emmet's shouting was starting to get on her nerves. "What do you mean?" she demanded. "We searched for hours, but we went too far. And on the way back we took a wrong turn and then these horrible lumpy things attacked us."

"LIES!" roared Emmet, showering Miranda with spit, and wagging a sausage-like finger in her face.

She flushed as red as a radish as all the other Dwarves shook their heads sadly and avoided her eyes as if they had caught her stealing.

"Stop calling us liars," cried Nicholas, the anger in his voice as sharp as the edge of a sword.

Emmet stood and spun on the boy. "Be quiet, lad. I know you lie."

Nicholas had no intention of being quiet. "I don't have to take this. And I don't care what you think. You're wrong. We haven't done anything, and we're not lying."

"Is that so?" sneered Emmet, his eyes glinting like ice. "Then look me in the eye, boy, and say you didn't disturb the Ku-Ku-Fun-Gi."

All three companions suddenly exchanged looks of horror. Miranda felt the blood drain from her face. "Nick, the lumps . . . does he mean?"

Anvil thought this was a good time to intervene. He squatted on his heels beside Miranda. "Not lumps, Miranda. Ku-Ku-Fun-Gi. Live in caves."

Nicholas gulped. "I-I th-thought they were just clumps of mould."

"AHA!" cried Emmet, triumphantly.

The three companions cringed at the looks the Dwarves gave them. They made them feel stupid and ashamed.

"We didn't mean to disturb them," said Miranda quietly, fighting to keep from crying.

"I don't understand why you're so mad," said Arabella. "It's not as if we murdered someone. Anyway, what difference does it make? They're not people, or animals. They're disgusting, slimy parasites."

Anvil bowed his shaggy head. "Not parasites. Symbionts," he explained. "Slimy. Not disgusting. Co-exist with rock. Draw weakness from rock. Breathe strength back. Good for both."

"Are you saying those Ku-Ku things are intelligent life forms?" asked Miranda, dreading the answer.

"Not things," stormed Emmet. "Ku-Ku-Fun-Gi! You killed them." He turned his back on Miranda and bashed his big fist into the rock wall.

"We didn't know," said Nicholas, realizing it was a poor excuse. Even as he said the words, he wished he were small enough to fit into a crack in the wall.

"If we killed them, how come billions more grew?" said Arabella. "How could that happen if they were dead? Answer me that."

Emmet whirled toward the girl, but Anvil raised his hand to forestall another outburst. "Stay, Emmet. I'll handle this." He looked at Arabella. "Ku-Ku-Fun-Gi attach to rock. Stay in same spot forever. Good for rock. Harmless, until disturbed. Then, replicate. Harm rock. Drain it. Rock dies."

"They sure sound like parasites to me," said Arabella.

Anvil disagreed. "No, rocks need symbionts."

"Right," scoffed Arabella. "Like I need warts."

Anvil sighed. The only people he knew in Canada were the children before him now. And if they were representative of children in this world, then human children must be very difficult, he thought. They argued about everything. He figured that the girl they called Bell could argue a Dwarf bald. But he didn't believe that they were bad or vicious. Otherwise Miranda and the others would not have followed the Druid to his world to help defeat the Demon and in doing so, save thousands of Dwarf children. But it still puzzled him how such courageous youngsters knew so little about the life forms in their own world. He sighed heavily as Miranda's hand lightly touched his sleeve. If he lived for another three hundred years he'd never understand them. But he couldn't help but like them.

"Mr. Anvil, won't the Ku-Ku-Fun-Gi go back to their normal relationship with the rocks now that we're not disturbing them?" asked Miranda.

"Not that simple," replied Anvil. "Can't stop them now."

"Let me get this straight," said Arabella. "The Ku-Kus and rocks have a symbiotic relationship, and it's a good relationship until the Ku-Kus are disturbed. When that happens, the Ku-Kus replicate and kill the rock. Am I right, so far?"

Anvil nodded.

"Why?" asked Arabella.

"Reflex," said Anvil. "Think they're being attacked. Can't differentiate between enemy and rock partner."

"What happens when the rock dies?"

"It crumbles, turns to dust."

"Is that what's happening now?" asked Miranda, not liking the sound of this.

"ARE YOU DEAF?" shouted Emmet. "Rock's dying. Cliff's turning to dust."

"But . . ." cried Miranda, a stab of pain burning her chest. "That means . . . all the Parliament buildings . . . the Library . . ." She stopped, knowing the rest, but not wanting to go there.

Anvil nodded sadly. "They'll weaken. Collapse," he said.

The realization of what they had done stunned Miranda, leaving her speechless. She couldn't take it in. Her country's Parliament buildings were going to crumble to dust all because Nicholas had kicked a mouldy lump of fungus. It didn't seem possible.

She looked at her friend, but the boy had his eyes locked on his feet. She knew how he felt. She knew, because it could just as easily have been her.

"How long before the buildings collapse?" she asked, praying for time.

"Don't know," said Anvil.

"Soon," said the other Dwarves.

"How soon?" demanded the three companions.

"Soon!"

Nick cleared his throat. What was his father going to say when he heard about this? "I-I'm sorry. I didn't know . . ."

"Didn't think," corrected Emmet.

"Emmet . . ." Anvil started.

"No," said Nicholas. "He's right. I didn't think. But even if I had thought about it, I probably would have done the same thing." He faced Emmet and met the other's harsh gaze. "Don't you see? It wouldn't have made any difference, Emmet, because I didn't know about the Ku-Ku-Fun-Gi."

"Good motto," snorted Emmet. "If you don't know it, kill it."

Miranda stood and touched the angry Dwarf's arm. "It's not just Nicholas's fault," she said. "We know what we did was wrong, but we didn't know it then. I don't think you have to worry about us ever bothering the Ku-Kus again. But tomorrow, what if I throw a stone into the Rideau Canal, and the water rises and drowns the whole city?" She bit her lip trying to find the right words for what she was thinking. "What I mean is, at the time, it seemed like that sort of thing, like swiping the heads off dandelions with a stick or throwing a stone in the river. So, please, just stop yelling and tell us what to do now. How can we stop the process?"

For a minute, Emmet stared at her. Then he nodded slowly and, as if the wind had suddenly left his sails, he sank onto the floor, all the anger gone from his body. He turned to his fellow Dwarves for answers.

But the other Dwarves were no help. They shrugged and exchanged glances. "Dunno," they said. "Never disturbed them."

"There's got to be a way to calm the Ku-Kus down," insisted Arabella, wearing the stubborn look that her friends knew all too well. "That's like saying that a butterfly fluttering its wings in Japan can cause a hurricane in Florida, and there's nothing anyone can do about it."

"But that's true," said Nicholas. "Everybody knows that."

Arabella tossed her head scornfully. "Well, I don't believe it."

"BE QUIET!" shouted Emmet, covering his ears with his large beefy hands.

"Oh, shut up, Emmet!" snapped Arabella. "If you can't help, then just keep quiet."

"I don't know about butterflies and hurricanes," said Miranda softly, keeping a wary eye on the surly

Dwarf and her temperamental friend. "But I agree with Bell. Surely there's something we can do to stop the Ku-Kus from destroying Parliament Hill."

Anvil chewed on his thumb thoughtfully. Then he looked at his fellow countrymen. "What about the Druid?" he asked.

"He'd know," agreed one of the Dwarves, nodding vigorously.

"Yup," chorused the others. "If anybody knows, he will."

"See," cried Miranda. "That's another reason we have to get to Bethany."

"What's that?" asked Anvil.

"That's the whole reason we came to find you," explained Miranda. "We think something is wrong in your world."

Anvil and the other Dwarves exchanged nervous glances. "Why do you think that?" he queried.

"Maybe it's nothing," said Miranda. "But I had a bad dream, and I saw King Ruthar. He wasn't dead."

"When?" asked Anvil.

"Last night."

Again, the Dwarves looked at each other knowingly. "Malcolm disappeared last night."

"What are you talking about?" asked Nicholas, scratching his head in bewilderment.

"Who's Malcolm?" asked Arabella.

When Anvil turned to the young companions, his face was grave. "Last night. Late. Malcolm was making rounds. Didn't return. Tracked him to the Portal." He reached into a fat leather pouch attached to his belt and held out his hand for the others to see. "Found these."

Nestled in his open palm were shards of what looked like blackened glass. "Something came through the Portal," he said. "From Bethany."

"What was it?" asked Miranda.

"Don't know. Smelled bad though. Like something dead a long time."

"Naim said there was no evil in Bethany," said Miranda, feeling her heart flutter in her chest like a trapped bird.

"True," said Anvil. "Until now."

"What about Malcolm?" asked Arabella.

The Dwarves went silent for a moment. It reminded Miranda of the day her school met in the gym and observed three minutes of silence for the thousands of innocent people killed when terrorists attacked and razed the World Trade Center in New York last fall. The mingled feelings of fear, anger, and sadness that she felt as she had watched the twin towers disintegrate into massive heaps of smoking rubble came back now. And she knew, without having to be told, that the Dwarves were grieving. They believed that Malcolm was dead.

Hate! Miranda thought, bitterly. Even though she was shut away in the Place with No Name, the Demon was still dangerous. Why did she want people to hate each other so much that they destroyed themselves as well as the ones they hated? It was so stupid. Nicholas said it was all about power—about evil people twisting the things people believed in and using others to get power for themselves. Miranda sighed. It was all so confusing it made her head spin.

She didn't know or care about power, or why people craved it. But she knew one thing and nobody could tell her differently. If you killed innocent people, it was wrong and it was evil. In her mind, it was as simple as that.

Miranda jumped when Anvil spoke her name, flushing when she realized that everyone was staring at her. "Sorry," she mumbled. "I was thinking about something."

"They want to know about your dream," prompted Arabella.

"There's nothing more to tell." Miranda paused as an image flitted through her mind. Then she gripped Anvil's arm. "Those black things. Let me see them again."

Anvil reached into the pouch at his belt and withdrew the shards of black glass or shell. Miranda stared at them for a long time. "I just remembered something," she said, squeezing her eyes shut in an effort to get it right. "In my dream, just before I woke up, King Ruthar gave the other man a small black marble or something . . . and it shattered . . .

and the man started screaming." She pointed to the black fragments in the Dwarf's hand. "The pieces looked like those."

Later, headed home, the companions walked quickly, heads bent, eyes fixed on the dark sidewalk. They didn't speak. To say that they felt terrible wouldn't begin to describe the turmoil in their minds. Miranda felt sick, butterflies churning in her stomach. Was this how a nervous breakdown felt? Go away, she told the butterflies. I can't get sick. There's no time.

What had they done? Who would have thought that kicking a lump of fungus would topple Canada's Parliament Buildings? How could such a small act have such catastrophic consequences? And, what about Malcolm? Were the Dwarves right? Was their friend dead? Was Hate, the Demon, responsible? Shut away in The Place with No Name, how could Hate have sent something evil through the Portal? What sort of creature was it? And how did the Demon communicate with it? Miranda had no answers, but she knew as surely as she knew the colour of her eyes that evil had found its way to the land of the Elves.

CHAPTER TEN

ROGUE DWARF

The giant black shape blended with the shadows of the thick trees bordering the lawn across the street from Miranda's house. Beside the monstrous figure, hunched among the evergreens, was the Dwarf. Whenever the Thug glanced at the squat, compact creature, his body shook with silent laughter. It was so ironic—recruiting a Dwarf, one of the enemy, to help destroy the Dwarves.

The Thug gently stroked the gold mark on his forearm with his long, sharp claws. It was the Demon's mark—a human skull fashioned from slivers of gold and pocketed into slits Hate had pierced in the creature's flesh, just under the outer layer of skin. The golden skull was a bond between Mistress and servant. As long as it remained in place, the

Thug felt the Demon's nearness like the sun on a lizard's back.

The monster's red eyes swept the darkened street in front of Miranda's house for signs of danger. Satisfied that they had not been spotted, he looked down at the Dwarf again, the laughter welling up inside him like a belch. The only thing Dwarf-ish about the little creature was its carcass. What was inside was anything but. Yet it gave the Thug pleasure to call it a Dwarf. He liked to think that it really was one of the filthy rock eaters over which he had control. After all, it was common knowl-edge that a Dwarf would cut out its heart before bowing to the Demon.

Two nights ago, when the Thug had breached the Portal under the Library of Parliament, he was as surprised to see the Dwarf as that creature was by his sudden appearance. The Dwarf was already reaching for the sharp sword at his belt when the Thug tossed the round black egg. He knew there wasn't one of the stinking hole-dwellers alive who could resist the glitter of a polished gemstone. And, the round glittering egg looked exactly like a rare black diamond. Instinctively, the Dwarf's hand had shot out, catching the egg and forming a fist over it. By then it was too late for the stupid stunted creature. If the Dwarf had ignored the egg and let it smash on the hard rock floor, he might have man-aged to escape and rouse his companions.

But he hadn't done that, had he?

Even as the egg burst in the Dwarf's hand, the black serpent that had been waiting, coiled within the shell, struck at the bare skin on his wrist. Death was swift but not merciful. As the poison attacked the Dwarf's nervous system and ate into his brain, like acid, the pathetic creature had thrashed about like a wounded bear, thick strands of froth spewing from its screaming mouth.

The Thug had watched, amused. He enjoyed the scent of terror, especially the tantalizing stench of Dwarf fear. By now, the poor fellow's companions knew Malcolm was missing. They were probably already searching the maze of tunnels. The Thug knew he must move swiftly. Hate's orders were simple. "Grab the girl and take the Bloodstones."

The creature stiffened as the front door of Miranda's house suddenly opened and a woman and the girl appeared on the front steps. He watched as they hopped into the vehicle parked in the driveway and the older woman guided the car onto the street and out of sight.

The sudden appearance of Miranda was a stinging reminder of the punishment Hate had inflicted upon the Thug for failing to rid the world of the girl once before. When his Mistress escaped from the Place with No Name in March, she had sent the Thug and three of its brothers to find Miranda and kill her. The girl was the only thing that stood between the Demon and freedom. But, for the first time since they had given themselves to evil, the Thugs had failed. And because this crafty child still lived, Hate was banished from her lands and condemned to suffer a slow death in the rank Elven prison. Thinking of the pain that his Mistress endured day after endless day preyed upon the Thug until he thought his black heart would explode. Pent-up rage made him give the Dwarf a vicious shove toward the dark house.

"Beware!" hissed the serpent that had taken possession of Malcolm's body. "I'll sskin you like a foxx and leave your bloody hide for the carrion crowss." As it strode swiftly across the street, the snake twisted the Dwarf's features into a sly, cunning leer, and turned its head toward the Thug.

The Thug bared his fangs and snarled at the Dwarf—his needle-sharp claws slashing at the trees, cutting deep grooves in the bark. But, less than a heartbeat later, he cringed in agony as thin rays of fire shot from the Dwarf's blazing eyes and burned clean through his skin to the bone.

"Remember which of uss iss called sslave," Malcolm hissed, enjoying the flood of rage and hatred spewing from its evil companion.

Despite his Dwarfish bulk, Malcolm moved like a shadow along the driveway and into Miranda's backyard. Mounting the steps to the terrace, he walked to a pair of paned French doors. He pressed his blunt face to the glass and peered into the room beyond. But the room was as black as the night and he saw nothing. Pulling the sword from his belt, he smashed the hilt against one of the glass panes. The thick glass shattered with a loud crack. Working quickly, Malcolm slid his pudgy hand through the opening, unlocked the doors and disappeared into the darkness.

"No, no and no!" said Dr. D'arte, her eyes on the red Jeep ahead. "You are not going back to Bethany."

"Why not?" asked Miranda. "I'll be all right. Nothing's going to happen to me there."

"No."

"Just tell me why," pleaded the girl. "Give me one good reason why you won't let me go."

Dr. D'arte turned onto their street. "Because I want you here."

Miranda laughed. "That's not a good reason. Come on Mom, don't you trust the Elves to keep me out of trouble?"

"Give it up, Miranda. You're not going, and that's final."

"You don't believe there's something wrong in Bethany. You think it's me, don't you?"

"I'm worried about you," said her mother. She reached across the seat and tugged on the girl's t-shirt. "Look how thin you're getting. And you're having nightmares again. For heaven's sake, Miranda, you're only ten years old. And you're starting to act and talk like a stranger. Of course I'm worried."

"Mom, I keep telling you I'm OK. And you know I like loose clothes."

Dr. D'arte sighed. "Everything was fine until you went to Bethany with the Druid."

"It wasn't Naim's fault," said Miranda defensively. "I didn't have to go."

It was her mother's turn to laugh. "Yes, you did," she said. "And we both know it." She steered the station wagon into the driveway and turned off the ignition. "I'm not blaming the Druid," she said. "Not really." She thought for a minute before taking Miranda's hand. When she spoke Miranda could barely make out the words. "I'm afraid if you go back, I'll never see you again."

The older woman's words shocked Miranda. She wanted to say something, but the thought of never seeing her mother again was so alien, she was struck speechless. She stared at her mother, the silence growing—separating them as surely as if a steel bar had been wedged between them. With a start, Miranda realized that her mother wasn't worried about something happening to her in Bethany, she was afraid that she'd lose her to the very place she ran away from before Miranda was born. Poor Mom, she thought.

"I could have sworn I turned the lights off before we left." Her mother was staring at one of the windows at the side of the house.

Miranda followed her gaze. There was light coming from somewhere inside. "No, you told me to turn out the lights. Which I did as we were going out the door."

Mother and daughter stared at each other. And then, as Miranda was wondering if, perhaps, she had left the hall light on after all, Dr. D'arte was out of the car and striding toward the front door. Miranda felt icy fingers on her neck as she grasped the door handle and scrambled after her mother.

"Mom, wait," she whispered, sprinting around the car. "Don't go in there."

Dr. D'arte halted and turned, waiting for Miranda to catch up. Even in the dim light, Miranda guessed from her mother's stern expression that she was quickly losing patience with her. Why did I have to tell her about the dream? She chided herself. Why did I have to go and make such a big deal about King Ruthar?

But her mom suddenly smiled and took Miranda's hand. They stood together on the front walk and stared at the light in the silent house. "Do you think someone's inside?" she asked.

Miranda looked up at her mother. Is she mocking me? Does she think I'm going to say it's the

Demon? Dr. D'arte was looking at her now, but Miranda took her time before replying. "I don't know," she said.

"Perhaps it's one of your friends from Bethany," said her mother, grinning.

"What do you mean my friends?" cried Miranda, her face burning. She wanted to snatch her hand out of her mother's grasp. But she didn't. "Mom, I don't understand. Why did you call them my friends? Why aren't they your friends, too?"

Dr. D'arte squeezed Miranda's hand. "I'm sorry. Old wounds opening up." Anticipating her daughter's next question, she continued. "Look, I was very angry when I left Ellesmere Island. I hated Ruthar because I didn't think he tried hard enough to rescue your father."

"I thought you were miffed at me, because you thought I was losing my mind," said Miranda, squeezing her mother's hand.

"I'm not miffed at you, and I don't believe you're insane," laughed her mother, returning the squeeze. "It's just that I thought I had buried Bethany and the Elves for good. Now, I find it's all coming back to haunt me. I don't want to lose you, Miranda." Then she laughed again. "Not before your next birthday anyway."

Miranda nodded. She wasn't nearly as confused as before. It bothered her when the older woman spoke of Bethany as if she hated everyone and everything on Ellesmere Island. Now, at least, she knew the answer. Or part of the answer.

"Are we going to stand out here all night?" asked her mother.

"Let's go round the back," suggested Miranda. "If I were going to burgle our house, that's how I'd get it."

They walked along the side of the house to a narrow wooden gate between the garage and the side door. Miranda unlatched the gate and they passed through into the garden. Sheltered from the streetlights, the backyard was dark and filled with shadows. While her mother checked the back door and the French doors that opened into her bedroom, Miranda scanned the yard and the blacker areas among the tall trees at the far end of the property near the white picket fence that separated her yard from Nicholas's. The moon cast a weak light on the ground, but nothing moved in the shadows. Everything seemed the same as usual. She jumped when her mother suddenly grabbed her arm and pulled her back toward the gate.

"What?" she cried, feeling cold in the warm air.

"Shhh!" whispered her mother sharply. "The glass in the door is broken. You're right. There's someone in the house."

CHAPTER ELEVEN

A NASTY SURPRISE

They quickly retraced their steps toward the gate that Miranda had left unlatched. But they never made it. A short, broad shape emerged from the shadows by the garage and stepped directly between them and the gate, blocking their only means of escape.

Dr. D'arte reached for a rake hanging on a hook at the side of the garage and advanced on the squat, dark intruder, waving the pronged end threateningly. "GET OUT OF HERE!" she shouted, furious that this creature had dared to invade her home, frightening her and her child.

"Hurumph." The intruder cleared his throat

before speaking. "Didn't mean to scare you," he said. His voice reminded Miranda of gravel pouring into a cement mixer.

"I said get out, NOW!" Dr. D'arte took a step closer to the dark intruder.

"Stop!" cried Miranda, her eyes sparkling like stars as she matched the gruff voice with the dark, squarish shape. She tugged on her mother's arm. "Don't hurt him, Mom. It's one of the Dwarves."

"Ah, yup," said the Dwarf. "Anvil sent me to . . ."

Dr. D'arte lowered the rake, but didn't put it back on its hook. "How long have you been here?" she asked, still suspicious of the stranger's sudden appearance.

The Dwarf seemed puzzled. "A minute. Just arrived. Saw you go through the gate. Followed."

"Did you see anyone else?"

"Nope."

Miranda looked from her mother to the Dwarf. "Somebody broke into our house while we were out," she said. "Whoever did it might be still inside."

"Show me," said the Dwarf, taking a few tentative steps toward Miranda, but keeping one eye fixed on her mother and the other on the rake clutched tightly in both hands. He didn't like the look of the sharp pointed tines and didn't relish the thought of having his Dwarfish rump skewered on a rake.

He followed the woman and the girl around the house and onto the terrace, pausing two or three times along the way to press his ear against the wood siding. Miranda rolled her eyes, wondering if the Dwarf could hear through walls. Reaching the French doors, he examined the broken pane and then slowly turned the doorknob. The door opened.

"What if they're still in there?" whispered Miranda.

The stout fellow thought for a minute, then he shook his large head. "Nope. Wouldn't break glass. Came to find something. Gone now."

"I'm scared," cried Miranda. "I can't go in there." She moved quickly to her mother's side and clutched her arm tightly.

The Dwarf looked at Miranda's mother. "I'll go. Check rooms. Make sure it's safe."

"Thank you," said Dr. D'arte, sounding relieved.

She and Miranda huddled on the swinging wicker sofa on the terrace and watched the lights go on in room after room as the Dwarf made his slow way from the top floor to the basement. Miranda held her breath, waiting for the helpful fellow to meet the robbers and for the inevitable sounds of shouting and crashing to spill from the house into the silent backyard. When the Dwarf finally stepped through the French doors onto the terrace, she felt lightheaded from lack of air.

"Nobody there. Nothing disturbed," he reported to Dr. D'arte.

"Did you check the closets and under the beds?" asked Miranda.

The Dwarf chuckled. "I did, Miss. Found this under your bed." He held out his hand, pressing a soft, furry mass into Miranda's arms.

"Look Mom, it's Bear," she laughed. "My stuffed animal," she explained, for the benefit of the Dwarf who was eying her curiously. Then she remembered something he had mentioned earlier. "Why did Anvil send you here?"

The Dwarf shuffled his feet. Miranda noticed he wasn't wearing boots. His big bare toes glowed like fat white slugs in the pale moonlight.

"Worried about stones. Said hide them. Keep safe, away from evil ones."

Miranda's hand shot to her neck, fingers automatically feeling for the thin chain and the tiny metallic pouch that held the six Bloodstones. She felt her mother's eyes on her and stifled a cry when her hands felt the bare skin on her neck, but no silver chain. With a sigh of relief, she remembered where she had left them.

"Where are the Bloodstones, Miranda?"

"It's OK, I know where they are."

"Stones safe?" asked the Dwarf, his voice low and scratchy.

"Yes, they're safe," breathed Miranda, thinking of the school's honour system and how no one had ever ransacked or stolen anything from the lockers.

"They're at school. I forgot them in my locker yesterday after gym."

It was just after eleven p.m. when the Dwarf announced that he was finished replacing the broken glass in the French doors with a board he had found in the garage. Miranda and her mother thanked him again, and watched as he stomped along the terrace and disappeared around the side of the house toward the gate.

Miranda opened the fridge door and yawned.

"Off to bed with you," said Dr. D'arte, firmly closing the door and guiding the girl to the foot of the stairs. "I'll be up in a minute."

For once, Miranda was too sleepy to argue. Clutching Bear under one arm, she clomped slowly up the stairs, her legs as heavy as lead, and moved like a sleepwalker along the hall to her room. She opened the door and froze. Bear dropped like a stone from her arms.

Someone had trashed her room.

The once pretty curtains were tattered beyond recognition. They hung in jagged swathes from rods that were curled and twisted like pretzels. The carpet had been slashed and ripped away from the wall. The room looked like it had been hit by a cyclone. The twin beds were smashed and flattened like pancakes, and the bedding shredded to rags.

Miranda whimpered when she saw her computer. It had been ground into fragments on the floor, as if an elephant had jumped on it. Huge gouges marred the walls. Her precious books—the books that she had read and loved since she was a toddler—were torn apart. The pages lay scattered about the room like autumn leaves.

Nothing had been spared. Except for the bear at her feet, her stuffed animals had been dismembered and their insides plucked out. The sight broke Miranda's heart. Tears trickled down her cheeks as she stared at the little downy heads, their glass eyes fixed on her, accusingly. They seemed to be saying, It's your fault. You weren't here.

"MOM!" Miranda sobbed, stumbling forward and falling to her knees amidst the wreckage. She heard footsteps clattering up the stairs. She recognized her mother's familiar tread, but there was another set of footsteps, heavier and clumping, mounting the steps just behind her mother. Nick, she thought.

Blood drained from her face and her body trembled as she thought about the Dwarf—the one who said Anvil had sent him. The one who had been so kind and helpful, even helping to nail a crude square of wood over the broken glass pane. He had gone through the house, room by room, and had reassured them that nothing had been disturbed. Had he missed her room somehow? Her mind was churning a mile a minute trying to work through the problem. No, she thought. I saw the light go on in my room. He knew!

But why had the Dwarves sent him to trash her room? It didn't take a genius to work out the answer. They hadn't sent him. And if that were true, then the Dwarf who had left here only minutes ago hadn't come from Anvil. As improbable as it seemed, Miranda believed the Dwarf was Malcolm, the one who hadn't returned from his rounds. The one whose boot Nicholas found in the tunnel under Parliament Hill. She remembered how white the Dwarf's bare toes looked in the moonlight. Anvil and the other Dwarves thought Malcolm was dead, but with every fibre of her being, Miranda knew that he was as alive as King Ruthar.

Something that smelled bad came through the Portal late on Sunday night. That's what Anvil had said. And whatever it was, it must have found Malcolm and overpowered him and made him evil, too. And then it had sent him to her house. But why?

As her mind raced with possibilities, she saw the weather-lined face of Naim, the Druid, in her mind as clearly as if he were in the room with her. His deep blue eyes were grave and he was nodding, as if he were encouraging her. And then for a fleeting moment, a look of sadness swept over his face. Miranda felt that he saw in her face the same accusing look she had seen in the glass eyes of the stuffed toys. It's your fault! You weren't here!

The hurt and confusion that swept over her the instant she opened her bedroom door and gazed upon the shambles turned to anger. Miranda's eyes were cold like green ice crystals when they met her mother's steady, but sad, gaze. She jumped to her feet, turned her back on the mess, and brushed past Dr. D'arte and Nicholas, who stood white-faced in the doorway.

"He wanted the Bloodstones, Mom," she said, her voice as emotionless as fire. "Since I'm the only one who can use them, what does he want to stop me from doing?" Her mother opened her mouth to speak, but Miranda shook her head. "The only thing I can think of is to stop me from using them. And since they only work in the old world, it sure looks like you're not the only one who doesn't want me to go to Bethany." She slumped, her limbs weak and weary. "Do you believe me now? Do you understand why I have to go?"

"But they didn't get the Bloodstones, Mir, because your mom said you left them in your locker at school," reasoned Nicholas, softly.

"Yes, that's where I left them," answered Miranda, snorting bitterly. "And I just told that Dwarf creature exactly where to find them."

"Come on Mir, Dr. D., let's go," urged Nicholas. "He can't get them if we get there first."

CHAPTER TWELVE

RACE AGAINST TIME

Nicholas made them wait while he sped through Miranda's backyard, scaled the picket fence, and disappeared through his back door. Miranda heard a muffled Woof! from Nicholas's black Labrador retriever. In less than a minute, the boy returned, proudly waving his most prized possession—the Elven sword, given to him by Laury, Captain of the King's Riders, the elite Elven guard.

Dr. D'arte was a careful but confident driver. She never went over the speed limit. But after cautioning Miranda and Nicholas to buckle up, she hit the gas, ramming the pedal to the floor. "Hold on!" she shouted over the sound of tires screeching on pavement. Then, she tore through the streets of Ottawa as if she were competing in the Indy 500. Miranda opened the window and gripped the edge of the seat until her knuckles were stiff, glancing worriedly out at the empty streets, expecting at any second to see flashing red lights accompanied by the shrill whine of a police siren.

They were lucky to arrive at the school alive. Dr. D'arte's hands shook uncontrollably when she finally pried them off the steering wheel. Miranda noticed the hard tension lines on her mother's face and the zombie-like expression put there by lack of sleep. If she could see her own face, she would have recognized the same pale, tight features, almost as if her teeth were permanently clenched.

The woman pulled up to the curb just past the school. She didn't like leaving the car unattended while they searched for a way into the building. But she wasn't about to let Miranda and Nicholas go off by themselves with that crazed Dwarf creature in the area. Switching off the ignition, she turned her head toward the youngsters to caution them about sticking together, but before she could open her mouth, or stop them, Miranda and Nicholas were out of the car, sprinting across the grass toward the side of the school.

"Lean on the horn if you see the Dwarf," said Miranda, over her shoulder, before disappearing into the shadows.

Fuming, Dr. D'arte leaped out of the car in pursuit of her headstrong offspring. Then she stopped, suddenly unsure of what she should do, her hand still gripping the door handle. The thought of the children all alone out there made her sick, but what Miranda said about keeping a lookout for the Dwarf made good sense. Her shoulders slumped in resignation.

"Why don't I just wait here," she said under her breath as she opened the car door and slid behind the steering wheel. She reached to pull the door shut. That's when she saw the pudgy fingers gripping the door and the square Dwarf face grinning at her through the car window.

Miranda stopped for a second and listened. She had been following fast on Nicholas's heels when she thought she heard something. It sounded like a dull crack. She remained as still as the shadowy building, but the sound wasn't repeated. Probably a bird stirring in the bushes, she thought, doubling her pace to catch up with her friend.

Nicholas circled the silent school and then ran along the side toward the fenced off playground and athletic field at the back. Miranda had never been near the school at night. Suddenly, the familiar building was an alien giant, unfriendly and frightening. Why did the night make things change? she wondered. Was it because the dark hid evil things that would be spotted right away in the harsh light of day? Was that why so many bad things seemed to happen at night? She shook her head to drive such thoughts away, and concentrated on Nicholas's running form, and the big problem of how they were going to get into the building.

Just before they reached the fence, the boy abruptly skidded to a stop and turned to Miranda. The movement was so sudden it caught the girl by surprise, prompting her to glance fearfully over her shoulder

"What?" she whispered sharply.

Nicholas gripped her arm. "Listen! I'm going to show you something. But you have to promise that you'll never tell anyone. . . and that goes for Arabella and Penelope."

Miranda wondered what Nick could show her about her school that she didn't already know. "OK," she said. "I promise."

Nicholas nodded. He turned and slipped into a narrow passage that led to the kitchen entrance. Kneeling, he caught hold of a rectangle of chicken wire covering a small window at ground level. Miranda was surprised that she had never noticed the window before.

"How do you know about this window?" she whispered, the sound loud in the still air.

Nicholas's teeth flashed white in the darkness and Miranda guessed he was grinning, but he remained silent as he worked the chicken wire free and then quickly lifted the window out of its frame as effortlessly as if he were removing a stamp from a letter. Before Miranda could question him further, he had scrambled through the opening.

"Come on! Hurry!" Nicholas hissed from somewhere beyond the gaping black hole of the window.

Miranda stuck her head through the opening.

"Not that way. Feet first," said the boy.

"How did you find out about this?" asked Miranda, when she was finally standing beside Nicholas, brushing unseen cobwebs off her clothing.

"Never mind," answered Nicholas, carefully fitting the chicken wire over the opening before setting the window back in its frame. "Just remember your promise. Come on, let's get the Bloodstones and get out of here before that Dwarf shows up."

But when they opened Miranda's locker, and Nick shone the flashlight inside, they were bitterly disappointed. The Bloodstones were gone.

"He couldn't have got here before us," whispered Miranda, tears of frustration filling her eyes. "He just couldn't."

"If he did, how'd he get in?" asked Nicholas, puzzled.

"It doesn't matter how he got in," stormed Miranda, not bothering to wipe the tears that were making dirty streaks down her cheeks. "Don't you see? He beat us. He's got the Bloodstones." She looked at her friend, hopelessness written across her face. "Nick, even if we can get to Bethany, it's no use. Without the Bloodstones, I can't help the Elves."

Nicholas sighed heavily, swallowing the sour taste of failure. "Listen, Mir, we can't give up now. If you really think there's evil at work in Bethany, we've got to warn Elester. We've got to tell him about the dream."

Miranda nodded slowly.

Instead of retracing their steps to Nick's secret window, the two friends left by the fire exit because that door opened only from the inside and was never barred. Outside, they walked like limp puppets, heads bowed, shoulders sagging, dragging their feet along the dusty ground. Even the thought of going to Bethany didn't lift Miranda's sagging spirits. The Bloodstones were gone and it was her fault. How could she have left them in her locker? How could she tell Elester she'd lost the Bloodstones? If he thought she was just a dumb kid, he'd be right. She blotted her teary eyes on her arm to conceal the hurt from her mother.

They moved like robots across the grass toward the sidewalk. Nicholas turned toward the spot where they had left Dr. D'arte and peered ahead. Then he came to a dead stop. "Where's the car?" he whispered.

"Where's Mom?" cried Miranda, looking up and down the deserted street, her heart dropping like a stone in a bottomless well.

CHAPTER THIRTEEN

ANOTHER
SURPRISE

Keeping to the shadows, they walked aimlessly about the dark, silent city, their spirits sinking lower and lower as the night wore on. The big question loomed in Miranda's mind like a mountain blocking her way. WHAT HAPPENED TO MOM?

"We've got to talk to the Dwarves," Miranda said finally, when she couldn't stand the worry and inactivity any longer. She knew her mother would never have left them stranded on the dark street in the middle of the night unless she had a good reason, or unless something had happened to her. Since both she and the station wagon were missing, Miranda had to believe that she drove away because . . . Because why?

It took them an hour to scale the cliff behind the Library of Parliament. And another hour after that, wending their way through the tunnels before they and the Dwarves found each other.

"Where's Anvil?" demanded one of the Dwarves.

"How should we know?" answered Nicholas.

"He went looking for you," said Emmet. The scowl on his face seemed to suggest that they had done something wrong, once again.

"We didn't see him," said Miranda. "But we saw Malcolm."

Seated cross-legged on the stone floor, circling a fire the Dwarves had lit to take the dampness out of the air, Miranda told her story. Emmet and his stout companions were struck dumb when they heard how Malcolm had broken into Miranda's house, and then gone to her school and stolen the Bloodstones from her locker. "And I think he's got my mother," she finished, her lips trembling as she fought to keep the panic at bay.

All the Dwarves, except one, jumped to their feet, stomping on the fire, impatient to scour the city for their lost comrade and Miranda's mother.

"Hold," said the Dwarf, who had remained seated. "Must plan."

"Hear! Yup!" roared the other Dwarves in unison.

"That's right, Drummy. Need a plan." Their thick-soled boots stomping on the stone floor sounded like the beating of war drums.

When the roaring and the sparks subsided, Miranda addressed the one the others called Drummy. "Now, more than ever, we need to get to Bethany," she said. "Can you help us?"

Drummy shook his head. "No, Lass. Sorry. Can't help. Portal's gone."

"What?" Miranda was stunned. "What do you mean, gone? Are you telling us the Portal has disappeared?"

"Where did it go?" asked Nicholas, totally dumbfounded.

"Gone!" barked Emmet, snapping his fingers in the boy's face. "Like this. Gone."

Nicholas scowled at the rude Dwarf before grabbing Miranda's arm and pulling her aside. "What are they talking about? How can a Portal just disappear?"

Miranda shrugged. "Nick, I don't know, but that's what they're saying. It's gone." She turned back to Drummy. "But, that means . . . Oh, this is awful." She touched his beefy arm. "It means you're stuck here. You can never go home."

"Stop being foolish, girl! Of course they can go home," said a deep, testy voice from the shadows.

"Who's there?" yelled Emmet, grabbing his sword and moving deeper into the tunnel toward the voice. Several of the other Dwarves exchanged looks, shrugged their burly shoulders, and followed their rash comrade, waving hammers, axes, and anything else that might serve as a weapon. "Show yourself, or taste the point of my sword!"

"Stop waving that thing at me, IMMEDIATELY!" commanded the voice. "Or you will be one very sorry little Dwarf."

For a long second, there was complete silence. Miranda went as still as a figure in a painting, but in the dim firelight her green eyes sparkled like stars. She straightened her back as if a heavy weight had suddenly been lifted from her shoulders.

A shadowy giant reared up on the tunnel wall as a black-clad figure emerged into the weak light cast by the dying fire. The figure was that of a man at least seven feet tall. He grasped a long wooden staff in his right hand. Despite the heavy black cloak that covered him from his head to his stained boots, Miranda knew him immediately, although she thought he looked thinner than when she had seen him last. There seemed to be less of him some-how, as if he were being used up.

The man's face was completely hidden beneath a loose-fitting hood. He halted in the outer rim of the light and peered about at the members of the little group sitting near the fire. Freeing his hands from under his cloak, he reached up and pulled the hood back, revealing a long face with sharp angles, etched with deep lines. Under trimmed white eyebrows, his sapphire blue eyes appeared black in the dim light as they came to rest upon Miranda.

"I knew you'd come," she said softly. And then, to her everlasting embarrassment, she covered her face with her hands and burst into tears.

Nobody spoke. Emmet coughed. Some of the other Dwarves shuffled their boots or looked up at the ceiling. Drummy took a step toward the girl, but Nicholas draped an arm protectively about her shoulders and his fierce glare was a warning to the others to keep their distance.

Ignoring the boy, Naim, the Druid, lowered his lanky form onto one knee. He reached out and placed his long hand on Miranda's head. "I have travelled far to reach you, child," he said, his voice cracking from weariness. "I feared I would arrive too late." Then he rose. "But I am here now and we have much to accomplish this night. But first, I will speak with Anvil and the others."

"Anvil's not here," said Emmet, glowering at Nicholas.

The Druid turned his back on the girl and moved closer to the fire, settling on a large, flat boulder next to the surly Dwarf. Still smarting with embarrassment over her crying fit, Miranda wrapped her arms about her knees and rested her head on her arms. She listened to the whispered discussion that was taking place around the fire, but she couldn't make out what they were saying. The urgent lift to their voices told her one thing though—Naim and the Dwarves weren't discussing the weather.

"Hello, it's good to see you, too," muttered Nicholas, the words oozing sarcasm.

Suddenly the ears of both youngsters perked up.

"Did Naim just say Kingsmere?" whispered Miranda, poking the boy's arm.

"It sure sounded like it," agreed the boy.

"Did you say Kingsmere?" she asked, getting up and joining the tight knot of Dwarves huddled about the Druid.

The Dwarves nodded. "YUP." They sounded like a gruff chorus.

"Well, what about Kingsmere?" prompted Nicholas, throwing his hands up in frustration.

The Druid's dark eyes fastened on the girl. "Do you know this place?" he asked.

"If it's the place I think you mean, I've been there dozens of times. But why do you want to know about Kingsmere?"

"Can you take me there?" pressed the Druid, ignoring her question.

"I guess," said Miranda. "But it's quite far."

"How far?"

Miranda looked to Nicholas for help.

"It takes about half an hour by car," said the boy. "Why?"

Naim brushed his hand over his face, as if to wipe away a painful memory. Miranda noticed that he still wore the large Druid's ring. In the firelight, the cabochon-cut stone looked as if it were filled with molten lava. She shivered, remembering the time she had held the ring in her hand, only to drop it in horror when she discovered that the "S" in the stone was a living fire serpent.

The Druid stared at the tiny tongues of flame for such a long time that the others wondered if he had forgotten about them. When he finally spoke, his voice was a harsh whisper. "There is much to tell. Three weeks ago, I left the Druid's Close with a unit of Riders. We were accompanying the Elven Crown to Bethany for Elester's Crowning. On the way, we were ambushed by some of Hate's creatures—creatures that have not darkened the skies for a thousand years. They overwhelmed us and stole the Golden Crown of Ellesmere."

Nicholas opened his mouth to speak, but Naim raised a hand, and the boy remained silent. He and Miranda exchanged quick glances.

"In Bethany, I learned that Elester had been sent away on patrol and was not expected back for several weeks. And then, I was told that my presence in the land of the Elves was no longer welcomed." He looked at Miranda. "I had planned to use the Bethany Portal to take you and your friends to Elester's Crowning." For a second, his eyes twinkled. "I thought you deserved to be present, and I know Elester would have enjoyed the surprise."

"Really?" breathed Miranda.

"Cool!" exclaimed Nicholas.

"But I was told to go back to my quarters, pack my belongings, and wait for the Guards to escort me to the harbour for transport off the island." He jabbed the fire with the end of his wooden staff. "Needless to say, I did not return to my rooms. I left as you see me. I walked out of the hall and headed straight for the Portal."

The old man's eyes clouded over and his breathing sounded laboured. "For three days and nights I have been trapped in the black space between Bethany and this world. I knew the instant I stepped through the Portal that something was wrong, but it was too late to retrace my steps. I sensed a disturbance in the wards that the Elves had put in place to keep the way open."

The Druid thought for a minute, searching for the words to help them understand what he had experienced, then he looked from face to face. "You journeyed through the Portal. You know that passage is a simultaneous process. At the moment you entered the Portal in Bethany, you were also exiting under the Library of Parliament. You did not experience a time lapse."

"It was like lifting your foot on earth and putting it down on the moon," said Miranda.

"Yes, but there are over two hundred thousand miles between the earth and the moon," said the Druid.

"The mean distance is three hundred and eighty-four thousand four hundred kilometres," quipped Nicholas.

"I've a mind to gag that boy," muttered Emmet, as everyone glared at Nicholas.

"As I was saying," continued the Druid. "I cannot explain what happened in the Portal. I can only say that when I put my foot down, the moon was not there. Nothing was there. I drained my powers trying to hold the wards together, and I lost my way many times. Finally, when I had neither the strength nor the will to fight any longer, the blackness took me and I knew no more until this night when I awakened on the cold stones in this place." He turned to Emmet. "Yet, you knew about the Portal. How?"

Emmet stomped one of his boots on the floor. "Night before last. Something bad came here. Killed Malcolm. Examined tunnel. Portal weakened. Fading. Knew then."

Naim leaned forward and clasped the Dwarf on the shoulder. "I am truly sorry about Malcolm," he said. "I knew him well. He was a fine fellow and a master stonecutter." He sucked in a mouthful of air. "I wonder why I lost my way but evil got through."

"I don't understand," said Nicholas, looking at the Druid. "Did the creature that came through the Portal damage it, or shut it down, or what? And, if it's not working, like Miranda said before you came, how are you going to get back to your world?"

"Those are intelligent questions, Nicholas," said the Druid, rewarding the boy with a thin smile. "Something, besides the Elves, is controlling or taking control of the Portal. What worries me is that whatever is interfering with the magic is doing it from Bethany."

"But, that means . . .?"

"It is a waste of time to speculate," said the Druid. "But I will answer your last question. I know that there is at least one other way into my world from here."

"That's why you asked about Kingsmere, isn't it?" cried Miranda, elbowing Nicholas excitedly. "There's a Portal there."

Nicholas's eyes widened like blinds going up. "Seriously?"

"If it has not been tampered with, yes, we can use the Portal at Kingsmere."

They talked for a while longer. The Druid's face darkened in anger upon learning how Malcolm had been subverted by evil. He listened intently while Miranda told him about her dream and about the Dwarf breaking into her house. She told him everything, except what the creature had done to her room. She knew that if she spoke of her stuffed animals, she'd start crying again.

"And now, something's happened to Mom," she finished, fighting to control her quivering chin.

"Mother's OK," said a voice, coming from outside the circle of light cast by the fire.

It was the Dwarf, Anvil.

"How do you know?" cried Miranda, jumping up and running toward the newcomer. "Have you seen her? Where is she?"

"Gone home," answered Anvil, thumping Miranda's back. "Saw her at school. Told her, go home."

Miranda felt faint as relief washed over her.

"Remember who your mother is, child," said Naim gently.

Miranda nodded. As usual, the Druid was right. She kept forgetting that her mother was an Elf, and could look after herself. "Are you still going to take us to Elester's Crowning?" she asked, dropping onto the floor beside the old man.

The Druid touched her arm. "I have another reason for wanting you to accompany me to my world, Miranda," he said. "But I must tell you that it is dangerous, perhaps more dangerous than even I know."

"It couldn't be worse than grabbing the Serpent's Egg, or calling Hate," said Miranda, shivering as images of the giant Fire Serpents and the Demon nibbled at the fringes of her mind.

"What do you want her to do this time?" asked Nicholas, suspiciously.

The Druid leaned toward Miranda, his eyes as dark as ink. "I need you to be my eyes," he said quietly. "I need you to guide me into the Dark Lands."

Miranda tried to keep a straight face, but Nicholas hooted rudely. "That's a good one," he laughed. "Mir gets lost crossing her backyard to my house."

"Not that sort of guide," snapped the Druid, impatiently. "I know where we are going and I know how to get there. I need you to use the Bloodstones to guide us through the passage into the Dark Lands and, if we make it, I will need your help to find the Elven Crown."

"Is that all?" asked Nicholas, his voice heavy with sarcasm.

The Druid turned to the boy. "Hold your tongue. This does not concern you." His eyes travelled back to rest on Miranda. "What do you say, girl?"

Miranda gulped, suddenly realizing that she hadn't told Naim the most important thing of all. "I can't help you," she cried. "I forgot the Bloodstones at school and Malcolm stole them."

"What?" The Druid's face turned black with anger.

"I'm sorry," cried Miranda, miserably. "I thought they'd be safe in my locker."

"Do not be sorry," said Naim. "You did nothing wrong. I am not angry with you. If I am angry, it is with myself. I feared someone would come after the Bloodstones, but when I saw you, I assumed, wrongly, that because you were safe, the stones were also safe."

He rose and paced back and forth before the fire. The others waited in silence, their eyes going from side to side, like fans watching a tennis match, as they followed him. Finally the man strode back to the fire. "This changes nothing. If Malcolm has the Bloodstones, they are on their way to Bethany. We must find them." He turned to Miranda. "What is your answer? Will you come with me?"

"What are the Dark Lands? Why is it so dangerous?"

"I have never been to that place. I know of only one person who made it there and back alive. For thousands of years, before the Demon was driven into the Place with No Name, she hid in the Dark Lands. She took the country from the Dars and made it hers."

"Who are the Dars?" asked Nicholas.

"There are no Dars," answered the Druid sadly. "The Demon destroyed that noble race."

"Does anything live there now?" asked Miranda, fear turning her limbs to mush.

"Yes," answered the Druid. "The winged creatures who took the Crown. There may be others. I do not know."

"What if we can't find the Crown, what then?"

"Ellesmere will be without a King, officially, but Elester will still rule until someone claims the Crown. Elven rulers traditionally pass the reins of power from father or mother to son or daughter. But they are not required by any law to do so. According to ancient Elven Annals, whoever wears the Crown rules the country. I am afraid that someone other than Elester is planning to claim both the Crown and the Elven Kingdom."

"Whew!" said Nicholas. "That's scary, especially when it's the Demon's creatures who already have the Crown."

"But the Crowning of the one who will wear it must be in Bethany, not earlier than six months after the death of the King or Queen."

"That doesn't leave much time," groaned Nicholas.

"That is why we must leave at once," said the Druid, his piercing eyes fixed on Miranda.

"What about school, Mir?"

Miranda didn't answer. Her thoughts were as jumbled and knotted as the roots of a tree. She hadn't told Naim about the Ku-Kus yet, and she was worried that maybe she should be looking for a way to save the Parliament Buildings, instead of running off to find the Golden Crown of Ellesmere. I'd better tell him now and get it over with, she decided.

When she had finished, the Druid asked Emmet to take him to the tunnel where the Symbionts had replicated. Miranda waited anxiously for his return. He's a powerful Druid, she thought. Surely he can do something. "Please, please!" she whispered. But when the Druid returned with the Dwarf, her hopes were dashed like paper ships on a shoal.

"I do not know how to reverse the destructive process of the Symbionts," he said, quietly.

"What are we going to do?" cried Miranda, looking at Nicholas and wondering what was going to happen to them when the Government of Canada discovered that they were responsible for the collapse of the Parliament Buildings. What sort of crime were they guilty of? Would they be sent to prison? She wrapped her arms about her stomach, feeling sicker by the second.

"I will ask my colleagues," offered Naim. "The Druids have knowledge of every living being. With luck, there may be time to find a solution before any visible signs of erosion are evident."

"But you didn't know about the Ku Kus, and you're a Druid," said Nicholas.

"Because I am a Druid, it does not necessarily follow that I know everything," answered Naim.

Miranda thought she heard Nicholas mutter something that sounded suspiciously like "You could have fooled me." But when she glared at her friend, he looked as innocent as a newborn lamb. She laid her hand on the boy's arm. "I'm going with Naim," she said. "I'd like you to come with us."

Nicholas grinned and clapped his hand over hers. "Just try and stop me!"

"What did you say about school?" asked the Druid, peering at the boy through narrowed eyes.

"Nothing," mumbled Nicholas.

Abruptly, the tall man reached for the pale wooden staff leaning against the wall of the cave. He shook hands with the Dwarves and then turned to the young companions.

"Come," he said. "Time is pressing, and we must reach Kingsmere tonight." He pulled the hood over his head and disappeared into the darkness.

Anvil, shuffling his boots and turning redder than a cooked lobster, thumped Miranda on the back and pressed something large and bumpy into her hand. "Good luck, lass. Take this. Might need it."

"Thanks," said Miranda, turning the curious thing over in her hand. It felt like a rock. Then she stuffed it into her backpack and ran to catch up with Nicholas and the Druid.

"I hope he's not planning to walk to Kingsmere," groaned Nicholas in her ear.

"Don't be stupid," laughed Miranda. "He's going to fly us there on his magic staff."

Behind, the sound of a boot scuffing on the stone floor made her spin around. She peered back along the tunnel, her imagination playing tricks on her, turning the shadows into giant, abstract shapes.

"Naim," she whispered, feeling her blood freeze. "There's something back there."

The Druid stopped and looked over his shoulder, his sharp eyes cutting through the darkness. "I, also, heard footsteps," he said. "But it is probably one of Anvil's men making sure we do not lose our way. Or it is Emmet." But when the big man set off again, Miranda noticed that his pace had quickened and she and Nicholas found themselves running to keep up.

"What's grumpy old Emmet following us for?" asked Nicholas. "We know the way out."

"He will be accompanying us," answered Naim.

"Oh, no!" groaned the youngsters, in unison.

CHAPTER FOURTEEN

BAD TIMES AT HOPEWELL ELEMENTARY SCHOOL

Hopewell Elementary School was in an uproar. It was Friday, the last day before the start of summer vacation. When Mrs. Von Kandi (a.k.a. Bonbon because of her resemblance to a marshmallow with legs), the school's cook, arrived at five-thirty in the morning, she was surprised to find that someone had left the kitchen door wide open. Determined to give the culprit a piece of her mind, she puffed her way from the cafeteria to the students' entrance, barrelling along the hallways like a freight train.

Mrs. Von Kandi stomped around a corner into the corridor that led to the grades four and five classrooms, and almost had a stroke. Someone had broken into the school and vandalized the students' lockers. Hand clutching her heart, she froze, her eyes moving slowly over the destruction. Locker doors lay helter-skelter on the tiled floor, warped and bent as if a giant had ripped them from their hinges. The contents of the lockers had been hacked apart and strewn on top of the busted doors. Gym clothes, books and binders, pens and photographs—all of the precious possessions of the grade four youngsters had been destroyed.

Who on earth was responsible? Surely, not one of the students. The cook knew most of the kids at Hopewell, and while they weren't exactly angels, she knew with absolute certainty that none was capable of such a malicious act. She shook her head and turned away, retracing her steps to another hallway to find a phone and await the arrival of the principal.

All morning, Arabella found her glance returning again and again to the only unoccupied desk in the grade four classroom. Where was Miranda? Did her absence have anything to do with the break-in at the school and the vandalized lockers? Had something happened to her? Had she gone to Bethany alone? She wouldn't do that. Would she?

By lunchtime, Arabella was so upset and worried, she felt physically sick. She went to the office and called her friend's house. Her angst grew as she listened to the phone ringing and ringing. It was the loneliest sound she had ever heard. After twenty rings, she hung up, vaguely wondering why the answering machine hadn't cut in.

Discouraged, she hurried to the cafeteria, looking for Nicholas, only to discover that he hadn't shown up for school either. As she was leaving the cafeteria, she felt, rather than saw, Penelope's eyes on her. She turned back, but the other girl looked away quickly, almost as if she were avoiding her. What was going on?

The afternoon dragged by in slow motion. It was the longest day of Arabella's life. Throughout the afternoon, she felt Stubby's eyes shift from Miranda's desk to her. When she tried to catch him staring at her, he lowered his eyes, but he wasn't quick enough to hide the sly smile that flitted across his face.

By the time the buzzer went at three p.m., Arabella was a total wreck. She stuffed her book and binder into her backpack and slipped out the back door, ignoring the shouts from her fellow classmates and "Hold on, you," from Stubby. He could give her a million detentions for all she cared. After tomorrow she never had to look at him again. She followed the detour away from the cordoned-off area around the destroyed lockers, flew out the side door, and ran toward Parliament Hill, her heart thumping wildly against her rib cage.

Penelope watched Arabella slip out of the class-room. She thought of following her, but something held her back. She also wondered why Miranda wasn't in school, but she figured she'd find out soon enough. Right now, she intended to hang around in case Stubby was up to something.

Yesterday afternoon, she had set out to follow Miranda and Nicholas. Her direct route happened to take her past her classroom windows. As she drew near, a loud crashing noise erupted in the classroom and spilled through an open window. Wondering what in the world was causing the din, Penelope peered cautiously into the room. What she saw made her gasp. She was so stunned that at first she didn't recognize Mr. Little, the grade four teacher. His face was twisted into a mask of hatred. Foamy spittle coated his open mouth and dripped from his bared teeth.

Fascinated and repulsed at the same time, Penelope couldn't tear her eyes off the man as he cleared a path to the back of the room, flinging desks and chairs aside as if they were blocks of Styrofoam. She watched in horror as he picked up a heavy textbook and wrenched off the cover before attacking the pages and ripping them from the binding. Then, he fell on the floor and took something from his inside jacket pocket.

The downy red hairs on Penelope's arms went as stiff as plastic bristles as Stubby banged his head against the wall, all the while pouring something from hand to hand. In the sunlight streaming through the windows, it looked like a stream of sparkling green water. But it was the laughter coming from the teacher's throat as his head hit the wall again and again that made the girl want to throw up. It wasn't a friendly laugh at all.

She almost went crazy trying to figure out what Stubby had been pouring from hand to hand. Something in the way the green blur caught the sunlight and seemed to glow as if it were alive, struck a chord in her memory. She had seen it before. But where? Where?

And then, a few minutes ago, when she least expected it, she solved the riddle. She happened to look at Stubby just as he twisted his lips into a cunning smile and stuck his yellow fingers between the top buttons of his shirt. Euwww! He's so disgusting, she thought, watching as the teacher clawed at the skin under his throat. She started to look away. That's when she saw it—a faint flash of something shiny, like sunlight striking a silver coin. And it came from the object Stubby had slipped from the opening between the buttons on his shirt.

Penelope's mouth dropped in astonishment as she made the connection between the green things in his hands yesterday, and the silver item he was now hurriedly stuffing back into his shirt. Somehow Stubby had got hold of Miranda's Bloodstones!

She knew it was true, even though it was impossible. Miranda never took them off, and no one else, except Nick and Bell, knew of their existence. So, how had they ended up around his scrawny neck?

Then, as if he felt her eyes physically touch him, Mr. Little looked at Penelope and flushed purple as he read the expression on her face. Oh-oh! she thought. He knows. She forced her lips to form an innocent smile and quickly dropped her eyes to her desktop. Replacing the fake smile with a frown, Penelope puzzled over the Bloodstones. Had the grade four teacher finally gone berserk and attacked Miranda? Was Miranda absent from school because she was hurt somewhere, or maybe even in the hospital?

Penelope couldn't answer her own questions . . . yet. But she knew two things for sure. One, Miranda would die before she gave the stones to Stubby. And two, she, Penelope, was going to get them back and return them to Miranda.

CHAPTER FIFTEEN

HORSE THIEVES

They left the tunnels of Parliament Hill behind and crossed the Rideau Locks, following a bicycle path to the Byward Market, a trendy mid-town area of flower shops, boutiques, restaurants, and a farmers' market.

The sun was still a pale thought in the eastern sky, but Miranda was amazed to see the fruit and vegetable vendors already bustling about setting up their outdoor stalls. The little group was now on York Street heading east toward Dalhousie Street. She knew the area well, but she wondered if Naim knew where he was going. This didn't look like the way to Kingsmere.

Miranda stared at the back of the man's head. His hair looked the same as the last time she saw him—perhaps a bit longer, and there was a lot more white streaking the black now. He wore it tied back against his neck in a ponytail, like the Elves. A feeling of sadness washed over her as she thought of his struggle in the Portal. What if the same thing happened to them at Kingsmere? What if they got lost in the blackness and could never find their way out? Shuddering, she drove the dark thoughts away.

Halfway along the block, between Dalhousie and Cumberland, on the north side of York Street, the Druid stopped abruptly before a white building. A sign swung from the corner of the building over a paved driveway that led to a small courtyard. The sign said: Cundell Stables, Est. 1869.

Miranda was amazed. She couldn't believe that she had lived in Ottawa all her life and never heard of something that had existed for over a hundred years. She looked at the sign again. "Wow!" she whispered, turning to the Druid. "These stables have been here for a long time, almost as long as Ottawa."

"Your city is but a child," remarked Naim.

"Actually, the city's older than that," explained Miranda. "But it was called Bytown before it became Ottawa." She looked at Naim, but he was staring into the courtyard and she could tell that he was no longer listening. She saw Nicholas looking furtively up and down the street, nervously brushing his hair out of his eyes.

"What are we doing here?" asked her friend, clearly upset.

The Druid returned a hard stare. "If you must know, we have to reach Kingsmere tonight. We need transportation. This is a stable. A stable has horses."

"Do you mean . . .?" Nicholas's eyes widened. "Are you saying that we're going to Kingsmere on horseback?"

"We either ride or walk," said Naim.

"Why don't we just take a taxi?" asked Miranda, a wave of exhaustion washing over her. The thought of having to ride on the back of a horse all the way to Kingsmere when she hadn't slept in over twenty-four hours brought tears to her eyes.

Naim put a hand on the girl's shoulder. He reached for Nicholas and drew the boy close. "I know that you are both weary. But we are an odd group and I think one of your human taxi drivers would remember us, and where he took us. He may tell others and the wrong ears may hear of our whereabouts. Horses do not tell stories."

"Will Malcolm come after me?" Just asking about the horrible Dwarf gave Miranda the creeps.

"If Malcolm has the Bloodstones, he will not be concerned with you. He will return to Bethany. But it is the creature I tracked through the Portal that worries me. The presence of evil was overwhelming. It was as if I were walking in the Demon's skin." For a second the Druid's hand tightened on Miranda's shoulder, but the girl didn't flinch or cry out. Then, to her relief, Naim released her shoulder, his arm dropping to his side like a heavy hammer. "We cannot use the Kingsmere Way until nightfall. You can rest on the journey."

"It's only five a.m.," Nicholas pointed out. "If we're going to get horses, we'll have to wait till the stables open. You can't wake people up this early."

"I have no intention of waking anyone, young man." And the Druid walked along the driveway into the courtyard.

Nicholas caught Miranda's arm and pulled her back. "Mir, if he's going to do what I think he's going to do, it's called stealing," he whispered.

Miranda whirled on her friend. "Shut up, Nick! You don't know what you're talking about. Naim wouldn't steal."

"Come off it," barked Nicholas, looking at Miranda scornfully. "He just said we're here to get some horses, didn't he? So, if he's not planning to steal them, you tell me how he's planning to pay for them?"

"Stop it," cried Miranda, forgetting to keep her voice down. "Why are you asking me, anyway? I don't know how he's going to pay for the horses. Maybe he's got money." She shrugged, as she peered through the arched passage. "But he'd never steal them."

Miranda wondered why Nicholas always acted so hostile whenever he was near the Druid. The last and only time they had been together, the boy almost drove the man out of his mind. He questioned everything Naim said, and argued constantly over nothing. They seemed to bring out the worst in each other. It was like putting fire with water. Then she grinned as she remembered something that had happened between Nicholas and the Druid when they had first journeyed to Naim's world. She turned to her oldest friend.

"I bet you're still mad at Naim for turning you into a stump." And she clamped a hand over her mouth to stifle her laughter.

Nicholas's neck turned red before his face. "You're wrong," he said, but his lowered eyes told Miranda that he was lying.

"Ha!" she whispered triumphantly.

The stump incident had made Nicholas furious for days. Miranda, Arabella and Penelope had laughed themselves dizzy when Nicholas told them how the Druid had turned him into a tree stump, and then had the gall to sit on him. But later, the day they had to return to Ottawa, Naim apologized to the boy, explaining that he only did it to save Nick's life. Then, Nicholas seemed content with both the apology and the explanation. But now, Miranda wasn't so sure.

She stood on the paved ground in the small courtyard, taking in her surroundings. The L-shaped stables wore a fresh coat of white paint. The window frames and stable doors were painted bright red. And the courtyard had been swept as clean as her mother's kitchen floor.

"Wait here," hissed the Druid, moving toward the stable doors. "And be quiet!" Then he disappeared inside.

He was gone for such a long time Miranda grew uneasy. She kept glancing over her shoulder like a guilty thief. What if Nick were right and Naim was planning to steal the horses? What if they got caught? Would the Druid listen to her if she asked him not to do it? She didn't like the thought of going to jail one bit. She didn't hear Nicholas come up beside her and she almost jumped out of her skin when he tapped her on the head.

But, before the boy could speak, the stable door opened and the Druid appeared leading a pair of horses. The moment she saw the animals, Miranda realized why it had taken Naim so long. He had spent the time saddling both horses and putting on their bridles. He had even wrapped their hoofs in burlap to muffle the clatter of their iron shoes on the pavement. Miranda didn't have much experience with horses, but she had learned to love the noble creatures on her last trip to Bethany.

She gulped at the sight of this pair. She had forgotten how big they were. These two were so huge and powerful they made Miranda feel small and vulnerable. Their coats were light brown. Their faces, manes and tails were as pale as the morning light. Miranda looked from one to the other. They were identical. She wondered how their owner could tell them apart. The horses snorted softly in the silent courtyard, eying the humans curiously. The Druid took their reins and walked them onto York Street.

"Do you realize what you're doing?" hissed Nicholas.

Naim ignored him, concentrating instead on checking the saddles.

"Maybe you can steal horses where you come from, but not here," pressed Nicholas. "Do you want to wind up in jail?"

"Hmm!" said Naim, looking at Miranda. "Do you have something to write on in that bag of yours?"

"Paper," said Miranda, pulling off her backpack and rifling through it to produce a pen and a clean sheet of paper.

"Write this. In the interests of National Security, we have taken Thunder and Lightning." He thought for a second.

Nicholas and Miranda exchanged glances, each thinking the same thing. How did he know the horses' names?

"New sentence. They will not be coming back, but rest assured that they will be treated kindly. Where is that stone Anvil gave you?"

Miranda pulled the stone out of her pack, hold-ing it up. "It's just a rock," she said, looking at the Druid questioningly.

"As you say, it is just a rock. But I am happy to see that you kept it. Now write: Please accept this stone in full and final payment. We remain in your debt. Do not sign it, but add a postscript."

Miranda wrote P.S. at the bottom of the piece of paper.

"The horses came willingly. Now kindly place the letter on the doorstep and weight it down with the stone."

Miranda obeyed, thinking that the owner of the stables was going to get a big surprise in a few hours when he opened the stable doors and discovered that his horses were gone. That would probably make him angry enough, but she thought he'd get even angrier when he read the note and saw the old rock. She hoped they'd be far away when the fireworks started.

Before he could stop himself, Nicholas burst out laughing. He wanted to say, "I can't believe you're doing this." Instead, he rolled his eyes skyward and wisely kept his mouth shut.

Miranda rode behind the Druid on Thunder. Nicholas stood on the ground, holding Lightning's reins and glaring up at the man. His face was as pale as Lightning's mane.

"I'm not riding with him," he said, tilting his head toward the Dwarf who was waiting at the intersection of Dalhousie and York, shuffling his boots impatiently. "Why don't you go back and get him his own horse?"

The Druid sighed. "Nicholas, I am weary and I do not have the strength to argue with you. I will say this once. You will ride with Emmet, or you will remain here. Now decide, quickly."

"Yeah, Nick, hurry up, before Naim turns you into a horse brick." laughed Miranda, enjoying the flush that spread over the boy's face.

In answer, Nicholas yanked the reins and led the pale brown horse along the street, toward the Dwarf, muttering under his breath. Moments later, seated in the saddle, with Emmet holding on to him for dear life, his dark mood brightened when the Druid urged him to take the lead. Nicholas was an experienced rider. He knew the cities on both sides of the Ottawa River like the back of his hand. He took them across the Ottawa River into the city of Gatineau, Quebec, via the Alexandra Bridge, behind the National Gallery. The few joggers they met on the pedestrian walkway stopped running to stare in amazement at the horses and their curious riders.

Nicholas was wide awake now—his dark mood gone as suddenly as morning mist. Figuring that the worst leg of the journey would be getting through Gatineau, he decided to set a zigzag course along streets north of Tache Boulevard, and flank the Gatineau Highway to Kingsmere.

Miranda tried to keep her eyes open, but her eyelids felt as heavy as bricks, and within a few minutes she was fast asleep, her head resting in an awkward position against the Druid's back. When she opened her eyes much later, she was surprised to find that they were paralleling the Gatineau Highway, traveling at a leisurely pace on the grass well away from the busy road.

"Tell me what you know of Kingsmere," said Naim.

Miranda took a minute to collect her thoughts. She knew Kingsmere well. She closed her eyes against the fierce glare of the mid-morning sun and gave the Druid a brief history of the place. It was the estate of William Lyon Mackenzie King, one of Canada's prime ministers. When the man died, he left hundreds of acres of forests, cleared land, and his former home and cottages to the government as a public park and trust for the citizens of Canada. The cottages were clustered on the shores of Kingsmere Lake in the Gatineau Hills.

"Describe the grounds," prompted Naim.

Miranda strolled the estate in her mind, describing what she saw. "It's mostly trees and fields, and great hiking trails. One of them winds down a hill and at the bottom you can look up and watch the falls. Moorside, one of the houses, is now a tearoom. When I go to Kingsmere with my mom, we always have tea and really yummy scones on the outside terrace. You can see the flower gardens from there. Mom said they're formal gardens. There's a rock garden, too, but it's secret and really hard to find. Besides Moorside, there are two, maybe three, other cottages and a farm . . ."

The Druid interrupted. "What I am looking for is something out of the ordinary, something that could be a Portal. Do you recall seeing such a thing—like twin oak trees, or a cave—anything that struck you as unusual?" Miranda felt the man shrug. "I am sorry, Miranda. I cannot help you. I do not know what form this Portal has taken. "

But Miranda's eyes were shining as excitement bubbled up inside her. "The ruins!" she cried. "It has to be one of the ruins!" She explained how the former prime minister collected architectural ruins and erected them on his property. "There's this old abbey with lots of archways. It's so cool."

"Humm," commented Naim. "An abbey. Yes, that could be just the thing. Good work, girl."

"Oh," laughed Miranda, "that's not all. Sometimes he'd bring back these gigantic door frames from famous buildings. My favourite is this humongous one made of stone. It stands alone at the end of the lawn just at the edge of the forest. There's something about it. It's mysterious. Oh, I can't explain it, but when you look at it from a distance, it's really like looking into a painting of trees in a far away place. And . . ." She paused, suddenly remembering the feeling that came over her whenever she was near the tall, stately archway. "This probably sounds dumb, but I know it's different from all the others. I just know it's the Portal."

"If you are right, Miranda, the Portal was there long before your Mr. King was born and long before your country had a name," said the Druid. "I would guess that the Portal inspired him to collect the other architectural ruins, but I doubt that he ever felt he had achieved the same result."

Miranda agreed, because she felt the same. The way the Abbey Ruins had been constructed to look as if the structure had always been at Kingsmere was truly amazing, but at the end of the day, they were just ruins. She could walk away from them without looking back. But the great, silent archway was different. It drew her like a magnet drew a nail.

They stopped frequently, to water the horses and work the stiffness out of their own limbs. Sometimes they walked for a mile or two, leading the horses on the soft grass. An hour before sunset, they turned off Kingsmere Road onto Swamp Road. Their destination lay only minutes away.

The serpent Dwarf hissed in rage. For a second the creature was tempted to vent its fury on its hulking mountain-sized companion, to strike at the Thug and sink its fangs into the slave's chest. But with a great effort, it controlled the urge. For reasons beyond the serpent's comprehension, Hate the Demon doted on her cold, silent assassins. The Dwarf didn't care what happened to the Thug, but he cared a great deal about his own skin. And he knew if he wanted to preserve his precious hide, he would be well advised not to anger the Demon. Hate never forgave.

Sensing the Thug's mounting frustration over their failure to reach the school ahead of the girl and snatch the Bloodstones from her locker, the Dwarf kicked his companion to get the other's attention. From their hiding place in a narrow alley in the Market, they had watched the girl disappear with the evil Druid. Hampered by the approaching daylight, they could not risk following her. But the Dwarf had another plan.

The Thug's eyes burned with hatred for the ugly little creature beside him, but he listened avidly as the Dwarf set out his plan. Then the huge black monster nodded once and slipped from the alley like a great cloud of smoke. The Dwarf followed, smiling wickedly.

CHAPTER SIXTEEN

TEA WITH MUFFY

Tears stung Arabella's eyes as she pounded on the door with her fist and left her finger glued to the bell. Her efforts to find Miranda had failed. Her best friend had vanished off the face of the earth. The minute school was out, Arabella had run all the way to Parliament Hill. Squeezing through the loose bar in the vent, she had braved the tunnels despite her rising panic, calling Anvil's name until she was hoarse. But there was no sign of the Dwarves. They, too, seemed to have vanished. And where was Nick?

From Parliament Hill, she took a bus to Miranda's house, but like her phone calls, no one answered when she rang the doorbell. Discouraged, and not knowing what else to do, she finally found herself outside Penelope's new twenty-ninth floor pent-house apartment.

"Please be home," she begged softly. And as she paused to listen for sounds inside the apartment, a terrible suspicion took shape in her mind. Was Penelope with Miranda and Nicholas? Had the three of them set out for Bethany without telling her? Jealousy cut her like a razor, releasing a bar-rage of emotions that threatened to choke her. Hurt turned to anger and anger became hate.

"If they did that to me," she muttered. "I will never speak to them again."

Arabella didn't know how long she stood in the hall outside Penelope's door, letting hatred consume her, but she was just about to turn and head for the elevators when she heard the high, shrill sound of a small dog barking from somewhere inside the apartment. The yapping grew louder as the animal bounded toward the door. The sound of excited sniffling replaced the ear-piercing barks as Muffy, Penelope's hateful miniature poodle, pressed its small black nose against the space at the bottom of the door.

"Muffsey Wuffsey, who's that?"

Hearing Penelope's familiar voice filled Arabella with shame. How could she have hated Miranda and her other friends so easily? Whatever made her think they'd conspire behind her back? How could she have distrusted them? She swallowed the bitter taste in her throat and hastily dried her eyes on her fists.

"Who is it?" demanded Penelope from the other side of the door.

"It's me. Bell."

Perched on a stool in Penelope's kitchen sipping hot tea laced with honey and warm milk, Arabella poured out her heart to the other girl. For once, Penelope didn't interrupt. She waited patiently until Bell wound down. When it was her turn, she told about Stubby's weird behaviour, and about the Bloodstones.

"This is so not funny," said Arabella, watching in fascination as Muffy greedily lapped up her tea from a tiny cup and saucer. The last time she had seen the little dog, Muffy's white fur had been dyed bright fuchsia. Now, the poodle was as green as a lime. She tore her gaze off the dog and looked at her friend. "How did he get the stones?" Then she grabbed the other girl's arm, squeezing it excitedly. "Penelope . . . the busted lockers . . . You don't think . . .?"

"Nothing that horrible man did would surprise me," said Penelope. "If he found the Bloodstones in Mir's locker, he'd have to trash the rest of the lockers to make it look like a random looting, with a lot of spite thrown in."

The two girls stared at each other over sips of tea. Arabella felt sick at the thought of Mr. Little attacking the lockers, but she was glad to be with Penelope. It felt good to be able to share her worries with a friend.

"You guys were planning to go to Bethany, weren't you?" said Penelope suddenly.

Arabella opened her mouth to deny the accusation, but decided to tell the truth. Her face was a study in guilt as she slowly nodded.

"And you weren't going to tell me."

"No," admitted Arabella, feeling rotten. She felt Muffy's hot little tongue lick her leg. She hooked a foot under the dog and slid her away.

"I'm not upset," said Penelope. "I just wanted to know."

"We didn't do it on purpose," said Arabella. "Mir believed that something bad was happening in Bethany, and things just went from there."

"It doesn't matter now," said Penelope. "What matters is finding Mir and Nick and figuring out how they're planning to get to Bethany. And, since they don't know how to open the Portal under Parliament Hill, they must know another way." She flashed Arabella a grin, her eyes twinkling with mischief. "And I think I know how to find them."

"How?" asked Arabella astonished.

"Didn't you notice how Stubby kept smiling to himself all day?" She didn't wait for Bell to reply.

"Well, after school yesterday, I decided to follow him. But he just went home. I hung about outside his apartment building for hours but he didn't come out. It was so boring I was just about to go home, when guess who appeared?"

"Just tell me," snapped Arabella.

Penelope picked up Muffy and cuddled her playfully. "Stubby. And guess where he went?"

"Penelope . . .!" said Arabella threateningly.

Penelope looked like a cat that had just caught a mouse. "Parliament Hill!" she said and waited for the other girl's reaction. She wasn't disappointed.

"You're not serious!" cried Bell. "No way!"

"So," said Penelope smugly, "why was creepy Stubby acting so pleased with himself all day?"

"Because he discovered something on Parliament Hill."

"Exactly! All we've got to do is follow him and he should lead us to Mir and Nick."

Arabella laughed. "You can be a real pain in the butt, but you are smart." Then she turned serious. "But how are we going to follow him?"

"That's easy," answered Penelope. "Chester, our chauffeur, will be here momentarily." Muffy wriggled out of her arms and raced around in a circle chasing her pom-pom tail.

"Of course," said Arabella, sarcastically. "How stupid of me not to know that." At that moment she felt something warm on her foot. Looking down, she was just in time to see Muffy shoot from under the stool and disappear into the dining room. She looked at her foot resting in a puddle. "Yuck! Muffy just peed on my foot."

Penelope laughed. "Sorry, she's a very BAD DOG!" She looked toward the dining room directing the last two words at Muffy. "Go in my bathroom and wash your foot. I'll get you a dry pair of socks."

"I don't suppose you'd consider leaving her at the kennels?" she asked, easing her backpack over her shoulder and heading toward the other girl's bedroom.

They perched on the edge of soft leather seats in the sleek black air-conditioned limo, parked across the street from Stubby's apartment building, and waited. Muffy was quiet for a change, curled about herself on a seat facing the girls, her tiny raisin eyes pinned to Penelope.

"How can you be sure he's home? What if he stayed at school and left from there?" Arabella was as tense as a coiled wire.

Penelope gave her a superior look. "Trust me, he's home."

Arabella's eyes were tired from peering at the entrance to the building on Prince of Wales Drive. The time crawled by and the waiting drove her mad. It surprised her, because when she was a little kid, she wanted to be a detective, like the heroine in her favourite books. Reading about some things definitely beats doing them, she thought, because the writer can condense the long hours of waiting into a sentence. The reality was boring. She wanted to jump out of the car and pace back and forth on the sidewalk, anything, not to have to sit here watching and waiting.

But the long wait finally paid off.

"It's him!" cried Penelope triumphantly.

Mr. Little stood on the steps of the apartment building and lit a cigarette. Taking several long drags, he threw the stub on the ground, crushed it with his foot and disappeared around the side of the building.

"Where'd he go? Can you see him?" asked Arabella, fearful of losing the man after their long vigil.

"His car's in the parking lot, just around the side, but he has to come this way. It's the only exit. Look for a white Mini."

Sure enough, a few seconds later, a small white car pulled out of the parking lot. Penelope tapped on the glass partition that separated passengers from the driver. "Chester, follow that car."

Keeping well back, they tailed Stubby to Hopewell Elementary School. The teacher parked on the street, locked the car and moved furtively toward the main doors.

"What's he stopping here for? Why'd he come back to the school? Do you think he's done something to Nick and Mir, and they're here somewhere?"

Penelope thought for a minute. "I don't think they're in the school, but I still think he knows where they are. He must have forgotten something."

"I hope you're right," said Arabella. "It's our only chance of finding them."

"Let's go see what he's up to," said Penelope, hopping out of the car. "We'll be right back," she advised Chester.

"And if we're not back in half an hour, get help," added Arabella, grinning impishly.

They ran across the grass away from the main entrance, along one side of the school toward the windows to the grade four classroom. It was early evening and still bright, but they could see the lights shining through their classroom windows. Cautiously, they peered through the end window, holding their breaths.

The room was empty.

"Where did he go?" asked Penelope, grabbing her friend's arm and looking about wildly, as if she expected the teacher to sneak up on them.

"Come on," hissed Arabella. "I bet he's taking the fire exit."

Not knowing the teacher's whereabouts, they suddenly felt vulnerable in the open space near the windows. Moving behind a border of tall shrubs that paralleled the exterior wall of the school, they crept toward the further wall where the building jogged to the left and blocked the fire exit door from view.

"We can see his car and the fire doors from here," whispered Arabella.

The fire door opened slowly and soundlessly, and Mr. Little, grinning like the Cheshire cat, slipped outside. If Arabella had any doubts about Stubby knowing where her friends were, one look at the man sent them scudding away like clouds on a windy day.

Suddenly a shadow loomed up behind the man. The girls shrank back in terror, fighting to control the screams rising in their throats.

It was one of the Thugs, a huge towering creature that looked like something out of a nightmare. Its red eyes burned with a dull glow in the early evening sunlight. The Thug put one clawed hand on the man's shoulder, spinning him around. Stubby's body went limp as a rag doll. His arms flopped to his sides and hung there. His legs buckled, and he would have fallen if the Thug had not tightened its grip on his shoulder.

The girls watched in horror, afraid to breathe. Stubby's back faced them and the creature was peering into the man's face so intently, Arabella felt as though it were seeing into his mind. After what seemed like hours, the Thug's clawed hand dropped from the man's shoulder. The creature turned away and disappeared, as if he had melted into the air. Stubby leaned against the door where he had fallen when the Thug released him. He remained like that for a long time. Then he shook himself as if he had suddenly awakened from a deep sleep. He peered about at his surroundings, letting his gaze rest on the clump of bushes where the girls were crouched, like human soccer balls, arms wrapped about their knees. Then, like one in a daze, he walked slowly toward his car staring curiously at the blood on his hand where he had rubbed his shoulder. But Arabella noticed his other hand reach for the Bloodstones that Penelope said were around his neck.

"I don't know what just happened," whispered Arabella, her voice shaky. "But at least he's still got the Bloodstones."

The girls waited until they heard the sound of Stubby's car driving away before they dashed back to Penelope's limo and resumed the chase.

CHAPTER SEVENTEEN

THE KINGSMERE WAY

Gazing at the creamy yellow cottages clustered on the shores of the lake in the dying sunset, Miranda felt again the familiar sense of peace and well-being that always seemed to come over her when she visited Kingsmere. She raised her head and took a deep breath. The air was fresh and clear, sweet with the mingled bouquets of pine and honeysuckle. Looking up, she saw that, even at sunset, the sky was bluer than anywhere else in the world—a pure, perfect blue that made her heart ache.

Magic! The word was there in her mind, as if it had been waiting for her to find it. It's true, she thought, wondering why she hadn't made the association before. It is a magic place. No other word would do. And then a thought suddenly struck her. The names. Kingsmere! Ellesmere!

"Naim," she said, feeling proud and elated by her discovery. "It's more than the Portal, isn't it? The Elves were here, weren't they? They built this place." She knew she was right.

The Druid laughed one of his rare laughs, and for a moment, Miranda pretended that there was no Demon—no evil. "The Elven magic has been growing stronger as we draw near Kingsmere," he said. "Yes, girl! The Elves were here and gone, but it seems their magic remained."

They were ahead of Nicholas and the Dwarf, Emmet. Thunder followed behind Miranda, bumping his nose against her back and nuzzling her hair. Miranda adored the big, sleek animal and giggled whenever he pushed at her clothing. "What do you want, Thunder, huh?" She turned and walked backwards for several steps, gently rubbing the creature's smooth velvety face. Nicholas walked alongside Lightning, one hand on the horse's mane. Emmet, the Dwarf, stomped heavily on Lightning's other side, purposely avoiding the boy.

"Do you believe Kingsmere is a magic place?" she asked her friend.

"No," muttered Nicholas, suddenly feeling the strain of the past twenty-four hours. "King was goofy. He said the ruins spoke to him."

The Druid turned to look at the boy. "There is magic here, Nicholas. I can feel it. Perhaps Mr. King felt it, too."

Nicholas shrugged. "Whatever," he muttered, too tired to care what the tenth prime minister of Canada felt about anything.

Miranda laughed. "You are so hopeless."

She turned back to Naim. "I've always felt there was something different about Kingsmere. I just didn't realize it was magic—until now. Even time passes differently. My mom and I come here a lot in the summer. We'd plan to stay an hour or two, but it's always dark by the time we leave."

"You may be right, girl" said Naim thoughtfully. "Elven magic works in strange ways." He inhaled deeply. "It is a beautiful place. You are fortunate to have this treasure."

"It's funny. Mom loves it here, but she doesn't know about the magic."

"She knows," said Naim quietly. "She knows."

"How come she never said anything?"

"That is a question for your mother," answered the Druid.

Miranda sighed. There were lots of things she wanted to ask her mother, but the timing was never right. But, perhaps this was a good time to tackle the Druid.

"Do you think King Ruthar is alive?"

"I know he is not," said the Druid.

"Then, why was he alive in my dream?"

Naim laughed again. "My dear child, why are you asking me? I do not know the answer." He grew silent then, looking at the western sky. The sun had set in a blaze of blues and purples and brilliant crimson streaks, as if a painter had taken a giant brush and boldly swept it across a blue canvas.

They joined Nicholas and Emmet in the Abbey Ruins, huddled in a tight knot near the famous doorway. The Dwarf disappeared abruptly, mumbling that he was going to take a look around for signs of Malcolm or other unwelcome creatures. They had come too far to let anything stand in their way now. Naim had said the Portal remained open for only a short time. They couldn't risk missing their opportunity or they'd have to wait a full month before they could pass through it. Miranda didn't quite understand why, but it had something to do with the full moon and a clear sky.

Finally, the Druid rose. He swung his heavy cloak over his shoulders and took Thunder's reins. "Let us go," he said. "It is almost time."

Miranda ran ahead, down the sweep of lawn, stopping where the ground dipped toward the Portal. She gazed in wonder at the great arched structure bathed in moonlight. It appeared almost white and luminescent.

"Where's Emmet?" hissed Nicholas, coming up behind her, his eyes scanning the treeline for the dark form of their taciturn companion. Lightning followed, hooves clop-clopping on the hard ground.

"Do not worry about Emmet," said the Druid, his eyes raking the arched structure. "He is around and will be here when it is time to go."

As they approached the Arc de Triomphe, he dropped Thunder's reins in Miranda's hand and motioned to them to wait until he returned. They watched him move cautiously toward the great yawning gap between the double columns. Then, he circled it, pausing several times to place his hands on the cold stone. Finally he turned to the others. "Come along," he whispered, and when the two young Ottawans approached, he laid a hand on their shoulders. "If there is a Portal in this place, Miranda was right. It is this structure and no other. I do not know if it will bridge the distances as it was intended to do, but when I touched the columns, I sensed a great power. That power has not been interfered with. So far, no evil has entered the Portal before us."

Miranda gripped the Druid's sleeve. The man gently removed her hand. "Do not fear for me. If it is not a Portal, then no harm has been done. I will pass under the arch and merely end up on the other side."

"What are we waiting for?" said Nick, shrugging

free of the Druid's hand and stepping up to the Arc. "Let's go!"

"Step aside, Nicholas. I will go through the Portal first."

The boy moved back reluctantly. There had been an edge to the Druid's tone that warned him not to argue. But to his surprise, Naim suddenly turned to him, and said kindly, "I do not know where this Portal exits. I must travel first to ensure that nothing is waiting for us on the other side. When I have gone, Miranda, wait a good minute or two and then follow." He looked at Nicholas. "You will lead the horse through the Portal after Miranda, and Emmet will come last."

Emmet had come up behind them unheard. Miranda still couldn't bring herself to like the silent Dwarf, but his presence made her feel safer.

Then the Druid took the reins from Miranda and led Thunder across the rough stone ground, up the steps, and through the Portal. His companions held their breath, half expecting to see the man and horse on the forest side of the opening staring back at them. But Naim and the horse were gone as if they had never existed.

A few minutes took forever. Miranda and Nicholas stood together in the warm June night. Miranda absentmindedly stroked Lightning's soft brown coat, as she gazed at the gigantic Arc, hypnotized by the blackness filling the space beyond the pale columns. Nicholas kept shifting his glance from his watch to the forest beyond the Arc. Night transformed the trees on the other side of the opening into writhing, formless shapes that reached for the youngsters with long black claws as if to snatch them and drag them into the dark.

When Nicholas nudged her, Miranda was so tense she felt she was about to shatter like a fragile, porcelain statue. "Go," he whispered, his voice thin and strained.

Swallowing her fear, she squeezed her friend's arm and moved toward the opening. A sudden movement off to the left of the Arc caught her eye and she turned her head sharply. A dark, thick shape seemed to drop to the ground and remain there, motionless. She couldn't see clearly, but for a second, she had a wild thought that it was the Dwarf, Malcolm. Shivering, she turned back to the Portal, walking faster now.

Then she saw it, a solid blackness rise from the still form on the ground, expanding rapidly and drifting toward the far side of the Arc. Miranda's heart stopped. It was a huge, monstrous creature and it was going to reach the opening before her. She broke into a run, racing up the steps as the gigantic serpent's head whipped around the columns and hovered above her, pushing into the archway. From somewhere behind, she heard the mingled sounds of Nicholas shouting and the horse screaming in fear. Then Miranda saw the great mouth snap open, revealing gleaming white fangs as long as her arm, but she couldn't stop now. Raising her arm protectively, she ducked to the side just as the serpent struck and then everything went as black as death.

CHAPTER EIGHTEEN

THE AUGURS

Miranda was terrified out of her mind. Where was she? Had the giant serpent swallowed her alive? If she had escaped the creature, this wasn't one bit like the passage from Bethany to Parliament Hill. Then, things had happened without any interruption. She clearly remembered walking between the two tall oak trees in the park outside the Council Hall, and in the same instant, she was home in Ottawa. But now, something was terribly wrong. She tried taking slow deep breaths to calm her racing heart, but she found herself gulping air like an asthmatic runner. She was lost, trapped somewhere in the blackness between Kingsmere and Bethany.

"NAIM!" She shouted the Druid's name over and over until her throat was raw. It had taken Naim three days to fight his way out of the darkness, using up every last ounce of his powers. But she wasn't a Druid. She was just a kid with no powers, except the Bloodstones. And they were gone. There wasn't a chance in a million that she'd ever fight her way out of this place, even if she knew what she was supposed to fight. She rubbed her arms vigorously. It had been warm, almost balmy, when she stepped through the arched Portal at Kingsmere, but now she was freezing.

And then she felt the ice on her flesh.

"Come this way! Quickly!" hissed a harsh voice. "And cover your arms."

Miranda was too stunned to move, until a strong hand gripped her shoulder and spurred her into action.

"Naim!" she cried, above the screaming of the wind. "Where are we? There's a big huge serpent back there . . . it's coming . . ."

The Druid's fingers dug into her shoulders. "What serpent?" he demanded, sharply. "But wait. Move aside to make room for Nicholas."

Miranda moved out of the way. "I don't know. It appeared out of the dark and moved to the Portal just as I . . ."

"What do you mean, it appeared out of the dark?" pressed the Druid.

"It happened too fast."

Suddenly a dark shape materialized before Miranda's eyes.

"Have I died?" wondered Nicholas. "MIR!"

Miranda grinned and grabbed the boy's arm. "No, you're not dead. But how did you get past the serpent?"

"What serpent?" asked Nicholas, looking at Miranda as if she were out of her mind.

"You mean you didn't see it?"

"Mir, I'm telling you, there wasn't any serpent."

Miranda turned to the Druid. "I'm not making it up," she said. "It came through the Portal from the forest side. It lunged at me and then I was here."

She hadn't realized that Emmet had come through the Portal until he spoke. "There was something," he said. "Scared the horse."

"That's right," cried Nicholas. "Lightning was terrified. I had to really work to get him through the arch."

"Come," said the Druid. "We will freeze if we do not find shelter."

"Wait!" cried Miranda. "Just tell me if we're trapped in the Portal!"

"What are you talking about?" snapped the Druid.

"Where are we? This isn't Bethany."

"Of course it is not Bethany."

A high-pitched laugh escaped from Miranda's throat before she could muffle it. She was giddy with relief, and weak from exhaustion and hunger. She was so glad to know she wasn't trapped in the

Portal that she decided she didn't care if she were on the moon. She was surprised when the Druid volunteered the information.

"I do not know how many Portals the Elves created from this world to yours," he said. "But I do know that each Portal leads to a different location. The Bethany Way connects to Parliament Hill. If you enter this Portal, you will exit at Kingsmere." He paused to brush the coating of sleet from his cloak. "If this blizzard is any indication, we are near the borders of the Dark Lands, nearer the Mountains of the Moon than the Waste." He glared at the girl. "I told you to dress yourself in something warm. Do it now, or you will freeze to death." Then he and the Dwarf moved out of range of the girl's hearing.

Miranda pulled a hooded shirt and her jacket from her backpack with numb, frozen fingers. But she wasn't thinking about the cold. They were near the Mountains of the Moon. And that was the best news. Dunmorrow, the mountain kingdom of the Dwarves, couldn't be far from here.

Although she was excited at the thought of seeing King Gregor again, her heart was heavy with sorrow over the tragic fate of Dundurum, the former Dwarf country. The fifteen-thousand-foot-high mountain had been sucked into the Place with No Name when the Elven Prince, Elester, drove the Demon into her rank, scabby prison. Luckily, the Dwarves had evacuated Dundurum and only the bodies of those killed by the Demon accompanied Hate on her wretched journey. That was only three months ago.

After the loss of Dundurum, the Dwarves negotiated a deal with Typhon, the black Dragon who guarded the treasure of his Dragon Clique, and had begun the process of relocating to Mount Oranono in the Mountains of the Moon on the day Miranda and her friends returned to Ottawa.

The Druid gathered the companions in a circle. "We will not survive this storm as we are. There is a place not too far from here where we can find shelter."

"Hmm, the Augurs!" said Emmet. "Not good."

Naim nodded. "What other choice do we have?"

"Freeze. Better choice," answered the Dwarf.

"I don't care if these Augurs are a bunch of homicidal maniacs," said Nicholas, shivering in his thin t-shirt. "Let's just get out of this weather."

"What are Augurs?" asked Miranda.

"Soothsayers," answered Emmet.

"What do you know, the Grouch is actually speaking to us," whispered Nicholas.

"They are that," agreed Naim, turning to the young Ottawan. "And more. They are eccentrics. When we get there, you are not to touch anything. Do you understand?"

"I guess," said Nicholas and Miranda.

"You will not ask questions, especially questions about the future, or do anything to agitate them, or it will be the worse for you."

"Are these Augurs human?" asked Miranda, fearfully.

The Druid laughed. "I'm afraid so," he said. "Now let us find this place before my old bones turn to ice."

Howling winds buffeted them, driving them a step back for every two they managed to take forward. Sleet pelted their bodies like sharp pieces of glass, stinging their faces and the exposed skin on their arms. The Druid shouted to the children to grip his cloak and walk behind him, using his great height and wide cloak to block the hurricane-force winds. Nicholas shrugged off the Druid's suggestion, but Miranda held onto the thick fabric as if her life depended on it.

When she stumbled from exhaustion and the man's cloak slipped from her frozen fingers, she cried out. Nicholas gripped her elbow, steadying her, but she could see in the boy's pale, icy face that he was also on his last legs. How much farther was this place? Then, as if she had asked the question aloud, Naim stopped and pointed through the driving sleet. At the sight of the soft yellow glow spilling out of the raging night ahead, they found new strength. At last, the weary, frostbitten travellers stood on the steps of a quaint cottage. Naim pounded on the door.

"Come in! Come in!" piped a plump, rosy-cheeked man, holding the door open with one hand and beckoning the travellers inside with the other. "Morda, love, we've got company." When he noticed the children, shivering as if they were in the throes of a grand mal seizure, teeth chattering behind lips that were blue and cracking from the cold, he grasped their hands and drew them into the welcoming warmth.

"Don't leave them standing out in the cold, old man. Bring them in." Miranda couldn't see the woman whose voice tinkled like the sound of happy laughter. The sound brought tears to the girl's eyes and made her heart ache with longing for a family—for grandparents, and aunts, and uncles, and cousins. "They're just in time for dinner."

Miranda hadn't noticed the mouth-watering aroma until the woman mentioned dinner. Now though, she realized she was starving. The thought of hot food made her light-headed.

The Druid made hasty introductions while the old man fussed over them. He stood the wooden staff and the swords in a stand by the door. Then, he took the Druid's sodden cloak and laid it over a rocking chair to dry by the fireplace. Despite the wet cloak, Naim's inner garments were as dry as a bone. Emmet stomped over to the fire and stood with his back to the flames, feet planted firmly on the wooden floor, arms folded across his chest. Miranda saw steam rising from the Dwarf.

The old man directed Miranda toward a small room near the door. "Better get those wet things off, young lady, before you catch your death. Look in the closet. Find something to wear while your things dry."

Miranda tore off her wet clothes, rubbed herself dry with a blanket-sized towel, and pulled on the first shirt she saw, adding another and another until she began to thaw. Then she slipped into a pair of giant baggy flannel pants, rolling them up at the waist and legs. She combed her hair with her fingers and looked quickly in the full-length mirror in a corner of the room. Scary, she thought, staring at her reflection in the glass. Her pupils were so enlarged they almost hid the green irises. Her bottom lip was cracked and bleeding, and small cuts dotted her face and hands where the ice pellets had stung her. Sighing heavily, she collected her own wet clothing and went to rejoin the others.

"You look goofy," whispered Nicholas, leaving to take his turn in the changing room.

"Shut up," Miranda whispered back.

When Nicholas came back into the room, Miranda couldn't help giggling. He looked ridiculous in a long, trailing yellow robe and thick, skin-hugging red tights. Even the usually stern Druid turned away and gazed at the ceiling beams before the boy caught his smile. Emmet stomped his boots and made a funny sound in his throat. Nicholas glared at the other companions, daring them to laugh. Then, he plopped down in the rocking chair and glowered at Miranda.

"Thanks for taking the only pair of pants," he whispered, his face burning redder than the flames in the fireplace.

"Oh!" said Miranda innocently. "Was that really the only pair?"

"Very funny," snapped the boy, wrapping the robe around his legs to hide the bright wooly tights. "Just wait. I'll get even."

The woman called Morda appeared in the kitchen doorway, wearing a smile that lit up the room. Miranda was surprised at the sight of her. From her laughter, she had pictured someone old and plump, with a round face and fine white hair through which her pink scalp was visible. The woman standing in the doorway was certainly old, and so beautiful Miranda couldn't look away from her. Her face was a perfect oval, framing a pair of amber-coloured eyes. Her hair was pale blonde, almost white. She wore it tucked behind her ears.

On the tray in Morda's hands were four steaming bowls. Miranda leaped to her feet and rushed to help the woman. She peered hungrily into each bowl before placing it on the table. In one was a mound of fluffy mashed potatoes with melted cheese and butter oozing out of the centre like molten lava. In another she saw bread stuffing. A third held sugar corn, and in the fourth was a hill of green peas. Everything smelled so delicious Miranda fought to control the urge to plunge her face into all of the bowls at once and gobble up the contents.

"Find your names and take your seats," said Morda. She patted Miranda's hand. "You are right here, dear." She indicated the place to her left, and disappeared into the kitchen.

Miranda noticed her name engraved on a flat piece of silver held in the beak of a small sterling eagle. She reached for it but pulled her hand away as she remembered Naim's warning. Surely he hadn't meant the place name holders, she thought. She looked at the old man waiting at the end of the table for the others to sit. "How did you know our names?" she asked, forgetting that Naim had also forbidden them to ask questions.

For a second, the old man looked bewildered, as if he didn't know what she was talking about. Just then, Morda returned, this time carrying a large platter with an enormous roast turkey or other fowl resting in the centre. It was the biggest bird Miranda had ever seen. She guessed it was as large as a pig.

"Cool," said Nicholas. "But exactly what sort of bird is it?"

"The kind that flies," answered the old man, winking at Morda as if they shared a private joke.

"Well, it certainly looks scrumptious," said Miranda, practically doubled over from hunger pains.

The old woman smiled with pleasure at the compliment and began sharpening a long carving knife on a whetstone. "Now, where are you from, child?" she asked, her hazel eyes sparkling yellow in the soft light.

"Ottawa," answered Miranda. "In Canada. It's the capital."

"Did you hear that, old man? Our guests are from Canada."

"Delighted to meet you! Wherever Canada is," cried the old man, picking up his wine glass and raising it in a toast. Realizing it was empty he got up and went to a small wooden corner cupboard. Bending over, he opened the bottom door and pulled out a bottle of clear red liquid. Miranda noticed it was almost empty.

The man waved the bottle at Morda. "This occasion calls for a drop of Pomegranate wine. What do you say, old thing?"

"We will not have wine," said Naim, curtly.

For a second there was complete silence. Miranda was surprised. The Druid was gruff and often impatient, but it was not like him to be rude, especially when the people he was being rude to had just saved their lives.

"Dear me," said the woman, laying the carving knife on the platter and patting the Druid's arm. "Whatever will our guests from Canada think?" She nodded to the old man. "Bring the wine, dearest."

"I said, no wine for us," repeated the Druid.

The room grew deathly still. Naim and the woman stared at each other for so long, Miranda thought she'd die of embarrassment. Desperate to change the subject, she slid her hand along the table toward the woman's arm and spoke without thinking. "Are you really an Augur? Can you tell the future?"

She felt the Druid's eyes shift abruptly from Morda to her. Too late, she realized her mistake. "W-what I-I m-mean . . ." she stammered, avoiding Naim's furious stare.

In a flash, Morda grabbed the carving knife, raised it and stabbed at the girl's hand. "IT'S NONE OF YOUR DAMN BUSINESS!" she shrieked.

Miranda gasped in shock, snatching her hand off the table less than a second before the sharp knife struck the wood. She felt the wind from the force of the blow on her hand as she stared at the weapon embedded at least an inch in the table. Frantically, she slid her chair down the table away from the old woman.

"Oh dear," sighed Morda, giving Naim a sad look. "Now see what you made me do?" She tugged on the knife, but it was stuck solid in the hardwood. She finally gave up and slumped back in her chair. "How can I carve the fowl without a knife?" she sobbed. "Ruined. Everything's ruined." Without warning, she picked up the bowl of mashed potatoes and hurled it down the length of the table to smash against the wall behind the old man. Miranda watched the bowl shatter, leaving a mess of potatoes and melted cheese sticking to the pale green wall. Then, Morda turned on Miranda. "And it's all your fault. Coming here. Telling lies, making up stories . . ."

"What are you talking about?" cried Miranda, her heart beating hard and fast. "I just asked a simple question."

"Do not argue," whispered Naim, his voice a harsh rasp. "Go to the door. I will get your things. We must leave here. Now."

"Would you just listen to the sly little weasel," hissed Morda. Then, her voice changed abruptly. "I just asked a simple question." Smiling like a wicked witch, she clawed at the turkey breast, ripped off a big chunk of meat, and stuffed it in her mouth.

Miranda felt colder than when they were outside in the blizzard as she recognized her voice coming from the old woman's throat. As one, the four companions pushed back their chairs and jumped to their feet, backing away from the table. Nicholas and Naim moved toward the fireplace where their clothes hung over chairs and on hooks in the stones. Miranda and Emmet eased toward the door, their eyes locked on the old woman, who continued ripping great chunks of meat off the turkey.

"Are you really an Augur? Can you tell the future?" The child's voice spilling from the woman was as obscene as the pieces of turkey sticking out of her mouth. Morda gripped the platter with both hands and smashed it down on the table, shattering it. Tearing at the turkey, her eyes never left Miranda. "YOU'VE GOT NO FUTURE!" she screamed, pointing a drumstick at the horrified girl. Her other hand was busy rummaging in a pocket of her dress. "You want to know the future?" she laughed, pulling something out of her pocket and holding it up in the air.

Miranda stared at the thing dangling from between Morda's thumb and index finger. It looked like a pair of limp, black lips.

"GIVE IT BACK THIS MINUTE, HAG!" spluttered the old man, jumping to his feet and knocking his chair over. He caught the wine bottle by its neck and smashed it on the edge of the table. He waved the jagged weapon threateningly at the woman. "HOW DARE YOU TOUCH MY THINGS!"

"IT'S NOT YOURS, IT'S MINE," squealed the old woman, hurling the bowl of stuffing at the man as she slapped the limp object against her mouth.

The change that came over her was mind-boggling. The grotesque mouth seemed to consume the woman's entire face. And the voice coming from the hideous black lips was a harsh, distorted monotone.

"Take five walking serpents, an heir, and a dream;
Add a revenant royal and a man's dying scream;
Combine with lost stones and the skin of a Fraud;

A ring of fire and a bloody rod;
A circle of gold; a pinch of hate;
A father's lie and a black crate;
A girl betrays, the Crown slays.
Stir with a stick and watch the walls fade,
When hers wears the Crown, Kings are unmade."

The words were scarcely out of the oracle mouth when the old man charged Morda, knocking her flat on her back on the floor.

His stubby fingers clawed at the black-lipped mouth, peeling it off the old woman's face. Then he leaped to his feet and tugged on the mouth, trying to wrench it free. But Morda hooked her fingers through the opening of the lips and held on for dear life.

"GET YOUR FILTHY HANDS OUT OF MY MOUTH!" roared the old man, pulling on the lips and stretching them until Miranda was sure they were going to snap in two.

"Emmet," she cried. "Quick! We've got to do something."

"Do something all right," muttered Emmet, scooping up the swords and the Druid's staff, and wrenching open the door. "Leave."

Miranda turned for one final look at the table with the shredded turkey lying on its side among the shards of platter before she sprinted out the door and into the raging storm. Curiously, she was no longer hungry.

CHAPTER NINETEEN

HOT ON THE TRAIL

"Stay back, Chester," warned Penelope. "If we're spotted, it's game over."

They were following the grade four teacher along Highway 5 and had just turned off the Old Chelsea exit, about thirty kilometres north of Ottawa. As their covert activities took them farther and farther away from the city, their spirits sank lower and lower. It was unlikely that their missing friends were holed up in the Gatineau Hills.

"Where's he going?" muttered Penelope to no one in particular.

Arabella's eyes were locked on the white Mini. Convinced that they were on a wild goose chase, she was ready to call it quits and tell Penelope to head back to Ottawa. As if Penelope had read the other girl's mind, she turned away from the window.

"Bell, we've come this far, we can't turn back now. Anyway, he can't be going much farther. There's nowhere to go at this hour, except one of the restaurants in Old Chelsea."

"There's Kingsmere," said Arabella.

"Yeah, during the day," said Penelope. "But it'll be closed now."

But when Mr. Little turned left off Old Chelsea Road onto the Gatineau Parkway and exited at Kingsmere Road, it certainly looked as if he were heading toward Kingsmere.

"Curiouser and curiouser," said Arabella, quoting from one of her favourite books as she leaned forward on her seat.

The girls stared at each other for a second, their spirits rising with excitement. What was taking Stubby to Kingsmere after the place had closed for the day?

"I told you he was up to something," quipped Penelope, slapping her friend's arm. Then she lowered the glass partition. "Chester, we know where he's going, so drop back. We don't want him to see our headlights."

When Chester switched off the lights and swung the long black car into the visitors' parking lot they located Stubby's Mini immediately. Penelope told the chauffeur to go back to Old Chelsea and wait there until she called him on his cell phone. Then she slung her backpack over her shoulder, stuffed Muffy into her jacket, grabbed a plastic bag from the floor, and hopped out of the car, Arabella on her heels.

They stood together in the darkness watching until Chester reluctantly drove away. Then, they studied the lay of the land on a wooden billboard and set a course for the main cottage, Moorside.

Penelope peered into the shadows on either side of the path. It wouldn't take much to convince her that the darker tree shapes were really a forest of giant, black Thugs waiting to spring at the girls as they went deeper among them. "I'm glad you're here, Bell," she whispered. "I couldn't do this if I were by myself."

"Me neither," said Arabella, grasping her friend's hand. "I'm scared enough with you here."

As they moved cautiously around a bend in the path, a light appeared in the distance ahead. Quickly, they stepped off the path and slipped among the trees, keeping their eyes on the bobbing light, their hearts thumping wildly. They waited just long enough to determine whether the light was receding or coming closer. Satisfied that it was moving away, in the same direction they were headed, the girls let out their breath and followed.

"It has to be Stubby," whispered Arabella, more anxious than ever to find out what he was up to, and if he was holding Nick and Mir captive somewhere out here. She quickened her pace, heedless of the uneven path and the thick roots half-buried in the soil.

"Be careful," cautioned Penelope in a half-teasing voice. "Don't trip and break a leg or I'll have to leave you here."

Arabella snorted rudely.

Moorside suddenly appeared before them like a pale phantom in the moonlight. "Hurry," whispered Arabella. "He's just gone around the back of the cottage."

The girls flattened themselves against the side of the building and crept toward the back where the tearoom was located. Reaching the corner, they were just in time to see Stubby stomping through the freshly-planted formal gardens.

"That creep," whispered Arabella, spitting in anger. "We should leave a note telling them who trampled their gardens."

Skirting the flower beds, they sprinted across the lawn and stopped. Not more than a dozen feet ahead, Stubby stood as still as a statue, his back to the girls. He was staring at a towering white archway down a hill at the edge of the forest. The girls stared, too. The sight of the white columns glowing eerily in the weak moonlight took their breath away. Then Penelope's eyes detected movement. She strained to identify the ghostly shapes moving near the gigantic structure.

Penelope pinched Arabella's arm. "Who is it?" she whispered.

Arabella pressed her mouth to Penelope's ear. "I don't know, but there's more than two people down there."

"It's got to be Nick and Mir. It's got to be them."

"Yeah, but who is that with them?"

"Horses," said Penelope, disappointment washing over her like sleep. She had made a big mistake. Stubby hadn't led her to Nick and Mir after all. She had been so sure he was involved in their disappearance. "It's not them," she whispered, tears of frustration clouding her eyes. "I'm sorry, Bell."

"Shhh!" hissed Arabella, watching the largest figure lead a horse shape through the archway. Then she turned and grabbed Penelope's arms, squeezing tightly. "It is them. I think that was the Druid I just saw go through the arch."

"Are you serious?" whispered Penelope. "I knew it. I knew it."

Arabella was desperate to get closer, but Stubby was standing directly between them and the archway. The girls watched as one of the smaller shadows walked up to the Arc and disappeared into the darkness.

"Where are they going?" asked Penelope, frantically pulling her cell phone out of its case on the side of her backpack.

"I can't see into the trees on the other side of the arch," said Arabella. "We've got to get closer."

Penelope tugged on her friend's arm, pulling her back and around the side of the house. "Chester, it's me," she whispered into the phone. "You can go home now. If my parents ask where I am, tell them you dropped me off at Miranda's house and I'm going to camp with her." There was a long pause. "Don't worry, I won't let them fire you. I've got to go now." She switched off the phone and stuffed it in her pocket.

"Won't they want to know which camp you're at?" Arabella asked, amazed that Penelope could lie to her parents so easily.

"Why should they want to know that?" asked Penelope. "Would you?"

"Well, yeah," said Bell. "I think most parents would want to know where their kids were going."

"Really," said Penelope. "Why?"

"Are you seriously saying that your parents never ask you where you're going? What if they had to get in touch with you?"

"Why would they have to get in touch with me?"

"How do I know?" snapped Arabella. "What if your father died, or something?" She wanted to shake the other girl until her teeth fell out.

"Bell, I don't see what you're getting so stressed about. If Daddy died, what good would it do to come looking for me? I can't raise the dead. I might as well finish what I'm doing and find out when I get home."

"You are so heartless!" Arabella stared at the other girl in shock.

"You don't know anything about me," said Penelope, absentmindedly reaching down the front of her jacket and stroking Muffy. "I'd be horribly sad, no matter when I found out. I'm only saying that it wouldn't make any difference to my father whether I cried my eyes out as soon as he died or a month later." She put her hand on Arabella's shoulder. "Anyway, if they really want to reach me, they can call my cell phone."

Arabella laughed quietly, shaking her head. Penelope was right, she really didn't know her very well at all. She decided to change the subject. "Have you given any thought as to how we're going to get the Bloodstones away from Stubby?"

"Don't worry, I've got a plan."

"Yeah," hissed Arabella. "That's what worries me."

When the third shape moved through the archway, Stubby finally stirred. He crept down the hill toward the short, stocky figure waiting alone near the dark opening.

"Here, take this." Penelope pressed the plastic shopping bag into her friend's hand. Then, before Arabella could stop her, she took off like a shot, racing toward Stubby as fast as her legs would move. Arabella waited for a good second before racing to catch up with the other girl.

Hearing the sudden sound of running shoes pounding on the grassy ground, Stubby wheeled around in time to see a dark shape practically on top of him, long arms reaching for his neck. He cowered, uttering a shrill scream as a small cold hand grabbed the chain about his neck and gave it a hard yank. Clutching his chest, Stubby lost his balance and toppled backwards onto the grass. Sobbing wildly, he scrambled to his feet just in time to receive a nasty shove from a second speeding dark shape. This time he landed face down in a smelly pile of manure.

"Serves you right, creep," hissed a nasty voice. And then the dark shape was gone, speeding down the hill in pursuit of the first attacker.

Arabella was still laughing when she caught up with Penelope. "You should have seen his face," she said. "He was scared out of his skin." She clasped Penelope's hand and ran toward the archway just as Emmet disappeared into the blackness. The girls didn't miss a step, they ran until they reached the opening and jumped over the threshold.

Stubby picked himself up slowly. He shook with fury as he pressed a hand against his raw neck. The D'arte brat had tricked him, sneaking up on him like that . . . assaulting him . . . almost strangling him. He'd fix her, and the other one. He'd get the precious gemstones back. They were much too valuable to be in the hands of a moron. He remembered almost passing out when he took them to be appraised. Priceless, that's what the jewelry appraiser had said. They belonged to him by rights now. He found them and the rule of law said Finders Keepers. He wanted them back, and he'd do whatever it took to get them.

He peered at the archway. They must have gone under and then snuck around through the trees to come at him from behind. What were kids doing out here in the dark? And who was the figure that went through the opening before the others? Were Miranda and her friend involved in witchery? Were they truly evil as he had always suspected? Well, this time he intended to find out.

He darted from tree to tree until he reached the Portal. He looked up at the stark beauty of the structure. Then he, too, stepped inside.

CHAPTER TWENTY

REUNION

The Druid drove the long wooden staff into a crack in the rock. Then he removed his cloak, and stuck the hood on the end of the staff. Holding one of the front flaps open, he motioned his companions inside the makeshift tent.

"This is so amazing," said Nicholas, disappearing inside the shelter.

"Miranda!"

Slumped sideways against a huge boulder, Miranda started, opening her eyes and looking about wildly. For a second, she thought they were still inside the quaint cottage, and Morda was coming toward her with the sharp carving knife raised to carve her like a turkey. When they abruptly left the Augurs' mad dinner party, Miranda was so relieved to have escaped in one piece that she didn't care about anything else. But then the shock set in. She kept seeing the old woman's beautiful features twist into an insane sculpture. And she kept hearing her voice coming from the woman's sneering lips.

What had destroyed the Augurs' personalities? What made them go berserk like that? Surely it had nothing to do with asking questions. Miranda thought that was just an excuse. The answers were more likely to be found in the almost-empty bottle of Pomegranate wine the old man had fetched from the corner cupboard. When she heard someone call her name, a feeling of sadness over the old couple's situation had replaced her initial shock. Heavy-hearted, stiff with cold, and weak from exhaustion, she stumbled into the cloak tent.

It was surprisingly roomy.

"You will not be comfortable, but at least you will be dry," said the Druid, holding out his hand where a tiny spark ignited and grew into a white flame.

Nicholas watched spellbound as Naim bent his knees and shifted the flame from his hand to the wet rock floor. It sputtered, like a cough, and then caught and blazed merrily.

"How did you do that?" gasped Nicholas. "Will you show me?"

The tall man chuckled. "That, my young friend, is a simple exercise I learned my first day at the

Druid's Close. What would you do if you had this knowledge?"

"I don't know," answered Nicholas. "It'd be cool to be able to do that."

"Cool is not the right answer," said Naim, flatly. "The fire will dry the rock. Spread the extra clothing on the ground and rest. I will be back shortly." As he was about to exit the tent, he turned to Nicholas. "And do not touch the flame."

"I wasn't going to touch it," said Nicholas. But he might as well have saved his breath because the Druid was gone.

Miranda grabbed a pile of clothes and had barely settled down before she sank into a deep sleep. A few minutes later, Nicholas's head lolled forward and he toppled sideways. His eyes closed and he saw his school buddies gaping in awe at the magic fire he had lit in the palm of his hand. His fire was blue.

King Ruthar smiled warmly, his green eyes glowing with goodness. He extended his arm, waiting for Miranda to take his hand. But she couldn't seem to reach him. She felt her legs moving—knew she was actually advancing toward him, but he wasn't getting closer. Something was very wrong

She sensed the presence behind her even before she heard the scuffling footsteps on the stone floor. Panic drove the air from her lungs, making her gasp as she spun to face the unknown menace. Strange, she thought, catching her breath and, at the same time, wondering how the King had managed to get behind her. He was close now. A few more steps and she'd be able to touch his outstretched hand. She smiled and took a step toward the man.

That's when he began to swell, growing bigger and bigger until his skin split, and something black and oily pushed its way out of his body. Miranda cringed in terror, her hands going up to cover her face. A hideous giant shape unfurled its length, like a rolled-up sail, and slowly thrust itself into the air until it loomed over the girl like a tall building. Its long black cloak billowed about it as if it were alive.

The creature's long tongue lashed wildly about the dark space under its hood, snapping at the air like a bullwhip. Blood, as black as tar, dripped from a pair of sharp fangs. In the blackness of its face, eyes like burning tail lights fixed on Miranda, and from their depths red-hot beams shot at her, charring her flesh to a crisp and driving her back. The Demon raised her head and hissed.

"Help me!" screamed Miranda, spinning about, poised to flee for her life. But she was too late. Hate struck. Raising one clawed foot, she brought it down on the girl, knocking her onto her back, pinning her to the floor, and pressing the air from her lungs. Cruel talons pierced deep into Miranda's chest. The cloying smell of death filled her throat, smothering her. And then, everything went black.

"Help, help! Somebody help me!"

"Mir!" yelled Nicholas. "What's happening? Hey! Stop that! Get off!"

Miranda struggled to free herself from the Demon's deathly grip, to get away from the sharp claws. She thought she heard Nicholas calling her name, but there were other voices too, angry and shouting.

Then a loud, gruff voice told the others to be quiet. Instantly, the shouting stopped and silence settled over the darkness.

Miranda knew that voice. It belonged to Emmet, the Dwarf. But what was he doing here? In a flash, she realized that she had been in the midst of a nightmare when the Druid's cloak had collapsed on her and Nicholas. But who, besides Naim and Emmet, was outside shouting?

And what was this wet, smelly creature pressing against her chest? The Demon? She caught the creature that was shivering uncontrollably, its sharp claws digging into her flesh. It couldn't be, and yet it was. "Muffy?" she said, and then she laughed out loud. "Penelope, what are you doing here?"

"Just taking a little stroll in the country," answered Penelope, joining in the laughter.

"Yeah, but we had trouble finding the country," added Bell.

"Just shut up and get us out of here," growled Nicholas, flailing his arms and legs at the heavy cloak. "I can't breathe."

"Yeah, and get Muffy off me," said Miranda.

Nicholas helped Emmet hang the collapsed cloak on the Druid's staff. The fire had vanished when the tent fell, or as Arabella explained, it went out when she and Penelope fell on the tent. Since Naim hadn't returned, they had to do without the magic flame. But the companions didn't seem to notice either the cold or the wet. They huddled on the hard rock floor exchanging stories of their adventures. Miranda laughed when Arabella recounted how she had knocked Stubby into the manure pile. During a rare lull in the excited chatter, Penelope pressed the small silver pouch containing the six oval Bloodstones into Miranda's hand. Miranda closed her fist over the stones as tears of gratitude welled up in her eyes.

"Now, if the Elves need help, maybe I can do something," she said.

Nicholas gave an animated account of their bizarre encounter with the Augurs, doing an excellent imitation of Morda slapping the hideous black mouth on her face.

Suddenly Miranda grabbed Nicholas's arm. "Nick, stop. I just thought of something."

"What?" The companions looked at her curiously.

"That poem Morda recited. Nick, do you remember what she said?"

"What are you talking about?" asked Arabella.

"The Augurs are soothsayers. They predict the future, like an oracle. Morda started to get agitated when Naim told her not to serve wine, but she really lost it when I asked if she could tell the future." Just thinking about the woman sent shivers up Miranda's spine. She turned to Nicholas. "You tell them."

Nicholas nodded. "You should have seen this demented person throwing bowls of food all over the place and digging into the turkey with her fingers. It was disgusting. Then she pulls this black flabby thing out of her pocket and sticks it on her face. It was this really incredible mouth and this scary man's voice spoke a poem about Ellesmere, and dead things, and blood. It was just a lot of drivel."

"No, Nick, you're wrong," said Miranda, her face lined with concern. "It wasn't a poem and it wasn't drivel. We've got to remember the exact words because I think they're really important. The way the voice said it, it was a recipe—a recipe for the fall of Ellesmere and the end of the Elves."

"You are both partly right," said the Druid, peering through the cloak flaps. "It is indeed drivel, as the boy said, but there is also truth in the prophecy. And yes, Miranda, it is a recipe, but do not be deceived by the words or the order in which the oracle mouth spoke them." He extended his arm, the children watching in amazement as a tiny white spark appeared in his palm and burst into flames. As before, he coaxed the flame from his hand onto the floor. His eyebrows rose at the sight of Penelope and Arabella, but he didn't acknowledge their presence in words.

"I do not like prophecies," Naim continued. "They are dangerous, often leading to disaster because fools work toward fulfilling them. The ultimate future of the inanimate universe may be set, in that this and the other planets and stars may be funnelled into a black hole in the skies; but the immediate future of living things of which we are a part is not set and can never be set. Remember that."

"I don't understand," said Miranda.

"Child," the Druid's voice was gentle. "The oracle can only list the ingredients that could signal the fall of the Elven Kingdom . . . if . . . if . . . if . . . There are too many ifs."

"But it could be true," insisted Arabella.

"Yes," admitted Naim. "But I know the Elves and therefore I do not believe it." He backed out of the tent. "There is usually a lull in the storm at daybreak, we must be away from here by then," he said. "Or face another full day and night on empty stomachs."

"Oh, oh, how could I have been so stupid," cried Penelope. "Don't go," she said to Naim. "I brought food." She reached for the plastic shopping bag, but Nicholas and Miranda got there first. The boy grinned impishly.

"I know we've had our differences, Penelope, but right now I think I'm in love."

"Puh-leeese!" said Penelope. And then, "Yuck!"

CHAPTER TWENTY-ONE

EXILE

Prince Elester stormed toward the Council Hall, his face hard with anger. Andrew Furth, his aide, and a dozen Riders followed in his wake, their hands steady on their weapons. They had just returned to Bethany after a month-long patrol of the island Kingdom's eastern shores. Word had reached the Elven capital of the discovery of several large boats, each capable of transporting a dozen passengers. The report said that the boats had been cleverly camouflaged and hauled into the stunted pines in an uninhabited area on the rugged Ellesmere coast.

Upon their arrival at Bethol-Aire, the easternmost garrison and the one responsible for defending that area of desolate coastline, Elester couldn't help but notice the look of surprise that spread over the post commander's face when the Prince asked for details of the landing. No, he was told, they hadn't spotted any boats. And no, they hadn't sent any message to Bethany.

Elester and his Riders had spent a month scouring the area, but their exercise had been in vain. Growing increasingly uneasy with each passing day, Elester had finally ordered the Riders to return home. He had barely leaped from Noble's back when one of the young Elven grooms tearfully blurted out that Laury, Captain of the Riders, had been taken before the Erudicia to answer charges of treason.

What is going on around here? Elester wondered, his eyes fixed on the half-dozen armed men and women on duty outside the Hall. They stood stiffly in patches of pale light reflecting from lamps on either side of the solid oak doors, warily watching the Prince and Riders approach. They were members of the Guard, the elite protectors of the King of the Elves. In a few weeks, when Elester wore the Crown of Ellesmere, they would protect him with their lives.

They looked as fierce as their reputations in their all-black uniforms. Knives were concealed in sheaths on their boots and belts, and each wore a sword of ice-tempered black steel with silver runes inlaid on the hilt.

A tri-cluster of silver oak leaves adorned the front of their black beret-like hats.

One of the men moved forward to intercept the Prince. Elester recognized him but did not know the soldier's name. Do not show anger, he cautioned himself. Do not show weakness or fear.

As the man approached, Elester slowed. "Good evening, friend. On whose authority has the Guard been called out at this hour?"

"Good evening, Prince," replied the man solemnly, touching his hat in salute. "I am sorry, but I cannot discuss the Elders' business with you." He was clearly uncomfortable, but he had answered the question cleverly. His eyes held Elesters' unwaveringly, but even in the dim light the Prince saw his grim soldier's face flush red.

"What is your name?" asked Elester.

"Coran, Sire. I am the officer in charge."

"Order the Guard back to barracks, and move aside, Coran," said Elester, keeping his voice steady. "I intend to know why the Erudicia calls one of my most loyal captains traitor, and meets in secret."

At first, the Prince hadn't believed the young Elven groom. The Erudicia, twelve of the wisest Elves in the Kingdom, were unquestionably trustworthy. They were chosen by the people to advise the King on important issues involving the security of the Kingdom and the safety of its citizens. Elester knew each of the twelve by name, and as his father before him, had the highest regard for their intelligent and reasoned advice. So why were they suddenly acting out of character—meeting like thieves in the night? And why hadn't Elester been advised?

Coran looked miserable. "I am sorry but I cannot dismiss the Guard, and you cannot enter the Hall."

Elester clenched his fists and fought to control his temper. "I will not ask again. Now get out of my way."

Coran clearly didn't know how to react. Elester looked for anger in the man's face but found none. If anything, the Guard was deeply troubled.

"You cannot pass," he said again.

"Tell me what is going on here, Coran?"

Coran glanced quickly back at the other Guards, who were watching the interchange without expression, but Elester noticed their hands now rested on their swords. When Coran faced the Prince again, he lowered his voice. "I do not know, Sire, but . . ." and his face burned a deeper red. "Apparently, our orders came directly from the King."

Elester laughed harshly. "What are you talking about, man? I am the only King on Ellesmere."

"You are not King yet," corrected Coran. "Until you wear the Crown, we are under the command of the Erudicia."

"That is a formality, nothing more. Which of the Elders dares to give orders in the King's name?"

"I only know what I have been told, Sire. It is said that Mathus speaks—er—with the King."

"What are you saying, man?" Elester's voice had a sharp edge. "My father is dead. The only things that speak for him now are the deeds he performed over his lifetime."

"I know," replied the Guard. "I was at the Battle of Dundurum. I saw the King fall. But . . ." He hesitated.

"But . . .?" pressed Elester.

"I do not know how to say this."

"Just say it." This time the Prince couldn't hide his impatience.

"Mathus says the King speaks to him and, Sire, the old man does not lie."

Elester felt ice form in his veins as he suddenly remembered the night Mathus came to him. He was stunned. "That is not possible," he said, seeing red. "I will see this imposter who speaks with my father's voice." His hand gripped the hilt of his sword, and he sensed the Riders stirring behind him, ready to follow his lead.

"Please do not do this," pleaded Coran, making no move to protect himself. "Neither I nor my men will raise arms against you." He gestured toward the Hall. "But there are over three dozen Guards inside those doors whom you will have to kill to gain entry into the Hall."

Elester's hand dropped from his sword and the quick look he gave the Riders told them to do the same. "Have no fear, Coran. We will not spill Elven blood. But I must speak with the Captain of the Riders. Where is he being held?"

"I will tell you, gladly for all the good it will do. Captain Laury is confined to barracks, under heavy guard." He paused, but opened his mouth as if he wanted to say more. Elester waited.

"Sire, I have known the Captain longer than you can claim years. He is honest and brave, and the men trust him. I do not believe what they are saying about him." He gestured toward the Hall. "And I am not the only one who thinks he is being framed."

"Good man," said the Prince.

"And another thing that troubles me, Sire, is that the Guards are unknown to us."

"What do you mean?" asked Elester, feeling the warm night turn chilly. "Are these not Elven Guards?"

"They are not," answered Coran. "I do not know who they are or where they came from. But there is something . . ."

Elester turned to the Riders. "I do not like this."

"Let us go and release the Captain," said Andrew angrily, stepping forward.

Coran raised his hand. "There is something else you should know, Sire. At dawn the Captain is being taken to a secret location."

"Sire," pleaded Andrew. "We must act now."

"Patience," said Elester. "I have one more question for our friend here." He turned to Coran. "I will get to the bottom of this, and if it is as serious as I believe, can I count on you and the Guards to stand with me when the time comes?"

"We are loyal to our country," answered Coran. "If you say that you will stand with us when we, too, are called traitors, that is good enough for me."

"Thank you, Coran," said Elester. "You have my word."

Elester and his Riders raced toward their barracks, keeping to the shadows. The night was deathly still, the moon invisible behind a thick cover of cloud. The Prince slowed and peered at the darkened building. There should have been a light on somewhere inside, but the only lights he detected were wavering flames from the open fireplace in the Riders' lounge area. Through the windows, the flickering tongues of fire created strange dancing figures on the barracks' walls. Elester stopped and listened intently, but his acute Elven hearing could not detect any sound of movement.

The barrack door stood open, but there was no sign of life. Elester ignored the warning screaming in his mind, instead taking a moment to note each detail. The open door was out of place. And there were no Riders clustered in twos and threes outside the building. If Laury was confined to barracks, where were the foreign Guards?

"Something is wrong," he said, his blood turning to ice. He gripped Andrew's arm. "Take some of the others and go around to the back."

The Prince moved purposefully toward the open barrack door, gathering speed with each step until he was running full out. Without being told, several Riders followed while the rest drew their weapons and spread out among the trees to keep a sharp lookout and warn against the unexpected.

As he ran, Elester scanned the grounds outside the barracks, peering longest into the shadowed areas. He saw nothing, but he sensed the lingering presence of something dark and malevolent. And strong! The power of the thing almost knocked the Prince off his feet.

"Hate!" he shouted, pulling his sword free and leaping through the open doorway into the lounge. Inside, the stench of hatred was overpowering. But Elester recognized another smell and his heart stopped. It was the coppery smell of blood—Elven blood.

"They are all dead," whispered one of the Riders, her voice filled with horror and disbelief. She reached for the light disk on the wall next to the door.

Elester gripped her arm. "Don't touch the lights," he hissed. "Use your sight. Count the dead. I must know what happened here."

Working quickly in the darkness, the Riders moved through the lounge and the sleeping quarters, their hearts heavy as the body count escalated.

Elester felt sorry for them. They were seasoned fighters, but nothing had prepared them for the sight of their slaughtered comrades lying in pools of blood on the barracks floor.

"Sir," hissed Andrew, who had made his way from the back of the building. "Over here."

Elester joined the other man, slipping on the sticky floor. He knelt, heedless of the blood that coated his knees, and looked at the broken, lifeless form in Andrew's arms. He squeezed his eyes shut to stop the tears before they started. This was not the time to show emotion. That would come later. When he felt in control again, he opened his eyes and gazed upon the dead man. It was Laury, Captain of the King's Riders, eyes open and fixed in a glassy death stare. For a second, no one spoke. Then the Prince laid his hand on the dead man's forehead and gently closed his eyes.

"Who did this?" asked Andrew, staring at the Captain, his face wet with tears but twisted with anger. "And why?"

"It is the work of the Demon," answered Elester, unhesitatingly. "But I do not know who is doing her work, or how she is directing it from the Dark Place."

And suddenly part of the answer to Andrew's last question hit him like a mountain falling on his head. He knew why Laury and so many Elves had been slaughtered. Angry with himself for not having figured it out sooner, he leaped to his feet.

"It is a trap!" he said, knowing he was as right as rain. It was a trap rigged to catch a Prince, and poor Laury had been the bait. Whoever did this terrible thing planned it to look as though Elester, in a fit of rage, attacked and killed his own soldiers, because he thought they were responsible for the death of Captain Laury. He also knew that Mathus and the others would be here soon. That had to be part of their plan, to catch him in the act of murder, covered in blood.

"Come on!" he said, fighting down despair, but letting his anger simmer. "We must get away." Then, thinking of what Coran had said about his dead father speaking to Mathus, the Prince caught Andrew's sleeve. "Burn this place. I will not leave our dead with their murderers. Better we burn the bodies."

Andrew looked at his leader's grim face and nodded, solemnly.

They lit paper and bits of clothing from the dying flames in the fireplace, dropping the burning brands onto cots, sofas, chairs, and wooden furniture. They caught quickly. Flames raced up the length of the curtains, consuming the fragile cloth like a hungry beast. By the time the Riders reached the back door, the inside of the barracks was an inferno.

"Head for the stables," said Elester, using his arm to wipe the sweat from his forehead. Followed by the Riders, he rushed outside and filled his lungs with clean night air.

Thud! Thud! Thud! Thud! Without warning, four brawny creatures dropped like boulders from the roof, landing amongst the Riders. Their clawed hands gripped long, pointed spears and their stupid faces looked like grinning globs of cottage cheese. Elester reacted instinctively, freeing his sword and charging the nearest lumpy-faced creature, who uttered a harsh bellow as the Prince's first stroke sliced deep into its soft, porous flesh.

"Trolls!" cried Elester, his thoughts as scrambled as eggs as he forced his mind to believe what he was seeing. Trolls on Ellesmere. And from the look of the fierce, pasty creatures, these were not the gentle, dark-fleshed Trolls who farmed the grasslands. These bigger, uglier creatures came from the Swampgrass. They were Bog Trolls, with hearts as black as the Demon with whom they were allied.

Until now, no Bog Troll had ever set foot on Ellesmere Island, home of the Elves. Elester was so stunned, he couldn't think straight. A million questions raced through his mind, but he didn't have one single answer. His chest hurt, and for a second, rage blinded him as his hate-filled eyes raked over the creatures that had slaughtered so many of his people. With a great effort, he controlled the anger and the hate. He must not let the Trolls sense that sort of weakness.

"Har! Har!" laughed a large Troll, obviously the leader. His voice was like a rockslide or a CD playing slowly backwards. He raised the spear and made a jabbing motion toward Elester.

"Har! Har!" chortled the other Trolls.

"What we got, eh, eh? A little princeling, eh?"

"Good, we kill princeling, eh, Grotch? Then we eat heart," said one of the other Trolls.

Elester thought he had never seen a more disgusting creature. He wondered what made their skins so pale and spongy. When his sword had pierced the flesh of the other one, it had felt like cutting into a rotten dew fruit. Was it because they lived in the swamps and rarely ventured into the sunlight? Could that explain the running sores he noticed on their bare flesh?

"Shut yer face, eh, Lepp." said Grotch, jabbing the one called Lepp in the ribs with his spear, but keeping his eyes on Elester and the Riders. He pointed a crooked claw at the Prince. "Dauthus wants this one, eh. Dauthus wants yer heart, princeling. You hear that, eh?"

Elester glanced at Andrew, tilting his head toward the stables. The other Elf nodded and began edging toward the outer rim of the group. At that moment, Elester crouched and came at Grotch, aiming a blow to the Troll's soft belly. Caught off guard by the suddenness of the Prince's charge, Grotch lumbered backwards. He raised the spear and stabbed at the Prince again and again. Elester rolled away from the deadly spear, coming up behind the Troll and thrusting deep into one of the creature's lumpy rear cheeks.

Grotch roared with rage, swinging his thick arms frantically, and jumping up and down to turn himself around to get at the Elf. Elester saw that there were only three Trolls standing and two of them were injured. But he knew that even an injured Troll was a dangerous foe.

"Run!" he shouted, and before the Trolls could react, the Prince and his Riders were gone.

CHAPTER TWENTY-TWO

A HISS OF SERPENTS

"What about the Prince?" Dauthus hated the cold underground chamber deep beneath the city of Bethany. He hated his cold, decomposing Elven host and its heavy, awkward human body. More than anything, the serpent longed to feel the heat of others of his kind coiling and flexing about the Demon's middle like a fatal, living belt. But if he ever wanted to see his Mistress, he had to free her from the Place with No Name. And there was only one way for that to happen. He, Dauthus, must wear the Crown of Ellesmere.

"I am ssorry, Masster," hissed Mathus, his ophidian eyes blinking from the corner to centre under fused eyelids in the Elder's face. "The Evil One ran away."

King Ruthar's body convulsed with Dauthus's rage. "Find him, Mathus, and kill him."

"Yess, Masster."

"Do you know what will happen to you if you fail?"

"No, Ssir, but I will not fail. I have poissoned the Elderss' mindss againsst the weakling."

For a moment, Dauthus thought of giving the other a sampling of the punishment Hate would inflict on it should it fail, but it was cold, and cold made the serpent sluggish. "Do the fools on the Erudicia believe that he slew the others?"

Mathus smiled slyly before responding. "Yess, the good-for-nothing Elvess call him murderer and traitor. They call him imposster."

Dauthus was pleased. He took a moment, allowing the feeling of pleasure to linger and warm his silky black body. "What about the Crown of Ellesmere?"

"It belongs to uss. It will be here ssoon."

"Good," said Dauthus. "Leave me now."

The serpent wearing Mathus's body turned and moved toward the door of the underground chamber.

"Wear a hood, Mathus. Do not show them your eyes," said King Ruthar, lying back on the cold marble slab.

When the Elder had gone, Dauthus wound himself into a tight coil. Everything was working according to the Demon's plans. Four of the eggs had hatched and were accounted for. One had killed the Elder, Mathus, the most trusted member of the Erudicia, and now wore his body and carried out his functions, turning the witless Elves against their Prince.

Dauthus had given one of the eggs to the repulsive Thug before he sent the creature through the Portal to Ottawa. The Thug's orders had come directly from the Demon. Get the girl and steal the Bloodstones. It was very clever of his Mistress to think of taking the magic away from the piddling human girl so she could not interfere with the Demon's great escape plans. Soon, both the girl and the stones would be placed in Dauthus's lifeless hands. He'd kill the girl and crush the stones to dust.

But what about the Prince? he wondered. Should he tell the Demon that the heir was still alive? Should he bother the Great One with such a trifling problem? No. The cowardly, snivelling boy had run away at the first sign of trouble, like a naughty child caught stealing. Dauthus opened his mouth and hissed gleefully. Ellesmere was an island after all. There were only three ways off. The first was through the Portal in the park outside the Hall, which was now under Dauthus's control. The second way was by boat, but the harbour was so heavily guarded, even something as small as a mouse couldn't get onto the docks. There was a third way the Prince could get off the Island and the serpent twitched just thinking about it. He could swim.

Dauthus had heard the stories the Elves told about the one called Dilemma who lived in the waters of Lake Leanora. He had never seen the creature, but he pictured it as a giant, black bloated thing, like a ball of thick oil. Its enormous eyes were all whites and completely useless and its skin was a network of throbbing veins like spiders' webs that trapped and held its prey while great slashing claws tore and shredded the victim's flesh, turning the lake as red as tomato pulp. The Elves said Dilemma's mouth was a gaping chasm with double rows of jagged teeth. Fish and other lake denizens fled from the monster in terror, and sometimes they were lucky, but a mere air-breathing human wouldn't stand a chance.

A sound nearby interrupted the serpent's thoughts. He uncoiled his sleek scaly length and manipulated the King into a sitting position. His reptilian eyes picked up the slight movement off to his left, in the darkness near one of the columns. He waited, tensed and poised to strike swiftly.

A short, squat figure emerged from the shadows. A filthy, stinking Dwarf. Dauthus spat in disgust, but he noticed the sharp axe clutched tightly in the creature's beefy hand and the sword hanging from his leather belt. Then a series of short, shrill hisses escaped from the serpent's open mouth. It actually sounded like laughter.

"Give me the Bloodstones." It was an order.

"The girl's got them," hissed the Dwarf that had once been Malcolm. "The Druid took her away."

"HOW DARE YOU FAIL ME!" As quick as a heartbeat, Dauthus struck at the Dwarf, spitting venom in the creature's face.

Malcolm dropped the axe and, uttering a shrill sound like a whistling kettle, pressed his hands against his sizzling skin.

"You are dead, brother," said Dauthus. "She will do more than burn a few holes in your worthless hide."

"I am not one of your toadies," wheezed Malcolm, keeping well out of the King's reach. "I followed orders. Didn't I find the girl? Didn't I search her house? I befriended her and she told me where she had left the stones. I went to her school and searched but they weren't there. The human child lied to me. She had them all the time."

"What of this Druid?" Dauthus knew how much his Mistress loathed the evil friend of the Elves. "How did he learn of our Mistress's plan? How did he know to go after the girl?"

"Don't ask me," hissed Malcolm. "Perhaps you said too much to the wrong human."

"Silence!" Dauthus's eyes smouldered. "You are sloppy, brother, and that makes you dispensable. So beware. Where are the Druid and the girl?"

"Hate's pet is tracking them."

"Find them, kill the Druid, and bring me the girl and the Bloodstones."

Malcolm spat on the floor at the King's feet and stomped from the chamber.

CHAPTER TWENTY-THREE

QUESTIONS FOR THE DRUID

The Ottawa companions alternated between riding and walking. The Druid and the Dwarf, Emmet, strode purposefully ahead as if they knew the route to Dunmorrow by heart. Miranda was in good spirits after the few hours of sleep she managed to catch, but she and the other youngsters were stiff and sore from the long hours they had spent hiking on the rugged trail and bumping along on horseback. Penelope complained loudly about blisters forming on her butt.

"Have you ever noticed that girls always complain about everything?" Nicholas muttered to Emmet.

The Dwarf gave him a surly look and stomped ahead at a faster pace, quickly widening the distance between him and the boy. Nicholas sighed. Well, he tried. Who said he had to be nice to that nasty little runt? He acted so smug and kept looking at Nicholas as if he were an idiot. Who cares? thought the boy. I'd like to know what he's done on this trip to make himself useful. Nothing, as far as I'm concerned. He might as well have stayed in the tunnels under the Parliament Buildings back home, for all the good he's done.

Nicholas shook his head to clear away the thoughts of Emmet. While he didn't like the fellow, he couldn't wait to get to Dunmorrow and see what King Gregor and the Dwarves had been up to in their new country. He remembered Dundurum with its wide boulevards carved out of the mountain with the same ache he felt when he thought of his grandfather who had died two years ago. His grandfather shouldn't have died and Dundurum shouldn't have vanished. He couldn't get over the fact that something as amazing as life could end in a second. Or that thousands and thousands of years of work and history could disappear in the wink of an eye. It wasn't fair!

As the company moved farther away from the borders of the Wasteland, the wind dropped and the stinging, driving sleet melted into a light drizzle. By early evening, patches of blue sky peeked through the thick clouds and the rain let up. The Druid looked at the exhausted zombie-like youngsters and pointed to a cluster of giant fir trees. "There is a clearing just beyond the trees. We will spend the night there."

"Yah!" cried Arabella, guiding Thunder through the trees. She slid off the big brown horse and almost tumbled over as her knees buckled upon hitting the ground.

Miranda simply let her legs collapse, and she dropped to the ground near a large evergreen tree. Penelope unzipped her jacket and Muffy scampered free, speeding like a bullet in a wide circle and barking as if she were warning the wild creatures of the forest to keep out of her area.

Nicholas and Arabella unsaddled the horses, rubbing them down with pieces of Nicholas's red wooly tights. They let the horses graze on the sweet grass. Emmet and the Druid held a whispered conversation, after which Emmet disappeared. Miranda felt guilty, slumped against the trunk of the evergreen, so she forced herself up and gathered wood for a fire. The kids cheered when Naim pointed the wooden staff at the pile of logs, igniting them into a cheery blaze. Penelope opened her plastic shopping bag and shared the last of the food she'd brought from Ottawa. The brie cheese and crabapple jelly sandwiches were a bit stale, but they disappeared in minutes, washed down with iced tea. Afterwards, to Penelope's amazement, everyone agreed that it was the best meal they'd ever eaten.

Later, while the Druid checked on the horses, Miranda and her friends sat cross-legged around the fire, chatting amicably and feeling warm for the first time since they had walked through the Portal at Kingsmere.

"Do you ever think about dying?" asked Nicholas suddenly, poking the fire with a long stick and releasing a shower of sparks that blinked like a swarm of fireflies before winking out.

"No," said Penelope. "What good would that do? Anyway, there are too many other things to think about."

"I do," said Arabella. "Sometimes. I think about what would happen to me if my parents got killed in an accident."

"What about you, Mir? Are you afraid of dying?"

Miranda didn't answer right away. She had been about to say yes, but something stopped her. "There's a difference," she said. "When I called the Demon at Dundurum, and she was suddenly there, I thought I was going to die, and I was petrified. But that was only because I was actually facing death. But I don't think so much about dying some day in the future."

"Do you believe in an afterlife?"

Miranda stared at Nicholas, whose face wore a thoughtful expression. She wondered what made him think of death all of a sudden. "I don't know," she said. "I'd really like it if there were."

"I bet the Druid knows," said Penelope. "Why don't we ask him?"

"Ask me what?" said the Druid, joining the children and lowering his lanky frame onto a boulder near the fire.

"Is there life after death?" asked Nicholas.

The old man stared into the fire without speaking. He looked so thoughtful that no one dared intrude on his thoughts. Then, he shook his head and raised his eyes to Nicholas. "I cannot answer your question, because I do not know the answer."

"Then," sighed Nicholas, "what's the point of everything, if there's nothing at the end?"

Naim chuckled. "That is a good question, my friend, and one that has been asked since the beginning of time. Sadly, your question is wiser than all of the answers." He turned serious, his dark eyes fixed on the boy. "You are very young, Nicholas. I suggest that you concern yourself with this life."

"That's just it," said Nicholas. "This life means nothing if that's all there is."

"Do you think so?" asked the Druid, lifting his eyebrows. "Let us agree, just for the sake of discussion, that there is nothing at the end. Do you think, then, that there is no point in making laws?"

"Well, no," said Nicholas. "It'd be pretty horrible if people could hurt each other and steal and do whatever they wanted."

"If there is nothing at the end, is there any point in researching cures for diseases? Or in forging friendships?"

Nicholas nodded, thoughtfully.

"You see, I can only answer your question with more questions. I would welcome an afterlife, but if I die and there is nothing, the answer is irrelevant because I will never know it."

"Whew," breathed Arabella. "This is deep stuff."

The Druid reached out and patted the top of Arabella's head. "It is that," he said softly.

"Why are there Druids?" asked Arabella.

Naim let out his breath. "I forgot how children from your world like to ask questions."

The children giggled and, as if they had been waiting for the opportunity, they suddenly bombarded the man with one question after another.

"Do all Druids carry a wooden staff?

"Why is there a black hole in the Milky Way galaxy?"

"Can you make us invisible?"

"How come we can only see lights from distant worlds millions of years later?"

"Is our planet going to get sucked into that black hole?"

"What's a continuum?"

Naim threw up his hands in despair, but his laughter warmed the children's hearts. "Enough! You have made me dizzy. I will answer Arabella's question." He used the staff to push himself to his feet. "The first Druid was Currer. He lived thousands of years ago at a time when the Demon ruled the Dark Lands."

The companions exchanged glances. This was news.

"What are the Dark Lands?" asked Penelope.

"I will get to that, in time," said the Druid, giving the girl a fierce look. "Taog, as the Demon called herself then, only left her lands to lure men into her service by promising them immortality. Many joined her, to their misfortune. Over hundreds of years, she managed to raise a mighty army of Thugs, the half-dead creatures with whom you are familiar. No one paid much attention to her, for the simple reason that they did not know what she was up to. There are not many ways open into the Dark Lands, and to the best of my knowledge, the only creatures who entered that place alive did so in the company of Hate. Except for Currer.

"I do not know how Currer made it through the violent storm that surrounds the Dark Lands, but he did. And he returned. He went in as a young man, a few years older than you, Nicholas, but when he came out a few months later, he was so old and shrivelled, even his friends did not recognize him. He lived only long enough to bring together three men and two women whom he trained to use their inner powers to fight evil."

He moved away from the fire and sat on the hard ground, resting his back against the sturdy trunk of a tree. "There have always been five Druids since Currer's time. We have pledged our lives to rooting out evil and destroying it."

"How long does it take to become a Druid?" asked Arabella.

"Forever," answered Naim, curtly, pulling his cloak tightly about his chest.

The man's silence signalled the young companions to turn in for the night. They curled up on the ground near the fire, each lost in his or her own thoughts. Muffy crawled into Penelope's arms, curled into a contented ball, and closed her tiny eyes. Miranda thought about the prophecy. Something about walking serpents made her uneasy. She tried to remember why she thought the serpent at Kingsmere had come from the black shape on the ground, and why Malcolm had popped into her mind then. Was Malcolm a serpent? No, he was a Dwarf. Nothing made sense. She stared at the sky until her eyes finally closed. As the little group drifted into exhausted sleep, the only sound disturbing the heavy silence was the crackling of the logs in the dying fire.

Muffy's shrill barks cut through the early morning silence like gunshots. Miranda sat up, her heart thumping like running footsteps. The fire had died, and it was so black she couldn't see her hand in front of her face, but she could hear her friends moving about, despite the sounds coming from Muffy. "Nick, what?"

Suddenly, Muffy went silent as Penelope clamped her hand about the dog's muzzle.

"Shhh!" whispered Nick. "I heard something in the trees, and then the Muffrat started barking."

"What is it?"

"I don't know, but I don't like it."

"I'm going to get Naim," whispered Miranda, crawling along the ground toward the spot where she had seen the Druid settle down for the night. "Naim!" she whispered.

"Be quiet. Do not move," came back the harsh reply.

Miranda turned to stone, sinking flat onto the ground. She blinked furiously, trying to see in the pitch black. Then a long snarling sound, low and ominous, rose out of the silence, and the blackness grew thicker in front of her face. It formed into a solid black shape like one of the giant trees bordering the campsite. A terrible chill swept through Miranda. The Thug had been there in the darkness all along. Invisible, watching, waiting.

The black shadow moved closer, paralyzing her. She stared, helplessly, as the creature's flaming red eyes grew bigger and bigger. She knew that death was only a heartbeat away and yet she couldn't make herself run. She closed her eyes and prayed there was an afterlife.

CHAPTER TWENTY-FOUR

NIGHT AMBUSH

A neon-green blur shot past Miranda and launched itself at the Thug, growling and snarling viciously, like a wild beast a hundred times its size. The poodle's brave, but stupid, attack jolted Miranda into action. She pushed herself into a crouched position and moved cautiously toward the trees. Her trembling hand reached for the small silver pouch about her neck. Clutching the Bloodstones tightly, she flattened her body against a thick trunk. At first she couldn't see anything. Then, as the magic seeing stone drew the girl's thoughts into itself, vague moving shapes began to solidify before her eyes into real living creatures. Miranda gasped. There were hundreds of them.

They were large, pale-skinned creatures, and they were everywhere, jabbing the ground with sharp spears. In their dark garments, their pale faces looked like lumpy moons floating through the darkness. What sort of beings were they? Miranda tried to locate her friends, but they were lost somewhere among the large, blocky shapes. She searched for the tall form of the Druid, but he, too, was nowhere in sight.

Then she heard him, and the sound of his voice was terrible. "LEAVE THIS PLACE, NOW!" he shouted.

A few seconds later, a stream of white fire exploded from the trees about thirty metres from Miranda. It slammed into one of the pale shapes, catapulting it into the air. Miranda watched in horror as the creature seemed to melt into the white flames, bellowing like a wounded boar until the fire consumed it. The sight made her sick. She had seen Naim unleash the Druid fire once before against the Wizard Indolent, and his awesome power had terrified her. He had terrified her then, and he terrified her now.

Using the Bloodstones, Miranda scanned the clearing, recognizing the sturdy form of Emmet, legs planted firmly apart, swinging a sword in one hand and an axe in the other. The creatures came at him unrelentingly. Like others of his kind, Emmet was a strong, fearless fighter, but there were so many of the strange, ugly shapes surging toward him, he couldn't possibly fight all of them. Then she caught the glint of metal out of the corner of her eye.

"Nick!" she shouted, but the cry was a mere whisper in a hurricane.

Nicholas had been hiding between two boulders behind the Druid when Naim ordered the assailants to turn back and leave this place. He wasn't too surprised when they ignored the old man's warning. Naim did not speak to the enemy again and Nicholas gasped when he saw him raise the staff and hose one of the creatures with white fire. Suddenly, the boy was tired of hiding, tired of being hunted by creatures he had never met. He stole out of his hiding place and moved toward the Druid. He stood in silence beside the tall, cloaked figure, noticing that the man's eyes were focused on the dozens of attackers surrounding Emmet. The Dwarf was putting up a good fight, but Nicholas knew it was just a matter of time before he was dragged down.

Another sheet of white fire shot from the Druid's staff, incinerating another assailant and badly burning several others. But Nicholas saw the problem immediately. Naim couldn't risk using the fire against the mob closing in on Emmet, for fear of killing the Dwarf.

"What are those things?"

"Trolls!" snapped the Druid, without turning his head. "Go and hide yourself, boy." His voice rumbled like thunder. "Now!"

"No," said Nicholas. "I'm going to help Emmet."

The man laughed a terrible laugh that turned the boy's pale face dark with embarrassment. It was the sort of laugh a giant might utter to an ant.

"I have my powers, Nicholas. You have nothing but good intentions. Now do as I say. Go!"

"No!" cried Nicholas angrily. "I've got my sword." And then, as if he suddenly remembered the Elven weapon, he pulled it from the scabbard on his belt, and before the Druid could stop him, he raced to aid the Dwarf.

Emmet's eyebrows rose in surprise when he saw the twelve-year-old boy charging through the press of Trolls, dodging a dozen spear thrusts, but he only grunted when Nicholas reached his side and turned to face their attackers. For a second, Nicholas stood transfixed, overcome with terror at the sight of so many hideous, lumpy creatures coming at him with their pointed weapons raised. He stared at the sword gripped tightly in his hand as if he didn't know how it got there or what he was supposed to do with it. Then, in a flash, the lessons he had learned from Laury, Captain of the King's Riders, came back to him.

"For the Riders!" he shouted, raising the weapon and aiming a swipe at the nearest creature. The sharp steel blade sliced through the Troll's flesh, severing the fellow's spear arm as effortlessly as cutting soft butter. Nicholas gagged at the dark stain on the blade of his sword, but he didn't have time to be sick, because one of the creatures smashed into him, knocking him flat on his back. Then it pounced, claws reaching to slash at its victim. Heart racing like a ticking bomb, Nicholas rolled to the side, out of the enemy's reach, and leaped to his feet.

In the light from another blast of Druid fire, he saw a pale shape loom up behind Emmet. He yelled a warning, but the Dwarf was fighting for his life against a horde of Trolls attacking from the front and sides. Knowing he couldn't reach the assassin in time, Nicholas raised his sword and let it fly. The weapon spun end over end through the air and stabbed into the creature's upper arm, cutting through muscle and wobbling back and forth as it lodged into the ribs in the Troll's side.

Howling in pain, the Troll dropped its spear and staggered away, trying to pull the sword free. Realizing he had thrown away his only means of defending himself, Nicholas ran to one of the fallen Trolls, searching the ground for a spear. He saw something sticking out from under the dead creature and grabbed the shaft to pull it free. Then, a pair of clawed hands gripped the boy and spun him around. Before he could aim a kick at his attacker, something hit him hard in the face. He was unconscious when the Troll hoisted him into the air and stuffed him into a large hemp sack.

"They've got Nick!" Miranda shouted, making a dash toward the boy. But she had taken only a few steps when a strong hand grabbed her arm and wrenched her back into the trees.

"Stay here," roared the Druid, keeping a firm grip on the girl's arm. "They want you, and the Bloodstones."

"But . . . Nick . . ." sobbed Miranda, helplessly.

And then, her heart stopped as the small form of Arabella appeared out of nowhere and flew at Nicholas's captor. "Hurry! Do something!" she screamed, struggling to free her arm from the Druid's iron grasp, and feeling every whack the Troll aimed at Arabella as if she were the one being slapped.

But Naim wasn't listening and Miranda soon saw why. He was looking for a weak spot in the wall of assailants that surged around them. Then, Miranda gasped, as the Druid expanded into a huge, terrible figure that towered over the Trolls. The front ranks fell back, bellowing in fear, and knocking those behind them backwards. In their haste to escape the looming giant with the deadly flaming staff, they trampled their fallen companions into the ground.

Miranda squeezed her eyes shut and concentrated on the fleeing Trolls. When she finally opened them, she was astounded to see the Druid split and multiply into a dozen terrifying figures who took off in pursuit of the attackers. In a few minutes they were gone. The air seemed to go out of the Druid and he turned to Miranda in surprise. "How did you do that?"

"What?" asked Miranda, truly puzzled.

"I do not know," said Naim. "But I felt myself becoming many. What did you do with the stones?"

"Nothing," said Miranda. "I just tried to think of something to keep the Trolls away."

"I do not have that power," said Naim, in a shocked whisper.

"I don't know what I did," shrugged Miranda. "But it worked." She looked around, surprised that there wasn't a single sign that a battle had been fought in this spot a few minutes ago. Nicholas and Emmet were gone, stuffed into sacks and taken away by the Trolls. There was no sign of Arabella and Penelope. Miranda hoped they were hiding in a safe place. There was no sign of the Thug. Not a single Troll body had been left in the clearing. "Where are all the Troll bodies?"

"Trolls always collect their dead," answered Naim, coldly.

"You said that Trolls hated their own kind. That can't be true if they care enough to take their dead home with them."

"That is not why they collect their dead," said the Druid, dreading where Miranda's questions were leading. He walked a short distance away and bent over as if he were examining the ground. But Miranda followed him.

"Why, then?" she pressed.

"Miranda, I do not wish to continue this conversation."

"Just tell me why, and I won't bother you anymore." And then the blood drained from her face. "They eat them, don't they?" she whispered. "That's why you won't tell me."

The tall man nodded, miserably. "But . . . ."

Miranda didn't wait for him to finish. "Those were the Bog Trolls, weren't they?" Miranda's voice was suddenly thin and strained, her eyes misty with tears. "The ones who killed my father?"

Naim took a deep breath and let it out slowly. Straightening his back, he turned to Miranda and nodded. "Child, they do not eat humans."

Miranda sniffled. "Do you promise?"

"I promise," said the Druid, solemnly.

Miranda was relieved to hear that the Bogs didn't eat humans. The thought that they might have devoured her father was too much for her to bear. But, talking about the Bog Trolls rekindled an idea that had been growing inside her for a long time. She had never known her father. All she knew about him was that he went into the Swampgrass alone, to negotiate peace with the Bogs and was never seen again. The Bogs said they killed him. But what if they lied? What if he were still alive—kept a prisoner in the swamp?

Miranda wanted to know the truth. No, she needed to know the truth. Now she was frantic to get the Druid to follow the Trolls back to their land to rescue Nicholas and Emmet, and find out what really happened to her father.

Thoughts of the father she had never known took her far away from the clearing and the Druid. It was the sound of someone sobbing that brought her back with a start. It was light enough to see now, and she wheeled about, searching the clearing for the source of the sound. Then she spotted the small figure sitting on the ground near the place where the Thug had attacked her earlier.

It was Penelope, rocking back and forth, her thin shoulders shaking uncontrollably. Miranda sprinted toward the girl, afraid of what she would find when she got there. Please let her be OK, she prayed, keeping her eyes on Penelope's heaving shoulders. Her eyes filled with tears when she saw the reason for the other girl's grief. The small green body lay motionless on Penelope's lap, its fur matted and stained with blood. Penelope stopped her rocking motion and raised her tear-streaked face.

"Look what they did, Mir. They killed Muffy."

CHAPTER TWENTY-FIVE

HARD DECISIONS

The Druid gently laid his hands on the still, bloody form, seeking a sign of life. Muffy's body was cold beneath her matted green coat. A very bad sign, thought Naim, shaking his head sadly. But then he felt it, a barely perceptible pressure on his hand, like a moth's wing brushing against his skin.

"The dog is alive," he said, amazed that such a fragile creature had managed to survive an encounter with one of the Thugs. "But she has been badly mauled and broken. She has lost a lot of blood from the gash on her side and the stump where her tail has been torn, or bitten, off. She is in shock and will not last another hour out here without some form of healing."

Penelope sniffled and clutched the Druid's sleeve. "Please don't let her die," she begged.

"I will do what I can to keep her warm and stem the bleeding," said Naim. "Now we must work together. I will hold the animal." He still couldn't bring himself to say poodle or Muffy. "You must find what I need." It was probably too late for the small dog, but assigning tasks to Miranda and Penelope would keep them busy and might take their minds off the dying animal.

He told them what he needed and they rushed to carry out his orders. Miranda gathered dried twigs for a fire. Penelope squirted water from a water skin into a flat pan and set it on the flames to boil. Then, together, they rooted through dozens of pockets inside Naim's cloak for healing herbs and roots, carefully avoiding those pockets they were forbidden to touch.

When the water was boiling, Penelope poured some into a container for cleansing the dog's wounds. Then she added a small amount to a tiny vial and added a pinch of something purple from a small pouch and set the vial aside to cool. She emptied four or five strange packets into the remaining water and stirred the ingredients with a stick, until it was a thick paste, like oatmeal.

Miranda held a tuft of Muffy's hair between her thumb and index finger and, picking up a small pair of scissors, tried to cut the hair away from the dog's wounds. But she was so afraid of causing the poor thing more pain, she couldn't control her trembling hands. "I can't do this," she cried.

"I'll do it," said Penelope, taking the scissors from Miranda's clammy hand. "I'm used to dogs." She bowed her head over Muffy, and used the scissors to snip away the sticky, matted clumps of hair around the wounded areas of the little body. Then she dipped the strips of cloth into the cooling water and cleaned away the blood, while Miranda gently slathered the thick paste on the deep wound in Muffy's side. They repeated the procedure on the stump where the poodle's pom-pom tail had once been and Miranda wound strips of cloth around and around the stump until it looked like a white ping-pong ball.

When the animal was bandaged and splints attached to its broken legs, Penelope held its mouth open while Miranda spilled a few drops from the vial down its throat. That done, Penelope wrapped the dog in the last of Nicholas's fluffy red tights to keep her warm, and gently eased the poodle inside the front of her jacket.

When they were done, the three companions looked at each other and sighed loudly. Naim stood and flexed his fingers, working out the stiffness in his knuckles from holding the dog in one position for so long. He turned to Penelope. "Now, you must leave us and go to Dunmorrow. The Dwarves will do what they can for your dog."

Miranda stared at the man in shock. "What do you mean leave us? She can't just up and go to Dunmorrow. She doesn't even know where it is."

"That is true," admitted the Druid. "But she will be with one who knows the way." He picked up the wooden staff and pointed it at the sky.

Miranda and Penelope followed the direction of the staff, squinting at the golden speck growing bigger as it hurtled toward them. A wide grin spread across Miranda's face but when she looked at Penelope, she was surprised to see the other girl staring in horror as the speck grew bigger.

"Oh, yikes!" cried Penelope, clutching Miranda's arm so tightly, Miranda yelped.

"It's OK," said Miranda, wondering what had come over her friend. "It's Charlemagne."

"Are you sure? It's not the Dragon?"

Miranda laughed. "No, it's not Typhon coming to get you."

Penelope lived in terror of Typhon, the gigantic Dragon who guarded the treasure for his Dragon Clique. Last trip, she stole a huge, valuable ruby from the Dragons' hoard and Typhon caught her, judged her, and found her guilty. The other kids never talked about the punishment in front of Penelope, but they still giggled about it behind her back.

The great, double-headed Eagle swooped over the trees, the wind whistling in its huge wings as it landed lightly on the ground a short distance from the three companions. Naim shielded his eyes from the glare of the sun on the creature's gold-tipped feathers, and strode toward the giant bird, a smile lighting up his usually stern face. When he reached the Eagle, he bowed solemnly.

"Hello, old friend," he said. "It is good to see you again."

The Eagle bowed its two heads. "The pleasure is mine," he answered politely. The voice was deep and rich. Miranda thought Charlemagne sounded very refined, like her image of a British monarch. But she shivered at the contradiction between the cultured creature and its instinctive hunting habits. As if the Eagle felt her eyes on him, one of the heads whipped toward Miranda.

"And that is the human, Miranda, if I am not mistaken?"

"Hello," said Miranda, bowing like the Druid. "Yes, it's me." She caught Penelope's arm and drew the other girl forward. "This is my friend, Penelope."

"Pleased to meet you," said one of the Eagle's heads, bowing and then stretching its wing to clasp the girl's hand.

Penelope walked to the Eagle and touched the feathers on the tip of his wing. "I am pleased to meet you, too," she said.

Charlemagne excused himself and walked off a short distance to converse with the Druid, but Miranda noticed the piercing Eagle eyes on one of its heads remained focused on the girls. The huge creature spread its massive wings and lifted into the air. It flew higher and higher, and then fell, circling faster and faster. Uttering a shrill cry, the Eagle swooped along the ground, fastened its golden talons about Penelope and soared above the trees.

Miranda watched until they disappeared, feeling strangely alone.

"It is time to go," said Naim, quietly.

"We're going to find Nick and Bell and Emmet?" asked Miranda, who had resigned herself to the probability that Bell had also been taken prisoner by the Trolls. "Aren't we?"

"No," said Naim wearily. "There is nothing we can do for them now. Our path leads east, to the Dark Lands."

"But . . . we can't leave them." Miranda was horrified. She didn't want to tell the Druid that one of the reasons she was so desperate to get to the Swampgrass was to find out the truth about her father. So, she folded her arms and glared at him. "I'm not going without them," she said.

Naim didn't respond right away. He whistled for the horses and packed the leftover herbs and roots into the pockets of his cloak. Then, he seated himself on the ground, stretched his long legs out before him, and rested his back against a boulder. "Come and sit, child," he said gently.

Miranda plopped cross-legged onto the ground, keeping a safe distance between her and the Druid. "What?" she asked, coldly.

"The Trolls are taking your friends to the Swampgrass. By now they have discovered that you and the Bloodstones are not among the captives. They have no interest in your friends, except to use them to capture you. They are counting on you rushing off to rescue them. We cannot do that, because we cannot fight the entire population of Bog Trolls. My powers are great, but not that great."

"Maybe not, but mine are," insisted Miranda. "You said so yourself. I can use the Bloodstones. I can make myself invisible and find Nick and Bell, and get them away."

"You cannot control the Bloodstones." The Druid sounded impatient, as if he should not have to state the obvious.

"I can, I can! You saw how I made the Trolls run away."

"Then explain how you did it."

Seeing her plan to learn about her father turn to dust, Miranda's eyes filled with tears and her body sagged in on itself. "I don't know. But, please, please, don't leave them."

The Druid rose and extended his hand. "Come. Things are not as bad for your friends as you think."

Miranda gripped his hand and he pulled her to her feet. "What do you mean?"

"The Eagle will speak to King Gregor about Emmet and the others. The fate of your friends is now in the hands of the Dwarves. They have the numbers to stand against the Trolls. I am only one."

Miranda scuffed the ground with the toe of her running shoe. She should have known that Naim wouldn't leave Nicholas and Arabella without doing something to rescue them. He might act hard, but he did not have a cold heart. But, without her friends as an excuse, what could she say now to make the Druid change his mind and go to the Swampgrass?

"I know that you care what happens to your friends, but I also know that is not the only reason you are so adamant to follow the Trolls." Naim walked over to Miranda, lowered himself onto his heels, and placed his hands on her shoulders. "Tell me if I am wrong."

Miranda lifted her green eyes and met the Druid's piercing sapphire gaze. She didn't have to say anything. He read the answer in her face.

"If I were in your shoes, I would want to know the truth, too. There is nothing wrong with that. But now is not the time."

"But why? I never get to decide anything." Miranda knew she was acting like a brat, but she couldn't hide her disappointment and it made her cross.

Naim thought for a minute. The child was upset, and he did not relish the thought of starting out on a dangerous journey with an angry, rebellious companion. Just thinking about it made him shudder. For a moment, the man was tempted to let the girl decide whether their path went northeast to the Dark Lands or west to the Swampgrass. Miranda was sensitive and intelligent. Surely, once she thought about it, she would make the right decision. No! he thought. This is not a game to be played on a whim. He turned back to Miranda and when he spoke, his voice was harsh.

"You already made your decision when you agreed to be my eyes into the Dark Lands."

Miranda's face drained of colour at the Druid's words. She clenched her fists, fighting the urge to scream at him, to tell him to go away and leave her alone. She hated him for reminding her of the reason she was here. She hated him for speaking the truth and making her feel ashamed.

"Are you angry with me?" asked the Druid, the harshness gone from his voice as suddenly as if Miranda had imagined hearing it.

She didn't trust herself to speak. She shook her head, avoiding the man's piercing stare.

"There is a reason why nothing must sidetrack us from our purpose," he said, offering an explanation like a peace offering. "I do not mean to be cruel, but your father has been missing for over ten years. Nothing catastrophic will happen if you wait a little longer to learn the truth about his disappearance. But if we fail to find the Crown and get it back, before the Evil Ones take it to Bethany, then you can forget about your father, because this world, as we know it, will end."

"How will it end?" asked Miranda.

"Remember: who wears the Crown, rules. If I am right—and I am right most of the time—the Demon intends one of her own to wear the Crown of Ellesmere. What do you think will happen if Evil reigns in the land of the Elves?"

"All the Elves will die," whispered Miranda.

"Yes," agreed Naim. "The Elves and Dwarves and humans in this world and the people in yours will all die because the seals about the Place with No Name will weaken and fail."

"Ohh!" whispered Miranda, as she suddenly realized why Naim was so desperate to get the Crown back from the Werecurs. Oh, she knew all along that it was important, but she hadn't realized how important, until this minute. Unbidden, images of thousands and thousands of faceless, half-dead beings filled her mind. She saw them clearly as they spilled out of the Nameless Place like black water gushing from a burst dam. "Ohh!" she said again. "I'm sorry. I didn't know . . . I didn't think about . . ." She raised her hands and held her head, driving the frightening images away. Slowly they faded from her mind, until only one remained. Miranda knew the huge black shape with knots of serpents roiling about her middle, and thick, black blood dripping from her long extruding tongue.

"The Demon will escape," she said, her voice barely as loud as a faint breath.

The Druid nodded grimly. "And this time, there will be no Elven magic to stop her."

"I'm sorry," said Miranda. "I feel sort of stupid, wanting my own way when I promised to help you. I guess I can wait a bit longer to find out what happened to my dad."

Naim put his hand on her shoulder. "Do not feel stupid, girl. It is not easy to choose between a parent and a journey that will certainly be dangerous and, perhaps, fatal."

Miranda followed him over to the pale brown horse. "I see now that I never had a choice—not really," she said, rubbing Lightning's side while Naim heaved himself into the saddle.

"I will make you a promise," said the Druid, gripping the girl's hand and hoisting her onto the horse behind him. "If we return from the Demon's Kingdom with our lives, I will go into the Swampgrass to learn what I can about Garrett."

Miranda couldn't find words to express her feelings, so she remained silent. It was a long time before she finally said, "Thank you."

The Thug fumed, his red eyes raking the girl's back as she walked up to the big ugly horse. A few more seconds and he would have grabbed her and, later, thrown the Bloodstones in the Dwarf's face. But the stupid Trolls had attacked before he gave the signal, and ruined everything. Then, like snivelling wimps, the imbecilic lumps ran away when the Druid did his harmless little trick. And now, Hate was furious. *Are you incapable of killing one measly child? Do I have to send another to do it for you?* she had shrieked in his mind, her fury stinging his flesh like burning oil. A shiver rippled along the Thug's hide as his Mistress's final words rang in his ears. *Do not fail me, or you will die.*

He scored the ground with his spiked feet, and sharpened the claws on the ends of his fingers on the nearest tree, slicing through the thick bark and gouging deep into the living wood. Was it his fault that the treacherous Trolls couldn't understand a simple command? *Wait for my signal.* That's what he had said. He hated Trolls. They were ugly, filthy creatures, unpredictable except for their stupidity, which was a constant. The Thug didn't understand why his Mistress needed them. He'd like to kill them all. But Hate didn't like dead Trolls. Their blood was different from humans and other creatures, and the Demon rejected it. As far as she was concerned, a dead Troll was just like a dead insect.

The Thug absentmindedly gashed the tree once more, his red eyes following the Druid and the girl as they rode from the clearing, the other horse trailing after them. Then he kneaded the skin over the gold skull on his forearm and followed, his eyes never moving off the girl.

CHAPTER TWENTY-SIX

THE
SWAMPGRASS

When Arabella saw the Troll whack Nicholas in the face and stuff him into a sack, she didn't think, she acted instinctively. Lowering her head, she charged, biting, kicking, and scratching the smelly creature. The sight of the tiny human child flying at him like an angry terrier with more courage than brains made the big Troll laugh impulsively, as though he were being tickled. But that didn't stop him from knocking the courageous girl senseless, picking her up by the arm, and dropping her into another sack. Then he kicked her.

A long time later, Arabella groaned and opened one swollen eye. She was in a dark place. The air smelled bad. Her head ached and her body was stiff and sore. Closing her eye, she thought about her predicament. She was still in the sack, and from the way she was bouncing about, she guessed that her captor had slung the sack over his shoulder and was moving at a rapid pace. Straining her ears, she listened for any sound that might tell her where they were going. But the Trolls never spoke and the only sounds she heard were the squishing of heavy feet plodding through water, and long hissing sounds like air escaping from a tire. Where were they taking her? And, what would they do to her when they got there? Was Nicholas still alive? Had Miranda and Penelope escaped?

She didn't know how long she'd been in the sack, a day or a week, but it felt like forever. She thought she'd go mad if she didn't stretch her cramped limbs soon. And then, suddenly, she heard loud guttural shouting, and the Troll stopped. She had been praying for this moment but now the thought of leaving the sack terrified her.

The Troll unslung the sack and shook it roughly. Arabella tumbled onto the wet, spongy ground. She peered through slits in her eyes, moaning in relief when she spotted Nicholas struggling to sit up. Emmet was there, too, his face black with rage. For the first time since she had met the grumpy Dwarf, Arabella was so happy to see him, she wanted to hug him.

One of the Trolls prodded her with his foot. "Har! Vag, ya filthy swine. What's this, eh?"

"Get off Bugg, ya piece of vomit," roared the Troll named Vag, who was obviously Arabella's captor.

Bugg gave Vag a vicious shove, but the other held his ground, raising his sharp spear and waving it in Bugg's face. "I'll tell Grotch, eh."

"Har, har!" bellowed Bugg, whipping a dagger from his belt and making a slicing motion at the other's mouth. "Ya can't tattle if yer tongue's gone, eh, what? Ya smelly bottom."

The other Trolls moved away from the captives, forming a ring around their squabbling comrades. They made bets, yelling and pushing, and calling each other names that were intended as insults but were merely disgusting. Using her elbows, Arabella pulled herself toward Nicholas. "I feel rotten," she said. Then she belched once, and threw up in the mud.

"Hey! Watch it!" cried Nicholas, as he and Emmet scrambled out of the way. Seeing the sheepish grin on Arabella's face, he found himself grinning too. "I guess you feel better now," he laughed.

"Sorry," said Arabella. "I think it was all that bouncing about in the sack. Are you guys okay?" She looked from the boy to the silent Dwarf.

"What do you think?" answered Nicholas, pressing his arms tightly against his ribcage. "I think something's broken."

"I'll live," muttered Emmet, ignoring the bloody cuts on his arms.

"This really sucks," said Nicholas, bitterly.

"No kidding," said Arabella. She turned to the Dwarf. "Emmet, what is this place?"

"Swampgrass," muttered the Dwarf. "Troll country. Bad."

Arabella looked about. If this was the Swampgrass, it was well named. In the gloomy half-light, she saw that they were on a wide strip of wet, soggy ground that was covered with long, sharp blades of grass. Overhead, strange, misshapen trees blotted out the sky, long leafless branches twisted and curled about each other like hands choking the life out of the wood. Arabella shivered, dropping her eyes from the ominous, living canopy.

Along both sides of the grassy area she saw hundreds of low, ramshackle buildings built on rafts. "I think we're in one of the Troll villages," she mused, and then giggled involuntarily.

"What's so funny?" growled Nicholas, eyeing his friend as if she had suddenly gone insane.

"It's not really funny," said Arabella. "I was watching this show on TV once and this guy said he had a recurring nightmare about being chased by irate villagers." She giggled again. "It's actually happening to us."

When she noticed that neither Nicholas nor Emmet was amused, she blushed furiously. "Never mind. You had to have seen it."

"It's not a village," whispered Nicholas. "Look at those shacks. There must be thousands of them."

The enormity of the city and the purposeful way the inhabitants bustled about overwhelmed him. He had never considered the Trolls a serious threat. The fact that they had captured and hauled him off to the Swampgrass hadn't altered his opinion. Like Arabella with her story of irate villagers, he had always thought of Trolls as stupid, bumbling idiots—comic creatures. But now, he wasn't so sure.

"Are there other cities like this?" he asked, dreading the answer. He took Emmet's grunt as a yes. "How many?"

"Twenty . . . thirty."

Nicholas whistled softly. That meant there must be hundreds and thousands of Trolls . . . maybe millions. The ones he could see were all males. Were there female Trolls? Did they live in families with children? Suddenly, he wrinkled his nose in disgust. "What's that horrible smell?"

Arabella held her nose and made a face. "You mean it's not you?"

"Ha, ha!" snapped Nicholas.

It was Emmet who finally answered the boy's question. "Swamp."

"Not that smell," said Nicholas. "The one coming from the buildings. It smells like a dead raccoon I found once."

Emmet let out a deep breath. "You smell bones."

Nicholas gasped. "What do you mean, bones?"

"Trolls build with bones."

Nicholas and Arabella exchanged horrified looks.

"Human bones?" squeaked Arabella.

Emmet grunted again.

Nicholas dropped his head into his hands. "I've got a really bad feeling about this."

"Over there," said Emmet, tilting his head in the direction of one of the floating shacks. "Guards."

Nicholas turned his head toward the spot Emmet had indicated. Like the other buildings, it was a floating structure. But the raft upon which it sat was moored away from the other buildings. Nicholas counted a dozen hefty Trolls planted on the raft, close to the building like giant trees. He felt his eyes drawn to the darkness that hung like smoke about it. His lips tightened as he noticed the black standard hanging limply from a pole on the roof of the building. "What's that flag?" he asked, praying for a breeze to straighten the standard so he could see what, if anything, was on it.

"The Demon favours black," said Emmet.

"Do you think it's where they keep prisoners?" asked Nicholas.

"Hmmm," replied the Dwarf. "No bars. Something else. Something that scares the Guards."

Emmet's eyes wandered slowly about his surroundings, his mind registering the unusual activity.

A mountain of weapons and sacks of provisions were being loaded onto great wagons, pulled by huge horned creatures he could not identify. As he watched, fascinated, one of the creatures roared and reared skyward, carrying the terrified Trolls who gripped the harness into the air with it. When its monstrous forelimbs thundered back to earth, the soggy ground gave way and in less than a minute, the giant creature, the loaded wagon, and a dozen Trolls vanished into the black swamp as if they had never existed.

"Whoa!" breathed the Dwarf, wondering if he had imagined the whole horrible scene. He looked about. A few feet away, the Trolls who had captured him and the children were still at it, fighting and pushing. They hadn't noticed, or if they had, it didn't faze them. The only sign that some great tragedy had just played out before his eyes was the echo of the gigantic creature's terrible death screams that filled the air for a long time before fading away forever. Nicholas and Arabella started at the terrible screams and looked about for the source, but saw nothing of what happened.

Emmet prodded Nicholas with his elbow. "Trolls are busy. Looks like they're readying for war."

But Nicholas wasn't listening. His mind was still focused on the dark box-like building. A wild thought raced through his mind. What if Miranda's father were still alive? What if he were shut up in that isolated shack, guarded night and day? And, what if he, Nicholas, found him . . . and rescued him? He could already see the look on Miranda's face when she met her father for the first time. He was so lost in his thoughts that he no longer heard the guttural sounds of the Trolls fighting and arguing. But a new sound brought him back to reality.

"WHAT IS THE MEANING OF THIS?" The high-pitched, whining voice came from behind the captives.

Instantly, the Trolls stopped fighting. They jumped back from each other as if they had been burned and fell silent, their white, lumpy heads whipping toward the voice. Nicholas turned and immediately saw the two human figures coming closer, but his eyes were drawn to the tall, hunch-backed shape in the long, tattered robes, gliding gracefully through the muck, as if his feet were not touching the ground. The boy's mouth dropped open and the colour drained from his face, leaving him as pale as a ghost. "Oh, no!" he groaned.

"Oh, no!" echoed Arabella, staring at the short man trotting beside the tall figure. "It's Stubby!"

"Forget Stubby," said Nicholas, harshly. "It's the other one you should be worried about. It's Indolent . . . the Wizard."

Arabella had never seen the nasty Wizard, but she knew him from the stories Nicholas still told about his imprisonment in the Castle of Indolence and how the Wizard had bewitched him and tried to turn him against his friends. Her eyes shifted from the grade four teacher to the tall, stooped man.

Indolent's garments were filthy. The upper front of his long, greenish-black robe was spattered with globs of congealed food and something else that looked like slobber. The hem was tattered and coated with mud. The Wizard's limp, stringy hair was a brash yellow, like egg yolks, and streaked with black. Arabella was sickened by the scattering of big, unsightly, blood-coloured scabs coating shaved patches on his pale scalp. Suddenly she gasped. A short black stick appeared magically in one of his hands where a second ago there had been nothing.

"Magic," whispered Arabella. "But . . . I thought . . ."

"Yeah," said Nicholas. "I thought he was finished, too. Wrong!"

"But Naim said he broke his wand and took away his power . . ."

"You saw that stick appear in his hand. If that's not magic, I don't know what is," said Nicholas, scooping up a handful of mud and rubbing it over his face, in a desperate attempt to prevent the Wizard from recognizing him.

But, he needn't have worried. The Wizard only had eyes for Arabella. He motioned to Stubby, who motioned to one of the Trolls, who grabbed the girl's arm and dragged her across the ground, dropping her in a heap at Indolent's feet.

The Wizard prodded Stubby with his elbow. "Is this the one?"

Stubby took one look and his face contorted in rage. "You fools," he screamed, digging his toe into the wet ground and kicking mud at Arabella. "You grabbed the wrong girl!" He aimed his next kick at the Trolls. "This isn't the D'arte brat. It's her little sidekick. Didn't I tell you she was ugly enough to sour milk?"

"All humans look ugly," mumbled one of the Trolls.

"Leave her alone," snarled Nicholas, who would have lunged at Mr. Little if Emmet hadn't grabbed his arm and held him back.

Noting the boy's frustration, Stubby smiled wickedly, grabbed a handful of Arabella's hair, and pulled her to her feet. Then he raised his other hand and slapped her across the face. "Where's Miranda?" he demanded.

The blow was hard enough to send Arabella reeling to the ground and bring tears to her eyes. Determined not to cry in front of this puffed-up little puke, she gritted her teeth and twisted her face into a wide grin. Then, she looked him in the eye.

"Go soak your head in the bog," she barked, aiming a mouthful of spit at his face.

Stubby leaped back, avoiding the jet of saliva. Shaking uncontrollably, he grabbed Arabella's shoulders and shook her until her teeth rattled.

"STOP!" commanded Indolent, thrusting Stubby aside as if he were one of the Trolls. He glided up to the girl, jiggling the stick at her as he moved.

Arabella's eyes opened wide in surprise when she suddenly found herself somersaulting through the air. She landed flat on her back on the wet ground, the wind knocked out of her. Nicholas thought she looked like a broken rag doll and his heart ached for her. His anger frightened him. It consumed him like fire, turning everything black. He wanted to kill Indolent.

"Be still, lad," hissed Emmet, gripping Nicholas's arm and squeezing until the boy winced in pain. Still the Dwarf held his grip, only dropping his hand when he saw the fire die in the other's eyes.

"Why did you do that?" demanded Nicholas, glowering at Emmet and rubbing his arm where the Dwarf's fingers had dug into his flesh.

"You know," was all Emmet replied.

Nicholas opened his mouth and then shut it abruptly. He locked eyes with Emmet and nodded slowly. He knew. He knew he had almost blown it. If the Dwarf hadn't stopped him, he would have lost his temper and said and done things that would have landed him and his companions in worse trouble than they were already in. He might have gotten them all killed. Thanks to the Dwarf, he had regained control of his feelings.

The Wizard's attention remained on Arabella. And, while that sounded bad for the girl, it meant that he and Emmet might not be guarded as heavily as if they were important.

Gritting his teeth, Nicholas watched Indolent smile like the good fairy and stretch out his arm to help Arabella out of the mud. Seeing that she was barely able to stand, the Wizard placed his hands on her shoulders to steady her. When he was satisfied that she wouldn't collapse, he snapped his fingers in her face and leaned toward the girl. Instantly, Arabella's head jerked up and up until she found herself face to face with Indolent.

"Don't look at him!" shouted Nicholas.

But the warning came too late. Arabella looked deep into the Wizard's eyes, amazed that Nicholas had never mentioned how black the irises were or how the whites flickered from pale yellow to orange, like a jaundiced flame. Before she could look away, she was trapped, like a fly caught in a spider's web.

Indolent rubbed his hands together gleefully. "Now, Little One, where is the D'arte girl?"

"Shut up, Bell! Don't tell him anything." Nicholas grabbed a clump of muddy earth and threw it at his friend, hoping to jolt her out of the spell the Wizard had cast.

Arabella flinched when the mud hit her neck, but she ignored the sting. For a second, a look of confusion washed over her face. Then it was gone, replaced by a satisfied, knowing sneer. Why had Nicholas said all those horrible things about this nice, gentle man? Well, the answer was obvious, wasn't it? She'd always known that her so-called friend had a nasty side—a spiteful, jealous side. Now that she thought about it, she had never really trusted him. In fact, she now saw clearly that she had always disliked him as much as he had always disliked her. She looked up at the Wizard and smiled. "She's with the Druid. They've gone to find the Crown of Ellesmere."

Indolent and the grade four teacher exchanged meaningful glances.

"Come with me, dear," said the Wizard, his voice as sweet as milk chocolate. "We can't have you coming down with a nasty bog fever. Come inside where it's warm. Little will find you something to eat." He turned to Stubby. "Put those two to work in the Drom Hole." Then, he reached for Arabella's hand. "I've got a surprise for you."

"What?" cried Arabella, skipping happily beside Indolent. "Please tell me."

"Then it wouldn't be a surprise, would it?"

Hearing Indolent use the same words he had once used on him disgusted Nicholas, but that wasn't what turned his flesh stone cold. As the Wizard grasped Arabella's hand, Nicholas had noticed the gold skull under the skin on his right forearm. The sight of the Demon's mark on Indolent horrified him. Was the Wizard's ego so inflated that he believed he could ally himself with Hate and not become one of her creatures? Was he so crazy that he believed he could use her to grab power for himself? The chill seeped into Nicholas's bones. His eyes narrowed and anger flared up inside him. He had found the answer to the question of where Indolent's new powers came from. He had to find a way to escape and warn the Druid.

Grasping Arabella's hand tightly, Indolent led her toward one of the buildings at the edge of the floating village. Stubby followed the pair, staring daggers at Arabella's back. He hated being called Little and he hated the thought of being ordered to serve Arabella. He was not some common housemaid or a waiter scrabbling for tips. He was better than that. He was educated—Indolent's equal. Afraid to voice his displeasure to the Wizard, he turned back and took it out on the Trolls. "You heard the man, oafs," he spat, kicking the closest one, and clapping his hands sharply. "Hop to it."

As the teacher strode past the prisoners, Emmet acted without thinking. He stuck out his foot and tripped him. Stubby landed on his stomach in the muck, face down in Arabella's vomit. It happened so abruptly, Nicholas burst out laughing, and for the first time since they had met, he saw a grin flash across the surly Dwarf's face.

"Not fair," he chortled, "save some of the big pieces for your Troll friends." Then he collapsed beside the Dwarf, laughing uncontrollably.

Stubby clambered to his feet, speechless with rage at the sight of his ruined, sodden clothes. He grabbed a spear from one of the Trolls and started toward Emmet, but something in the Dwarf's face halted him in his tracks, making him take a step backward. For a second he stared at Emmet, his entire body shaking as if he were in the throes of a violent seizure. The Dwarf returned his gaze, a mere hint of a smile curling the corners of his mouth. Finally Stubby's eyes dropped. The teacher backed away until he was satisfied that a safe distance separated him from the Dwarf. Then he hurled the spear at Emmet and hot-footed it after the Wizard.

"That was cool," said Nicholas, wiping tears of laughter from his mud-streaked face. "I wish I'd thought of it."

"Felt good," snorted Emmet, thumping Nicholas on the back.

"Get up, ya sumps, eh," boomed Vag, grabbing the prisoners by the scruff of their necks and setting them on their feet. "Down the Drom Hole, har, har, eh." He slipped thick ropes about their necks and gave them a shove. "Get!"

"What are they going to do to us? " Nicholas whispered to Emmet.

The Dwarf shrugged. "Something bad."

Vag and five or six other Trolls marched Nicholas and Emmet over the grassy bog. As they trudged through the muck, the spongy ground swelled and trembled beneath them. The pressure of their feet on the sodden earth produced long hissing sounds as air and water were forced out. Nicholas broke out in a cold sweat at the thought of sinking through the thin layer of water-bloated earth into the black waters below. He glanced sideways at Emmet, and knew from the Dwarf's grim face that he, too, was fighting an urge to run.

They had gone about five kilometres, when Vag suddenly yanked on the ropes, almost strangling the captives. The landscape had changed as they moved deeper and deeper into the swamp. The Troll shacks on either side of the strip of waterlogged ground gave way to high mossy banks. Now, the pungent smell of mould that Nicholas had noticed when they entered the swamp replaced the revolting reek of the buildings and grew so pervasive it stuck in his throat, making him cough harshly. He tried breathing through his mouth, but the odour stayed on him like thick lotion. It coated his tongue and seemed to seep through his very pores.

"Chokedamp," muttered Emmet, coughing harshly. "Like cancer. Kills everything."

Vag nudged Nicholas with the point of his spear, directing him toward a small hole in the bank. "Drom Hole," he rumbled, slipping the rope from the boy's neck and stuffing a rough cloth sack in the top of his jacket. Then he thumped Nicholas in the chest with one of his thick fingers. "Go. Get Drom stones."

Nicholas stared at the hole in horror. "No way," he shook his head. "You can't make me go in there."

"HAR, HAR!" laughed the Trolls, whacking each other's head with their spears, as Vag picked up the boy and stuffed him headfirst into the black hole.

CHAPTER TWENTY-SEVEN

THE DROM
HOLE

Nicholas was stuck. In the narrow, dank hole, he felt as if the earth were tightening about him, slowly crushing him to death. His ribs hurt, he couldn't breathe, and he was more afraid than when he had stood beside Emmet fighting the Trolls. Then something bumped his sneakers and he found himself sliding a couple of feet forward in the darkness.

"Move, lad." Emmet's voice was muffled and seemed to be coming from a great distance.

Relieved that he was not alone, Nicholas sucked in his breath, killing his tender ribs in the process, dug his fingers into the mud, and slowly inched his way ahead. Once or twice, something big and slimy slipped through his fingers, causing him to start frantically. He wasn't scared of creepy crawly things he could see and identify, but the unseen slimy things slithering over his flesh gave him the creeps. He prayed that nothing poisonous lived in the bog—or, to be precise, in the Drom Hole.

A long time later, he stretched to get a grip in the mud and his hands met air. He froze, afraid of what might be waiting at the bottom of the hole. How deep was the drop? What if he let go and couldn't get back up? How would he ever get out?

"I'm at the end, Emmet. I can't feel anything. It just drops off. It's pretty scary."

Emmet wrapped his big hands around Nicholas's ankles. "I got you, boy. Go slow."

Nicholas pulled himself ahead and dropped his upper body until he felt solid ground beneath his hands. "Okay," he shouted. "Let go." He wriggled the rest of his body through the hole, and then he reached back in, locked his hands about the Dwarf's wrists and pulled until Emmet dropped the few feet onto the ground.

Silently, they huddled together in the damp, black place, afraid to move for fear of getting lost and never finding their way back to the hole again.

"I understand about the Thugs," said Nicholas, still curious about the Trolls. "How they gave themselves to the Demon so they'd live forever, but what about the Bog Trolls? Are they human, or what?"

"No," replied Emmet. "River Trolls are human. Evolved. Know right from wrong. Follow customs. Frame laws that make conduct predictable. Not erratic and capricious like Bogs. Don't commit murder. Aren't violent. Care for their young."

Nicholas was amazed. He'd never heard Emmet utter more than a few words at a time. He remained silent, hoping the Dwarf would continue. He wasn't disappointed.

"For Bog Trolls, wrong is right. Worship Demon, but don't belong to her like Thugs and Hellhags. Violent, ignorant creatures. Hate all other races. Hide their women and offspring. Treat them as slaves. Kill them for breaking rules. Kill them for speaking . . . laughing. Women won't disobey. Too ignorant. Like giant children. Frightening." Emmet sighed. "No," he said again. "Bog Trolls aren't human."

Nicholas thought for a second. "Are they evil like the Demon?"

Emmet shook his head. "No," he said. "Not like Demon. Ignorant evil. Insane evil."

Nicholas leaned his head against the wall of the burrow and thought about what his companion had told him. The more he learned about the Trolls, the greater his fear of them grew.

"What we need is a light," he muttered a long time later, wrapping his arms tightly about his chest. He felt a lump inside his t-shirt, scratching his skin. Reaching under the shirt, he pulled out the rough cloth. It was the sack the Troll named Vag had stuffed into the neck of his jacket. It must have slipped under his clothing when he pulled himself through the black hole.

"What are we supposed to be doing in here? Why did they give us these sacks?"

"Ugly Troll said find Drom stones."

"Do you know what they are, because I sure don't?"

"Might know it. Different name."

Nicholas thought about what the Dwarf said. "It's a little late now, but we should have asked them to show us one of the stones." He took a deep breath and let it out slowly. "I guess it doesn't matter, because even if we knew what they looked like, we'd never find them without a light?"

"Hummfff," mumbled Emmet, thoughtfully. "Trolls want Drom stones. Must be valuable."

"Is that what you think they're guarding back there in that shack?" said Nicholas, thoughtfully. He still believed, or perhaps hoped, that he was going to find Miranda's father, but until he learned more he didn't want to talk about it.

"No," said the Dwarf. "Guards scared. Not scared of Drom stones."

Tired of the endless hours in the dark with nothing to do, Nicholas removed his jacket and pulled his t-shirt over his head. Using his teeth, he made a hole in the material and began tearing the shirt into thin strips.

"Here," he said, pressing the strips into Emmet's hand. "Tie them together at the ends. It won't be very long, but, if I hold one end and wait by the hole, you can take the other and hunt for these Drom stones."

"Arr," said Emmet, falling silent again as he knotted the strips of Nicholas's t-shirt into a make-shift rope.

Clutching one end of the rope, Emmet moved carefully about in the dark, feeling the ground for anything that didn't squirm or wriggle. The Dwarf was used to rock tunnels, but he had no liking for this place. He hadn't said anything to Nicholas, but he knew that the hole they crawled through wasn't a natural phenomenon. Something had tunneled through the earth, creating both the hole and this large, dark burrow. He couldn't imagine what sort of creature it was, but, judging by the size of the place, it was big.

"Ahh!" he yelled, as his hand collided with some-thing rough and cold. He ran his fingers over the object and then jumped back as if he had touched a hot burner.

Nicholas stood by the Drom Hole, shifting his weight from one foot to the other to prevent insects and other unseen critters from crawling up his legs. The dark was so overpowering—so tangible—he was afraid it had become permanently imprinted on the lenses of his eyes, and even in bright sunlight, he would never be able to pierce the black film. He hated every second in the lightless hole. He wondered what would happen if he had to spend the rest of his life in this utter, impenetrable darkness. Would his eyes adjust, or would they grow bulbous and turn white and useless, like the sight organs of creatures that lived at the bottom of the ocean? He wished that he could see what Emmet was up to. What if something caught and ate the Dwarf, and then followed the rope back to him? Emmet couldn't have picked a worse moment to shout in alarm, and wrench the rope out of the boy's hand.

"Emmet?" cried Nicholas, dropping to his knees and scrabbling about for the rope, as if his life depended on finding it.

"Bones," swore Emmet. "Dead a long time."

"What kind of bones?" asked Nicholas, fighting to keep his voice calm, but feeling cold sweat run down his back and under his arms.

"Human, I think."

When the Dwarf bumped into him a few seconds later, Nicholas almost died of fright. "Don't do that," he scolded.

"Here," said Emmet, finding Nicholas's hand and pressing a charcoal-sized object into his palm.

"What is it?" asked the boy, turning the hard object over in his hand. "You think it's one of those Drom stones?"

"Don't know," answered the Dwarf. "Found seventeen. Need to go farther."

"Do you really think these things are valuable?" asked Nicholas, an idea starting to take shape in his brain.

"Trolls think so."

"Well," said Nicholas, grinning in the darkness. "The Trolls are too big to fit through the hole, so there's no way they'd ever find out how many stones we really find, right?"

"Hmmm," said Emmet.

"What I mean is, if we bring back five stones each and say that's all we found, they can't prove we found more, right?"

"Steal stones?"

"I wouldn't exactly call it stealing."

"What, then?"

The Dwarf's blunt questions flustered Nicholas. "Okay, it's probably stealing. I admit it. At least to the Trolls. But . . ." He searched for the words to explain that taking the stones, when they weren't the Trolls' in the first place, wasn't the same kind of stealing as the Druid taking the horses from Cundell Stables in Ottawa and leaving a rock in payment. That was serious. This was more like taking honey from a bees' hive, or eggs from a hen.

"Sneaky," grunted Emmet, sounding suspiciously as though he were laughing. "I like it."

"You do?" asked Nicholas, pleased by the Dwarf's unexpected praise.

"Yup."

"Hey," laughed Nicholas. "Who knows, we might be rich."

Emmet counted out seven stones and passed them to Nicholas, who dropped them in his sack. Then he placed the sack on the ground directly under the Drom hole. "So we can find them easily," he explained, before crawling into the hole and worming his body back the way they'd come.

The prisoners lost count of the days. Nicholas's life was an endless, boring existence that took a toll on his mind and body. The only thing that kept him from going stark, raving mad was the steadily growing pile of Drom stones. Early every morning, Vag and a half-dozen Trolls marched him and Emmet through the sharp grass and mud to the Drom Hole, and stuffed them into the dark tunnel. Late at night, when the companions emerged from the hole, the Trolls were waiting to march them back to the village where they were locked in a mean, windowless hovel on one of the rafts.

Their one meal a day was barely enough to keep them alive. At first Nicholas had turned his nose up and pushed the bowl of Troll food aside. It smelled rotten and he was determined not to eat anything his captors put before him. But Emmet urged him to swallow the disgusting fare to keep his strength up.

The boy lost weight, until his loose, dirty clothes looked as if they were two sizes too large. His energy drained away and his spirits sank deeper than the black waters of the swamp. He ached to see clear blue sky and feel the sun warm his cold flesh. But he never complained. During the long nights, silent except for the sounds of the Dwarf scraping at the wooden flooring, Nicholas kept his mind focused on rescuing Miranda's father, and escaping from this dismal, life-draining place.

Then, one night, as the two prisoners huddled in the dingy, slummy shed, Emmet moved next to the boy and whispered. "Can you swim, lad?"

"Of course," Nicholas whispered back. "Why?"

"Dug us a hole, I did," said the Dwarf, proudly.

With mounting excitement, the prisoners examined the opening Emmet had scraped through the bottom of the raft. Escape was no longer a hopeless dream, but an actual, tangible possibility. The thought of getting away from the Trolls gave Nicholas a new interest in living. Even his fear of the black waters of the swamp couldn't dampen his enthusiasm.

"I'm going in," he whispered, barely able to stop himself from slipping into the water and swimming away as fast as his arms and legs could move.

"Be careful," cautioned Emmet. "Can't see down there. Go slow." When Nicholas didn't reply, he gripped the boy's arm and held it firmly. "Say it, lad."

"OK, OK," said Nicholas, twisting his arm until the Dwarf released his hold. "I'll be careful."

Quickly, he removed his outer clothing. Then, he gave his companion a light tap on the shoulder and disappeared into the cold, ink-black water. Emmet knelt on the damp flooring and peered into the black hole, waiting for the boy to return. He waited and waited. He was still waiting when he heard harsh shouts and the heavy thudding of Troll boots approaching, but there was no sign of Nicholas. Through the jagged opening in the floor, the black swamp water was as still as a sheet of glass.

CHAPTER TWENTY-EIGHT

THE DARK SHACK

With a heavy heart, Emmet turned toward the thick door of the shed. Something was happening out there, but what? Had they caught the boy? That seemed to be the only explanation for the sudden activity. The Trolls would be here soon. If they hadn't already got hold of the boy, they'd discover his disappearance soon enough. And the hole in the floor.

The Dwarf almost jumped out of his skin when something grabbed his ankle in the darkness. A second later he heard a soft splash as Nicholas's head bobbed to the surface. Quickly, Emmet caught the boy's arms and started to pull him through the opening.

"No," breathed Nicholas, coughing water from his throat. His voice was harsh with fear. "We can't stay here. We've got to get away. Now!"

The Trolls had almost reached the shed.

"Come on, man," said Nicholas, impatiently.

Still, the Dwarf hesitated.

"What are you waiting for? I said we've got to go now."

"Can't swim," said Emmet.

"What do you mean, you can't swim?" demanded Nicholas, incredulously.

"Mean what I said. Can't swim."

"Just get in," urged Nicholas. "Hold onto the opening. Take a deep breath. Trust me, Emmet, I won't let you drown."

Without another word, Emmet took a deep breath, held it, and dropped feet-first through the hole. His heavy Dwarf boots acted as a weight and, to his everlasting horror, he found himself sinking like a boulder to the bottom of the swamp.

Nicholas felt the rush of water as the Dwarf plummeted past him. He was a strong swimmer, but the pitch-black water unnerved him. He had to get to the Dwarf quickly and lead him to the surface before Emmet panicked and drowned both of them with his superior strength. Nicholas dove straight down, his arms stretching in front of him. He almost shouted with relief when his fingers touched Emmet's coarse Dwarf hair. Instinctively,

Nicholas reversed the dive, wrapped one arm about his drowning friend's neck and shot to the surface, coming up under the raft and banging his head hard on the rough wood. Without stopping, he used the boards to propel his body to the end of the raft. Then, he propped Emmet's head out of the water.

The Dwarf didn't move.

Nicholas's heart was pumping wildly from the exertion plus the long hours in the cold water. "Emmet!" he hissed, thumping the Dwarf's back, knowing it was probably the wrong thing to do, but too overwrought to think clearly.

The Dwarf's body twitched. He was alive.

Nicholas rolled Emmet onto his back and pulled him through the water. He had to get them away. Judging by the shouting all about him, he knew the Trolls had already discovered the absence of the two prisoners. Weak from exhaustion and cold, he gritted his teeth and moved soundlessly away from the shack, following a direction that he prayed would take them close to the Drom Hole. If he could only get himself and Emmet there before the Trolls thought to post a guard outside the tunnel, they'd be safe. At least they'd be safe from the Trolls, whose size prevented them from following the fugitives through the narrow tunnel. Nicholas refused to think about what they'd do once they reached the burrow. It was too depressing.

Hours later, numb with cold, he collapsed on the sodden ground of the burrow next to the Dwarf, who hadn't spoken a word since jumping into the water. They were safe for now. But how long could they survive in the damp burrow, in wet clothing? He must have slept then, because the next thing he remembered was somebody shaking him roughly. Thinking the Trolls had found him, he clenched his frozen hands and punched his attacker.

"No need for that," muttered Emmet, gripping the boy's wrists.

"Well, cut it out," cried Nicholas, pushing the Dwarf away.

"Put these on," said the Dwarf, pressing a bundle of dry clothing into Nicholas's arms. "Went back. Borrowed 'em."

Nicholas felt his eyes sting with tears. "Th-thanks," he stammered, unable to find words to tell the other how thankful he was for the unexpected gift.

"Need 'em. Keep warm, or die."

The dry garments hung loosely on Nicholas's lean body, but they were thick and warm and lifted the boy's sagging spirits.

"Now," said Emmet, when they were settled. "Tell me what you saw."

"I saw what's in the shack," said Nicholas, the hair on his arms rising as he relived his nighttime adventure in the black waters of the Swampgrass by narrating it to the Dwarf.

When his head had broken the surface without causing the slightest ripple, he was amazed to find that he had travelled so far underwater. Before him, like a monstrous black box, squatted the iso- lated building. Elsewhere in the swamp, Nicholas saw lights from fires and lanterns. But, in the area surrounding the guarded shack there was nothing but blackness. Even the reflected light from nearby fires did not penetrate the dark area. It seemed to Nicholas as though a piece of the swamp had been cut out, leaving only emptiness. He scanned the dark area, trying to locate the Troll Guards that, earlier, had encircled the shack like a living wall. He saw nothing.

Nicholas had moved closer, using the floating platforms to propel himself slowly through the water. He didn't know if Trolls possessed sight as keen as Elves, but he had kept his head lowered, just in case. He was sure his white face on the black water would glow like a light bulb, warning the guards of his approach. A sudden harsh shout erupted from nearby, making him start violently. He forced himself to remain calm, counting to ten before moving forward again. As silent as a shadow, he passed a group of Trolls crouched around a large flaming cauldron. Their harsh voices grated on his nerves. He hid in the smoke, listening for any sudden changes in the night sounds, changes that meant danger to him. But no one saw him.

Ahead, the blackness seemed to reach out to him, drawing him into itself like water to a drain. Despite the chill, sweat ran down his scalp, mingling with the stagnant waters of the swamp. Nicholas went more swiftly, his eyes glued on his destination. He was almost there—he could make out the outline of the building now—a menacing presence, like something evil come to life. He could see the black standard hanging limply in the still air, but he no longer wondered to whom it belonged. He knew. As Emmet had observed, the Demon favours black.

Nicholas stopped, studying the open water between him and the platform upon which the lone building rested. He estimated that about fifty feet separated the raft from other floating structures. He'd be at his most vulnerable in the open water. He peered about, searching for the Troll Guards. Where were they? He watched for several minutes, then he took a slow, deep breath and dropped beneath the surface.

He swam slowly, imagining himself as a giant predator—a great white shark gliding stealthily and purposefully toward his unsuspecting prey. Moments later his fingers bumped the raft upon which the dark building rose. Cautiously, he raised his head above the water. His heart raced like a ticking bomb when he spotted one of the Guards only a few feet away. Then he saw the others. He counted eight Trolls. There must be others around the other sides of the raft. Or hiding inside the building. They towered over him like giant stone figures, silent and still, their thick hands gripping sharp weapons.

RUN! His mind screamed at him, and he almost obeyed. NO! He mouthed the word silently. NO! He had come too far to run away now. He was going to solve the mystery of the isolated shed—find out what was hidden there—what was so important that hefty Trolls guarded it night and day.

He hesitated a moment longer, his lean face set with determination. Then he inched through the water along the side of the raft toward the back of the building. Peering about for Guards, he noticed that the sounds he had heard before and the glow from dozens of fires and lights were gone. He felt that he had entered a vacuum—an unnatural place where nothing from outside could penetrate the deathly black space. Gripping the edge of the raft, he eased out of the water and flattened his pale body against the outer wall of the building. Near the corner, he saw a doorway. Quiet as a grave, he crept along the wall until he stood next to the opening. Then, steeling himself, he thrust one hand into the blackness. There was no door blocking his way, just a thick black drape fashioned from some heavy, coarse material. He parted the curtain and peered inside.

A dim light, invisible from outside, shone from a lantern suspended from a beam in the ceiling. The pale halo was enough for Nicholas to see that the room was empty, except for the crude mattress in the corner and the motionless figure lying there, its face to the wall. He slipped quickly into the room, letting the heavy drapes drop shut behind him. His eyes were riveted on the unmoving shape as he crept across the room. I was right, he thought, excitement rising through his fear. It's Mir's dad. His mind raced with other possibilities, but he chased them away. This was the only thing that made sense.

Nicholas dropped onto his knees beside the inert form. Gently he reached out and touched its shoulder, prepared for the struggle when the prisoner woke up suddenly. But there was no resistance. At the touch, the body rolled onto its back. Nicholas scuttled back, his face a mask of disbelief at the sight of the wide, staring eyes in the vacant Dwarfish face.

Then he heard it—a low hissing sound. And it was coming from the Dwarf. Nicholas froze in horror as the Dwarf's dead eyes blinked and its body twitched grotesquely. It's Malcolm! thought Nicholas as the blood in his veins turned to ice. The Dwarf's head jerked toward the boy, its horrible eyes wobbling insanely as they tried to focus on the intruder.

Run! Run! But Nicholas couldn't move. Suddenly, the Dwarf's body went limp and Nicholas saw something black appear in its slowly open-ing mouth. Using the last of his strength, Nicholas pushed himself to his feet and raced through the draped doorway to freedom.

Too panicked to care about the need for stealth, he had jumped into the black swamp creating a resounding splash that brought the Troll Guard on the run. Then he swam faster than a fish, slap-ping at the water noisily, coughing up the filthy swamp, afraid that, at any moment, his fear would pull him under.

Exhausted, Nicholas slumped against the damp wall of the burrow, surprised to find his clothes damp with sweat. Emmet remained silent, but he whistled softly. The tale the boy told stunned him. Serpents in league with the Demon . . . here in the Swampgrass. And using poor Malcolm's body as a host. The boy was lucky to have escaped with his life. He hoped Nicholas never learned just how lucky he was. But there was no time for musings. They had to warn King Gregor.

"Can't stay here, lad," he said.

"I've got to go back," whispered Nicholas, almost as if the thought had just occurred to him.

"No," said Emmet. "Nothing back there."

"Bell's still back there," snapped Nicholas. "In case you forgot."

"She's bewitched, lad," said Emmet, sadly. "Waste of time."

"I don't care," said Nicholas. "I'm not going without her."

The Dwarf sighed. Why were human children so unbelievably wise one minute and so astoundingly stupid the next? He shook his head. It was a great mystery—way beyond his understanding. "I'll go back."

"No," said Nicholas. "It has to be me. She won't listen to you."

He hid among the twisted roots of the swamp trees, his eyes fixed on the building into which Indolent had led Arabella the day they were captured. As he continued his lonely surveillance, he realized that he hadn't set eyes on his friend since that day. He hadn't thought it strange, until now. With a shudder, he suddenly wondered if she were still alive.

At that moment, the door of the shed opened and Arabella stepped cautiously outside. She looked about, suspiciously, and then stepped off the float onto the soft ground. Probably making sure I'm not around, thought Nicholas, bitterly. He watched as she came directly toward the place where he crouched. She stopped suddenly, a short distance away, and stared at the stunted trees, almost as if she knew he was there.

Nicholas seized the moment. He slipped out from among the trees, and waited as still as the air in the swamp. Noticing Arabella's expression switch from puzzled to recognition, he called out to her. "Bell, it's me. Nick."

"Get away from me," cried Arabella, raising her hands protectively and taking a step backward.

"Bell, wait," said Nicholas, knowing he was wasting his breath, but desperate to break the Wizard's hold on the girl. "We . . ." He shut his mouth abruptly, hurt by the hatred that flared up in Bell's dark eyes. He realized he couldn't risk telling her anything. She'd blab to the Wizard in a second. She wouldn't be able to help herself. "Just do one thing," he said, quietly. "Look at his arm. You'll see the Demon's mark. He's evil, Bell." Then Nick bowed his head and turned his back on his friend, feeling sad because he was angry with her even when he knew what had happened to her wasn't her fault.

"Shut up! You're the one who's evil," screamed Arabella. "And I don't ever want to see you again. Do you hear me? I hate you."

Nicholas turned back. "Oh, yeah," he shouted, too angry to care about getting caught. "Why don't you visit the dark shack, Bell. You'll find one of your friends in there."

The Troll grabbed Nicholas's arm, twisting it until the boy cried out. It was Vag, the one who had captured Arabella.

"Teach ya not to run away, eh." Vag swatted Nicholas on the side of the head, knocking him to his knees.

Nicholas shook his head and sighed. "I am so fed up with getting whacked," he muttered, twisting like an eel out of the Troll's grasp, landing a kick to the giant creature's knee, and breaking into a run.

Emmet was waiting for him outside the tunnel. He listened as Nicholas told him about Bell, then he stomped his heavy boots in the mud and thumped the boy hard on the back. "Sorry, lad."

Nicholas nodded. "You were right, Emmet. But I had to try."

When they reached the burrow, the first thing Nicholas did was count the Drom stones they had collected, even though he had counted them the night before. "Forty-five." He stuffed them back into the sack.

Earlier, they had decided to follow the cavern as far as it went and then try to dig their way to the surface. During their imprisonment in the dank burrow, they had inched forward, gradually exploring deeper and deeper in the buried cavern. They never heard a sound except their own voices, muffled and harsh in the thick, mildewed air.

Twice, Nicholas had stumbled upon a pile of bones, stripped clean by the process of decomposition, or something else—something living in the burrow. Horrified, he stood frozen as the piles collapsed. The clatter of bone tumbling over bone sounded hollow, as if the marrow had been sucked dry a very long time ago. Then, he was glad of the darkness.

Now, Dwarf and boy hurried away from the grisly skeletons, blocking thoughts of what had made the piles of bones from their minds. They pushed on, running their hands over the smooth mud wall.

What we need is a light," complained Nicholas, slipping the cloth sack from one shoulder and slinging it over the other. "I'd give my share of Drom stones for the Druid's staff right about now."

They had been moving cautiously through the burrow for close to an hour when Emmet suddenly gripped the boy's shoulder so tightly, Nicholas grunted in pain.

"Quiet!" whispered the Dwarf. "Listen! Back there. Something's coming."

The creatures that had tunneled through the wet, grassy bank and shaped the burrow over long years had evolved from the gases and scum that collected in pockets under the sodden soil. They were neither thinking beings nor part of a larger, grand plan. They just were. The Trolls called them Droms. They were pale, translucent things, sightless, like man-sized earthworms. One end was all mouth. Existence consisted of tunnelling and consuming the mud and the unwary insects and other swamp life forms whose movements they tracked. They tunneled and they ate—and they were always very, very hungry.

For several days now, the creatures had known of the two humans. The dull thudding of footsteps on the damp earth floor created tremors that reached the Droms, stirring the creatures' blood and whipping them into a frenzy. Without hesitating, the Droms changed courses, and from every direction, began tunnelling toward the intruders.

CHAPTER TWENTY-NINE

THE DRAGON'S GIFT

Penelope was bored to death. She had been at Dun-morrow for over a week, and so far, she hadn't even seen King Gregor yet. The Dwarves were too busy rebuilding their new country to find time for her. Oh, they saw that she had everything she needed. She was allowed to go where she chose and do as she pleased. But, what she really wanted was to be with her friends. There was no one to talk to, and she was lonelier than she had ever been. The night she had arrived with Charlemagne, she had dinner in the Lodge, but a thousand Dwarves shuffling their feet and staring at her was so unnerving she took all of her meals in her quarters after that.

The good news was that Muffy had survived her attack on the Thug and was mending nicely, according to the Dwarf healers, who had set the poodle's broken legs and put casts on the damaged limbs. Penelope had made everyone write cute sayings and sign their names on Muffy's casts. The little dog wore a halo about her neck, to prevent her from biting at the stitches under the plaster. Her side had been medicated and stitched together, and the stump where her tail had been was a white ball of bandages.

Yesterday, the healers released Muffy. On the way to Penelope's quarters, the little dog hobbled slowly on her mistress's heels, bringing smiles to the faces of the Dwarves they passed on the newly carved streets of Dunmorrow.

After lunch, and Muffy's rest, Penelope set out on her daily trek, following a different route from the previous day's wanderings. She walked for an hour. Then, worried that Muffy was tiring, she decided to turn back. But when she saw the wide stone stairway leading up to another level of the mountain, she forgot all about her decision. Scooping Muffy into her arms, she mounted the steps, almost absentmindedly, her thoughts far away with her friends. Had Miranda and the Druid reached the Dark Lands? Had they found the Crown of Ellesmere? Were they already on their way to Dunmorrow? Tears filled her eyes as her thoughts turned to Nick and Bell, taken by the Trolls. She couldn't bear to think of what the nasty Trolls would do to them, if they were still alive.

The stairs ascended higher and higher, spiralling toward the top of the mountain. The long climb had tired the girl and she was glad to see the steps end at a long corridor with high stone ceilings. A large sign hung over the entrance to the corridor. It was printed in giant letters. NO HUMANS BEYOND THIS POINT. TRESSPASSERS WILL BE DINNER.

Ignoring the warning, she gently set Muffy on the stone floor and stared into the restricted passage. Her arms were stiff from carrying the little dog and she took a minute to rub them vigorously. Then she suddenly shivered. She knew who had put up the sign. Typhon, the Dragon. She remembered hearing the stone carvers near her quarters mention that the Dragon wasn't in residence. She hadn't realized they were talking about Typhon, until now. A nagging voice told her to turn back, but she paid no attention. She wasn't going to do anything. She just wanted to look. She took a step into the passage.

Muffy was reluctant to go any farther. She dug her wobbly legs into the stone and tugged on the lead. Penelope signed. "It's okay, Muffers," she said as she picked up the protesting poodle.

Inside the Dragon's haunt, Penelope went from chamber to chamber, searching for the treasure rooms. When she finally found the first of many, she stood in the doorway, her eyes wide with excitement. Muffy slipped from her arms, uttering a shrill yelp as she landed awkwardly on the floor. But for once, Penelope didn't notice. Her wide eyes were soldered to the sparkling gems and piles of gold jewellery. Slowly she entered the cave. Then she knelt on the stone floor and picked up a handful of loose emeralds, diamonds, and rubies, letting them flow through her fingers like multi-coloured liquid.

Now that she was here, Muffy buried her head in a basket overflowing with deep blue-black sapphires, taking a second to press her cold black nose against each stone. Then, she limped about the cave, barking shrilly.

Penelope was busy wrapping herself in a long length of gold cloth that felt like water on her bare arms. In a corner of the room, she saw a gilt mirror lying on its side against the wall. Still holding the cloth, she stood the mirror upright, stepped back, and draped the gold fabric over her shoulders, like a long train, grinning at her image in the mirror. "Look, Muffs," she said, and the little dog came to her mistress and sniffed the rich material, wagging her bandaged stump, excitedly.

As the afternoon slipped by, Penelope found a miniature gold crown with tiny citrines and tourmalines set into the delicate band. Laughing, she set the crown on Muffy's head. It fit perfectly. When she reached out to remove it, the dog growled and limped away to hide among the treasures with her prize.

Draped in real gold and bedecked from head to toe in jewellery that would have paid the national debts of every country in her world, Penelope stood in the entrance to another cavern transfixed by the sight of a mountain of gold and silver crowns, tiaras, diadems and coronets, inlaid with large, twinkling stones of every size, shape and colour. She tried on a particularly ornate crown that slipped over her head and hung about her neck.

When Muffy growled from deep in her throat, Penelope spun about, startled. There, filling up the mouth of the cave was a monstrous creature, with great burning eyes and a stream of fire wafting from its gaping nostrils. It was Typhon, the Dragon.

"THIEF!" roared Typhon, spitting a ball of fire at the girl.

Penelope shrieked, leaping aside an instant before the fireball exploded in the spot where she had been standing. The size of the crater told her that, if she hadn't moved, she'd be dead. She stared at the humongous Dragon, hating herself for looking and acting guilty when she hadn't really done anything wrong.

"I-I w-wasn't s-stealing," she cried.

The Dragon's huge head whipped toward Muffy, who was growling like a wolf, and snapping at one of the creature's clawed toes. Quick as lightning, Typhon's mighty forearm shot out. His gigantic clawed hand closed over the little animal. But that didn't stop Muffy from barking. She barked all the way to the Dragon's mouth. Just as Typhon was about to pop the poodle, casts, halo and all, into his cavernous maw, Penelope fell to her knees, tears running like rivers down her cheeks.

"Please don't eat her," she pleaded. "Please, we were just playing. I wasn't stealing, honest."

"YOU LIE!" The Dragon lashed his thick tail from side to side practically demolishing the entrance, causing huge boulders to rain down upon his thick, black, scaly back.

"Please, don't hurt Muffy. I'll clean your treasure. Just don't hurt her. She's already hurt enough. So, please, please let her go. I'll do anything."

"ANYTHING?"

"Yes," said Penelope, clinging to the Dragon's hesitation like a drowning sailor clinging to a life ring.

"COME," commanded the Dragon, backing out of the entrance.

Penelope followed meekly, scrambling over the fallen boulders. She kept far enough behind to avoid being crushed to death by the creature's wicked tail. Typhon led her to a large cavern on the side of the mountain where one of the cave's mouths led directly to a wide ledge outside. In the middle of the room, an enormous black stone, streaked with red and flecked with gold, rested on its side on a cushion in a bathtub-sized basket.

Typhon pointed at the stone. "Watch it until I return. Do not take your eyes off it. Do not touch it. Do not lose it, or you will be very sorry, and so will your little friend. Do you understand?"

Penelope cowered at the sound of the threatening words, but she nodded. She even dared to speak. "W-when w-will y-you be back?"

"WHEN I'M BACK," boomed Typhon, opening his claws to release Muffy. Then with a final lash of his tail, he squeezed his huge shape through the small opening and disappeared outside.

"Okay," said Penelope to herself. "Take your time."

As soon as the Dragon left the cave, a feeling of relief washed over the girl, like sleep coming to an insomniac. Her legs went as limp as cooked spaghetti and she sank onto the floor against the wall of the cave. Muffy hobbled to her for comfort. She held the shaking animal, straightened the halo, and stared at the giant stone. Would the Dragon really let them go if she did what he wanted? What if he didn't come back for a week? How would she and Muffy survive that long without food? Was Typhon serious when he said not to take her eyes off the stone? She had to blink, didn't she?

Suddenly, a loud crack! brought her to her feet. She felt disoriented, as if she'd been jolted out of a deep sleep. Had she fallen asleep? Taking heart that the stone was still there, she dropped Muffy and walked about the cave, wondering what had made the noise. Finding nothing amiss, she placed the palm of her hand against the cold surface of the stone and walked around it. What kind of gemstone was it? she wondered. The Druid had said that Dragons worked hard to earn their treasure. Had the stone been given to Typhon in payment for a job? What, exactly, did Dragons do?

Crack! She pulled her hand off the stone and jumped away as if she'd been bitten. She backed against the wall and stared in horror as the stone cracked again and a wide seam spread along its length. The sound was coming from the stone. In a flash, Penelope knew that the object she was guarding wasn't a gemstone at all. It was a giant egg. A giant Dragon egg. And it was hatching.

"Oh my gosh! Oh no!" she cried, twisting her hands together and racing frantically to the mouth of the cave and back to the egg. "This can't be happening? What am I going to do?"

Hearing the note of panic in Penelope's voice, Muffy growled and peered about the cave for the cause of her mistress's distress. Her tiny, dark, raisin eyes fell on the egg as the seam split apart and a head poked through the shell. Then, whatever hair remained on Muffy's body bristled and she froze, eyes locked on the creature struggling to break out of the egg.

Penelope was having a fit. Her mind was running in a dozen different directions at the same time. This huge baby Dragon could gobble up her and Muffy in one bite. This wasn't part of the deal she made with Typhon. How could he have left her alone with a Dragon egg? He should have told her. And, he should have told her what to do, so she wouldn't be having a nervous breakdown. She had to think of something before that creature was out of the egg. But what? She didn't know anything about Dragons. What did they eat? What if it went outside and fell off the mountain? Could baby Dragons fly?

The black Dragon pushed the rest of its body through the shell and uncurled its long tail. It was at least twice as tall as Penelope, who noticed the small bumps on its back where its wings hadn't grown yet. So much for the flying question. The creature blinked several times as if to adjust its eyes from the blackness of the egg to the dim light in the cavern. Then it saw the girl and went as still as Muffy.

Penelope stared at the huge infant. She remembered Miranda once saying that babies were cute, but Penelope doubted that she had ever seen a baby Dragon. This creature was not cute. It was a primitive, scary thing, and the girl didn't have a clue how to deal with it. Her heart pounded against her rib cage so violently, she almost fell down, as the Dragon took its first unsteady steps toward her.

Muffy was still scared stiff and as silent as death. That's probably why she's still alive, thought Penelope, praying that the dog would stay scared.

"STAY!" she shouted. But the Dragon stretched out its long neck until its face was an inch from Penelope's. Its nostrils quivered as it sniffed the girl and the jewellery heaped about her neck.

Sweat broke out on Penelope's forehead and trickled down her face. Then the baby Dragon uttered a scratchy sound, and pressed its nose to the girl's face. Oh, no, she thought. What does it want? It's going to bite my head off. It's going to breathe fire on my face. Weak with fear, she worked up her courage and touched the Dragon's nose. It was hot. Does it have a temperature? Is it sick? Oh dear! Why had she come here? Please, just let me get out of this alive and I promise I'll never tell another lie, I'll stop stealing. I'll study harder and give up my CDs, I'll even give all my money to the poor—well, maybe not all of it, but I'll give a lot of it away.

The Dragon seemed fascinated by the brilliant glittering stones in the ropes of necklaces around Penelope's neck. It seemed particularly interested in a sparkling yellow diamond attached to a thick chain. Penelope pulled the chain over her head and dangled the precious gem in front of the Dragon's nose. Totally mesmerized, the infant's head moved back and forth as its eyes followed the stone. Maybe it'll go to sleep, thought Penelope, desperate for Typhon to return. The diamond stopped swinging while she changed hands. That's when the baby Dragon snatched the jewel and plopped it in its mouth.

"NO!" yelled Penelope, her fear of Typhon greater than her fear of the baby. She gripped the baby's jaws and tried to pry them open. "Drop it!"

The Dragon looked at her, blinked, and swallowed the stone. Then, distracted by the daylight reflecting through the mouth of the cave, the creature made a beeline for the opening. Penelope choked on her tears and raced after the creature, knowing that she'd never reach the opening before the newly hatched Dragon tottered onto the narrow ledge outside.

Suddenly, from out of nowhere, Muffy hurled herself between the giant infant and the mouth of the cave.

Penelope opened her mouth to scream at the little dog, but her throat was paralyzed with fear, and no words came out. She watched in horror as the baby Dragon stumbled toward Muffy—a whale coming at a minnow.

Muffy barked. The Dragon hesitated. Muffy barked again, and advanced one step at a time toward the curious infant. Still, the Dragon hesitated. Muffy drew nearer. The baby Dragon took a wobbly step back.

Penelope had been holding her breath for so long, she thought she was going to black out. She couldn't believe what she had seen. And neither could Typhon, who had been watching from the mouth of the cave. Slowly, the monstrous Dragon squeezed his length through the small opening and expanded to his full size. He rolled a massive boulder in front of the entrance. Then, he slowly turned, his blazing eyes traveling from Penelope to Muffy. For a long time, no one spoke.

"It ate one of the jewels," said Penelope, miserably. "I'm sorry."

"Come," said Typhon, his horrible, contemptuous voice oddly quiet.

He led the girl to one of the treasure chambers. "Give me the jewels," he said.

Penelope removed the necklaces in one sweep. The rest of the jewels followed. Finally, she slipped the golden crown over her head and placed it in Typhon's hand.

The Dragon took her to another chamber. "Wait here," he said, entering the cavern and rooting through piles of dirty, blackened junk. Penelope watched from the doorway. After the treasure chambers, this had to be where Typhon kept the garbage. She had never seen such a mess. Finally, Typhon seemed to find what he had been searching for. He dug something out of the pile and turned to the girl.

"You like crowns," he said. "I believe that you spoke the truth. You did not come to steal from me.

Take this. I pay my debts with a gift and a favour. Now go."

Penelope picked up Muffy and ran along the passage. She couldn't get away fast enough. Only when she was safely descending the stairs did she stop for a second to look at the Dragon's gift. It was the ugliest thing she'd ever seen—a cheap, dented crown. It was shiny black, and felt like plastic. Suddenly she started laughing. She had wanted the golden crown that had fallen around her neck. So Typhon gives her a piece of junk. She wondered if that was the going rate for Dragon babysitters.

"Come on, Muffsey. Let's go." But all the way back to her quarters, she wondered what the Dragon had meant when he said he pays his debts with a favour. Did he owe her a favour, or was it the other way around?

CHAPTER THIRTY

PUZZLING OVER THE PROPHECY

The roiling blackness was an impenetrable wall. Miranda swung one leg awkwardly over Lightning's back and slid to the ground, a feeling of dread gushing up inside her like a geyser.

"What is it?" She asked her travelling companion, unable to break her eyes away from the twisting, roaring phenomenon.

Behind her, she was aware of the Druid dismounting and rubbing down the horses. She felt a twinge of guilt at not helping with the task, but the power of the thing shielding the Dark Lands mesmerized her.

"Some say it is a war of the elements," answered the Druid, appearing beside her and laying his hand on her shoulder. "A great Cataclysm, and it has raged about the Dark Lands since the Demon first made her presence on earth known. The first Druid wrote in his journal that if you stare at it too long, you will lose all sense of equilibrium and be drawn into its mass."

As Miranda struggled to tear her eyes away from the Cataclysm, she realized the truth in the Druid's words. It took every ounce of will to break contact. "I wonder how he knew that," she said, blinking rapidly.

"Unless . . ."

"In his journal, he described his great struggle to keep from being subsumed into the storm, but he also knew that as he battled, it grew stronger, leaving him weakened. In the end, though, he went back, and it reached out and took him."

"That's horrible," cried Miranda. "He could be in there now."

"I do not know what is in the storm."

Miranda shuddered and, keeping her eyes averted, waved her arm toward the black swirling cloud. "I can't guide you through that. If we go in there, we'll die."

"I believe that you are, perhaps, the only one who can get us into the Dark Lands."

"You're wrong. I can't." Miranda's fear made her angry. She felt like a bug on the forest floor in the midst of a raging forest fire. Why were people always expecting her to do things she couldn't do? Why her? How had they managed before she came along? "I can't do it," she said again.

She waited for the sound of the Druid's harsh words. But when he finally spoke, his voice was gentle. "Child, I would not ask you to do something if I believed you were unable."

"That's not true," cried Miranda, turning away, knowing she was being petulant, like the child he had called her. "You made me get the Serpent's Egg, and when that wasn't enough, I had to go into Dundurum and trap the Demon so Elester could shut her away."

"Look at me, Miranda."

Reluctantly, Miranda turned her head toward the Druid and looked into his blue-black eyes. Why did she let him make her feel guilty?

"Is that how you remember what happened the last time I brought you to this world?" Naim's voice matched the sadness in his eyes. He knew that the girl was afraid. He didn't blame her because he knew she probably wasn't as afraid as she should be.

Miranda looked down at her feet. Slowly, she shook her head. "No," she said, the word a mere whisper.

"Have you been holding your anger at bay all this time?" asked the Druid, quietly.

"No, no!" cried Miranda. "I'm not angry. I've never been angry, except at the Demon . . . at evil. Naim, I'm scared."

Naim peered at the girl through narrowed eyes, as if he were trying to read her thoughts. He wasn't absolutely convinced that she hadn't been harbouring resentment against him. After all, she was only ten years old, and he had expected and was expecting more from her than he had ever expected from an adult. Hadn't she already done enough?

"It is not fair, as you and your companions would say, is it?" he asked.

"I guess," answered Miranda. "I never did anything to the Demon. I just don't understand why she wants to destroy everything." She sighed loudly. "I hate evil. I wish the Demon would die so evil would end."

Naim threw back his head and chuckled. "Evil does not need the Demon to thrive, child."

"If evil doesn't come from the Demon, then where does it come from?" asked Miranda, thoroughly confused.

"It just is, Miranda, like weeds."

"But you fight evil. How can you just go on fighting and fighting, day after day, knowing that you can never, ever, ever destroy all the evil?"

"I, too, hate evil. My entire life is dedicated to fighting it in its many guises. But let us imagine for a moment what the world would be like if the constant threat of evil were removed and our tragic struggle ended."

"Everything would be perfect," breathed Miranda. In fact, that was the sort of world she and her friends dreamed about.

"Exactly," said the Druid, as if a perfect world were a bad thing.

"What do you mean?" demanded the girl.

"Think about it," answered the Druid. "A perfect world—where enjoyment comes without effort, without struggle. I would be very afraid that by its own perfection, your ideal world would bring about a new kind of evil."

"I don't understand," said Miranda.

"Nor do I," answered the Druid, sadly.

While Naim tended to the horses, Miranda, at his bidding, gathered wild mushrooms, which grew in the soil near the roots and on the lower bark of certain trees. Miranda liked to eat mushrooms, but she couldn't tell the difference between a toadstool and a chanterel. When their chores were done, the Druid carefully weeded out the poisonous toadstools from the edible mushrooms, pointing out the differences for Miranda's benefit. Then, he lit a fire and they sat side by side on a dried-out log in silence, toasting the odd-shaped fungi on long sticks.

Despite the Druid's warning not to place too much stock in the words, Miranda couldn't help thinking about the prophecy given by the oracle mouth. And then, an image that had been lurking just below the waters of her conscious mind suddenly surfaced. She started, and the stick dropped from her hand into the flames.

"Walking serpents," she whispered, thoughtfully, as if she were trying to remember the words to an unfamiliar song.

Miranda turned to the old man. "I know what walking serpents means!"

"What are you talking about, child?"

"The prophecy!" cried Miranda. "Remember the serpent I told you about—the one that tried to stop me from going through the Portal?"

"I remember," said Naim. "What of it?"

"It didn't come out of the dark, like I thought. It came out of a dark shape that was lying on the ground. I remember thinking it was Malcolm."

"And you think the serpent was animating Malcolm for its own purposes?"

"Yes," said Miranda, her voice strong with certainty. "I think that's what the oracle mouth meant by walking serpents."

The Druid stared into the flames for a long minute. "If you are right—and I believe you are—this means that the serpent Penelope's dog caught on Ellesmere Island did not die of its injuries."

Miranda stood and moved closer to the fire. But the heat from the bright flames could not take away the chill that stole over her body and set her teeth chattering. Her mind was racing a mile a minute as she tried to remember the exact wording of the prophecy. "If the serpent is animating Malcolm . . ." She hesitated, searching for words to express her thoughts. "What I mean is . . . well . . . that's just one walking serpent. The prophecy said five walking serpents. Does that mean there are four others?"

The Druid shook his head. "I do not know," he said. "But the thought of others frightens me."

They talked for a while longer and then the Druid moved away from the fire, pulled his dark cloak tightly across his chest and settled on the ground, his back resting against the trunk of a thick evergreen tree. "Sleep now," he said. "Worrying will get us nowhere. We have a long ride if we are to reach the pass into Hate's Kingdom by this time tomorrow."

Miranda couldn't sleep. She was edgy and worried about the prophecy and about what tomorrow had in store for them. She moved the long stick through the embers, stirring up sparks that flew into the air, flared briefly, and died abruptly, like good intentions. Although the moonless night hid the Cataclysm, the black barrier was a disturbing presence in Miranda's mind. It seemed to know that she was near, and she felt it raking the air to find her.

"Come. It is time to go." The Druid's voice was filled with weariness, as though he had not slept for many nights.

Miranda opened her eyes and sat up, surprised that she had actually slept. She looked toward the northeast and her heart missed a beat. The black spinning mass was so close, she felt that if she stretched out her arm, it would disappear into the blackness and snap off. And surely it hadn't been that massive last evening. Why, if she peered long enough, she could identify the things moving within the blackness.

"Miranda . . .?"

The sound of her name startled her. She tore her eyes away from the Cataclysm and followed the Druid toward the horses. Her stomach felt hollow and her heart was a heavy weight in her chest.

They rode Thunder until early afternoon, when they stopped to stretch their stiff limbs. Within a half hour, they resumed their journey, this time on Lightning. Miranda could hear the black storm now. It rumbled like a continuous roll of thunder. The horses heard it too. They stomped nervously, their ears pressed flat against their heads. As they drew ever closer and the blackness expanded, blotting out the northeastern sky, she couldn't help but feel that she and the Druid and the two Ottawa horses were shrinking smaller and smaller, and soon the blackness would reach out and consume them.

At dusk, Naim suddenly reined Lightning to a stop. "We must leave the horses here," he said.

Miranda understood why they couldn't take the horses any farther, but her eyes spilled tears when it was time to say goodbye. Somehow, the dark journey seemed darker, more dangerous, with two than with four. Naim removed the tack from the horses, and swung the saddles, leather bags, and bridles over a thick maple limb. Then, he called the loyal animals, and placing a hand on each long, downy face, he spoke softly to the two Ottawa horses. Miranda couldn't hear the words, but she thought he was probably thanking them for carrying them so very far. Then he picked up the wooden staff and turned into the storm.

"And watch out for Trolls," cautioned Miranda, giving each animal a last, gentle rub. Then, she followed the Druid, one hand wrapped tightly about the small silver pouch holding the Bloodstones.

The light brown horses stood as still as if they were carved from Bronze, staring after the man and the girl, long after the blackness swallowed them.

CHAPTER THIRTY-ONE

ATTACK OF THE DROM

Nicholas clenched his jaw tightly to stop his teeth from chattering. Whatever was behind, following them in the black lair, was getting closer. For the hundredth time, he wished they had a light. Being able to see their stalker, even if it were the Demon herself, would be better than the images his mind conjured up. Sometimes, he imagined it was a giant spider tracking them, following their scent— its hairy legs making the dragging sound that sent shivers racing up his spine. At other times, he pictured a gigantic rat, long claws scuttling on the spongy ground—its limp tail curling behind like a dead snake.

Emmet led the way. Holding one end of the makeshift rope, he paused frequently to get his bearings. He knew all about rock and tunneling through mountains, but he was uneasy in the dank, dark burrow. He had no idea what sort of creatures made the swamp their homes. Were they savage things—all teeth and claws, or benign life forms—timid and elusive? Tightening his grip on the rope, he advanced cautiously. Without warning, he pitched forward and fell head over heels into a deep depression.

Suddenly, Nicholas felt the rope in his hand stretch and go taut, before snapping apart.

"Emmet!" he hissed. "Where are you?"

When the dwarf answered, his voice was muffled as if he were speaking through a thick wall. But Nicholas didn't miss the tone of urgency. "Get down! Be quiet!"

The boy obeyed instantly, dropping onto his stomach on the ground and sliding his body ahead in the darkness. When he felt the ground give way, he stretched his arms and reached into the pit. "Emmet?" he whispered loudly, knowing he was on the verge of panic, but unable to control his fear.

"Don't move," ordered the Dwarf. "Listen!"

Nicholas listened. The dull, scratchy sound he had been concentrating on came from behind, but now he heard similar sounds all about them, as if the mud walls of the burrow had come alive. They were trapped. He held his breath and flattened his body against the damp earthen floor. Despite the chilly dampness, sweat formed on his neck and back as he fought to remain motionless. But it was almost impossible to keep still when his instincts were screaming at him to run away as fast as he could.

"Give me your hand, boy."

At the sound of Emmet's voice, Nicholas forgot his fear for a moment and hurried to obey. Inching forward until he couldn't go any farther for fear of joining the Dwarf in the pit, he dug his toes into the soft earth and leaned into the darkness—stretching one arm and groping about until he touched a calloused hand. Locking hands with Emmet, he braced himself to pull the man out of the hole. That's when the first creature broke through the earthen wall.

Instinctively, Nicholas wrenched his hand out of the Dwarf's grasp and froze, his nerves as tense as a violin's strings. He sensed the thing going still also, waiting near his toes for the slightest movement that would pinpoint the location of its prey. Desperately, he tried to force his body into the soft ground in a wild, hopeless attempt to hide from the creature. Seconds crawled by like hours. Nicholas cursed the darkness and the helpless feeling that washed over him like a breaker crashing against a shoal. The urge to run came back with a vengeance. But what if he ran smack into one of the creatures? He knew he couldn't just lie here praying the thing near his ankles would overlook him. He had to do something. But what? How could he fight them without a weapon? It was too late now to think about recovering his sword from the Trolls.

Nicholas's eyes stung with bitter tears of frustration. He was utterly defenceless, but he was also determined not to die in this dark place where no one, including his parents, would ever know what happened to him. The thought of ending up as a pile of brittle bones, like the other poor creatures that had died all alone in this terrible place, made him choke in terror. Nothing could be worse than that. Nothing! For a second he thought of Miranda. Had her father died here? Were his bones among those he and Emmet had stumbled over in the darkness? Please, no! he thought. No! Sudden anger replaced the fear that had paralyzed his limbs. He reached into the pit. "They're here," he whispered. "We've got to face them sooner or later."

Emmet caught the boy's arm and squeezed his understanding. "Let's make it sooner," he replied, planting one sturdy boot against the wall of the depression and, using Nicholas's arm as a rope, walked up the wall of the pit.

Pain shot across Nicholas's shoulders as the stocky Dwarf climbed out of the pit. His arm felt as if it had been pulled out of its socket and stretched about a foot longer, but he didn't have time to worry about it, because the creature near his feet stirred suddenly—agitated into action by the sudden movement of the humans. Breathing heavily, Emmet scrambled onto the ground. "Get up, lad," he hissed as he moved away from the boy.

Nicholas stared after the Dwarf, and it suddenly dawned on him that he could see. Then he heard loud, gruff voices.

The army of Dwarves swarmed through the burrow, swords and axes raised to slash and chop at the worm-like creatures that covered the floor like a sea of living milk, and poked from the walls and roof like pale, giant thumbs. Although the Droms were sightless, they seemed to sense the brightness of the lights attached to the Dwarves' heads. The sudden combined light stunned them like a herd of deer frozen in the glare of headlights.

The sight of the giant, translucent beings sickened Nicholas, leaving a bad taste in his throat. He doubled over and gagged, trying to spit the reek from his mouth.

"YO!" shouted Emmet, waving his arms and wading through the fixed creatures toward his fellow countrymen. "Took your sweet time getting here. Toss me an axe, Cyrus."

Grinning, the Dwarf looked over his shoulder for the boy. What he saw stopped him in his tracks. All about him, the Droms were recovering from their stunned condition, and Nicholas was slowly disappearing into the cavernous mouth of one of the creatures, whose body convulsed as it sucked the boy into its white, slug-like length. He realized that the lad was paralyzed with terror. Nicholas's unblinking eyes bulged from their sockets and looked like golf balls. Emmet shook his burly head, neatly caught the axe thrown by Cyrus, and stomped back for the boy, the axe rising and falling again and again as he hacked a path through the Drom.

"It's okay, lad," he shouted, reaching for Nicholas's wrist. "Grab hold!"

Nicholas blinked stupidly as the Dwarf clamped his strong hand about the boy's wrist and yanked hard. He tried to speak, but fear had stolen his voice.

Holding Nicholas with one hand and the axe with the other, Emmet chopped at the Drom until the creature's convulsions slowed and then stopped. Muddy sludge splattered on Nicholas's legs and back with each fall of the axe. Satisfied that the wormy thing was dead, Emmet stuck the axe in his belt and, using both hands, pulled Nicholas free. Nicholas sprawled on the ground as motionless as the dead Drom. He couldn't feel his legs and he was too scared to look in case they were still inside the Drom.

"Get up!" Emmet ordered. "Now, boy."

"My legs . . ." croaked Nicholas, trying to push himself up, but too weak to move. "Are they . . .?"

Emmet snorted. "You got two legs, boy. Now use them." His impatience evaporated as it suddenly dawned on him that Nicholas's legs were numb as a result of being squeezed in the Drom's strong, pulsing muscles. Gently, he slung the boy's arm over his shoulder and raised him to his feet. But it was no use. Nicholas tried, but he couldn't control his legs. They buckled under his weight like over-cooked string beans.

"YO!" shouted Emmet, half-dragging, half-carrying the boy toward the other Dwarves.

Several Dwarves hurried to either side of Nicholas and took him from Emmet, moving swiftly through the Drom and along the burrow back the way they had come.

CHAPTER THIRTY-TWO

THE DARK LANDS

"There!" shouted the Druid, pointing ahead.

The roar of the seething Cataclysm drowned out his words, but Miranda stared where he pointed, squinting into the gloom. They stood at the edge of the storm. Although the black, swirling cloud obliterated light, she could just make out the two gigantic columns that framed the gateway into the Kingdom of Hate, the Demon. As they drew nearer, the columns gradually revealed details that had not been visible from a distance. In fact, Miranda saw now that they were not columns at all, but two immense statues—giant guardians from another age—carved from stone as black as midnight.

She couldn't take her eyes off the towering sentinels. Her eyes travelled up the length of the one closest to her and a gasp escaped from her lips at the sheer enormity of the figure, looming up and up until its head disappeared into the roaring twister. In the presence of such awesome power, she felt as small as a mote.

Pagan runes and awful images of monsters attacking all manner of creatures, great and small, were etched deep into the stone. Miranda didn't have to be told, she knew instinctively that the runes corresponded to the images and had been carved by something totally evil.

The Druid turned to her. "They were the last of their kind," he explained, tilting his head toward the silent sentinels. "Until the Demon set her sights on Dars-Healyng, these lands belonged to the Dars, a proud race of giants."

"What happened to them?" asked Miranda.

"Hate gave them a choice. Join her or die. They died."

Miranda waved her arm at the giants. "You mean the Dars are dead . . . every last one of them?"

"Yes," answered Naim, his voice heavy with sorrow. "These two were the last."

"Why do you keep talking about them as if they weren't statues?" said Miranda.

"Because they are not mere statues," answered Naim. "The Demon burned them with heat so intense it turned them into solid rock."

"Are you saying that these figures were once alive?" Miranda shivered at the thought of the unspeakable pain the creatures must have endured at the hands of Hate, the Demon. Sadness for the giants' fate and anger at the Demon boiled inside her. Once, she had thought that the Demon might, one day, be sorry for the horrible things she had done. Miranda knew different now. Hate was hate. And nothing she or anyone did could ever change that. There was no love in Hate. No pity or mercy. There was just hate.

"I hate her," she whispered, horrified by the blackness sweeping through her like fire. Quickly, she turned her thoughts and her eyes to the closest figure. When she noticed the black stone serpent, its tail coiled tightly about the tragic statue as if it were crushing the figure in a death grip, the hair on the back of her neck bristled. It repulsed and fascinated her at the same time. She moved closer. Why were there so many snakes in the service of the Demon? Why snakes?

The Druid opened his mouth to warn Miranda not to touch anything in this place, but before the words formed in his throat, she reached out and pressed her palm flat against the pitted surface of the Dar.

Then a scream escaped from her lips as her hand stuck fast to the burning/freezing stone. Shocked, she reacted instinctively, snatching her hand away and tearing the skin from her palm. The sharp pain that shot through her hand felt a hundred times worse than the time she had stuck her tongue on a frozen metal door handle at home in Ottawa.

The Druid rushed to Miranda's side, grasped her wrist, and peered at the raw flesh. He shook his head angrily. "I am sorry," he said. And, as Miranda stared at him in surprise, he added. "I should have foreseen that the Demon would set traps for the unwary."

"It's not your fault," whimpered Miranda, tears forming in her eyes as she and the old man stared at the torn skin sizzling on the rough, black stone figure. In seconds, the strips of skin were reduced to ashes that drifted off the stone and floated to the ground like fine black mist.

While Naim searched his cloak for something to ease the girl's trauma, Miranda gripped her wrist with her good hand, turned her face away from her companion, and cried soundlessly. Even the air brushing over the raw skinless palm was unbearable.

"If this is Hate's idea of a trap," she sniffed, finally, "she's pretty stupid. Losing a little skin off my hand isn't going to stop us." She grimaced. "It just hurts a lot."

Naim leaned forward and gently placed his hands on Miranda's shoulders. "I do not mean to frighten you, but you must tell me at once if you feel weak and tired."

Miranda stared at him, furiously blinking away the last of her tears. "Why? What do you mean?" Her eyes widened in horror as she grasped the meaning of the Druid's words. "What? What? Was there something on the stone? Am I going to die?"

"I do not know," answered the Druid, spreading a green tincture on a soft white cloth and applying the dressing to Miranda's palm.

Relief was instantaneous. All traces of pain vanished in a heartbeat. Miranda felt laughter bubbling up inside her. "Don't worry," she said. "I'm okay. I couldn't feel like this if I were dying."

But the Druid didn't share the girl's elation. His face wore a worried expression as he watched her. "Still, you are to tell me of any changes that come over you," he repeated.

"All right, all right," laughed Miranda, thinking how much like her mother he sounded when he was worried.

Then, without warning, she swayed and fell lifeless to the ground.

"MIRANDA!" Naim was at her side in a flash. He thought his heart would break as he dropped to his knees, placed his hand on the back of the girl's neck, and gently lifted her head. Silently, he cursed his failure to take care of the child. And she was a child. The other one, Arabella, had accused him of using children to do his dirty work. Well, it was true, wasn't it? He was using Miranda to do something beyond his powers.

"I will not let the Demon take you," he said in a terrible voice.

His mind raced, searching through his vast store of knowledge for a remedy to counteract the poison he believed had entered the girl's body through her skinned palm the moment she touched the black figure. Another part of his brain seethed angrily at his failed attempt to find the Elven Crown and return it to Ellesmere. Miranda was sick . . . probably dying. Without her, the quest was over, finished. Suddenly, his hand, supporting her head, felt the tendons in her neck go taut. Then her body shook and a burst of laughter erupted from her throat.

"NEVER, NEVER DO THAT AGAIN," roared the Druid, releasing his hold on her neck and rising to his feet.

Miranda couldn't stop laughing. Her head bumping on the rocky ground only made her laugh harder. "You . . . should . . . have . . . seen . . . the . . . look . . . on . . . your . . . face," she managed, between fits of giggling.

"Do you think this is a game?" The Druid's voice was ice.

"No," giggled Miranda, rolling onto her side and fighting to suppress her laughter. "Not a game."

Naim sighed. Then he turned and strode toward the opening between the giant sentinels. Slowly,

Miranda got to her feet. She tried to keep a straight face, but couldn't hide the grin as she trotted after the Druid, her eyes locked on his ramrod-stiff back.

As she passed between the black statues, keeping to the centre of the opening, well away from the creatures, a sudden infinitesimal movement on the surface of one of the figures caught her eye. Whipping her head about, she froze and peered at the statue. She could have sworn she had seen something move along the blackness. Her eyes travelled slowly up the figure's length. Nothing. Miranda blinked. She must have imagined it. She stared at the carved serpent until her eyes hurt with the strain. Surely she had been able to see its head before. But now it was gone. She looked up and there it was, hovering like a fanged thunderhead a few feet above the Druid.

"NAIM! WATCH OUT!" she screamed.

Naim came to a sudden stop and looked up. When he saw the creature swinging back and forth just above his head, his heart stopped. He remained as still as a stone, his eyes caught and held by the serpent's cold hypnotic stare. Miranda watched, sick with fear. Naim was a Druid with unimaginably terrible powers, but next to the monstrous serpent, he looked as helpless as a tiny bird, too mesmerized to fly away from its own imminent death.

The two combatants remained locked in their silent, motionless battle for such a long time that

Miranda almost screamed from the tension. The serpent opened its mouth and Miranda heard a deep hissing sound over the roar of the cataclysm. Then, like lightning, the monster snake struck, its great head a blur as it swooped down at the Druid.

Miranda gasped at the swiftness of the attack. She'd never seen anything move so fast. But Naim was faster. Dropping into a crouch, he leaped aside and raised the pale wooden staff in one smooth movement. White fire crackled from the tip of the staff. Quickly he glanced at Miranda. "Go!" he shouted, pointing the staff at a narrow passage in the rock, his voice gobbled up by the hissing and roaring sounds.

The serpent recoiled and hung suspended above the Druid, poised to strike again. Miranda darted toward the passage, body tensed to receive the deadly bite that she expected to feel at any moment. When she was safely inside, she fell against the rock wall, arms wrapped tightly across her stomach, legs weak and unsteady. She looked back for the Druid, but a wall of darkness seemed to drop between them. She struggled to go back, but the black wall blocked her way.

"Naim!" she cried, pounding her fists into the blackness. Then, she sank onto the ground and waited for the Druid to appear. But he didn't come.

CHAPTER THIRTY-THREE

DRUID
V.
SERPENTS

The serpent struck again, knife-like fangs glistening like glass. Naim raised the staff, pointing it at the great head. White fire erupted from the tip and streaked toward the creature, forcing it up and back. The serpent twisted and swerved, easily evading the deadly flames. The fire shot past the attacker and slammed into the second Dar figure, blasting a boulder-sized chunk of ebony stone from the charred giant's shoulder. The black scoria tumbled to the earth, crashing in a tremendous cloud of dust on the rocky ground. Naim jumped back to avoid being crushed to death by the giant boulder. He pressed one arm over his nose and mouth, but the black dust stung his eyes and found its way into his breathing passages, choking him.

The serpent hissed. Die! it thought, triumphantly. Die, Druid! The nictitating membrane, the third eyelid it shared with other reptiles and birds, slid across its ophidian eyes like a curtain drawn across a window, momentarily dimming the glow from a pair of burning red eyes. The curtain opened. Fire the colour of blood shot from the creature's eyes straight at the Druid, who was still blinking dust from his own stinging eyes. But he felt the heat and leaped out of the way less than a second before the red serpent-fire exploded into the ironstone wall directly through the spot where he had been standing. A bus-sized section of the wall disintegrated into rubble, spraying the area with sharp spikes of stone.

"I cannot stop this creature!" Naim whispered, his eyes frantically combing the wall for the passage where he had sent Miranda running. Where was it? It should be there, just off to his left. But the opening was gone. At the same time, he sensed a change in his surroundings—a disturbance caused by a great power. It was as though a barrier had suddenly dropped between him and the girl. But he could not let his thoughts linger on that. He had to find a way to defeat the monster snake or escape somehow.

The deadly sentinel dived at him again, its forked tongue drawn back into its throat as it readied to sink its giant fangs into the man's flesh. Suddenly the creature froze. Behind it on the other Dar statue, it felt the tremor as a ripple ran along the oily length of its serpent companion.

His enemy's behaviour puzzled Naim. Something important had just taken place. But what? Why had the creature stopped its attack so abruptly? The Druid shook his head. He couldn't think about that now because the serpent's terrible mouth was already descending. Naim pointed the staff again, calling on his Druid powers to keep it trained on the serpent's head—no matter how the creature twisted and gyrated. Then, like water gushing from a fire hose, white flames spewed from the staff. The serpent dodged and weaved, recoiling swiftly, but this time it wasn't fast enough. The fire homed in on the creature, drenching the hard plates just below its gaping jaws, searing the flesh away and leaving an open wound that wept large droplets of a pale fluid laced with blood as black as oil down the serpent's length.

The screaming hiss that came from the creature's open mouth pierced the air, slicing into the rocks and stabbing deep into the ground. A wide crack opened at Naim's feet, knocking him off balance and onto his knees at the very edge of the abyss. Shaken, he peered down into nothingness. Then he staggered wearily to his feet and braced himself to meet the next onslaught. He didn't have long to wait.

Lusting for the Druid's blood, the serpent lunged at the man. Naim aimed the staff, but a boulder crashing to the ground a few feet away slowed his reaction, and before he could move, one great fang caught him on the shoulder and tore through his cloak and into his flesh. The force of the strike lifted him off his feet and hurled him backward to land in a heap at the base of the rock wall.

Despite the throbbing pain in his shoulder and the blood creating an ever-widening stain on the front of his cloak, Naim was on his feet instantly. He had to find a way to end the battle soon. He was weary—his reflexes no longer sharp, but dull and sluggish. And his ebbing strength was barely enough to evoke the magic fire. For a second, he wondered if the giant fang that had pierced his flesh was hollow and filled with venom. Well, he would know soon enough.

His thoughts turned to Miranda. Would she know enough to go on without him, if he were unable to get to her? He should have talked to the child—told her all that he knew of the Dark Lands, so that she would be aware of the pitfalls that might be waiting for her. But, then, what did he really know about the Demon's kingdom? Only what he had read in the First Druid's journals, and they were woefully lacking in particulars.

The second serpent struck so swiftly, the Druid was caught by surprise. It came at him from the side, its broad flat head cannoning into the man, knocking him off his feet. The wide mouth snapped shut inches from his face, and Naim reeled from the fetid odour issuing from the gaping cavity.

Summoning a burst of super-human strength, Naim brought the staff down hard on the flat part of the snake's head, between mouth and eyes. He felt something crack as the blow landed true, then he leaped aside and backed quickly away, never taking his eyes off the creature's cold, burning eyes.

Get back! hissed the first attacker, slowly uncoiling itself from the mountainous Dar figure. He's mine!

Naim tensed, his eyes locked on the first serpent as it slithered purposefully down the Dar, but aware of the second recoiling at the edge of his vision, getting ready to strike. He breathed heavily. He had barely managed to stay alive battling one of the creatures. How could he fight two of them?

No! hissed the second serpent answering its companion. Mine! And it lashed out at the Druid, like a deadly fist. Naim saw the abrupt movement out of the corner of his eye and he raised the staff, praying desperately that the other creature wouldn't choose this moment to come at him from the front. Sparks danced from the staff, coalescing into a raging white ball—liquid fire that flew at the monster zooming in on its doomed prey.

The white ball burst against the serpent's armor-like scales and spread along its body like a match dropped in a river of gas. The serpent shrieked, springing high into the air, twisting and writhing in an attempt to outmanoeuvre the fire that consumed it. Then it dropped like a stone, smoke and flames streaming from its burning flesh. Down, down it plunged, its red eyes hot with hatred for the small, black-cloaked figure gripping the Druid staff.

Blinding red serpent-fire flashed from the creature's eyes, miraculously missing the Druid, but flattening the towering rocks about him into small pebbles and creating a storm of gritty dust. The human stood alone amidst the rubble. There was nowhere left for him to hide. Despite the pain from its cracked upper jaw, and its burned skin, the crazed serpent hissed with pleasure. It could already feel its fangs sink deep into the man's tender flesh. And what a feeling! It had endured the long fast, and now, not even the Demon herself could separate it from its prize.

It was almost on top of the Druid when it felt its downward momentum slowed as some powerful force caught and gripped its body. The great head whipped about.

"He's mine!" hissed the first serpent, its sharp fangs embedded in its companion's body, scaly tail coiled about the Dar like a vise.

"Mine!" The second serpent lunged at its companion, eyes focused on the gaping, weeping, wound in the other's throat.

For a second, Naim was too stunned to move. He stared in horror as the two titans clashed, coiling about each other and rolling over and over through the loose rocks, great tails lashing frenziedly. Realizing that he was still holding the staff aloft, his hand dropped like a heavy weight to his side. Then, holding one hand tightly against his bleeding shoulder, he turned and ran as fast as the wind, hands brushing the rock wall, seeking a way through the solid mass to reach Miranda. If he had looked behind, he would have noticed the trail of blood he left in his wake.

CHAPTER THIRTY-FOUR

THE DEMON'S GARDEN

"Please let him be okay," whispered Miranda. It seemed like hours had passed since she had sought the safety of the narrow passage in the solid rock. She was sick with worry. What if Naim didn't come? What then? How was she supposed to find the Crown of Ellesmere when she didn't even know where to look? Surely if he were still alive, he'd have been here by now. An image of the grim-faced Druid facing the monstrous serpent filled her mind and brought tears to her eyes. She felt guilty doubting Naim's magic, but she didn't think it was enough this time. The snake was too powerful, bigger than anything she had ever seen, bigger even than the Demon. Her shoulders sagged in resignation. "He's not coming," she said.

Ahead, the blackness swirled. Miranda stood up and peered along the narrow passage, but her eyes could not penetrate the dark. She felt that she was encased within the dark wall—had become part of it and would never find her way back to the light. She took a few tentative steps deeper into the passage. Then she heard the voices.

Mirannndaaa!

Miranda hesitated, listening intently. The voices pierced her heart, filling her with sadness.

Mirannndaaa!

"Who are you?" she asked, reaching instinctively for the Bloodstones.

Do not listen! warned the stones in her mind.

Help us, Mirannndaaa!

Clutching the Bloodstones, she tried to shut out the voices, concentrating instead on the darkness, letting her thoughts fly before her down the passage. Gradually, the darkness shifted, opening a path in front of her. It was like looking at objects through night-vision goggles.

Come to us, Mirannndaaa. Please help us!

Where are the voices coming from? she wondered, peering through the eerie half-light. Then, she looked up into the Cataclysm and paled in horror. Nothing in her young life had prepared her for the sight that met her eyes. The voices were coming from the storm. No, the voices were coming from people trapped within the raging blackness. It was a storm of human shapes—hundreds and thousands of them. For a second, Miranda couldn't speak, couldn't breathe. All she could do was stare at the teeming mass of battered and broken bodies. It was more than she could bear.

"I've got to help them," she breathed, feeling that she couldn't live with herself if she turned her back on the poor, suffering creatures.

Yes! cried the voices. Help us!

You cannot help them! She felt the Bloodstones pulse like tiny beating hearts in her closed palm.

"What do you want?" she cried.

You! They want you! screamed the Bloodstones. Run! Run!

A young woman hurtled toward Miranda, twisted limbs reaching out, straining to grasp the girl's hand. Miranda's first impulse was to grab hold of the woman and pull her down and out of the storm, but it was the look in the other's eyes that prompted her to obey the Bloodstones and run for all she was worth. The doomed creature's eyes were cold and lifeless—unblinking orbs glazed in a grotesque death gaze.

Miranda raced along the cut, keeping her eyes down and off the teeming mass of creatures that had come to the Demon because they believed they were not like others of their kind. They were not content to work and struggle, and raise families to work and struggle, knowing that at the end death awaited them as surely as night follows day. No, they were different, special, filled with a burning need to prove their superiority over other, lesser beings. Hate didn't even have to go looking for them. They always found her.

Miranda ran on, oblivious to the whining, imploring voices. Miraculously, she dodged giant boulders and long, tapered spears of ice or glass that shot out of the Cataclysm like sharp knives, smashing against the towering walls and pounding deep depressions in the hard earth. She knew that without the Bloodstones to guide her, she would have been lost by now, probably crushed flatter than a page in a book beneath one of the flying boulders. But, amazingly, she always knew when to leap aside. It had to be the Bloodstones warning her, but she didn't understand how.

The cut into the Demon's kingdom was a place of chaos and destruction. Miranda kept her eyes glued on the path ahead and her thoughts on staying alive. She couldn't allow herself to think of food or water, or a soft bed upon which to lay her stiff, aching limbs. Just keep going, she thought. There is nothing here.

Miranda jumped as something skittered across her path and disappeared among the loose stones. Besides the ghastly human shapes caught in the whirling Cataclysm, she wondered what sort of things lived in this place. Nothing friendly, she decided, picking up speed to put a safe distance between her and whatever was back there.

Abruptly, the cut widened and Miranda found herself in a fair-sized clearing. For some unfathomable reason, the storm that swirled about the Dark Lands didn't rage here. And the light was better. She stopped and took a deep breath. She'd made it this far. Perhaps she could find the Crown after all. She peered cautiously about the clearing, looking for danger. She breathed easier when she saw that it was deserted.

Slowly, she moved forward, her eyes darting from one end of the clearing to the other. What a horrible place, she thought, shuddering as her gaze came to rest on a colossal black tower that dominated the far end of the Demon's gloomy garden.

"Miranda!"

Miranda stopped and spun around at the sound of the deep male voice.

A dark-cloaked figure was standing beside a large stone table, his hand resting upon a black crate. Miranda's heart skipped a beat. The Crown! Quickly, she glanced over her shoulder back the way she had come, mentally calculating the distance between her and the passageway. She was a fast runner, but could she get there before the stranger overtook her?

Her eyes switched to the stranger. He hadn't moved. He was still in the same spot, watching her.

He was tall, perhaps even taller than the Druid. The dark cloak hid his outer garments. Miranda peered under the broad hood, but her eyes met only blackness. Where had he come from? She could have sworn the clearing was deserted less than a moment ago. Was it magic? Was he an illusion sent to trap her? He didn't seem threatening. But, then, who was he? What was he doing here? And, how did he know her name?

"Do not be frightened," said the stranger, reaching with one long hand to draw back the dark hood.

At least he has hands, thought Miranda, gripping the Bloodstones so tightly, they protested by pulsing violently. A second later, she gasped as the hood dropped from the stranger's head and she found herself staring at an Elven man. It was Prince Elester. But, no, she could see that this man and the Prince were not one and the same. Elester was leaner, and younger. Yet, there was something familiar about him . . .

"Who are you?" she asked, her voice soft with wonder. "What are you doing here? How do you know me? Did Elester send you?"

The man laughed. "I have heard that children from your world ask a million questions. I see that my friend spoke the truth."

The man's easy laughter softened his grim Elven features and made Miranda want to laugh with him. But, while he seemed nice enough, this was the land of the Demon and she wasn't about to trust him until she was satisfied that he meant her no harm. She flashed him a brief thin-lipped smile. "Well?" she pressed, crossing her arms against her chest and tapping her foot impatiently on the ground.

The tall stranger laughed again, holding up his hands in a gesture of peace. "Patience, child. I will answer your questions."

Miranda nodded. "Who are you?" she demanded again.

"I am Elven, like you, Miranda."

"Are you from Bethany? Do you know Elester?"

"Yes," answered the stranger. "But I have not seen my home or my friend in years."

"How did you get into the Dark Lands?"

The man gestured toward the narrow cut. "Through there," he said, grinning at the girl's serious expression. Anticipating her next question, he continued. "And, yes, being an Elf, I can find my way in the darkness."

"Why did you come here? How do you know me?"

The man stiffened and a look of sadness darkened his face. He didn't reply right away, and when he did, his voice was little more than a low whisper. "Those are the most difficult questions," he said, turning away from Miranda.

Miranda waited. The Bloodstones were quiet now, inert objects like ordinary pebbles. The stranger was staring at the black tower, but from his expression, Miranda knew that he wasn't seeing the structure. His thoughts were far away. Finally, he straightened his broad shoulders and turned.

"May I ask you a question?"

"I guess," said Miranda.

"Has your mother ever talked to you about your father?"

Miranda shrugged, wondering what the man was getting at. What did her father have to do with any of this?

"Has she?"

"Yes," said Miranda.

"What has she told you?"

"That he's dead."

"What would you say if I told you that your father was not killed by the Trolls?"

"I'd say you're lying," she cried out angrily.

"It is true, Miranda."

She believed him. Deep in the secret places of her heart she had always known he was still alive, somewhere. The story Naim and her mother told about how he had supposedly met his death didn't ring true. How could an intelligent man, who had fought the Trolls for years, who had studied their ways and knew them better than anyone, go into the Swampgrass alone? And, when he didn't return, why hadn't King Ruthar sent an army of Elves to free him?

"You know I speak the truth," said the stranger.

"Where is he?" Suddenly, Miranda was more frightened than she had ever been in her life. She was terrified that something was going to go wrong and destroy the fragile fabric of her hopes and dreams. Her father was alive. Please let it be true, she pleaded silently.

"He is here," whispered the stranger.

Miranda wheeled about, bright green eyes searching for another presence in the clearing. She looked everywhere, turning in a complete circle until her eyes met the darker green eyes of the stranger. "But . . . I don't understand. There's no one here but you and me," she said.

"Yes," said the tall man, his smile lighting up the bleak clearing like a burst of sunshine.

"You . . ." Miranda stared at the man as if she were seeing him for the first time. She had thought he looked familiar. Now she knew why. It was like looking at herself, the family resemblance was obvious. "You're my father." She thought her heart would burst through her chest. She wanted to run to him, but she suddenly felt shy and awkward. Would he like her? She glanced at her torn and dirty clothing and combed her fingers through her limp, straggly hair.

The man nodded, tears clouding his eyes, turning them a deep green like a meadow brook. "And you are my Miranda," he said. Then he smiled again and, this time, Miranda's found herself grinning too, as if father and daughter shared a private joke. Abruptly, she thought of the prophecy . . . something about a father and lies. She wracked her brain, but she couldn't remember how it went.

"I gave Ruthar the Bloodstones for you."

Miranda opened her palm and looked at the small green ovals nestled there. "Take them back," she said. "They're yours."

"Keep them, Miranda. They belong to you now."

"No," she insisted. "I want you to have them." She grinned. "They'll be mine someday, anyway." She held out her hand and moved toward her father.

"Stop!" warned a cold voice from behind. "That thing is not your father."

Miranda spun around. A dozen tall cloaked figures spilled from the cut into the clearing, moving out to come at the man from three sides. One figure ran lightly across the distance toward Miranda. She knew him.

"Elester!" she cried, and then she saw the anger in his face. "No!" she screamed. "You're wrong. It's him. It is!"

"Hurry," urged the voice of the man who called himself Miranda's father. "Give me the Bloodstones. They're mine." His voice was soft, but his face suddenly twisted and turned ugly with rage.

"Get over there!" snapped Elester, giving Miranda a hard shove in the direction of the cut, and striding purposefully toward the man, his sword gleaming dully in the gloom.

But Miranda stood her ground, hurt and confusion showing on her dirt-streaked face. "Who are you?" she shouted.

Then the man laughed, a horrible laugh that froze Miranda's heart. "I am your father," he said.

In the blink of an eye, a dozen arrows lodged in the man's chest. For a second, nothing happened. Then, the creature's eyes opened wide in surprise and he toppled over backwards and lay still. Miranda stood paralyzed as Elven Riders rushed to the motionless body and carried it into the middle of the clearing. Elester sprinkled a white powder over the form and set it ablaze. The Elves stood in a tight circle around the blazing corpse, heads bowed against their chests. They remained like that, unspeaking, until the body and the serpent hiding inside it were reduced to ashes.

"Take the Crown from the crate," said Elester, removing his cloak and tossing it to Andrew. "Wrap it in that."

The young Rider rushed to carry out the Prince's orders. He and some others broke the seals on the crate and removed the Golden Crown and wrapped the cloak about it. Then, grinning like a fool, Andrew picked up a flat rock and placed it inside the iron crate. The Riders resealed the box and left it where they found it.

Throughout it all, Miranda remained motionless, oblivious to what was happening around her, wandering in a faraway place in her mind where no one could ever hurt her again. When the blackness came, she was glad.

CHAPTER THIRTY-FIVE

TREE DEMONS

Miranda dreamed that she was running through a thick forest, desperately searching for something, but she couldn't remember what it was. She sensed another presence in the deep woods. She couldn't see it, but it was there, coming behind her like an icy wind. And it was hunting her. Suddenly, the ground at her feet disappeared and she was tottering on the edge of a wide gorge. On the other side, a man was shouting and waving his arms frantically.

"Who are you?" she called across the distance.

The man's answer came to her on the wind.

"Your father."

"I can't get across," cried Miranda.

"Jump!" said the man.

"It's too far." And it was too far. Even in a dream state, Miranda knew she'd never make it.

"Jump!" repeated the man. "Jump! Jump!"

Miranda closed her eyes and jumped. And, as she dropped like a brick, one thought flashed through her mind again and again. He knew! He knew it was too far!

Then something grabbed her arm, and the sickening falling sensation vanished. Miranda opened her eyes and dared to peer at her rescuer.

"Ahh!" she breathed, relief flooding through her as she recognized the stern face of the Druid. But then she twisted her arm from his grasp and drew back. "Is-is it really you?"

"Do not be afraid," said the Druid. "I am real enough, child."

Miranda noticed the shine on his cloak near his shoulder. She knew it was blood, dried now. "You're alive." She wondered why she suddenly felt like crying.

"Of course I am alive," the man snapped, and then the harshness left his voice. "And so are you, I am happy to see."

She looked about, taking in her surroundings. It was night. Overhead the stars winked through the canopy of tall trees. The air smelled fresh and minty, tinged with the scent of hardwood burning on a nearby fire, and the mouth-watering aroma of something cooking. The only sounds that reached her ears were the burblings of a small brook and the crackle of the flaming hardwood logs. Gradually, it all came back to her; the chaotic race through the cut; the menacing black tower looming like the Demon over the clearing; her father . . . no, the man who pretended to be her father . . . Miranda pressed her hands into her eyes. "Oh, Naim," she whispered. "I wanted it to be him. I wanted it so badly."

The big man nodded slowly, reaching for Miranda's small hand and enclosing it in his fist. "Elester told me everything," he said, his anger clipping the words and turning them into bullets.

"He wanted the Bloodstones."

"Yes," agreed the Druid. "Without the stones, you are less than nothing to the Demon."

Miranda sniffled. "I believed him. Once, I even thought of the prophecy, the part about a Father's lies, but I didn't listen."

"I am truly sorry, child."

"Don't be," said Miranda, sniffling again as she pulled the silver pouch from the neck of her shirt and gripped it tightly. "He didn't get them. And that means I'm still a threat." She stared at the tiny pouch for a second before slipping it back inside her shirt. "They didn't warn me," she said, looking at Naim questioningly. "They just went still. I wonder why."

"I have no knowledge of the Bloodstones," said Naim. "Ask Elester when he returns." He planted the Druid staff in the earth and pushed himself to his feet, groaning with the effort. "Come now. You must eat. We have a long journey before us."

"Wait, what about the Crown?"

Naim flashed one of his rare grins. "The Crown is safe."

"Where is Elester, anyway?" asked Miranda, following the Druid's shadow to a small fire blazing cheerfully within a circle of stones, a safe distance from the trees.

"Gone," said the Druid, pointing at an iron pot sitting on one of the flat stones bordering the fire. "Eat."

"Gone," whispered Miranda, mimicking the Druid and sticking out her tongue at his back. She found a tin plate and spoon, and scooped out several ladles of the thick stew. Then she plopped on the ground by the fire and ate until she thought she'd burst. When she had finished, she rinsed the plate and tin spoon in the brook and went looking for Naim.

She found him, deep in whispered conversation with several cloaked figures, their heads close together. She opened her mouth to call his name, but instead, slipped behind a large tree trunk and crept toward the circle of men. Why were they whispering? The answer was obvious and it hurt worse than a slap. They were whispering because they didn't want her to hear what they were saying. The hurt flamed into anger. After coming all this way, after going into Hate's kingdom to find the Crown, how dare they treat her like a stupid kid! She crept closer. Once, she saw Naim stiffen and peer into the trees. She froze, hardly daring to breathe. Only when she saw him turn back to the others did she move closer.

Suddenly she stopped, a wicked grin stealing over her face. Quickly, she reached for the soft, silver pouch and poured the six Bloodstones into her hand. Cupping them tightly, she focused on the thick stand of trees looming above the conspirators like giant guardians. She cloaked the great evergreens in long black garments, then she made them grow, sending them shooting higher into the moonlit sky. Next, she willed their branches into long, clawed limbs, and planted burning red eyes in the blackness. Then, she waited, the fist clutching the Bloodstones pressed against her chest.

Suddenly, the world about her exploded.

"DEMONS!" shouted one of the men.

Mingled with the shouts, Miranda heard the sound of swords slipping from sheaths and the thunk as weapons sliced through illusory black garments and lodged deep in the hard wood.

Giggling, Miranda turned away and ran toward the camp. She had taken only a few steps when the Druid's stern voice stopped her in her tracks.

"Come here, at once!"

Shame turned her face red and hot as a crimson sunset. But then, her anger flared again. She clenched her fists and marched out of the trees, stopping a few feet from the Druid. For a moment, Druid and Elven girl glowered at each other, but it was Miranda who finally lowered her eyes.

"Is this your doing?" Naim's voice was as emotionless as frost as he fought to control his anger.

"You mean this?" asked Miranda innocently, waving her arms toward the Elven Riders. She was pleased to see that many of them were still struggling to dislodge their sword blades from the thick bark of the trees. The Druid didn't speak. He was glaring at her as if he didn't know her . . . as if she had murdered someone. His silence fuelled her anger. "Yes! OK? I did it. Are you happy now?"

For a second, absolute silence fell over the forest. The tall, dour men stared at the small girl, their faces registering astonishment and amusement at the same time. Then a figure detached itself from the others and moved toward Miranda. Dropping onto one knee, the Prince of Ellesmere gently gripped her shoulders.

"But why, Miranda?" he asked, his eyes boring into her, his concern for her making her feel mean.

"B-because," stammered Miranda, all the anger dissolving as quickly as it had flared up.

"I do not understand," said Elester.

"Because I came to find Naim . . . and then I saw all of you whispering like you didn't want me to hear

. . . and then I knew you didn't trust me . . . and it made me angry because I came all this way to help you . . . and then nobody asks me to come when you're having a secret meeting in the woods . . ." She looked past Elester from one dark face to another until her eyes, shining like burning emeralds, rested on the tall form of the Druid. "You said I'm less than nothing without the Bloodstones. You didn't come to Ottawa for me, did you? You needed my magic."

"That is not what I said," sighed the Druid, heavily. "And yes, I needed the Bloodstones." Then, gripping the staff until his knuckles were white, he strode into the forest, a tall dark figure blending with the shadows.

"Look at me, Miranda," said Elester, taking the girl's hands in his. "We have no secrets here."

"But, I thought . . ." Miranda felt sick. She wanted to look away, but her eyes wouldn't obey. "Then, why were you whispering?"

"Because we are still in the shadow of the Dark Lands, and the Demon's hunters are astir."

"Oh," she said, her face going white as a ghost as she realized what she had done.

"Yes," said Elester. "My men thought they were being attacked, and their shouts announced our location to the Werecurs."

"Oh, no!" cried Miranda. "These Werecurs are coming, here?"

Elester nodded.

"I'm sorry," said Miranda, her voice thin with dread. "I was angry. I didn't know."

Elester patted her shoulder and stood. He wasn't about to scold her. She was still hurting from her encounter with the false one. That her hurt would turn to anger was not unexpected. Nothing he said could make her feel worse than she already felt. She knew what she had done was wrong. He read it in her eyes. "Do not be too hard on the old man," he said. "He needed the Bloodstones, but know that he would give up his life to protect yours." He reached for her hand. "Come now. You can rest while we ready the horses."

"No," said Miranda, removing her hand from the other's firm grasp. "I want to wait for Naim. And I need to be by myself for a little while."

Elester nodded, and turned toward the camp. "It is good to see you again, Elven girl," he added over his shoulder.

Sickened and ashamed of her behaviour, Miranda waited for the Druid to return. She knew she wouldn't rest until she told him how sorry she was. A short time later, the Druid found her, fast asleep, curled up on the ground near the spot where he had entered the forest. The man sighed as he cradled the girl in his arms and carried her back to the camp, wrapping his heavy cloak about her to protect her from the dew-drenched grass. Then, he dropped onto the ground by the fire, his back against a dead tree, staring at the dying flames until the embers turned cold and the gray early morning light drove away the darkness and the shadows. When Elester touched his shoulder, he rose slowly to his feet, his shoulders sagging from the weight of his long struggle against the Dark Ones.

"We must go now," said Elester. "Wake the girl."

CHAPTER THIRTY-SIX

THE WINGED HUNTERS

They rode in silence, following the foothills of the Mountains of the Moon. They rode swiftly, bared heads bowed low over the horses' manes. Miranda was in her usual place behind the Druid, who had been overwhelmed to discover that the Elves had brought along his own mount. Miranda had wrapped her arms about Avatar's great downy face. The big red roan had saved her life once and she loved him from the bottom of her heart. The horse seemed to remember the girl, because he pressed his soft nose into her neck and whickered animatedly. She was happy to see Thunder and Lightning trotting contentedly behind the Riders. Now, she idly stroked Avatar's side as she searched her mind for words to say to the Druid. Finally she spoke.

"Naim?"

"Hmm?"

"I'm sorry I turned the trees into monsters."

"Hmm."

"Are you still mad at me?" She wished she could see his face.

"I am not angry." Naim knew the girl had to talk—get things off her chest. He waited, knowing he wouldn't have long to wait.

"My mom calls what I did 'acting out.' She said kids do it when there's no other way to get the mad out." She stared at the Druid's back.

"Your mother was always wise," said the Druid.

"She's a psychiatrist," chirped Miranda, proudly.

"I do not know that word," said the Druid.

Miranda thought for a second. "It's like an Elven Healer, only she works with mental disorders."

"Do you know why you were acting out?" asked Naim.

"I think," said Miranda. "I remember it hurt so bad when I knew that man wasn't my father, I didn't think about getting angry. Then, when you woke me up, I remember I felt like kicking things, but I didn't. After, when I saw you and Elester and the others in the woods, I finally found something to kick. But I wasn't really mad at you or the Riders."

"No," agreed Naim. "You were angry with that creature and with yourself for believing the lies he told you."

"I guess," answered Miranda, knowing that he was right. "So you're not angry at me?"

"I am not angry."

"Really?"

"MIRANDA, I AM NOT ANGRY!"

"Well, you don't have to shout," quipped Miranda, grinning mischievously.

"HUNTERS!" shouted one of the Riders.

The company reined in their horses and wheeled about. Miranda frowned, squinting into the sky toward the Dark Lands. She saw nothing. She tugged on the Druid's cloak. "Where?" she asked, her heart pounding. She had heard about the Werecurs, but had forgotten about them when they had not shown themselves in the Dark Lands.

"There!" said Naim, pointing the staff at a black smudge in the eastern sky.

It looked like a thundercloud. But, as Miranda stared, she saw that it came with a purpose, defying the wind and streaking through the sky like a great, black inkblot spreading across a blotter. Elester rode back, urging his mount to a stop alongside Avatar. Noble stretched his long neck toward Miranda and nuzzled her hand.

"They have not spotted us," said the Prince, his eyes focused on something in the distance. "There!" he said, pointing south.

Miranda squinted as she scanned the vast countryside. "What?" she asked.

"Movement," said Elester. "At the edge of the forest."

"You are right, my friend," said the Druid, glancing from the forest to the Werecurs.

Elester homed in on the tiny figures, his keen Elven eyes focusing like binoculars. "It looks like a company of Dwarves," he said. "They are not aware of the danger yet."

"Can't we do something?" cried Miranda. "Warn them, or . . ."

Elester exhaled loudly. "They are too far away."

"Naim?"

When the Druid didn't reply, Miranda reached for the Bloodstones. She felt them stir in her hand, pulling, trying to absorb her being into their cool heat. She held herself back, but let them take her thoughts. Then, astonishingly, she was flying, actually streaking like a meteor toward the band of Dwarves, the hills and flatlands a blurred green patchwork quilt below. She thought she recognized fine streaks of red running through the green, but she was moving too swiftly to focus. Faster and faster she went, too stunned by what had just happened to think about what she would do, or if she could do anything, when she reached the unwary travellers.

Naim felt the girl's body slump against his back. Startled, he reached back and caught her arm, preventing her from slipping off the great horse. "Miranda! Elester, the girl."

Elester leaped from the saddle and caught Miranda. He laid her on the ground, his hand pressed against her neck seeking a pulse, as the Druid dismounted and hurried to join him.

"She lives," he said, but his face wore a puzzled frown. "There is something wrong here," he said, looking at the older man. "Tell me what happened."

"Nothing happened," answered the Druid, impatiently, feeling Miranda's unblinking eyes fixed on him. He rubbed his hand over his forehead, pushing the straggling strands of black and white hair off his face. "Well, man, out with it. What is wrong?"

"Miranda is alive, but she is not here."

The Prince's words fell on the Druid like ice water. "What do you mean, she is not here?" he demanded. "Where is she?" Suddenly he was afraid of Elester's reply. Then he noticed the girl's small clenched fist, and he knew the answer. He thumped the ground with the blunt end of his staff. "THUNDER!" he boomed. "That child is using the Bloodstones!"

Elester nodded slowly. "Somehow, she has learned to travel without form."

Naim gripped the wooden staff. "But she is a just a child, Elester. The Stones are inert in her world. How has she learned this art? Since she has been here, she has not been out of my sight for longer than a few hours." He squeezed his eyes shut for a moment before continuing. "She does not realize the danger."

"True." Elester agreed with the Druid. The Bloodstones were a potent magic and Miranda was using them capriciously. "She is not directing the Stones, rather she is trusting them to lead her."

The Druid sighed. "I should not have given them to her. I should have thrown them away."

"They were never yours to give, or to throw away," said Elester, gently. "They belong to her, and eventually, they would have found their way into her possession."

Naim turned away from the girl's motionless form and her steady, sightless gaze. She is right to look at me like that, he thought. I am to blame for all that has happened to her. Shielding his eyes with his hand, he peered across the hills. "What do you see, Elester?" he asked.

Elester motioned to Andrew, the young Elven aide who had discovered Laury's body amongst the carnage in the Riders' barracks in Bethany.

"Stay with the girl," he said, and then he joined the Druid.

Miranda dropped to the earth. Forgetting, or not realizing, that she was an insubstantial being—a thing composed of thought and air—she tensed in anticipation of her body slamming into the ground. When she landed as gracefully and as lightly as a butterfly balancing on the petal of a buttercup, she couldn't have hidden her grin if she had found herself in the middle of a host of Demons.

She landed directly in the path of the company of Dwarves. She estimated their number at around thirty. Not enough. A thousand Dwarves wouldn't stand a chance against the swarm of Hunters. She sprinted to intercept the small party, waving her arms and pointing behind them at the death cloud expanding by the second. As she ran, she shouted at the top of her lungs. "LOOK BEHIND YOU!"

But the Dwarves didn't react. They marched toward her, oblivious to their peril. Abruptly, Miranda stopped, staring at the approaching company, her mouth open in shock. They couldn't see her! She had come to save them and they couldn't even see her. Still, she ran until she was among them, dashing from one to the other, screaming in frustration. Her hands flashed through their sturdy bodies as she tried to grab hold of their clothing. She had to make them listen.

Then she saw Nicholas.

She flew to him, hoping against hope that she could reach through the layers of mist that separated them. Here was her friend, the boy she had known all of her life. If anyone could hear her, it was Nicholas.

"Nick!"

No reaction.

Back where her body rested on the ground, Andrew noticed the girl's knuckles turn white as her fist tightened about the Bloodstones.

Nicholas slowed. He tilted his head and listened intently. He felt uneasy, as if he had missed something important. Danger! Run! For a second, he thought of Miranda. Then he shook his head, wondering why he felt as if he were being sucked into the black swamp. Danger! Run!

Something was wrong. Nicholas felt something stirring the air about him—something that had no form but was as real as flesh and bone. He didn't know what it was. He couldn't see it. But he knew it was there and it was trying to warn him of . . . Danger! Run!

He paused and looked about. Then he gripped Emmet's arm and pulled the Dwarf to an abrupt halt. "What's that?" he asked, pointing at the black smudge in the sky.

"HEAD FOR THE TREES!" yelled Emmet, yanking his arm out of the boy's grasp and giving Nicholas a hard push.

"EMMET, WHAT'S GOING ON?" shouted the boy.

"HUNTERS, BOY! MOVE!"

Nicholas and the others raced toward the dense forest, but Miranda could see that they were too late. The Werecurs struck like a hurricane. She watched helplessly as the Demon's hunters dove at the fleeing Dwarves, sharp claws slashing, cruel teeth snapping.

"NO!" she screamed, as all about her Werecurs swooped upon Dwarves, driving their wicked claws through flesh as they snatched up the bodies and soared into the sky, shrieking in triumph. Miranda couldn't stand it. Blindly, she charged at the winged creatures, her fingers reaching and curling to rip the flesh from their foul bones. But she was as helpless as a breath and her hands grappled with thin air.

Let go! Let go! The Bloodstones screamed in her head.

Miranda resisted, until she saw one of the creatures homing in on Nicholas. Her friend watched the monster come for him, but was unable to move. His fear of the creature paralyzed him, making him an easy prey. Miranda let herself go, let the Bloodstones consume her. She felt the change come over her immediately, filling her with unimaginable power. Ignoring the Werecurs, her eyes swept across the clearing, taking the measure of each Dwarf. Then, they settled on Nicholas and she released the power.

The Dwarves stopped fleeing and turned to face the predators. The Werecurs screeched gleefully. They flew in short circles, weaving like great drunken bats. Abruptly, the Dwarves and Nicholas disappeared. The screeching became howls as the Werecurs turned upon each other, biting and clawing in rage over the loss of their prize. Then, where seconds ago the Dwarves had been running for their lives, a throng of mammoth creatures sprang up from the earth. They were hideous things with hungry eyes and white foam bubbling from slits in their crazed faces. As they closed in on the grounded hunters, claws like stilettos shot from their twisted limbs. The Werecurs screamed in terror, their huge fleshy wings flapping like sheets on a clothesline in a high wind. Trampling their weaker brethren, they turned and ran away, hopping and flapping and finally rising into the sky.

Nicholas couldn't believe his eyes when the horrible winged creature suddenly turned away, as if it could no longer see him. The boy seized his chance and ran toward the shelter of the trees, his legs pumping faster than his racing heart. He knew that something had happened back there—something he didn't understand. He wondered if he'd ever know what made the Hunters give up the hunt.

Miranda concentrated on her monsters, sustaining the illusion until the Werecurs were a blur in the distance. She peered into the trees for a glimpse of Nicholas, but he had disappeared along with the Dwarves. Then, she was flying again, back over the green fields that were laced with long thin red ribbons. Thank goodness Nicholas had escaped the Trolls. But she was deeply troubled. What had happened to Arabella?

CHAPTER THIRTY-SEVEN

DUNMORROW

The sun had set in a spectacular blaze of crimson when Prince Elester called a halt for the night, and the company of Riders smartly set up camp and saw to their horses. Miranda helped them, offering to look after Avatar and Noble and the two Ottawa stallions. As she rubbed down the horses with soft, sponge-like cloths, and talked to them, giggling whenever they nibbled at her clothing or nudged her with their soft noses, she felt the tension leave her body for the first time in days. It was pleasant, uncomplicated work, driving away the nightmares and soothing her mind.

Elester found her there. He stood and watched as she playfully scolded the four spirited animals and he marvelled that, for a few precious moments, the terrors had gone, allowing Miranda to be a carefree child again.

"Come, Miranda," he said softly, saddened to be the one to spoil the moment and bring the fears flooding back. "We have spotted Nicholas and the Dwarves." He thought he saw the girl's thin shoulders sag slightly as if a heavy weight had suddenly settled there. She gave each horse a last gentle stroke before turning away.

Miranda was so happy to see Nicholas, she laughed and cried at the same time. Nicholas, too, was overcome, although he tried to hide it by coughing hoarsely.

"It was you!" he whispered later, when they finally found themselves alone. "Somehow, it was you. But how did you . . . ?"

Miranda grinned. "Don't ask. We couldn't warn you. You were too far away. And we couldn't let the Werecurs see us, because of the Crown. I didn't even think. I just grabbed the Bloodstones and suddenly I was there."

"I knew," said Nicholas. "Really. That's what made me look back. I felt danger and then I thought of you."

"No kidding?"

"Really," repeated Nicholas.

"Where's Bell?"

Nicholas shook his head. "I tried to get her to come with us, Mir, but . . ."

"You mean she's still there?" Miranda couldn't stop the tears that filled her eyes and spilled down her cheeks. "You left her there?"

"Not his fault," said Emmet, coming up beside Nicholas and laying his large hand on the boy's shoulder.

Elester clasped the boy's hand firmly. "It is good to see you again, Nicholas."

"Where's Laury?" asked Nicholas, his eyes searching for his friend among the other Riders. When the Prince hesitated before answering, Nicholas felt his heart fluttering like a bird in a cage. Later, he said that was when he knew something bad had happened.

"I am sorry," said Elester, after he told the boy how the Captain of the Riders had met his death.

Nicholas nodded. "Me too," he said. And then he turned away and walked alone for a long time, trying and failing to make sense out of all the violence and bloodshed. It was a long time before he joined Miranda and the others about the fire and then, the companions talked till the early hours of the morning. Nicholas told them that Indolent, sporting the Demon's mark on his arm, seemed to be leading the Trolls. He told how the evil Wizard had bewitched Arabella. Finally, he told them what he had seen in the dark, isolated shed.

"Miranda does not believe that Malcolm has been subverted by the Demon. She believes that whatever killed the Dwarf is using its body as a host," said the Druid. He turned to Miranda. "Tell Elester about your dream, the part about Ruthar."

Miranda nodded. "I followed this old man down into an underground room where King Ruthar was lying on a long table. The man held the King's hand and then, King Ruthar sat up and gave him a small black thing that looked like a marble. As the man looked at the thing in his hand, it burst apart and then he started screaming." She stopped for a second, searching her mind for any missing details. "Oh, when King Ruthar opened his mouth, I saw a serpent's tongue."

For a moment no one spoke. Then, Elester whistled softly. "This is incredible," he said. "It explains so much." He looked at Miranda. "The man you followed, did you recognize him?"

"Yes," answered Miranda. "I knew his name in my dream, but I don't remember now. I think he was one of the Erudicia."

"Mathus!" said Elester, remembering, again, the night his father's oldest friend had come to his room. The old man was fretting because he kept hearing the dead King calling to him. Elester hit his fist against his palm. Then he told the others about the strange visit from Mathus in the middle of the night. "It fits with your dream, Miranda." But he was beginning to wonder if it really were a dream. "When he left me, he probably went straight to my father. I meant to send someone to check that everything was as it should be, but then the Erudicia sent me . . ." He thought for a second. "Got rid of me, now that I think of it . . . by sending me off on a wild goose chase."

"I still don't understand what's going on," said Nicholas, who had been listening avidly. "Why are the Demon's creatures using dead people as hosts? What is it they want?"

"What they have always wanted," answered Naim. "To destroy us."

"Trolls getting ready for war," said Emmet.

With a mounting sense of urgency, the others listened as Emmet gave details of the massive war machine being assembled in the Swampgrass.

"Did you learn where they plan to strike first?"

Emmet shook his head.

"Dunmorrow," said Hirum, slapping his hand against his knee. "Trolls hate Dwarves."

"I wonder," said the Druid, staring into the flames. "From what Nicholas and Emmet have told us, the Trolls are not making the decisions in the Swampgrass."

"What are you thinking, old friend?" asked Elester.

"I am thinking that five days from now, you will be crowned King of Ellesmere." The Druid paused long enough for the others to stir restlessly.

"So?" said Nicholas.

Naim ignored the boy. "And I am thinking about something I read in the Elven Annals. Who wears the Crown, rules.

Elester stared at his old friend. "You think they will strike Ellesmere?"

The Druid nodded. "I do."

The Prince stood and strode toward the Riders, many of whom were already asleep, wrapped in their heavy travel cloaks. He glanced over his shoulder. "I am going home," he said.

They left within the hour. The Riders shared their mounts with the Dwarves, and Nicholas rode Lightning, who seemed to remember the boy. This time, he was pleased to let Emmet climb onto the horse's back behind him. Miranda had to laugh at the sight of the miserable Dwarves clinging to Nicholas and the tall Elven Riders for all they were worth.

A day and a half later, they rode through the arched entrance into a huge courtyard in Dunmorrow, mountain kingdom of the Dwarves.

Miranda gazed at the lofty peak, struck speechless by its beauty and majesty. It was not at all like Dundurum, the Dwarves' former country. Mount Oranono wasn't black, but white—a pure, blinding, dazzling white that shone with the brightness of polished silver. She looked at Nicholas and noticed that her friend's eyes were as round as loonies as he stared in wonder at the awesome spectacle.

The Dwarves were busily carving out their new country in Mount Oranono, one of the hundreds of peaks that comprised the Mountains of the Moon, or as the Dwarves called them, the White Mountains.

The White Mountains fell under the guardianship of the Dragon Typhon, Chief of a clique of gargantuan black fire-breathing Dragons. After the Dwarves' land was sucked into the Place with No Name along with the Demon, Typhon offered the Dwarf King a ninety-nine-thousand-year lease on Mount Oranono. Gregor, King of the Dwarves, had accepted the terms of the lease, even the one stating that the Dwarves would redo the Dragon's haunt, which was located near the rocky summit.

The White Mountains were formed in the Permian period, toward the end of the Palaeozoic era, between the Carboniferous and Triassic periods, which lasted forty-five million years. They had been standing before the Permian extinction gave rise to the dinosaurs, before the Elves came from Empyrean, before evil fell on the world. The veins of white gold and fine silver running through the rock gave the mountains their brilliance.

"Nick! Mir!" came an excited voice from the courtyard.

Nicholas groaned as Penelope raced across the open courtyard. Miranda burst out laughing when she spotted Muffy's green body bouncing in Penelope's arms. She was glad the little dog had survived the injuries inflicted by the Thug. When she had helped clean and dress Muffy's wounds, she had not expected the animal to last on the long journey to Dunmorrow. She was amazed to see that it had completely recovered. She removed Naim's staff from its straps alongside the saddle and whacked her friend on the leg, sliding it back in its place before the Druid noticed.

"Ow!" growled Nicholas, rubbing the sore spot on his leg and glaring at Miranda. "What did you do that for?"

"Stop being mean to Penelope."

"I'm never mean," said Nicholas.

"Yeah, right," laughed Miranda. Then she became serious. "Muffy attacked the Thug and almost died. That's why Naim sent them to Dunmorrow. So just try to be nice for once."

"Okay, I'll try," muttered Nicholas. "As long as she doesn't start whining or making really stupid comments."

"The King is waiting," said a Dwarf guide, but when Miranda started to follow the adults, Naim turned to her. "Stay here. We will join you in the lodge."

"But, I want to come with you," said Miranda, knowing she was pouting like a child, but not caring.

"Not this time," said Naim firmly, turning and striding after the others.

Nicholas draped his arm about Miranda's shoulder. "Don't mind him, Mir. Come on, I'm starving."

The Ottawa friends followed their guide along a broad street. They stopped now and then to admire the fine stonework of a score of Dwarf stone carvers. Miranda's eyes filled with tears of joy when she noticed that the walls on both sides of the street were reserved for the Dwarf histories. It had hurt as much as the death of a loved one when the Demon's army had destroyed Dundurum along with thousands of years of Dwarf history that had been told through pictures painstakingly carved into the stone walls, year after year, from the time of the first Dwarves.

Something in one of the carvings caught her eye and she went to take a closer look. It was a picture of a girl standing alone in the midst of unbelievable devastation. Coming toward the girl was a terrifying, four-armed monstrosity, at least twenty times her size. With a shock, Miranda realized that she was the girl in the carving. For a second she saw it in her mind as clearly as if it had happened a minute ago. She was there, alone on the ruined street near the Dwarf capital of DunNaith. She saw the black monster narrowing the distance between them, long claws dripping with blood from a deep wound the creature had inflicted in its own chest. She saw, again, the fire in the Demon's eyes and the white, blood-flecked fangs gleaming like ice picks in the creature's hideously grinning mouth.

Miranda turned away, unable to stop the trembling in her legs. She couldn't get over how tiny she looked next to the Demon. How had she ever mustered the courage to trap Hate? If she had seen it carved in stone first, she could never have done it.

"Hey, look!" cried Nicholas, excitedly. "I'm here, too."

He tapped the Dwarf carver on his shoulder and pointed to a boy waving a short sword as he charged into a pack of hairless, four-limbed creatures. "That's me," he said, his chest swelling with pride.

The Dwarf carver grunted noncommittally and went on with his work.

"I think it would be more accurate if you were running away," said Penelope, stifling a giggle.

Miranda joined in the ribbing. "Or peeing your pants," she laughed.

Nicholas flushed red. "I don't see you here, Penelope," he sneered. "But, I guess they don't have a small enough space to show what you did."

"Shut up," snapped Penelope. And Muffy backed her up by growling viciously at Nicholas.

"Yeah, Nick," echoed Miranda. "That's mean. Shut up."

Their guide led them to the lodge, a huge brightly-lit communal dining room furnished with long harvest tables placed in rows from one end of the long stone chamber to the other. Unlike Elves, who prefer to dine late in the evening, Dwarves eat at the same time every day, exactly 6:00 p.m. Since it was now several hours past sunset, the lodge was deserted. Andrew and the other Riders were already there and they called to the youngsters to come sit with them.

"I hope they have sauerkraut and sausages," said Nicholas, thinking of the last meal he had enjoyed with the Dwarves. "I really liked that."

"Euww!" said Penelope. "I hate sauerkraut. It causes gas."

"You are so revolting," said Miranda. "Be quiet."

During the meal, which, to Nicholas's delight and Penelope's horror, turned out to be sauerkraut and smoked sausages, the youngsters shared their adventures. While Muffy ravenously attacked Penelope's dinner, the girls listened, horrified, as Nicholas recounted his ordeal as a prisoner of the Trolls in the Swampgrass. Nicholas and Penelope felt their faces turn pale as death as Miranda told of her journey into the Dark Lands. And all three companions giggled hysterically over Penelope's encounter with Typhon, the Dragon. Then they fell silent, their high-spirits flattened by a single thought that stuck their minds simultaneously. Arabella wasn't here to tell her story.

Suddenly, the lodge door burst open and Gregor XV, King of the Dwarves, stomped into the room, followed by the Druid, Prince Elester, and Emmet, in that order. There was a great deal of boot thumping and backslapping as the old friends met. The King's face turned as red as raw beef when he saw Miranda. He expressed his pleasure by giving her three hard whacks on her back that sent her reeling. "GOOD! GOOD!" he roared, a silly grin plastered on his blunt Dwarf face.

Then Muffy farted.

For a second, a heavy silence settled over the lodge as everyone stared at the tiny dog. Penelope, turning the colour of her hair, tried to catch the poodle, but Muffy, sensing trouble, wriggled out of the girl's grasp and scooted off to hide under a chair at the other end of the room.

Naim flashed Penelope a dark look as he and Elester followed Gregor from the room.

"We'll get her," offered Andrew, motioning the Riders to spread out as they advanced toward the miniature green terror.

Miranda thought she'd die laughing at the sight of the big, tall Riders closing in on the teeny animal. Just as one Rider lifted the chair away and Andrew dropped onto his heels and reached for the dog, Muffy bared her teeth and pounced. Caught off guard by the poodle's ferocity, Andrew toppled over backwards. Muffy landed on his chest, leaped onto the floor, sunk her teeth into the Rider's leather boot, and tugged with all her strength. By this point, all of the Riders, except the object of Muffy's attention, were holding their sides, doubled over with laughter.

Then the Druid appeared in the doorway.

Sensing a new threat, Muffy released her hold on Andrew's boot and, barking shrilly, tore across the room, a small green streak. Naim didn't even see her coming. The dog leaped for the staff, but missed and caught her teeth in the wide sleeve of the Druid's cloak. Naim started, staring at the creature hanging from his cloak, growling savagely.

"Penelope," he said, his voice deadly quiet. "Take this beast away from here before I turn it into . . ."

". . . a balloon," shouted Nicholas.

". . . a stump," laughed Miranda.

". . . a mat," finished the Druid.

Penelope hurried across the room and caught Muffy's weight in one arm; her other was busily dislodging the creature's teeth from the Druid's cloak. Fighting to keep a straight face, she flew out the door, "Bad Muffsey!" echoing in her wake.

Naim glared at the other occupants of the room. The Riders glanced sheepishly at the Druid as they filed through the doorway, but they couldn't hide the grins that softened their battle-hardened faces.

"Find your rooms and go to them, now," The Druid commanded Miranda and Nicholas. "Rest, and be ready to leave in three hours."

"Yes, sir!" snapped Nicholas, saluting stiffly as he and Miranda marched past the tall man. Then he whispered out of the corner of his mouth. "He's still a big pain in the butt. I'd love to toss Muffrat in with him for the night. The fumes would kill him."

"Shhh," cautioned Miranda. "He'll turn you into something if he hears you."

"Do you know where we're going?" whispered Nicholas.

"Yep," said Miranda, sharing her knowledge with her friend. "We're going to Ellesmere Island." What she didn't share with the boy were her fears that they'd never get there in time.

CHAPTER THIRTY-EIGHT

RETURN TO ELLESMERE ISLAND

Still half asleep, the companions waited in the pre-dawn silence for the great iron doors, sealing the entrance to Dunmorrow, to slide open. The men were tense, anxious to be on their way. It was a long ride to the old docks on the northeastern coast of Lake Leanora, where the Elves maintained a fleet of ships, in compliance with the terms of their alliance with the Dwarves. Then they stepped through the massive arched doorway into a world of utter chaos and wild confusion.

"Cool!" breathed Nicholas, his eyes wide as he stared about in wonder.

Miranda was speechless. She couldn't find words to describe so many Dragons. They were everywhere, in the sky and on the ground, thousands of giant creatures, steam escaping from their cavernous nostrils turning the air into a sauna. And what a noise they made. Miranda couldn't hear herself think. This is what pandemonium means, she thought. Then, she realized that the Dragons were blocking their way. The Dragons had them trapped. "Oh no!" she cried, racing toward the Druid.

She saw King Gregor, with Naim and Elester at his heels, striding purposefully toward a colossal creature, who, she noticed, was raking its hind claws impatiently over the stone. She ran after them, leaping aside as a spark bigger than her head flew from the Dragon's claws, almost setting her ablaze.

"Morning," mumbled Gregor. "Bit early for your kind?"

The huge Dragon looked at the stocky Dwarf and spat a ball of flame off to the side. "It's about time you showed up," he roared. "We were just leaving."

"Well," muttered Gregor, worried about this many Dragons leaving droppings all over his front yard. "Don't let me keep you."

"Are you coming or not?" roared the Dragon. "I'll count to five. One . . ."

"What are you talking about?" asked Naim, stepping toward the Dragon.

"Get back, Druid. This does not concern you."

"Tell us what you are doing here," said Elester.

"We're here to take you to Ellesmere," snapped Typhon, as if he were speaking to a child. "Why else would we be here, at this hour?"

"But . . . who . . .?" the Prince was speechless.

"I do not do this for you, Elven Prince," snapped the Dragon, his eyes flashing with contempt. "Or you," he added, whipping his head toward the Druid.

"Excuse me," came a small voice. Penelope stepped up to the Dragon. "He's here because of me. I asked him to fly us to Bethany. He owed me a favour, so. . . ."

Everyone stared at the girl, incredulously.

The Druid broke the silence by chuckling softly. "Perhaps the sun has begun to shine on us," he said, clapping Elester on the shoulder. "With the Dragon's help, we will reach Bethany in time."

Miranda grabbed Penelope's arm and dragged her away from the others. "What's this about a favour?"

"It's true," said Penelope. "I told you about the Dragon's egg."

"Yeah, but you never mentioned any favour."

"I didn't?" said the other girl, innocently. "Oops! It must have slipped my mind."

"You are so not nice," laughed Miranda. "Anyway, don't tell me if you don't want to. I just think it was so cool, the way you said, He's here because of me. You should have seen the look on Naim's face."

"Actually, I did see it," giggled Penelope. Then she relented and told Miranda about the favour.

It took two full days to outfit the restless Dragons with harnesses and attach straps to secure the passengers. But finally the work was finished. King Gregor ordered everyone, including the Dragons, to catch a couple of hours' sleep and be ready to depart just before dawn. But while others obeyed the King's orders, Miranda and her friends were too keyed up to think about sleeping. They met in Miranda's room to share their fears and doubts. Tomorrow was the day Elester was supposed to be crowned King of the Elves. They also knew that that wouldn't happen without a fight.

Early the next morning, the first of the Dragons dropped from the cliffs, spread its enormous wings, and took to the sky. Others followed until the air over the White Mountains was a solid mass of black flying creatures. Up, up soared the Dragons, tunneling through clouds, climbing to where the air turned colder than a winter's day. They circled once and dropped like stones, levelling out to fall in behind the lead Dragon, carrying among them the entire Dwarf army—over thirty thousand seasoned soldiers.

And, it was Typhon who led the epic formation. On the great Dragon's back, strapped to a harness fitted over the creature's ribbed spine, were Miranda and Penelope, along with the Druid, Prince Elester and the Dwarf King, Gregor. Andrew rode with them, his arms wrapped tightly about Prince Elester's cloak, which hid the glow emanating from the Golden Crown. Nicholas had chosen to share the Dragon carrying Emmet and a dozen Dwarves outfitted for war. The boy's lean face sported a wide grin all the way to the Elven Capital.

Miranda spotted the gleaming white rooftops just before noon. She pinched Penelope and pointed ahead. "Bethany!" she shouted. "We're almost home." As her friend flashed her a curious look, Miranda, too, thought about what she had said. Why had she called the Elven Capital home? Was that how she really felt?

Her heart leaped into her throat as Typhon went into a steep, spiraling dive and the ground and buildings below rushed to meet them. Miranda squeezed her eyes shut to blot out the terrifying spectacle, but closing her eyes didn't take away the dizziness or lessen the sick feeling in the pit of her stomach. Then, the mighty Dragon pulled out of the dive and skimmed over the treetops, flying toward a wide patch of green lawn. Miranda opened her eyes. Below, hundreds of people were pointing and staring into the sky. She looked over her head and gasped. The cloud of Dragons had turned the blue sky over Ellesmere Island as black as pitch.

Peering ahead, she recognized the Council Hall nestled amidst the tall oak trees that marked the northern boundary of the park. Her heart beat faster when she spotted the Elven flag waving from a tall flagpole in front of the Hall. Emblazoned on a snow-white background was a pair of oak trees standing solid and straight, like proud guardians. Halfway up the thick trunks, a red heart reminded Miranda of an expression her mother used frequently—Heart of Oak. Above the trees, forming an arch, the Empyrean Crown blazed with the radiance of a small sun.

Then it was the activity in the park that caught and held her attention. Thousands of Elven men, women, and children were crowded about a raised platform. Twelve chairs stood in a row at the back of the platform, behind a larger, single chair—a simple, beautiful chair. With mounting dread, Miranda felt as though the scene spread out below—the Guards, the platform, the props—was a giant stage. And the Elven people were arriving for the main event—the Crowning! So, the Crowning was proceeding on schedule. The big question was: whom were they planning to crown?

Typhon came to earth just outside the entrance to the park. All about, Dragons were circling, searching for space to land and unload their human cargos. The creatures' spanking great wings caused a howling gale that whipped the trees into a frenzied ocean of green and tore great chunks of grass and earth out of the ground. Squinting to protect their eyes from the flying leaves and soil, Miranda and the others unbuckled the straps that had held them in place throughout the flight, and slid down ropes, landing heavily on the ground beside the gigantic Dragon.

"As ever, my friend," said Elester, touching the Dragon's clawed forelimb. "I am in your debt."

"Now that we're here, we might as well stick around. Things could get interesting," said Typhon, the Dragon.

"That's an understatement," sighed the Elven Prince.

"What about snacks for my kin?" rumbled the Dragon.

Elester thought for a second. "Do they fancy Werecur?"

Then the Prince was gone, sprinting across the park, and pushing through the crowds toward the empty chair on the raised platform. Following like hounds on the tail of a fox were the Druid, using the wooden staff to nudge people aside, the two Ottawa girls, and the company of Riders, including Andrew clutching his precious package. As they ran, Miranda glanced about for Nicholas, but the boy was lost somewhere in the midst of the Dwarf ranks.

King Gregor stomped heavily. He meant to protect Elester, but he didn't want to fight Elves. He breathed easier when Coran and thousands of Riders suddenly swelled the ranks of the Dwarf army.

Suddenly, a hush fell over the park. Everything went as still as death. The breeze died. Birds stopped singing. The trees froze as if petrified. For Miranda, it was as if the whole world had abruptly stopped breathing. The heavy oak doors of the Council Hall opened slowly. Black-clad, somber-faced Elven Guards filed from the building, lining up along both sides of the path leading from the Hall to the raised platform. The silver runes on the hilts of their swords winked like gemstones in the early afternoon sun.

Miranda kept her eyes on the open door. She watched the twelve members of the Erudicia, the King's Advisers, emerge from the Hall one after another and walk in a stately procession to occupy the twelve chairs at the back of the platform. Miranda stared at them, trying to remember the name that went with each face. These men and women were the wisest Elves in the Kingdom. They looked kind and good in their long white hooded cloaks. She noticed that only one Adviser wore the hood over his head. All of the others were bareheaded. She didn't like the way the hooded man kept his head down as if he were hiding something.

When Arabella came through the doorway, Miranda froze and cried out. Alarmed, the Druid slowed and glanced at the girl. Seeing the blood drain from her face, he ran to her and gripped her shoulders, as if he intended to shake her.

"What is it?" he asked, his fingers digging into her flesh.

"It's Bell," whispered Miranda. "She's here."

"Stay with the Prince," ordered the Druid, clutching Andrew's arm, his face as dark as a storm cloud. Then he turned to Miranda. "Come with me."

Miranda held on to the sleeve of his cloak, running to keep pace with Naim's long, determined strides. She wondered what he was going to do. Could he break the spell Indolent had put on Arabella? Poor Bell, she thought. She doesn't even know she's bewitched.

They skirted the park and avoided the teeming crowd by passing among the tall oak trees that formed a natural border along one side of the park. The trees hid the Hall, but as they emerged into the open, it was visible again. Miranda looked about for Arabella, but the girl had gone.

"There she is," she cried, pointing at a short, dark-skinned girl standing at the side of the building, next to an oleander tree. Her back was facing them, but Miranda could see that she was using a long stick to doodle in the packed earth at the base of the tree.

"Do not let her know that you know her," cautioned the Druid.

"Why?" asked Miranda.

"Because Indolent will have turned her against you."

"But, what if she recognized me?"

As if she sensed their approach, Arabella started and glanced over her shoulder. The stick dropped from her hand. "If you know what's good for you, you'll get out of here, now," she snapped at them, coldly.

Miranda recoiled as if the other girl had slapped her.

"We're just trying to be friendly," said Miranda. "Are you here for the Crowning?"

Arabella's face twisted in fury. "Do you think I don't know who you are?" she sneered. "Mir-an-DA!"

Miranda blinked back her tears. The way Arabella spat out her name made it sound coarse and ugly. She nodded slowly, and took a small step forward. "And you're my best friend, Bell."

Arabella laughed—a horrible, grating sound that set Miranda's teeth on edge. "Get away from me. You pretend differently, but I know you're one of them."

"Arabella!" The word sounded like a whip cracking. "Look at me."

Arabella's vacant, haunted eyes shifted from Miranda to the Druid.

"GET AWAY FROM THE GIRL!"

Miranda almost jumped out of her skin at the high-pitched, hysterical voice that came from behind, near the back of the Hall. She and the Druid wheeled about at the same time, the staff in Naim's hand already raised to strike. Out of the corner of her eye, she saw Arabella cringe and fall back against the side of the Hall, throwing up her hands as if to ward off an unseen blow. Miranda ached to run to her friend and hold her, but she was afraid it would only make things worse.

"YOU!" screeched the Wizard Indolent, his face contorted with rage and hatred.

"It is over, Indolent," said the Druid, with the certainty of Death knocking at the door.

Miranda's blood curdled. This other, chilling, unfeeling side of Naim terrified her. She wished he would just wave the staff at the Wizard and turn him into a stump, like he did to Nicholas. Wouldn't that solve everything?

"Oh, no you don't!" ranted Indolent. "Not this time, Druid!"

Naim laughed. Miranda thought it sounded cruel and heartless and it did nothing except stoke the flames of Indolent's fury. The Wizard snapped his fingers. In a flash, a short, black, tapered stick appeared in his hand. He waved it at the Druid. Naim laughed again. "Next to me, your power is a trifling thing—a nothing," he said, still speaking in the same deadly quiet voice.

"Ha, ha!" squealed the Wizard, hopping from foot to foot gleefully, as if he knew something the other did not.

Blue flames spurted from the tip of the black stick and flicked toward the Druid like long tongues. Quicker than Miranda's eyes could follow, Naim stood the staff on the ground in front of him. The blue fiery tongues slammed into the air about the staff and rebounded, shooting back toward the Wizard like a blazing wave. Indolent shrieked and leaped aside, barely avoiding being consumed by his own Wizard-fire.

Mesmerized by the battle between the magical combatants, Miranda's heart stopped when something hit the back of her head and fingers scratched into her scalp, pulling her hair. She drove her elbow back, jabbing her attacker hard in the ribs. She heard a thin groan and felt the hand drop from her head. Clenching her fists, she spun around, and came face to face with her grade four teacher. For a second, Miranda couldn't believe her eyes. "What are you doing here?" she asked incredulously. "How did you get here?"

"Shut up," snapped Stubby. "Just tell me where the stones are!"

"In your dreams," said Miranda. Suddenly, her eyes opened wide and a knowing look spread over her face. "Aha!" she cried. "You followed us to Kingsmere. That's how you got here. And now, you and the Wizard Idiot are new best friends."

"I said shut up, you little . . . aaak . . ."

Miranda blinked. Mr. Little seemed to be getting littler before her eyes. She blinked again. He was growing smaller—shrinking and shrinking, until his head slipped down under his shirt and he disappeared inside his clothing. She glanced at Naim. He had to be responsible for shrinking Stubby. But, the Druid didn't appear to notice the girl. His eyes were focused on Indolent as the two men circled each other like wary predators.

Blue fire exploded from the black stick and formed a seething mass of burning gases. For an instant it hovered in the air, like a giant balloon. Then, with terrifying speed, Indolent launched it at the Druid. This time, Naim wasn't nearly fast enough. A movement at the edge of his range of vision distracted him momentarily. By the time he switched his attention back to the Wizard Indolent, it was too late. The blue flaming ball whammed into him with the force of a giant's fist, lifting him off the ground and flinging him backwards. He heard Miranda scream as he collapsed on his back on the ground, frantically slapping his cloak to put out the fire.

But, he was back on his feet in an instant. "I said it was over." Then he thumped the ground with the blunt end of the Druid staff. White sparks erupted from the pale wood and spread from end to end, turning the staff into a long white flame. As Miranda watched, the smoke rising from Naim's singed cloak turned the white burning staff the colour of blood. Naim raised his arm and spun the staff as if it were a baton. Faster and faster it whirled, until it formed a solid shield of fire. Slowly, he advanced on the Wizard. "Her power will not protect you from me," he said. "Or did the one you now serve neglect to mention it?"

"I SERVE NO ONE!" spat the Wizard, grabbing a clump of long, stringy hair in his fist and pulling it out by the roots.

Miranda gagged, repulsed by the unclean creature.

"Wrong!" said the Druid, from behind the flaming shield. "You have always served yourself, and now, you serve the Demon. I will tell you how she rewards her servants, Indolent."

"SILENCE! I will not listen to the scurrilous rantings of a deranged ninny—a drivelling laughing stock."

Miranda tensed, waiting for the Druid's wrath to come down on Indolent like a sledgehammer. She breathed easier when she heard him chuckle.

"As you wish," said the Druid. "You did not heed the advice I gave you in the past, but I will say it again. It is not too late for you. Remove the Demon's mark from your flesh and leave this place. Do not look back." A tiny spark of white flew from the blazing shield and struck the Wizard's stick.

"LEAVE HIM ALONE!" screamed Arabella, flying at the Druid like a small, raging dervish.

"No, Bell!" Miranda reached out and caught Arabella's arm, yanking the girl to a sudden stop.

Arabella turned on her, but Miranda seized the girl's wrists and held on so tightly she was afraid she'd break the bones. "Bell, please, I don't want to hurt you."

Indolent flicked the black stick to get rid of the Druid's spark. He flicked it again and again, but he couldn't dislodge the tiny flame that seemed to burrow into the hard black wood. Then, he glared at the Druid. "What have you done?"

He watched, stupefied, as the black wand began to disintegrate in his hand, crumbling into dust and blowing away in the breeze. For a second, he stared at his empty hand as if, by staring, the magic stick would suddenly reappear. Then, a long, wailing scream escaped from his throat and he turned and fled into the trees.

"Do you mind?" said Arabella, wrenching her arm out of Miranda's grasp. "What are you doing, Mir? That hurts." She looked about

Miranda's heart leaped with joy. She released Arabella's wrists and turned to the Druid. "Naim! You did it! You broke the spell!" She grabbed her friend and hugged her, squeezing the air out of her lungs. "Oh Bell, thank goodness! I'm so glad you're back."

"Let me go," gasped Arabella. Then, her body began to tremble uncontrollably as it all came rushing back—the Trolls, Stubby slapping her face, and the Wizard Indolent.

"You are safe now, child," said the Druid gently.

"I remember things," said Arabella, her eyes stinging as they filled with tears. "Nicholas! Where's Nicholas?"

"He's here. He escaped with Emmet."

"I was horrible to him, Mir. I told him I hated him."

"It's okay, Bell. He knows you couldn't help it. Remember, Indolent did the same thing to him."

"Did I do anything horrible to you?" she asked. "You're still my best friend, aren't you?"

Miranda and the Druid exchange quick looks. Then Miranda laughed. "I'm probably your only friend."

"Come. Let us go. We must be there for Elester's Crowning."

"What?" cried Arabella, her face turning grey.

"We got the Crown, Bell. Naim and I got it from the Dark Lands."

"No!" said Bell. "Listen! I don't know what you've got, but it's not the Empyrean Crown. I know, because the real Crown is here."

CHAPTER THIRTY-NINE

THE CROWNING

Prince Elester's heart hammered in his chest as he ran toward the raised platform. No one challenged him or tried to stop him. Something is wrong, he thought, glancing quickly over his shoulder, as if he expected not to see the others. But they were there, following like shadows. The Riders scanned the crowds, alert for danger. Andrew Furth hugged the Crown in one arm, keeping the other free for Penelope, who held on like a bulldog with a stick. Reassured, Elester quickened his pace, locking his eyes on the hooded man occupying one of the twelve chairs at the rear of the platform. Mathus! he thought sadly, recalling the night the man had come to him worried because he imagined he heard the dead King's voice in his head.

Silently, the young Prince berated himself for having ignored the old man's premonitions.

The Prince glanced toward the Council Hall just as a tall figure appeared in the open doorway. Then, he felt his world reeling as he recognized his father. This cannot be happening! he thought, torn between a burning urge to run to the man who had nurtured him throughout his life, and a cold anger at the monster that was responsible for the slaughter of his Captain and the other Riders.

King Ruthar moved slowly, awkwardly, between the straight rows of Elven Guards, stumbling and almost falling as he mounted the few steps to the platform. Head bowed as if weighted down by an unspeakable sadness, the old monarch made his way to the single chair and carefully lowered himself into the seat.

Elester was only steps away from the base of the platform when, suddenly, a score of fierce Guards moved quickly between him and the King.

"MURDERER!" roared the hooded Adviser, jumping to his feet, and pointing at the Prince. "KILL HIM!"

Several Guards stepped to either side of Elester and gripped his arms. The Prince did not struggle. He looked around to check on Penelope, then he looked at the men blocking his way, his green eyes scanning each hardened face. He read anger there, and disbelief—perhaps sadness, too. He was their Commander. He knew them, many personally. He had fought alongside them, shared their meals, shared their troubles. He had never considered how they might feel about him. He had simply led them to the best of his ability, because that was the only way he knew.

From the time he took his first steps, the principles by which his father lived and ruled—principles of truth, honour, and courage—had been instilled in him until they were indelibly imprinted on his psyche. He had never asked another to do what he was unwilling to do. He had always assumed that those under his command knew that he would give his life to save theirs. Did they believe that he had killed his own men? Were they capable of carrying out Mathus's order? Would they kill him?

He would never know the answer, because at that moment the King stood and raised his right hand. Elester noticed the jerky, irregular gesture, as if the body were a puppet being manipulated by invisible strings attached to its limbs. "Do not kill him," the King commanded. "Let the one who is no longer my son watch."

Then, he turned to two giant cloaked figures waiting motionless at the foot of the steps, and bowed even lower, his head twitching obscenely. Elester peered about at the crowd. What was wrong with them? Were they so blinded by false hope that they couldn't see that this creature was not their King— that the two heavy-set figures were not Elves? The lumbering creatures mounted the steps, sharing the weight of the black iron crate.

Elester held his breath, feeling sweat roll down his neck. What had happened to the Druid and Miranda? He wished they were here beside him. He wanted them to share the moment when the creature opened the black crate. For an instant, he was back in the Demon's garden, ordering Andrew to break the seals around the box and remove the Crown. He recalled the mischievous grin that flashed across the young Rider's face as he replaced the Crown with a rock. Then they had resealed the crate and left it where they had found it.

The hulking forms in their black cloaks resembled giant vultures hunched over their prey as they bent over the crate and removed the seals. The crowd fell silent again as the creatures gripped the iron handles and slowly lifted the heavy container. They carried it to the King, who was waiting as motionless as a beast about to pounce on its victim. King Ruthar reached out and lifted the lid. Immediately all heads turned away, and hands flew up to shield eyes from the blinding yellow light that radiated from inside the open crate.

Elester's body went cold as he glanced quickly at Andrew, his face asking the question that was stuck in his throat. Andrew held up the cloak, creating a small opening through which the Prince clearly saw the Golden Crown shining like melted gold. Then the young Rider shrugged as if to say, I do not understand what is happening.

The King dipped both hands into the crate and drew out the dazzling golden light. At that moment, a thick, black cloud crossed in front of the sun, and darkness fell on Ellesmere Island. Elester's heart turned to lead in his chest. He watched, helplessly, as King Ruthar raised the Elven Crown and held it poised above his head. They had failed. The Crown hidden in the folds of his travel cloak was a counterfeit. The Demon had tricked them, luring them away from Bethany and into the Dark Lands on a wild goose chase, while the Werecurs carried the real Cap to Bethany.

"DEMON!" he shouted, desperately struggling to free his arms from the Guards' iron hold. "Show your face, servant of Hate."

A gasp rose from the crowd and a thousand heads turned toward Elester. The older Elves exchanged looks and sighed, loath to believe that their Prince's hands were red with the blood of his own people. Elester looked from face to face. "Since when have the dead come back to life on Ellesmere?" he shouted. "My father died at Dundurum." He pointed at the imposter holding the Crown over his head. "That creature was sent by the Demon to destroy us!"

The Prince recoiled, shaken as his countrymen and women turned away, their faces clouded with shame . . . or anger . . . or disgust. He looked at

Andrew and the Riders, but he could not read their expressions. Then he noticed Penelope, tears coursing down her cheeks and dropping from her chin. He smiled, gently. "It is not over yet, child."

"Y-you're w-wrong," stammered Penelope, her eyes fixed on the dead King. "L-look!"

On the platform, King Ruthar lowered his arms and set the brilliant Crown on his bowed head, holding it in place with his twitching hands. Then, a soft hissing sound escaped from the King's lips, growing in volume as he slowly raised his head. Smoldering like live coals in their beloved ruler's face were two red eyes—Demon's eyes.

Stunned, the Elven people surged back, screaming and crying in terror. But the burning red eyes held them—hypnotizing them like birds beguiled by a snake. They watched in horrified silence as the creature began to twitch and swell as if something inside were expanding and pushing against the frail human casing. Then the King's body began to slough away, decomposing into pulp, and the sleek black serpent emerged triumphantly, the Empyrean Crown shining like a star atop its flat head.

As if this were the signal they had been waiting for, an army of Trolls swarmed from the forest behind the Council Hall. They pressed into the open areas along the sides and back of the platform and turned their ugly, hate-twisted faces to the Elves.

"We're too late!" cried Miranda, skidding to a stop

and bursting into tears of despair. Beside her, the Druid and Arabella were silent, staring at the great gloating monster that had destroyed the Elves.

"Wait here," said Naim. "I must find Elester and the others. As long as the Prince lives, he is dangerous. They will try to kill him."

Miranda wiped her face on her arm and scanned the crowd, searching for Elester and her friends. But she couldn't locate them among the thousands of tall golden-haired Elves. She dared look back toward the platform, hoping with all of her heart that there was still a faint ray of hope. But, when she saw the size of the Troll army packed about the platform and others surging from the forest like a river, hope died. Her eyes rested on the huge hissing creature aglow with the light emanating from the Elven Crown, and she started to cry again. Her trembling hand flew to her neck, seeking the small silver pouch, as if only the Bloodstones could protect her from the evil that filled the air in the beautiful park.

Abruptly, she felt the stones pulse through the fine metal. Quickly, she opened the pouch and poured the six precious pebbles into her palm.

It is not the Crown!

The words ripped through her mind.

It is not the Crown!

"What is it?" cried Arabella, noticing Miranda stiffen and go as white as flour.

But, Miranda didn't hear, she was already running toward the platform where she had last spotted the Druid's tall, cloaked form. Arabella sighed heavily and took off in pursuit.

The nictitating membrane closed across Dauthus's eyes as the serpent tilted its head to one side and waited for a sign that the Elven magic that sustained the walls of the Demon's prison was weakening—disintegrating like the dead King's useless shell. His black skin rippled with pleasure. Soon, she would be free. Any second now, her voice would fill his head, driving away the horrible blackness. Would she praise him? he wondered. The serpent hissed softly as he waited, dreaming of his reward. Nothing happened . . . still he waited.

"It's not the Crown!"

The voice cut into Dauthus's thoughts, as irritating as a pinprick. The serpent whipped his head about, his red eyes locking on the source of the irritation. He glared at the child, standing motionless before the platform, the flame in his eyes growing brighter. But, suddenly a series of short hisses escaped from his throat, like puffs of steam bursting from a kettle. Dauthus was laughing.

An instant later, the Golden Crown on his head sputtered and the brilliance seemed to fade. Startled, Dauthus's body convulsed and the Crown slipped and dropped, rolling until it bumped against the edge of the platform. "GET IT!" he hissed at Mathus. But, as the hooded Adviser bent over to snatch the Crown, the gold finish began to fleck away and within seconds, the Crown eroded into dust.

"I told you it wasn't the Crown!" repeated Miranda. She knelt on the ground, and reached into the knapsack she had torn off Penelope's back as she had raced past the startled girl. Then she stood and raised the battered black Crown—the "piece of junk," the gift given to Penelope by Typhon, the Dragon.

"This is the Empyrean Crown," she said, her green eyes shining. Then, she turned and took a step toward Elester, blushing furiously when she realized that every eye in the park was fastened on her.

"Bring me the Crown, Miranda."

The voice stopped Miranda in her tracks. Desperately, she fought to resist the command, but she couldn't move. She thought she heard Naim calling her, his voice thin and afraid, but then it was gone, swept away by her overpowering urge to give the Crown to the serpent. She hesitated, as if she couldn't make up her mind what to do. The words of the prophecy flashed into her mind. A girl betrays.

Then, almost reluctantly, she turned back, ignoring the gasps from the crowd and the desperate cries of her friends. At a sign from Dauthus, the Trolls pressed back, clearing a path for the girl. Miranda was numb with fear. But, somehow she made it to the platform steps, where Mathus was waiting, his hands reaching to take the Crown from the stupid child. A girl betrays.

For a second, Miranda gripped the Crown tightly and looked about, her eyes wide and frightened. Then, she placed the black crown in the Adviser's hands and turned away, weaving among the Trolls and hurrying past her friends, ignoring their shocked and saddened faces as she ran toward the wooden bench hidden among the oleander trees by a small pond.

Hate's servant recoiled, winding about himself until his gaping mouth was level with Mathus's chest. He dipped his head and waited while the Senior Adviser, with trembling hands, crowned Dauthus King of the Elves.

"What have you done, child?" whispered the Druid to no one, his voice sounding as old and weary as his ancient limbs.

A horrible, hissing shriek exploded from the serpent. The creature's red eyes rolled back in his head. His body heaved as wave upon wave of pain washed over him. He writhed about the platform, thrashing wildly, unable to dislodge the black Crown that was slowly burning into his flesh.

"GET IT OFF!" he screamed.

Mathus hurried to obey, but after he had taken a few steps, he paused for a moment, staring at his dead brother. Then, he hissed softly, almost sadly, and walked rapidly away.

With a dazzling flash, the battered, black covering burst from the Crown, exposing the white flames leaping from the golden Cap. The fire surged through the creature's head and, like molten lava, flowed into its body, until it reached the tapered tail and erupted from the snake's flesh. But Dauthus was dead long before his carcass exploded, and rained infinitesimal specks of black scales upon the stunned Trolls.

Huddled on the wooden bench among the sweet-scented oleander trees, Miranda didn't see the great cloud of Dragons take to the sky in pursuit of the Werecurs. She didn't see Typhon, and the rest of his frightening kin, swoop down and drive the Trolls out of the city and into the waters of Lake Leanora, home of the great, bloated creature the Druid had named Dilemma.

EPILOGUE

Late in the afternoon, on the third day after the debacle in the park outside the Council Hall, Elester Conaire Mor placed the Gold Empyrean Crown upon his head and sat quietly in an intricately carved wooden chair, under a magnificent oak tree, while the new Senior Advisor of the Erudicia proclaimed him King of the Elves.

There was not a single dry eye in the park.

For as long as they lived, Miranda and her Ottawa friends would remember this day with a longing they could never express in mere words, or ever satisfy. The sky was brilliant cornflower blue, so perfectly glorious, it hurt. The sturdy oaks appeared taller, the leaves greener, than ever before. The sun shone brighter, and the air smelled sweeter.

The kids cheered until their voices gave out, grinning happily as they wiped away the tears of joy that streaked their faces. They held their breath as the Elven Flag was raised, and the standards of past Elven Kings were unfurled. Then they, along with tens of thousands of men, women, and children, raised their voices and sang the words to songs they had never heard, in a language they did not know.

At exactly midnight, under a gibbous moon, the celebrations began.

They feasted first, taking their places at the longest table Miranda had ever seen. Stretching from one end of the park to the other, its white table linen glowed in the soft candlelight from tall silver candelabra. The fine Elven silver bowls, holding a profusion of wild flowers, gleamed like white fire in the moonlight. There were great silver-domed platters heaped with roasted pheasants stuffed with apricots, pea-sized crispy potatoes infused with cream, pyramids of stuffed green, red, and yellow peppers, sweet yellow corn, grape leaves filled with rice and dates, and dozens of other dishes that Miranda couldn't identify.

On the evening of the fourth day of feasting and dancing, Miranda and her exhausted friends sat around the fireplace in the living room of the girls' cottage, talking late into the night. By the time Nicholas left to return to the Riders' barracks where he was billeted, they had decided that it was time to go home.

The next morning, Miranda got up with the sun. She slipped quietly out the door and made her way to the park. She found the Druid sitting on the soft grass at the edge of the pond, watching five ducklings bobbing like corks behind their mother. He looked up as Miranda dropped into a cross-legged position on the grass beside him.

"We're going home today."

"Yes," said the Druid, as if he already knew.

They sat together in silence, like old friends comfortable in each other's presence. This was the first time Miranda had a chance to corner the Druid since that unforgettable day when she had given the Golden Crown to Dauthus. She had a lot to say and very little time in which to say it.

"Can I come back?" she asked, finally breaking the silence. Then, she hurried on without waiting for the Druid's answer. "It's the Bloodstones. You were right when you said I don't know how to control them. But I can't learn that in Canada because they don't work there. I have to be here." She took a deep breath as if she were about to jump into the pool. "So, can I come back, and if so, will you teach me how to control the power?"

Naim looked at her for a long time before answering. "No," he said, gently.

"Why not?" cried Miranda.

"Because, for now, your place is with your mother and your friends." Seeing that Miranda was about to argue, he raised his hand. "Listen to me, Miranda. I said for now your place is home. Later, when you are older, you may ask again."

"Then will you say yes?"

The Druid chuckled. "Then I will probably say yes. Now, tell me, did you know what would happen when you gave the Crown to the Demon's servant?"

Miranda shrugged. "I didn't know. I was going to give the Crown to Elester . . . and . . . honestly, I still don't know what made me change my mind. I remembered the words of the prophecy. A girl betrays, a Crown slays. I wasn't sure what it meant, but I think the Bloodstones let me know that I was supposed to betray Elester so the Crown could slay the serpent. It didn't make sense the other way . . . I mean if I betrayed the serpent and the Crown slew Elester. I wasn't the serpent's friend, so how could I betray it?"

"But you did not know," pressed the Druid quietly.

"No," said Miranda. "But everything turned out OK, didn't it?"

Naim sighed. "Yes, child, it did. You prevented a terrible battle that would have decimated the Elves and the Dwarf army."

"Seriously?" said Miranda, peering at the Druid to see if he were teasing her. "How?"

"If you had given the Crown to Elester, the serpent would still be alive. It would have unleashed the Trolls and summoned the Werecurs. With the Dragons' help, we may have been able to defeat them, but not without a great loss of lives. By letting the Crown slay the Serpent, the Trolls and others suddenly found themselves without a leader."

"I had to run away," said Miranda thoughtfully. "I was afraid because I couldn't face what was going to happen when the serpent was crowned. I've never killed anything, until now." The thought still made her sick.

The Druid patted Miranda's hand. "Is that what you think? That you killed the serpent?" He laughed softly. "My dear girl. I am sorry to disappoint you, but you had absolutely nothing to do with that creature's demise. The Demon killed it long before the creature emerged from its egg. And then she used it for her own evil ends." He paused for a moment. "That thing was not some noble, dangerous creature like a Fire Serpent, or a Dinosaur, or a Dragon. It was Hate, as surely as if she, herself, were present."

Miranda felt a heavy weight fall from her shoulders. She wondered if the sixth Bloodstone had known about the power of the Crown to reject evil. Perhaps, someday, when she learned more about the magic, she would discover the answer.

The Druid was also thinking about the Bloodstones. Miranda was intelligent, but he did not believe that she had acted on her own initiative when she gave the Crown to the serpent. No, he thought. It was the Bloodstones. Their powers were truly awesome—beyond anything he had ever known. That's what made them dangerous in the hands of a child. Yes, he thought. She must learn how to control the magic. And there is only one place where she will learn that . . . the Druid's Close.

"We've been looking everywhere for you," said Arabella, dropping onto the grass and dipping her fingers into the water. Nicholas and Penelope appeared seconds later. Penelope dropped Muffy's lead and the little dog dashed to the edge of the pool, barking and growling at the baby ducks.

"So, what happens now?" asked Nicholas, proudly polishing the blade of his new short sword on his sleeve. Last evening, at a special ceremony in the Riders' barracks, Andrew Furth, acting on orders from the King, initiated the first step in Nicholas's training that would, one day, make him a full-fledged Rider.

"What happens now, indeed," said the Druid, getting up slowly. "The King is expecting you."

They followed Naim across the park and along a narrow clay footpath that wound like a ribbon through a thick stand of willow trees. Miranda hadn't been this way before, and she wondered where Naim was taking them. Abruptly, the trees ended and they found themselves on the shores of Lake Leanora.

Slipping out of their running shoes, they ran along the pink sand beach and waded in the water as the Druid strode purposefully toward a low white house further down the beach. Miranda noticed the wide covered verandah wrapped about the front and side of the house, and the tall, golden-haired figure standing there, watching their approach.

They sank into fat cushions in comfortable wicker chairs, sipping iced tea from heavy crystal goblets as they said farewell to King Elester. Everybody laughed at the sight of Muffy greedily slurping her beverage from a small crystal bowl on the floor.

"Without your help, I would not be King today," said Elester. "And many more of my people would have died."

"But, Sir," said Nicholas. "What about Indolent? He's still alive."

"And Malcolm and Mathus?" added Arabella. "They got away, too."

"Don't forget the Thug thing that hurt Muffs," said Penelope.

"There's something else," said Miranda, feeling her flesh crawl. "The oracle mouth said five walking serpents. I count Malcolm, Mathus, Dauthus and that Elf who said he was my father. That only makes four. There's still one more egg out there."

For a second, no one spoke. But the quick look exchanged between the King and the Druid told her they were worried.

"I will not rest until we find them," said Elester, finally. "You can return to your homes knowing that we will be especially vigilant. The Demon will not catch us napping again."

"I have a question," said Miranda. "Naim couldn't get into the Dark Lands without the Bloodstones, so how did you get in?"

Elester laughed. "It was easy. I followed you."

Before they left, Elester made Nicholas, Arabella, and Penelope stand. Then he made them citizens of Ellesmere and placed a silver medallion, with two raised oak trees under a Golden Crown, about their necks. Next, he turned to Muffy who, for once, sat as still as a statue, except for the rapid wagging of the stump where her tail was beginning to grow back. "This little one is as fearless as a Dragon and has the courage of a lion. She is now an Elf-hound." With that he hung one of the medallions about the poodle's neck. Finally, he turned to Miranda. "You do not need a medal to remind you that Bethany is your home, Miranda D'arte Mor."

"Is that my real name?" asked Miranda, her voice soft with wonder.

Elester nodded. "You and I share last names, Elven girl."

A huge crowd awaited them outside the Council Hall. Miranda giggled when she saw King Gregor and Emmet sitting on a flat stump at the side of the building. She turned to the Druid. "I can't believe you did that," she said.

"What else would you have me do with the unpleasant fellow?" asked the Druid.

"Hey, guys," called Miranda. "What about Stubby?"

Her friends burst out laughing when they learned that the Druid had turned Stubby into a stump. Even Nicholas thought it was funny, as long as it had happened to someone else.

"Well?" said Miranda. "What are we going to do?"

"Let's think about it," said Penelope.

"For about ten years," said Arabella.

"Let's leave the little weasel here," said Nicholas.

So, they left Stubby in Bethany.

It took a long time to say farewell to everyone. King Gregor stomped his sturdy boots and thumped the Ottawa companions hard on their backs. "Come again. Stay. Dunmorrow." Then he left to join the Dwarf army and the Dragons for the long flight back to Mount Oranono. Nicholas was glad to hear that Emmet was returning to Ottawa with them.

Just as Miranda was about to step between the pair of tall oak trees, she suddenly stopped dead, spun about, and ran over to the Druid. "What about the Ku-kus? You said you'd ask the other Druids . . ."

"I spoke with my colleagues," said Naim. "Do you have anything . . .? Nicholas! Come here, lad."

When Nicholas joined them, Naim asked what was in the sack over the boy's shoulder.

"Drom Stones," said Nicholas. "The Trolls made us hunt for them and we kept some. The Bogs got all excited whenever we brought some out of the Drom Hole, so they must be extremely valuable."

The Druid raised his head and laughed. "Valuable to the Trolls, Nicholas, but I am afraid you have not found your fortune. The Trolls use them like coal, because wood will not burn in the swamp."

Nicholas flushed and looked about for a place to dump the black stones.

"Open the sack," said Naim. Then he reached inside and muttered words that neither Nicholas nor Miranda understood. Removing his hand, he slapped the boy gently on the shoulder. "I needed a vessel for the Druid magic," he explained. "The Drom stones were perfect. If you place them among the Symbionts, I think, over time, they will stop replicating and settle down."

"Whew!" Nicholas and Miranda exchanged relieved looks. "Thank you," they said, meaning it with all their hearts. Then, Miranda touched Naim's arm. "You won't forget your promise?"

The Druid nodded, his eyes misting as he watched the young friends hold hands and take a step between the two oak trees. Then he turned and made for the stables where the stallion, Avatar, waited impatiently.

They left Emmet and the Ottawa Dwarves and made their way to the side-tunnel and the Ku-Ku-Fun-Gi. They were shocked by the damage the fungi had caused in such a short time. The ceiling and walls of the tunnel beyond the entrance had crumbled and collapsed into a heap of rubble. Working quickly, they scattered the Drom Stones and then stood back, hoping for a sign from the creatures that the Druid's magic was working. Miranda felt sad—still finding it hard to believe she and her friends were responsible for what the Ku-Kus had done.

Nicholas stared at the Symbionts, fascinated. "But, how did the Dwarves get them off us?" he muttered, shaking his head.

"I'm sorry, Nick," said Arabella, on the way home.

"For what?"

"For the things I said to you in the Swamp-grass."

Nicholas draped his arm about her shoulder. "That wasn't you, Bell."

"Maybe not, but I'm still sorry."

Back home, Dr. D'arte mentioned that someone had broken in to a stables in the Market, taken two horses, and left a big rock on the owner's doorstep. "The rock turned out to be an uncut ruby worth fifty horses," she said.

Miranda burst out laughing. Wait till Nicholas hears this, she thought.

"What's so funny?" asked Dr. D'arte. "Do you know anything about this?"

"Don't ask, Mom," laughed Miranda. "Believe me, you don't want to know."

Hidden in a copse on the side of a hill over-looking the Elven capital, Malcolm, the Dwarf, hissed softly. Dauthus had failed to carry out the Demon's plans. Now he was dead. There was nothing to show he had ever existed, except a few scorched scales. The creature winked its red eyes, and twisted the Dwarf's mouth into a wicked grin. Poor Dauthus. Poor misguided fool. He thought he was so important to Hate's plans—so busy giving orders that he never, for a second, suspected that the Demon had another plan.

The Dwarf patted one of his pockets and felt the small black egg. Then, hissing with pleasure, he kicked the huge creature beside him. It was time to meet Mathus and find a way off Ellesmere Island.

Be sure to read

The Twisted Blade

Book Three of

The Serpent's Egg Trilogy

"*The Twisted Blade* is a thrilling, suspenseful conclusion to The Serpent's Egg Trilogy. It had me cheering inwardly at every victory." Brittany D., age 10

Also watch for The Mole Wars Series
by J. FitzGerald McCurdy

The Fire Demons (Book One)
The Black Pyramid (Book Two)

For the past five billion years,
something's been trapped within the
earth…. Now it's breaking free.